THE STORYTELLER'S PACK

A FRANK R. STOCKTON READER

THE STORYTELLER'S PACK
A FRANK R. STOCKTON READER

ILLUSTRATED BY BERNARDA BRYSON

CHARLES SCRIBNER'S SONS *New York*

"Where, indeed, in our literature shall we find such a body of honest humor, with its exaggeration deep in the nature of things, and not in the distortion of the surface? The salt which seasons it, and may be relied on to keep it wholesome is the unfailing good humor and charity of the author. The world, as he sees it, is a world peopled with tricky sprites and amusing goblins. When he was telling tales for children, these gnomes and fairies and brownies were very much in evidence. He does not bring them into evidence in his stories for mature readers, except occasionally, as in 'The Griffin and the Minor Canon'; but they have simply retired into the recesses of the human spirit. They do their work still in initiating all manner of caprices and whimsical outbreaks; but they are concealed, and this storyteller, who knows of their superabundant activity, goes about with a grave face the better to keep their secret."

WILLIAM DEAN HOWELLS

Contents

List of Illustrations

Introduction

FRANCIS RICHARD STOCKTON was born in Philadelphia on April 5, 1834, to William Smith Stockton and Emily Hepsibeth Drean. His father was Agent for the Phildelphia Almshouse and later Steward, but his passion was Wesleyan theology. He wrote innumerable pamphlets on religion and temperance and devoted so much energy to the formation of the Methodist Protestant Church that he apparently neglected his job, for he was dismissed in 1844 for general mismanagement of the Almshouse. Fortunately, his mother owned a farm and helped provide for the large family—six children by William Stockton's first wife and seven by Emily Drean Stockton.

Frank Stockton, the oldest son of the second group, was lame from birth and delicate. He entertained himself and his brothers and sisters with stories while walking to school and would "take up the thread of a story and carry it on from day to day until the thing became a serial."

"I was very young when I determined to write some fairy tales because my mind was full of them. . . . These were constructed according to my own ideas. I caused the fanciful creatures who inhabited the world of fairy-land to act, as far as possible for them to do so, as if they were inhabitants of the real world. I did not dispense with monsters and enchanters or talking birds and beasts, but I obliged these creatures to infuse into their extraordinary actions a certain leaven of common sense." He began to submit stories to magazines in high school and built up an impressive collection of rejection slips.

Stockton graduated as a Bachelor of Arts from the Central High School of Philadelphia in 1852 and took up the trade of wood engraving. With his brother John Drean Stockton, a steel engraver who later edited the Philadelphia *Post*, he opened up a shop and managed to support himself with commissions from magazines and newspapers. His engravings, ornate and busy in the style of the period, were competent if unoriginal. However, he was interested enough in the trade to patent an engraving tool that cut parallel lines at the same time. Soon the publication of his first story, "The Slight Mistake," in the Philadelphia *Courier*—"an imitation of Dumas and other favorite French authors," as Stockton himself said—encouraged him to spend more time writing.

Sometime after William Stockton's dismissal from the Almshouse, Stockton's mother established the West Philadelphia School for Young Ladies. It was there that Stockton met Mary Ann (Marian) Edwards Tuttle, an English teacher from South Carolina. They were married on April 30, 1860, and lived in New Jersey during the Civil War. Stockton, never deeply concerned with politics, abhorred war but sympathized with both sides. If he had a political belief, it was in peace through compromise. He believed in freeing the slaves gradually and indemnifying their owners, and he felt that the South should be permitted to secede. He printed privately "A Northern Voice for the Dissolution of the Union" in 1861, in which he suggested that the Union should be comprised only of those states that consented to join it, but withdrew the pamphlet from circulation when Fort Sumter fell in April. His wife was Southern, and he had relatives fighting on both sides. It is interesting that he wrote no fiction during the war years.

After the war, the Stocktons moved to Philadelphia to help out the family, and Stockton became a steady contributor to *Riverside Magazine*. When *Hearth and Home* was founded in 1868 under the direction of Mary Mapes Dodge, she hired Frank Stockton as her assistant. To fill out the magazine, he wrote not only stories but articles on subjects varying from pest control and dressmaking to interior decoration. His first book, *Ting-a-ling*, a collection of fairy tales for children, originally published in *Riverside Magazine*, came out in 1870, and in the same year he gave up engraving. In 1873,

Scribners started *St. Nicholas,* a magazine just for children, with Mary Mapes Dodge as editor. The first children's magazine to print stories that were simply entertainment and not moral tracts, *St. Nicholas* was an immediate success with children all over the world. Mark Twain, William Dean Howells, Louisa May Alcott, Mayne Reid, Howard Pyle, and Frances Hodgson Burnett were among its contributors. Stockton, as Mrs. Dodge's assistant, had much of the editorial responsibility, and in the early days he helped pad the magazine with stories and articles written under the names of "Paul Fort" and "John Lewees." But the work he considered his best was always signed with his own name.

The Stocktons, who loved the country, returned to New Jersey in 1874 and bought a small farm near Rutherford, where they dabbled with raising chickens and livestock. Stockton's novel *Rudder Grange,* an episodic account of a young married couple who decide to live on a canal boat to save money, is based on their own domestic mishaps. Stockton never actually lived on a canal boat, but Pomona, the servant girl who makes the hero cringe when she reads English melodramas syllable by syllable at the top of her voice, was real, and so were the heroine's experiments with breeding chickens and furnishing her home. *Rudder Grange* was written in 1873 and 1875 and published successfully as a series of stories but was rejected in book form by several publishers, including Roberts Brothers, a Boston publishing company, who "felt the public pulse, and . . . regretted to remark that it did not beat in warm throbs for me," Stockton remarked.

By 1876 Stockton, who was working long hours at the *St. Nicholas* office and writing in his free time, found reading tiring and painful. His eyes improved after a vacation in Florida and the Bahamas, but they immediately got worse when he started work again. He was forced to resign from *St. Nicholas,* and for several years he could barely read or write. He would dictate his stories to his wife in the morning for two or three hours and spend the rest of the day thinking out what he would say the next morning, down to the last exchange of dialogue. Once a story was down on paper, he rarely revised it.

In the meantime, his reputation was growing. He was receiving $150 for a short story in *St. Nicholas* and $300 a story—a large sum in those days—from other magazines. *Rudder Grange* was published by Scribners in book form in 1879 and established him with the American public, which demanded more stories about Pomona. *The Floating Prince and Other Stories*, one of his finest collections of fairy tales, was published in 1881 and was immediately popular with both children and adults. Then Stockton wrote a short story called "In the King's Arena" for a dinner party. He had so much fun at the party that he never got around to reading the story, but it was published by *Century Magazine*—after some hesitation on the part of the editors, who were not sure what to make of it—with a new title, "The Lady or the Tiger?" The story caught on, and Stockton returned from a long tour of Europe to find himself deluged with letters, all demanding to know the fate of the hero. Interviewers pursued him for an answer. Stockton, who had rewritten the ending five times to make a solution impossible, would hedge: "If you decide which it was—the lady or the tiger— you find out what kind of a person you are yourself." In the *Ladies' Home Journal* he wrote: "During the first construction of the story I had no thought but that I should finish it, state which door was opened by the young man in the arena, and give the reasons why his ladylove, the princess, directed him to one portal rather than to the other. But when I reached the point of the story at which the princess must decide which door she should point out to her lover, I found myself in a greater quandary than that in which she would have been had she really existed, for I had not the advantage of being either semi-barbaric or a woman. . . ."

At first he reacted to the fuss with a mixture of enjoyment and dismay. Critics were hailing the story as a masterpiece and as a new departure from the prevalent dialect story. But when it reached the absurd point of Stockton's attending a party where two figures carved in ice cream—a lady and a tiger—were set in front of him, in the hopes that he might dig his spoon into one, he began to be disquieted. Suddenly he found that he was again collecting rejection slips. Editors would write him polite letters in which they regretted that the work he submitted was not up to the standard set by "The Lady or the Tiger?" "In other words, I found that I had ruined my own market by furnishing one story which I could not quite live up to . . . ." Stockton added: "I wrote 'His Wife's Deceased Sister' in the bitterness of my soul at that period, as a protest against the assumption that when a man does his very best he places himself under the obligation to do as well on every succeeding occasion or starve to death for lack of ability to do so." Stockton was inevitably carried away by the clamor, for despite its popularity, "The Lady or the Tiger?" is not one of his finest stories: It is a whimsicality that depends on a gimmick.

Almost three years later, sequels to the story, written by determined amateurs, were still pouring into the *Century* office. L. F. Tooker, who had to wade through them all, describes Stockton at that time: "I recall the manner in which he used to make his appearance, coming quietly into the room and slipping in a sidelong way peculiar to himself, into the chair that stood by my desk, just inside the door. His features were strong, his eyes dark and unusually large, and his voice was grave, deep in tone, even musical. His face in repose was sad, and had about it the drawn look of those who know habitual pain, though I am sure that he always spoke of himself as being in the best of health. His laugh, though hearty at times, had the peculiar characteristic of being almost soundless." And Robert Underwood Johnson, in *Remembered Yesterdays*, described him as having "a sallow skin, piercing dark eyes, straight black hair, a nose a bit awry and a sensitive mouth whose twitchings gave notice of a good story. He was lame, one leg being shorter than the other, but there was always a dignity in his limping walk. He laughed much and enjoyably but almost noiselessly at the humor of other persons as well as his own—a real achievement for a humorist."

Stockton managed to re-establish his market with several collections of short stories and fairy tales, including "The Transferred Ghost," "The Bee-Man of Orn," and "The Queen's Museum." Some, like "The Queen's Museum," "The Griffin and the Minor Canon," "The Bee-Man of Orn," and "Old Pipes and the Dryad," are among the best fairy tales ever written. Stockton was often stilted when writing about real situations, but he was always comfortable among his dwarfs, gnomes, and pigwidgeons; his humor, quiet irony, and the "leaven of common sense" in his fantasies make them seem more real than most of his novels. In 1886, *Century* published his most popular long work, *The Casting Away of Mrs. Lecks and Mrs. Aleshine,* a little masterpiece about two middle-aged Robinson Crusoes who paddle to a desert island on the Pacific after their ship has gone down and find a full larder. Stockton is quoted as saying: "It is much more to my liking to write about middle-aged women than young women. The older ones have more character; you can make them do most amusing things." The incongruity of the two calm respectable widows and their exotic surroundings made the book such a success that Stockton felt forced to write a sequel, *The Dusantes,* although he believed that sequels were always inferior to the original.

Stockton's eyes continued to trouble him, but he was able to afford a secretary and would dictate to her from his hammock or in the cupola of the Holt, a house with a little farm just outside Morristown, New Jersey. He wrote novels, short stories, nonfiction, and several science-fiction works, including "The Great Stone of Sardis," in which the hero discovers that the center of the earth is an enormous diamond. It would be interesting to know if F. Scott Fitzgerald knew of the book when he wrote "The Diamond As Big As the Ritz." Although Stockton lifted much of his scientific material from the Encyclopaedia Britannica, he was prophetic in describing the voyage of a ship to the North Pole underwater, for the submarine *Nautilus* actually made such a journey in 1958. *Rudder Grange* went on selling, and Stockton wrote several sequels about Pomona. One of his nonfiction works, "The Buccaneers and Pirates of Our Coast," is still a favorite with children although its original editors criticized it for being too tame. Stockton had a weakness for pirates.

In 1899, the Stocktons moved to Claymont, an old house near Charles Town, West Virginia. There Stockton wrote his last work, a collection of short stories entitled *John Gayther's Garden and the Stories Told Therein*, in which John Gayther, an old gardener, and the people he works for and their friends—including Pomona and her husband Jonas—are used as a device linking miscellaneous stories. The book was published posthumously. Stockton visited New York in 1902 and continued to Washington to attend a banquet given by the National Academy of Sciences. He became suddenly ill during the dinner and was carried to his hotel, where four days later he died of a cerebral hemorrhage. It was left to his wife to finish *John Gayther's Garden:* "The stories are all told. The winter has come . . . and John Gayther walks alone in his garden."

II

Frank Stockton was not a wide reader. In his childhood he loved the fairy tales of Hans Christian Andersen and read the works of Victor Hugo, William Thackeray, Jane Porter, Alexandre Dumas, Oliver Goldsmith, and Honoré de Balzac, but his favorite authors were Daniel Defoe and Charles Dickens. "In front of all who have created fiction stand, firm and unmoved, Defoe and Dickens, who, as I look upon it, have established the great principle that the author who believes in his story will tell the best story and the author who believes in his characters and loves them will make them real beings who shall live with his readers and be held by them always as companions and friends." He was indifferent to current authors and seldom read their works, although he did read and admire Mark Twain. It was in an essay praising him that Stockton wrote: "Anyone with a lively fancy may invent odd and even amusing characters and incidents, but the humorous situation of the highest order cannot be created; it must be evolved from a real situation." The statement also describes Stockton's work, for he said his own writing fell into two groups: "One, the world of fancy invaded by the real; the other, the world we live in as seen through spectacles of more or less fantastic colors." In an article in *Author,* he mentioned his method of work:

"First I lasso an idea. It may be a startling climax—an effect, the causes leading up to which will of themselves develop a narrative. With the main idea fast in my possession, the rest is comparatively easy. I plan the story generally in my head, though I sometimes sketch it out roughly on a sheet or two of paper. I never take the trouble to work out the details. I crowd the interest in characters toward a certain point in the narrative.

"Occasionally they protest and declare that they would not do what I make them do. Generally I like to see a character. I like a physical type, but I never copy anybody. Yet, strangely, I have to think of some fact, of some acquaintance. The moral character is worked up by selecting traits from various men or women known to me. . . . I dislike to rely on reading, because the ideas evolved are the offsprings of another mind. I always feel however new the thought that comes to me may be, that the author I am reading had had it in his mind and rejected it."

William Dean Howells, who wrote several articles on Stockton, commented on those "realistic novelists who permit their characters to break all of the Ten Commandments in turn, but use their most strenuous endeavors to keep them from breaking the one imperious commandment, Thou Shalt Not Transgress the Law of Average Experience. Mr. Stockton's characters, on their part, never trouble themselves about the Ten Commandments—morality is sort of a matter of course with them—but they break the realist's great commandment in the most innocent and unconscious manner." Stockton, mischievously speaking through a character in *John Gayther's Garden* confirms this:

"Now you must understand . . . that when people who are really in earnest, especially people in fiction, go forth to find things they want, they generally find them. And if it is highly desirable that these things should be out of the common they are out of the common. A great deal of what happens in real life, and almost everything in literature, depends on this principle."

Stockton's characters sail imperturbably toward their unlikely destinations. They are good souls living in a benign world, and the best of them are incurable optimists. They usually prove to be right against all odds—for instance, the character in "The Remarkable Wreck of the *Thomas Hyke*," who insists not only that everything will turn out all right but that he is enjoying himself even when the ship has sunk below the water. Stockton's wise people—notably griffins, hermits, sailors, a sphinx or two, and middle-aged ladies—create order in the most ludicrous circumstances. Stockton's favorite device is to make the reader accept outrageous events and coincidences with a straight face. Mrs. Lecks and Mrs. Aleshine, for example, are such obviously respectable, practical, and unruffled ladies that the reader is prepared to accept their hilarious adventures. Stockton generally preferred shy young men and respectable widows as his heroes and heroines—the reader could never accuse them of any flights of fancy, and their calmness in impossible situations made their entanglements even funnier. Often Stockton would carry the irony even further, as in "The Transferred Ghost," in which it is the plaintive, respectable—and not at all frightening—ghost who is haunted.

Stockton's real interest was in people and the creatures in his world of fantasy. His plots are simple and sometimes repetitive, and his novels, which are generally a series of short episodes strung together, show that he was obviously happier within the limits of a short story. Very seldom, too, does he describe scenery with any real enthusiasm or sensitivity. At times it is a necessary backdrop to a love story, as in "Our Story," but he is much more comfortable inventing the dreadful wilds in "The Griffin and the Minor Canon." He relies on dialogue to describe his characters. Again and again he writes about the sea—old captains and sailors' widows constantly appear in his pages. It has been suggested that writing about the sea excused him from describing an exact geography, but his pre-occupation with the sea is much more than that; on reading his stories one gets the impression that to Stockton the men who sail the ocean are a race apart—they are his Mississippi pilots, free, unfettered by country or convention, weathered by practical experience.

When Stockton found a plot he could use, he would often use it over and over with slight variations. This is particularly true of his tales of shipwreck—and he loved shipwrecks. Of course, they provided endless possibilities for throwing characters together and spinning tall tales. "The Remarkable Wreck of the *Thomas Hyke*" is perhaps the best of them all, but its device—staying on a ship after less sensible men have abandoned it—appears in many stories, including "The Water-Devil." Stockton uses this device in his land stories in another form; the heroes return to what they already know is safe and established, whether it is a backyard or a principle. (Stockton's heroes are continually finding romance in their own backyard, sometimes even literally, as in "My Unwilling Neighbor," where the hero's house is torn from a hill in a storm and slides into the garden of his beloved.) Stockton always disclaimed that he attached morals to his stories, and, indeed, in *John Gayther's Garden*, Pomona's farmer husband says:

"My opinion about morals to stories is that the people who read them ought to work them out for themselves. . . . Some people work out one kind of moral, and others work out another kind. It was a pretty big job to write that story, which I had to do the most of, and I don't think I ought to be called on to put in any moral, which is a good deal like being asked to make bread for the man who buys my wheat."

But there are certain themes—or patterns—in Stockton's work that approach being morals, and the principle of sticking to what

one already knows is perhaps the one that crops up most. Another
is the right of the individual to live his own life without interference.
Stockton apparently disliked busybodies, for the meddlers in his
writing always learn their mistake. Sometimes he even spells the
moral out; in a short story called "The Clocks of Rondaine," an
old woman tells the little girl who has tried in vain to synchronize
the clocks in the village: "Never ask people as old as I am to alter
the principles which have always made clear to them what they
should do or the clocks which have always told them when they
should do it." The Junior Sorcerer discovers in "The Bee-Man of
Orn" that the Bee-Man has returned to his original form, even
though he has interfered to give him a fresh start in life. And the
Queen in "The Queen's Museum" is gently reprimanded for forcing
her passion for buttonholes on the people: " 'The longer your
Majesty lives,' said the Stranger, 'the better you will understand
that we cannot make other people like a thing simply because we
like it ourselves.' "

The morals in Stockton's stories are never harsh; evil is always
tame and rarely enters his world. There is a certain honesty even in
his dishonest characters, and there are usually reasons for their behavior. Only in a few tales—"The Griffin and the Minor Canon" or
" 'His Wife's Deceased Sister' "—is there a real note of bitterness.

But once in a while there is an anxious note in Stockton's insis-
tence on returning to what is already safe and established, and it
occurs too often to be a coincidence. Usually one finds it in a story
dealing with some kind of creative vision. The hero of "A Tale of
Negative Gravity" has to get rid of the marvelous invention that
gives him so much pleasure because people think he is mad. In "The
Magic Egg," in which the hero convinces a whole audience that he
is performing magic, his fiancée, who realizes the truth, tells him:
"Everything was a sham and a delusion; every word you spoke was
untrue. . . . Now I know nothing was real . . . not even the man."
And he loses her. In " 'His Wife's Deceased Sister' " the hero is
forced to sacrifice his precious manuscript because it is so good that

it might endanger his publishing market. There is something wistful in Stockton's praise of Mark Twain: "Mark Twain's most notable characteristic is courage. Few other men—even if the other men could think of such things—would dare to say the things that Mark Twain says." Stockton's bitterness over the rejection of his work after the publication of "The Lady or the Tiger?" does not seem enough to explain his repetition of theme: he places his truths in the mouths of fantastic creatures and children (children are constantly being held up as examples of logic and wisdom); he rarely analyzed his own work or even that of other writers; he set his limits and made few innovations. He decided not to be courageous.

Perhaps this is why the reader seldom encounters strong emotions in Stockton's writing. If evil is alien, so is tragedy. As for love, William Dean Howells remarked caustically: "Mr. Stockton is rarely more droll than when he lets his lovers disport themselves as lovers. It sometimes seems as if he looked up lovers' words in the dictionary." His shy young heroes, who are never particularly heroic, manage to win their ladies through a series of accidents or with the help of determined women like Mrs. Lecks and Mrs. Aleshine, who know a good match when they see one. In "My Terminal Moraine" the hero, trapped under ice, hears his sweetheart Agnes, whom he has been forbidden to see, chipping through the ice to him, and he is on the verge of proposing when she clears a hole—and offers him sandwiches! To Stockton passion is something semi-barbaric, as in "The Lady or the Tiger?" His young ladies are generally lukewarm goddesses to whom the heroes always defer, even if that means sacrificing their creativity. Presumably their lukewarm world is a safer one.

Stockton's personal dislikes are only hinted at. Because he has a weakness for truants and is constantly ironic about school, one suspects that he did not enjoy his school days. More than once he makes it clear that children—especially truants—have more wisdom than their elders, and sometimes he will even reverse their positions, as in the very funny episode in "The Accommodating Circumstance," in which the hero finds himself enrolled in a school run by boys. In one of Stockton's novels, a comic character says:

"Happening one day to pass a house with open windows, I heard the sound of children's voices speaking in unison, and knowing that this must be a school, I looked in, compelled entirely by that curiosity which often urges us to gaze upon human suffering . . ."

Even suffering is accepted passively. It cannot be much fun for the poor Minor Canon to be stuck in the dreadful wilds, but he never protests or comments on the ordeal. There is a certain stoicism in all Stockton's characters.

As an adult, Frank Stockton is said never to have entered a church except to attend a wedding or a funeral. Obviously he disliked his father's inflexible Methodism, for when he writes about a church, it is only to set the scene for a ghost or a fairy tale. He seldom mentions politics. He did write two stories about the Spanish-American War, but they are stories in which not a single life is lost and everything ends amicably. In his science-fiction novel *The Great War Syndicate*, a group of sensible businessmen form a syndicate to direct a war that has broken out between England and the United States, and only one life is lost. Concepts of government crop up frequently in the fairy tales, where they are turned inside out and upside down; in "The Floating Prince," a young prince anxious to set up a kingdom recruits school boys as aristocrats, a tiny fairy as his prime minister, and a group of distinguished citizens as his common people. The King in "The Banished King" discovers that he is precisely what is wrong with his kingdom—and hands his throne over to the Queen. But outside of fantasy Stockton avoids criticism of society.

Stockton's fictional world, in other words, is a deliberately limited one; he never thought of himself as anything more than a storyteller or identified his work with the mainstream of American literature in the nineteenth century. But his sense of humor, gentle irony, and informal style have made many of his fairy tales and stories timeless. Writing at a time when most children's books were still instructive and saccharine, he never condescended to children; he addressed them as adults. The critic, William Chislett, Jr., once said that Stockton "wrote first for children and then went on explaining things to the same children grown up." He chose to explain to children and adults that the world was a happy one. The delightful hermits, sailors, middle-aged women, children, and creatures of fantasy that inhabit his comedies only stumble across an occasional—and never very alarming—obstacle, for as Marian Stockton wrote:

"He had not the heart to make his stories end unhappily. He knew that there is much of the tragic in human lives, but he chose to ignore it as far as possible, and to walk in the pleasant ways which are numerous in this tangled world."

A Note About the Selection

The stories in *The Storyteller's Pack* are all fiction, and all are complete in themselves. We decided, for instance, not to include *The Dusantes*, Stockton's sequel to *The Casting Away of Mrs. Lecks and Mrs. Aleshine*, because it is inferior to the original story and adds little to it. Our collection gives examples of Stockton's fairy tales, ghost stories, and sea yarns, and different facets of his humor. Occasionally a story is included for another reason —no anthology of Stockton would be representative without "The Lady or the Tiger?", and " 'His Wife's Deceased Sister' " seems necessary for an understanding of Stockton's life and work, even though it is not one of his best tales. Although the stories are loosely grouped by genre, they are also arranged so that the theme or subject of one story leads into the next. "The Lady or the Tiger?" is again an exception, but there are similarities in the stories that precede and follow it—"Our Story" and " 'His Wife's Deceased Sister.' "

—*The Editors*

THE STORYTELLER'S PACK

A FRANK R. STOCKTON READER

Do take the tomb, Good Father, for it's as much yours as mine. . . .

The Bishop's Ghost
and the Printer's Baby

AROUND THE WALLS of a certain old church there stood many tombs, and these had been there so long that the plaster with which their lids were fastened down had dried and crumbled so that in most of them there were long cracks under their lids, and out of these the ghosts of the people who had been buried in the tombs were in the habit of escaping at night.

This had been going on for a long time, and at the period of our story the tombs were in such bad repair that every night the body of the church was so filled with ghosts that before daylight one of the sacristans was obliged to come into the church and sprinkle holy water everywhere. This was done to clear the church of ghosts before the first service began; and who does not know that if a ghost is sprinkled with holy water it shrivels up! This first service was attended almost exclusively by printers on their way home from their nightly labors on the journals of the town.

The tomb which had the largest crack under its lid belonged to a bishop who had died more than a hundred years before, and who had a great reputation for sanctity; so much so, indeed, that people had been in the habit of picking little pieces of plaster from under the lid of his tomb and carrying them away as holy relics, to prevent disease and accidents.

This tomb was more imposing than the others and stood upon a pedestal, so that the crack beneath its lid was quite plain to v⋯ and remarks had been made about having it repaired.

Very early one morning, before it was time for the first service, there came into the church a poor mason. His wife had recently recovered from a severe sickness, and he was desirous of making an offering to the church. But having no money to spare, he had determined that he would repair the bishop's tomb, and he consequently came to do this before his regular hours of work began.

All the ghosts were out of their tombs at the time, but they were gathered in the other end of the church, and the mason did not see them, nor did they notice him; and he immediately went to work. He had brought some plaster and a trowel, and it was not long before the crack under the lid of the tomb was entirely filled up and the plaster made as smooth and neat as when the tomb was new.

When his work was finished, the mason left the church by the little side door which had given him entrance.

Not ten minutes afterward, the sacristan came in to sprinkle the church with holy water. Instantly the ghosts began to scatter right and left and to slip into their tombs as quickly as possible, but when the ghost of the good bishop reached his tomb, he found it impossible to get in. He went around and around it, but nowhere could he find the least little chink by which he could enter. The sacristan was walking along the other side of the church, scattering holy water, and in great trepidation the bishop's ghost hastened from tomb to tomb, hoping to find one which was unoccupied, into which he could slip before the sprinkling began on that side of the church. He soon came to one which he thought might be unoccupied, but he discovered to his consternation that it was occupied by the ghost of a young girl who had died of love.

"Alas! Alas!" exclaimed the bishop's ghost. "How unlucky! Who would have supposed this to be your tomb?"

"It is not really my tomb," said the ghost of the young girl. "It is the tomb of Sir Geoffrey of the Marle, who was killed in battle nigh two centuries ago. I was told that it had been empty for a long time, for his ghost has gone to Castle Marle. Not long ago I came into the church, and finding this tomb unoccupied, I settled here."

"Ah, me!" said the bishop's ghost. "The sacristan will soon be around here with holy water. Could not you get out and go to your own tomb? Where is that?"

"Alas, good father," said the ghost of the young girl, "I have no tomb; I was buried plainly in the ground, and I do not know that I could find the place again. But I have no right to keep you out of this tomb, good father; it is as much yours as it is mine, so I will come out and let you enter; truly, you are in great danger. As for me, it doesn't matter very much whether I am sprinkled or not."

So the ghost of the young girl slipped out of Sir Geoffrey's tomb, and the bishop's ghost slipped in, but not a minute before the sacristan had reached the place. The ghost of the young girl flitted from one pillar to another until it came near the door, and there it paused, thinking what it should do next. Even if it could find the grave from which it had come, it did not want to go back to such a place; it liked churches better.

Soon the printers began to come in to the early morning service. One of them was very sad, and there were tears in his eyes. He was a young man, not long married, and his child, a baby girl, was so sick that he scarcely expected to find it alive when he should reach home that morning.

The ghost of the young girl was attracted by the sorrowful printer, and when the service was over and he had left the church, it followed him, keeping itself unseen. The printer found his wife in tears; the poor little baby was very low. It lay upon the bed, its eyes shut, its face pale and pinched, gasping for breath.

The mother was obliged to leave the room for a few moments to attend to some household affair, and her husband followed to comfort her, and when they were gone, the ghost of the young girl approached the bed and looked down on the little baby. It was nearer death than its parents supposed, and scarcely had they gone before it drew its last breath.

The ghost of the young girl bowed its head. It was filled with pity and sympathy for the printer and his wife. In an instant, however, it was seized with an idea, and the next instant it had acted upon it. Scarcely had the spirit of the little baby left its body than the spirit of the young girl entered it.

Now a gentle warmth suffused the form of the little child, a natural color came into its cheeks, it breathed quietly and regularly, and when the printer and his wife came back, they found their baby in a healthful sleep. As they stood amazed at the change in the countenance of the child, it opened its eyes and smiled upon them.

"The crisis is past!" cried the mother. "She is saved, and it is all because you stopped at the church instead of hurrying home, as you wished to do." The ghost of the young girl knew that this was true, and the baby smiled again.

It was eighteen years later, and the printer's baby had grown into a beautiful young woman. From her early childhood she had been fond of visiting the church and would spend hours among the tombs reading the inscriptions and sometimes sitting by them, especially by the tomb of Sir Geoffrey of the Marle. There, when there was nobody by, she used to talk with the bishop's ghost.

Late one afternoon she came to the tomb with a happy smile on her face. "Holy father," she said, speaking softly through the crack, "are you not tired of staying so long in this tomb which is not your own?"

"Truly, I am, daughter," said the bishop's ghost; "but I have no right to complain. I never come back here in the early morning without a feeling of the warmest gratitude to you for having

She had died of love.

given me a place of refuge. My greatest trouble is caused by the fear that the ghost of Sir Geoffrey of the Marle may some time choose to return. In that case I must give up to him his tomb. And then, where, oh where, shall I go?"

"Holy father," whispered the girl, "do not trouble yourself; you shall have your own tomb again, and need fear no one."

"How is that?" exclaimed the bishop's ghost. "Tell me quickly, daughter."

"This is the way of it," replied the young girl. "When the mason plastered up the crack under the lid of your tomb, he seems to have been very careful about the front part of it, but he did not take much pains with the back, where his work was not likely to be seen, so that there the plaster has crumbled and loosened very much; and with a long pin from my hair I have picked out ever so much of it, and now there is a great crack at the back of the tomb, where you can go in and come out just as easily as you ever did. As soon as night shall fall, you can leave this tomb and go into your own."

The bishop's ghost could scarcely speak for thankful emotions, and the happy young girl went home to the house of her father, now a prosperous man and the head printer of the town.

The next evening the young girl went to the church and hurried to the bishop's tomb. Therein she found the bishop's ghost, happy and content.

Sitting on a stone projection at the back of the tomb, she had a long conversation with the bishop's ghost, which, in gratitude for what she had done, gave her all manner of good advice and counsel. "Above all things, my dear daughter," said the bishop's ghost, "do not repeat your first great mistake; promise me that you will not die of love."

The young girl smiled. "Fear not, good father," she replied. "When I died of love, I was, in body and soul, but eighteen years old and knew no better; now, although my body is but eighteen, my soul is thirty-six. Fear not; never again shall I die of love."

He spent his whole time in the company of bees.

The Bee-Man of Orn

IN THE ANCIENT COUNTRY of Orn there lived an old man who was
called the Bee-man, because his whole time was spent in the company of bees. He lived in a small hut, which was nothing more
than an immense beehive, for these little creatures had built their
honeycombs in every corner of the one room it contained, on the
shelves, under the little table, all about the rough bench on which
the old man sat, and even about the headboard and along the
sides of his low bed. All day the air of the room was thick with
buzzing insects, but this did not interfere in any way with the old
Bee-man, who walked in among them, ate his meals, and went to
sleep without the slightest fear of being stung. He had lived with
the bees so long, they had become so accustomed to him, and his
skin was so tough and hard that the bees no more thought of
stinging him than they would of stinging a tree or a stone. A
swarm of bees had made their hive in a pocket of his old leathern
doublet; and when he put on this coat to take one of his long
walks in the forest in search of wild bees' nests, he was very glad
to have this hive with him, for if he did not find any wild honey,
he would put his hand in his pocket and take out a piece of a comb
for a luncheon. The bees in his pocket worked very industriously,
and he was always certain of having something to eat with him
wherever he went. He lived principally upon honey; and when he
needed bread or meat, he carried some fine combs to a village not
far away and bartered them for other food. He was ugly, untidy,
shriveled, and brown. He was poor, and the bees seemed to be his
only friends. But, for all that, he was happy and contented; he
had all the honey he wanted, and his bees, whom he considered the
best company in the world, were as friendly and sociable as they

9

could be, and seemed to increase in number every day.

One day there stopped at the hut of the Bee-man a Junior Sorcerer. This young person, who was a student of magic, necromancy, and the kindred arts, was much interested in the Bee-man, whom he had frequently noticed in his wanderings, and he considered him an admirable subject for study. He had got a great deal of useful practice by endeavoring to find out, by the various rules and laws of sorcery, exactly why the old Bee-man did not happen to be something that he was not and why he was what he happened to be. He had studied a long time at this matter and had found out something.

"Do you know," he said, when the Bee-man came out of his hut, "that you have been transformed?"

"What do you mean by that?" said the other, much surprised.

"You have surely heard of animals and human beings who have been magically transformed into different kinds of creatures?"

"Yes, I have heard of these things," said the Bee-man. "But what have I been transformed from?"

"That is more than I know," said the Junior Sorcerer. "But one thing is certain—you ought to be changed back. If you will find out what you have been transformed from, I will see that you are made all right again. Nothing would please me better than to attend to such a case."

And, having a great many things to study and investigate, the Junior Sorcerer went his way.

This information greatly disturbed the mind of the Bee-man. If he had been changed from something else, he ought to be that other thing, whatever it was. He ran after the young man and overtook him.

"If you know, kind sir," he said, "that I have been transformed, you surely are able to tell me what it is that I was."

"No," said the Junior Sorcerer, "my studies have not proceeded far enough for that. When I become a Senior, I can tell you all about it. But, in the meantime, it will be well for you to try to discover for yourself your original form, and when you have done that, I will get some of the learned masters of my art to restore you to it. It will be easy enough to do that, but you could not expect them to take the time and trouble to find out what it was."

And with these words he hurried away and was soon lost to view.

Greatly disquieted, the Bee-man retraced his steps and went to his hut. Never before had he heard anything which had so troubled him.

"I wonder what I was transformed from?" he thought, seating himself on his rough bench. "Could it have been a giant or a powerful prince or some gorgeous being whom the magicians or the fairies wished to punish? It may be that I was a dog or a horse or perhaps a fiery dragon or a horrid snake. I hope it was not one of these. But, whatever it was, everyone has certainly a right to his original form, and I am resolved to find out mine. I will start early tomorrow morning, and I am sorry now that I have not more pockets to my old doublet, so that I might carry more bees and more honey for my journey."

He spent the rest of the day in making a hive of twigs and straw, and having transferred to this a number of honeycombs and a colony of bees which had just swarmed, he rose before sunrise the next day, and having put on his leathern doublet and having bound his new hive to his back, he set forth on his quest, the bees who were to accompany him buzzing around him like a cloud.

As the Bee-man passed through the little village, the people greatly wondered at his queer appearance with the hive upon his back. "The Bee-man is going on a long expedition this time," they said; but no one imagined the strange business on which he was bent. About noon he sat down under a tree, near a beautiful meadow covered with blossoms, and ate a little honey. Then he untied his hive and stretched himself out on the grass to rest. As he gazed upon his bees hovering about him, some going out to the blossoms in the sunshine and some returning laden with the sweet pollen, he said to himself, "They know just what they have to do, and they do it; but alas for me! I know not what I may have to do. And yet, whatever it may be, I am determined to do it. In some way or other I will find out what was my original form, and then I will have myself changed back to it."

And now the thought came to him that perhaps his original form might have been something very disagreeable or even horrid.

"But it does not matter," he said sturdily. "Whatever I was, that shall I be again. It is not right for anyone to retain a form which does not properly belong to him. I have no doubt I shall discover my original form in the same way that I find the trees in which the wild bees hive. When I first catch sight of a bee tree, I am drawn toward it, I know not how. Something says to me, 'That is what you are looking for.' In the same way I believe that I shall find my original form. When I see it, I shall be drawn toward it. Something will say to me, 'That is it.'"

When the Bee-man was rested, he started off again, and in about an hour he entered a fair domain. Around him were beautiful lawns, grand trees, and lovely gardens; while at a little distance stood the stately palace of the Lord of the Domain. Richly dressed people were walking about or sitting in the shade of the trees and arbors; splendidly caparisoned horses were waiting for their riders; and everywhere were seen signs of opulence and gaiety.

"I think," said the Bee-man to himself, "that I should like to stop here for a time. If it should happen that I was originally like any of these happy creatures, it would please me much."

He untied his hive and hid it behind some bushes, and taking off his old doublet, laid that beside it. It would not do to have his bees flying about him if he wished to go among the inhabitants of this fair domain.

For two days the Bee-man wandered about the palace and its grounds, avoiding notice as much as possible but looking at everything. He saw handsome men and lovely ladies; the finest horses, dogs, and cattle that were ever known; beautiful birds in cages and fishes in crystal globes; and it seemed to him that the best of all living things were here collected.

At the close of the second day the Bee-man said to himself, "There is one being here toward whom I feel very much drawn, and that is the Lord of the Domain. I cannot feel certain that I was once like him, but it would be a very fine thing if it were so; and it seems impossible for me to be drawn toward any other being in the domain when I look upon him, so handsome, rich, and powerful. But I must observe him more closely and feel more sure of the matter before applying to the sorcerers to change me back into a lord of a fair domain."

The next morning the Bee-man saw the Lord of the Domain walking in his gardens. He slipped along the shady paths and followed him so as to observe him closely and find out if he were really drawn toward this noble and handsome being. The Lord of the Domain walked on for some time, not noticing that the Bee-man was behind him. But suddenly turning, he saw the little old man.

"What are you doing here, you vile beggar?" he cried; and he gave him a kick that sent him into some bushes that grew by the side of the path.

The Bee-man scrambled to his feet and ran as fast as he could to the place where he had hidden his hive and his old doublet.

"If I am certain of any thing," he thought, "it is that I was never a person who would kick a poor old man. I will leave this place. I was transformed from nothing that I see here."

He now traveled for a day or two longer, and then he came to a great black mountain, near the bottom of which was an opening like the mouth of a cave.

This mountain he had heard was filled with caverns and underground passages, which were the abodes of dragons, evil spirits, horrid creatures of all kinds.

"Ah me!" said the Bee-man with a sigh. "I suppose I ought to visit this place. If I am going to do this thing properly, I should look on all sides of the subject, and I may have been one of those horrid creatures myself."

Thereupon he went to the mountain, and as he approached the opening of the passage which led into its inmost recesses, he saw, sitting upon the ground and leaning his back against a tree, a languid youth.

"Good day," said this individual when he saw the Bee-man. "Are you going inside?"

"Yes," said the Bee-man, "that is what I intend to do."

"Then," said the Languid Youth, slowly rising to his feet, "I think I will go with you. I was told that if I went in there I should get my energies toned up, and they need it very much; but I did not feel equal to entering by myself, and I thought I would wait until someone came along. I am very glad to see you, and we will go in together."

So the two went into the cave, and they had proceeded but a short distance when they met a very little creature, whom it was easy to recognize as a Very Imp. He was about two feet high and resembled in color a freshly polished pair of boots. He was extremely lively and active and came bounding toward them.

"What did you two people come here for?" he asked.

"I came," said the Languid Youth, "to have my energies toned up."

"You have come to the right place," said the Very Imp. "We will tone you up. And what does that old Bee-man want?"

"He has been transformed from something and wants to find out what it is. He thinks he may have been one of the things in here."

"I should not wonder if that were so," said the Very Imp, rolling his head on one side and eying the Bee-man with a critical gaze.

"All right," said the Very Imp. "He can go around and pick

out his previous existence. We have here all sorts of vile creepers, crawlers, hissers, and snorters. I suppose he thinks anything will be better than a Bee-man."

"It is not because I want to be better than I am," said the Bee-man, "that I started out on this search. I have simply an honest desire to become what I originally was."

"Oh! that is it, is it?" said the other. "There is an idiotic moon-calf here with a clam head, which must be just like what you used to be."

"Nonsense," said the Bee-man. "You have not the least idea what an honest purpose is. I shall go about and see for myself."

"Go ahead," said the Very Imp, "and I will attend to this fellow who wants to be toned up." So saying, he joined the Languid Youth.

"Look here," said that individual, regarding him with interest, "do you black and shine yourself every morning?"

"No," said the other, "it is waterproof varnish. You want to be invigorated, don't you? Well, I will tell you a splendid way to begin. You see that Bee-man has put down his hive and his coat with the bees in it. Just wait till he gets out of sight, and then catch a lot of those bees and squeeze them flat. If you spread them on a sticky rag and make a plaster and put it on the small of your back, it will invigorate you like everything, especially if some of the bees are not quite dead."

"Yes," said the Languid Youth, looking at him with his mild eyes "but if I had energy enough to catch a bee, I would be satisfied. Suppose you catch a lot for me."

"The subject is changed," said the Very Imp. "We are now about to visit the spacious chamber of the King of the Snap-dragons."

"That is a flower," said the Languid Youth.

"You will find him a gay old blossom," said the other. "When he has chased you round his room and has blown sparks at you, and has snorted and howled and cracked his tail and snapped his jaws like a pair of anvils, your energies will be toned up higher than ever before in your life."

"No doubt of it," said the Languid Youth; "but I think I will begin with something a little milder."

"Well then," said the other, "there is a flat-tailed Demon of the Gorge in here. He is generally asleep, and, if you say so, you can slip into the farthest corner of his cave, and I'll solder his tail to the opposite wall. Then he will rage and roar, but he can't get at you, for he doesn't reach all the way across his cave; I have measured him. It will tone you up wonderfully to sit there and watch him."

"Very likely," said the Languid Youth; "but I would rather stay outside and let you go up in the corner. The performance in that way will be more interesting to me."

"You are dreadfully hard to please," said the Very Imp. "I have offered them to you loose, and I have offered them fastened to a wall, and now the best thing I can do is to give you a chance at one of them that can't move at all. It is the Ghastly Griffin and is enchanted. He can't stir so much as the tip of his whiskers for a thousand years. You can go to his cave and examine him just as if he were stuffed, and then you can sit on his back and think how it would be if you should live to be a thousand years old and he should wake up while you are sitting there. It would be easy to imagine a lot of horrible things he would do to you when you look at his open mouth with its awful fangs, his dreadful claws, and his horrible wings all covered with spikes."

"I think that might suit me," said the Languid Youth. "I would much rather imagine the exercises of these monsters than to see them really going on."

"Come on, then," said the Very Imp, and he led the way to the cave of the Ghastly Griffin.

The Bee-man went by himself through a great part of the mountain and looked into many of its gloomy caves and recesses, recoiling in horror from most of the dreadful monsters who met his eyes. While he was wandering about, an awful roar was heard resounding through the passages of the mountain, and soon there came flapping along an enormous dragon, with body black as night and wings and tail of fiery red. In his great foreclaws he bore a little baby.

"Horrible!" exclaimed the Bee-man. "He is taking that little creature to his cave to devour it."

He saw the dragon enter a cave not far away, and following, looked in. The dragon was crouched upon the ground with the little baby lying before him. It did not seem to be hurt but was frightened and crying. The monster was looking upon it with delight, as if he intended to make a dainty meal of it as soon as his appetite should be a little stronger.

"It is too bad!" thought the Bee-man. "Somebody ought to do something." And turning around, he ran away as fast as he could.

He ran through various passages until he came to the spot where he had left his beehive. Picking it up, he hurried back, carrying the hive in his two hands before him. When he reached the cave of the dragon, he looked in and saw the monster still crouched over the weeping child. Without a moment's hesitation, the Bee-man rushed into the cave and threw his hive straight into the face of the dragon. The bees, enraged by the shock, rushed out in an angry crowd and immediately fell upon the head, mouth, eyes, and nose of the dragon. The great monster, astounded by this sudden attack, and driven almost wild by the numberless stings of the bees, sprang back to the farthest portion of his cave, still followed by his relentless enemies, at whom he flapped wildly with his great wings and struck with his paws. While the dragon was thus engaged with the bees, the Bee-man rushed forward, and seizing the child, he hurried away. He did not stop to pick up his doublet but kept on until he reached the entrance of the caves. There he saw the Very Imp hopping along on one leg and rubbing his back and shoulders with his hands, and stopped to inquire what was the matter and what had become of the Languid Youth.

"He is no kind of a fellow," said the Very Imp. "He disappointed me dreadfully. I took him up to the Ghastly Griffin and told him the thing was enchanted and that he might sit on its back and think about what it could do if it was awake; and when he came near it, the wretched creature opened its eyes and raised its head, and then you ought to have seen how mad that simpleton was. He made a dash at me and seized me by the ears; he kicked and beat me till I can scarcely move."

"His energies must have been toned up a good deal," said the Bee-man.

"Toned up! I should say so!" cried the other. "I raised a howl, and a Scissor-jawed Clipper came out of his hole and got after him; but that lazy fool ran so fast that he could not be caught."

The Bee-man now ran on and soon overtook the Languid Youth.

"You need not be in a hurry now," said the latter, "for the rules of this institution don't allow the creatures inside to come out of this opening or to hang around it. If they did, they would frighten away visitors. They go in and out of holes in the upper part of the mountain."

The two proceeded on their way.

"What are you going to do with that baby?" said the Languid Youth.

"I shall carry it along with me," said the Bee-man, "as I go on with my search, and perhaps I may find its mother. If I do not, I shall give it to somebody in that little village yonder. Anything would be better than leaving it to be devoured by that horrid dragon."

"Let me carry it. I feel quite strong enough now to carry a baby."

"Thank you," said the Bee-man, "but I can take it myself. I like to carry something, and I have now neither my hive nor my doublet."

"It is very well that you had to leave them behind," said the Youth, "for the bees would have stung the baby."

"My bees never sting babies," said the other.

"They probably never had a chance," remarked his companion.

They soon entered the village, and after walking a short distance, the Youth exclaimed, "Do you see that woman over there sitting at the door of her house? She has beautiful hair, and she is tearing it all to pieces. She should not be allowed to do that."

"No," said the Bee-man. "Her friends should tie her hands."

"Perhaps she is the mother of this child," said the Youth, "and if you give it to her she will no longer think of tearing her hair."

"But," said the Bee-man, "you don't really think this is her child?"

"Suppose you go over and see," said the other.

The Bee-man hesitated a moment, and then he walked toward the woman. Hearing him coming, she raised her head, and when she saw the child, she rushed toward it, snatched it into her arms, and screaming with joy, she covered it with kisses. Then with happy tears she begged to know the story of the rescue of her child, whom she never expected to see again; and she loaded the Bee-man with thanks and blessings. The friends and neighbors gathered around, and there was great rejoicing. The mother urged the Bee-man and the Youth to stay with her and rest and refresh themselves, which they were glad to do as they were tired and hungry.

They remained at the cottage all night, and in the afternoon of the next day the Bee-man said to the Youth, "It may seem an odd thing to you, but never in all my life have I felt myself drawn toward any living being as I am drawn toward this baby. Therefore, I believe that I have been transformed from a baby."

"Good!" cried the Youth. "It is my opinion that you have hit the truth. And now would you like to be changed back to your original form?"

"Indeed I would!" said the Bee-man. "I have the strongest yearning to be what I originally was."

The Youth, who had now lost every trace of languid feeling,

took a great interest in the matter and early the next morning started off to inform the Junior Sorcerer that the Bee-man had discovered what he had been transformed from and desired to be changed back to it.

The Junior Sorcerer and his learned masters were filled with enthusiasm when they heard this report, and they at once set out for the mother's cottage. And there by magic arts the Bee-man was changed back into a baby. The mother was so grateful for what the Bee-man had done for her that she agreed to take charge of this baby and to bring it up as her own.

"It will be a grand thing for him," said the Junior Sorcerer, "and I am glad that I studied his case. He will now have a fresh start in life and will have a chance to become something better than a miserable old man living in a wretched hut with no friends or companions but buzzing bees."

The Junior Sorcerer and his masters then returned to their homes, happy in the success of their great performance; and the Youth went back to his home, anxious to begin a life of activity and energy.

Years and years afterward, when the Junior Sorcerer had become a Senior and was very old indeed, he passed through the country of Orn, and noticed a small hut about which swarms of bees were flying. He approached it, and looking in at the door, he saw an old man in a leathern doublet, sitting at a table, eating honey. By his magic art he knew this was the baby which had been transformed from the Bee-man.

"Upon my word!" exclaimed the Sorcerer. "He has grown into the same thing again!"

The Queen's Museum

THERE WAS ONCE a queen who founded in her capital city a grand museum. This institution was the pride of her heart, and she devoted nearly all her time to overseeing the collection of objects for it and their arrangement in the spacious halls. This museum was intended to elevate the intelligence of her people, but the result was quite disappointing to the Queen. For some reason, and what it was she could not imagine, the people were not interested in her museum. She considered it the most delightful place in the world and spent hours every day examining and studying the thousands of objects it contained; but although here and there in the city there was a person who cared to visit the collection, the great body of the people found it impossible to feel the slightest interest in it. At first this grieved the Queen, and she tried to make her museum better; but as this did no good, she became very angry, and she issued a decree that all persons of mature age who were not interested in her museum should be sent to prison.

This decree produced a great sensation in the city. The people crowded to the building and did their very best to be interested; but in the majority of cases the attempt was an utter failure. They could not feel any interest whatever. The consequence was that hundreds and thousands of the people were sent to prison, and as there was not room enough for them in the ordinary jails, large temporary prisons were erected in various parts of the city. Those persons who were actually needed for work or service which no one else could do were allowed to come out in the daytime on parole; but at night they had to return to their prisons.

It was during this deplorable state of affairs that a stranger entered the city one day. He was surprised at seeing so many prisons, and approaching the window in one of them, behind the bars of which he saw a very respectable-looking citizen, he asked what all this meant. The citizen informed him how matters stood, and then, with tears mounting to his eyes, he added, "Oh, sir, I have tried my best to be interested in that museum, but it is impossible; I cannot make myself care for it in the slightest degree! And, what is more, I know I shall never be able to do so; and I shall languish here for the rest of my days."

Passing on, the Stranger met a mother coming out of her house. Her face was pale, and she was weeping bitterly. Filled with pity, he stopped and asked her what was the matter. "Oh, sir," she said, "for a week I have been trying, for the sake of my dear children, to take an interest in that museum. For a time I thought I might do it, but the hopes proved false. It is impossible. I must leave my little ones and go to prison."

The Stranger was deeply affected by these cases and many others of a similar character, which he soon met with. "It is too bad! too bad!" he said to himself. "I never saw a city in so much trouble. There is scarcely a family, I am told, in which there is not some uninterested person. I must see the Queen and talk to her about it." And with this he wended his way to the palace.

He met the Queen just starting out on her morning visit to the museum. When he made it known that he was a stranger and desired a short audience, she stopped and spoke to him.

"Have you visited my museum yet?" she said. "There is nothing in the city so well worth your attention as that. You should go there before seeing anything else. You have a high forehead and an intelligent expression, and I have no doubt that it will interest you greatly. I am going there myself, and I shall be glad to see what effect that fine collection has upon a stranger."

This did not suit the Stranger at all. From what he had heard, he felt quite sure that if he went to the museum, he would soon be in jail; and so he hurried to propose a plan which had occurred to

The people hadn't the slightest interest in her museum.

him while on his way to the palace.

"I came to see your Majesty on the subject of the museum," he said, "and to crave permission to contribute to the collection some objects which shall be interesting to everyone. I understand that it is highly desirable that everyone should be interested."

"Of course it is," said the Queen, "and although I think that there is not the slightest reason why everyone should not feel the keenest interest in what the museum already contains, I am willing to add to it whatever may make it of greater value."

"In that case," said the Stranger, "no time should be lost in securing what I wish to present."

"Go at once," said the Queen. "But how soon can you return?"

"It will take some days, at least," said the Stranger.

"Give me your parole to return in a week," said the Queen, "and start immediately."

The Stranger gave his parole and left the palace. Having filled a leathern bag with provisions from a cook's shop, he went out of the city gates. As he walked into the open country, he said to himself, "I have certainly undertaken a very difficult enterprise. Where I am to find anything that will interest all the people in that city, I am sure I do not know; but my heart is so filled with pity for the great number of unfortunate persons who are torn from their homes and shut up in prison that I am determined to do something for them, if I possibly can. There must be some objects to be found in this vast country that will interest everyone."

About noon he came to a great mountainside covered with a forest. Thinking that he was as likely to find what he sought in one place as another and preferring the shade to the sun, he entered the forest and walked for some distance along a path which gradually led up the mountain. Having crossed a brook with its edges lined with watercresses, he soon perceived a large cave, at the entrance of which sat an aged hermit. "Ah," said the Stranger to himself, "this is indeed fortunate! This good and venerable man, who passes his life amid the secrets of nature, can surely tell me what I wish to know." Saluting the Hermit, he sat down and told the old man the object of his quest.

"I am afraid you are looking for what you will not find," said the Hermit. "Most people are too silly to be truly interested in anything. They herd together like cattle and do not know what is good for them. There are now on this mountainside many commodious and comfortable caves, all of which would be tenanted if people only knew how improving and interesting it is to live apart from their fellowmen. But, so far as it can be done, I will help you in your quest, which I think is a worthy one. I can do nothing for you myself, but I have a pupil who is very much given to wandering about and looking for curious things. He may tell you where you will be able to find something that will interest everybody, though I doubt it. You may go and see him, if you like, and I will excuse him from his studies for a time, so that he may aid you in your search."

The Hermit then wrote an excuse upon a piece of parchment, and giving it to the Stranger, he directed him to the cave of his pupil.

This was situated at some distance and higher up the mountain, and when the Stranger reached it, he found the Pupil fast asleep upon the ground. This individual was a long-legged youth with long arms, long hair, a long nose, and a long face. When the Stranger awakened him, told him why he had come, and gave him the Hermit's excuse, the sleepy eyes of the Pupil brightened, and his face grew less long.

"That's delightful!" he said, "to be let off on a Monday; for I generally have to be satisfied with a half holiday, Wednesdays and Saturdays."

"Is the Hermit very strict with you?" asked the Stranger.

"Yes," said the Pupil. "I have to stick closely to the cave; though I have been known to go fishing on days when there was no holiday. I have never seen the old man but once, and that was

when he first took me. You know it wouldn't do for us to be too
sociable. That wouldn't be hermit-like. He comes up here on the
afternoons I am out and writes down what I am to do for the next
half week."

"And do you always do it?" asked the Stranger.

"Oh, I get some of it done," said the Pupil; "but there have
been times when I have wondered whether it wouldn't have been
better for me to have been something else. But I have chosen my
profession, and I suppose I must be faithful to it. We will start
immediately on our search; but first I must put the cave in order,
for the old man will be sure to come up while I am gone."

So saying, the Pupil opened an old parchment book at a
marked page and laid it on a flat stone, which served as a table,
and then placed a skull and a couple of bones in a proper position
nearby.

The two now started off, the Pupil first putting a line and hook
in his pocket and pulling out a fishing rod from under some
bushes.

"What do you want with that?" asked the Stranger. "We are
not going to fish!"

"Why not?" said the Pupil. "If we come to a good place, we
might catch something that would be a real curiosity."

Before long they came to a mountain brook, and here the Pupil
insisted on trying his luck. The Stranger was a little tired and
hungry and so was quite willing to sit down for a time and eat
something from his bag. The Pupil ran off to find some bait, and
he stayed away so long that the Stranger had quite finished his
meal before he returned. He came back at last, however, in a state
of great excitement.

"Come with me! Come with me!" he cried. "I have found something that is truly astonishing! Come quickly!"

The Stranger arose and hurried after the Pupil, whose long
legs carried him rapidly over the mountainside. Reaching a large

hole at the bottom of a precipitous rock, the Pupil stopped, and exclaiming, "Come in here and I will show you something that will amaze you!" he immediately entered the hole.

The Stranger, who was very anxious to see what curiosity he had found, followed him some distance along a narrow and winding underground passage. The two suddenly emerged into a high and spacious cavern, which was lighted by openings in the roof. On the floor, in various places, were strongly fastened boxes and packages of many sorts, bales and bundles of silks and rich cloths with handsome caskets, and many other articles of value.

"What kind of a place is this?" exclaimed the Stranger in great surprise.

"Don't you know?" cried the Pupil, his eyes fairly sparkling with delight. "It is a robber's den! Isn't it a great thing to find a place like this?"

"A robber's den!" exclaimed the Stranger in alarm. "Let us get out of it as quickly as we can or the robbers will return and we shall be cut to pieces."

"I don't believe they are coming back very soon," said the Pupil, "and we ought to stop and take a look at some of these things."

"Fly, you foolish youth!" cried the Stranger. "You do not know what danger you are in." And so saying, he turned to hasten away from the place.

But he was too late. At that moment the robber captain and his band entered the cave. When these men perceived the Stranger and the Hermit's Pupil, they drew their swords and were about to rush upon them, when the Pupil sprang forward, and throwing up his long arms, exclaimed, "Stop! It is a mistake!"

At these words, the robber captain lowered his sword and motioned to his men to halt. "A mistake!" he said. "What do you mean by that?"

"I mean," said the Pupil, "that I was out looking for curiosities and wandered into this place by accident. We haven't taken a thing. You may count your goods, and you will find nothing missing. We have not even opened a box, although I very much wanted to see what was in some of them."

"Are his statements correct?" said the Captain, turning to the Stranger.

"Entirely so," was the answer.

"You have truthful features and an honest expression," said the Captain, "and I do not believe you would be so dishonorable as to creep in here during our absence and steal our possessions. Your lives shall be spared, but you will be obliged to remain with us; for we cannot allow anyone who knows our secret to leave us. You shall be treated well and shall accompany us in our expeditions; and if your conduct merits it, you shall in time be made full members."

Bitterly the Stranger now regretted his unfortunate position. He strode up and down one side of the cave, vowing inwardly that never again would he allow himself to be led by a hermit's pupil. That individual, however, was in a state of high delight. He ran about from box to bale, looking at the rare treasures which some of the robbers showed him.

The two captives were fed and lodged very well; and the next day the Captain called them and the band together and addressed them.

"We are now twenty-nine in number," he said; "twenty-seven full members and two on probation. Tonight we are about to undertake a very important expedition, in which we shall all join. We shall fasten up the door of the cave, and at the proper time I shall tell you to what place we are going."

An hour or two before midnight the band set out, accompanied by the Stranger and the Hermit's Pupil; and when they had gone some miles the Captain halted them to inform them of the object of the expedition. "We are going," he said, "to rob the Queen's

museum. It is the most important business we have ever undertaken."

At these words the Stranger stepped forward and made a protest. "I left the city yesterday," he said, "commissioned by the
Queen to obtain one or more objects of interest for her museum;
and to return now to rob an institution which I have promised to
enrich will be simply impossible."

"You are right," said the Captain, after a moment's reflection.
"Such an action would be highly dishonorable on your part. If
you will give me your word of honor that you will remain by this
stone until our return, the expedition will proceed without you."

The Stranger gave his word, and having been left sitting upon
the stone, soon dropped asleep and so remained until he was
awakened by the return of the band a little before daylight.
They came slowly toiling along, each man carrying an enormous
bundle upon his back. Near the end of the line was the Hermit's
Pupil, bearing a load as heavy as any of the others. The Stranger
offered to relieve him for a time of his burden, but the Pupil would
not allow it.

"I don't wish these men to think I can't do as much as they
can," he said. "You ought to have been along. We had a fine time!
We swept that museum clean, I tell you! We didn't leave a thing
on a shelf or in a case."

"What sort of things are they?" asked the Stranger.

"I don't know," replied the Pupil. "We didn't have any light
for fear people would notice it, but the moon shone in bright
enough for us to see all the shelves and the cases; and our orders
were not to try and examine anything but to take all that was
there. The cases had great cloth covers on them, and we spread
these on the floor and made bundles of the curiosities. We are
going to examine them carefully as soon as we get to the den."

It was broad daylight when the robbers reached their cave. The
bundles were laid in a great circle on the floor, and at a given sig-

nal they were opened. For a moment each robber gazed blankly at
the contents of his bundle, and then they all began to fumble and
search among the piles of articles upon the cloths; but after a few
minutes, they arose, looking blanker and more disappointed than
before.

"So far as I can see," said the Captain, "there is nothing in the
whole collection that I care for. I do not like a thing here!"

"Nor I!" "Nor I!" "Nor I!" cried each one of his band.

"I suppose," said the Captain, after musing for a moment,
"that as these things are of no use to us, we are bound in honor to
take them back."

"Hold!" said the Stranger, stepping forward. "Do not be in
too great a hurry to do that." He then told the Captain of the
state of affairs in the city and explained in full the nature of the
expedition he had undertaken for the Queen. "I think it would be
better," he said, "if these things were not taken back for the
present. If you have a safe place where you can put them, I will in
due time tell the Queen where they are, and if she chooses she can
send for them."

"Good!" said the Captain. "It is but right that she should bear
part of the labor of transportation. There is a disused cave a mile
or so away, and we will tie up these bundles and carry them there;
and then we shall leave the matter to you. We take no further interest in it. And if you have given your parole to the Queen to return in a week," the Captain further continued, "of course you'll
have to keep it. Did you give your parole also?" he asked, turning
to the Pupil.

"Oh, no!" cried that youth. "There was no time fixed for my return. And I am sure that I like a robber's life much better than
that of a hermit. There is ever so much more spice and dash in
it."

The Stranger was then told that if he would promise not to be-
tray the robbers he might depart. He gave the promise, but added

sadly that he had lost so much time that he was afraid he would not now be able to attain the object of his search and return within the week.

"If that is the case," said the Captain, "we will gladly assist you. Comrades!" he cried, addressing his band. "After stowing this useless booty in the disused cave and taking some rest and refreshment, we will set out again, and the object of our expedition shall be to obtain something for the Queen's museum which will interest everyone."

Shortly after midnight the robbers set out, accompanied by the Stranger and the Pupil. When they had walked about an hour, the Captain, as was his custom, brought them to a halt that he might tell them where they were going. "I have concluded," said he, "that no place is so likely to contain what we are looking for as the castle of the great magician, Alfrarmedj. We will, therefore, proceed thither and sack the castle."

"Will there not be great danger in attacking the castle of a magician?" asked the Stranger in somewhat anxious tones.

"Of course there will be," said the Captain, "but we are not such cowards as to hesitate on account of danger. Forward, my men!" And on they all marched.

When they reached the magician's castle, the order was given to scale the outer wall. This the robbers did with great agility, and the Hermit's Pupil was among the first to surmount it. But the Stranger was not used to climbing, and he had to be assisted over the wall. Inside the great courtyard they perceived numbers of Weirds—strange shadowy creatures who gathered silently around them—but not in the least appalled, the robbers formed into a body and marched into the castle, the door of which stood open. They now entered a great hall, having at one end a doorway before which hung a curtain. Following their Captain, the robbers approached this curtain, and pushing it aside, entered the room beyond. There, behind a large table, sat the great magician, Alfrarmedj, busy over his mystic studies, which he generally pursued in the dead hours of the night. Drawing their swords, the robbers rushed upon him.

"Surrender!" cried the Captain, "and deliver to us the treasures of your castle."

The old magician raised his head from his book, and pushing up his spectacles from his forehead, looked at them mildly, and said, "Freeze!"

Instantly they all froze as hard as ice, each man remaining in the position in which he was when the magical word was uttered. With uplifted swords and glaring eyes they stood, rigid and stiff, before the magician. After calmly surveying the group, the old man said, "I see among you one who has an intelligent brow and truthful expression. His head may thaw sufficiently for him to tell me what means this untimely intrusion upon my studies."

The Stranger now felt his head begin to thaw and in a few moments he was able to speak. He then told the magician about the Queen's museum and how it had happened that he had come there with the robbers.

"Your motive is a good one," said the magician, "though your actions are somewhat erratic; and I do not mind helping you to find what you wish. In what class of objects do the people of the city take the most interest?"

"Truly I do not know," said the Stranger.

"This is indeed surprising!" exclaimed Alfrarmedj. "How can you expect to obtain that which will interest everyone when you do not know what it is in which everyone takes an interest? Go, find out this, and then return to me, and I will see what can be done."

The magician then summoned his Weirds and ordered them to carry the frozen visitors outside the castle walls. Each one of the rigid figures was taken up by two Weirds, who carried him out and stood him up in the road outside the castle. When all had been properly set up, with the Captain at their head, the gates were shut, and the magician still sitting at his table, uttered the word "Thaw!"

Instantly the whole band thawed and marched away. At daybreak they halted and considered how they should find out what all the people in the city took an interest in.

"One thing is certain," cried the Hermit's Pupil: "whatever it is, it isn't the same thing."

"Your remark is not well put together," said the Stranger, "but I see the force of it. It is true that different people like different things. But how shall we find out what the different people like?"

"By asking them," said the Pupil.

"Good!" cried the Captain, who preferred action to words. "This night we will ask them."

He then drew upon the sand a plan of the city—with which he was quite familiar, having carefully robbed it for many years—and divided it into twenty-eight sections, each one of which was assigned to a man. "I omit you," the Captain said to the Stranger, "because I find that you are not expert at climbing." He then announced that at night the band would visit the city and that each man should enter the houses in his district and ask the people what it was in which they took the greatest interest.

They then proceeded to the cave for rest and refreshment; and a little before midnight they entered the city, and each member of the band, including the Hermit's Pupil, proceeded to attend to the business assigned to him. It was ordered that no one should disturb the Queen, for they knew that what she took most interest in was the museum. During the night nearly every person in the town was aroused by a black-bearded robber, who had climbed into one of the windows of the house, and who, instead of demanding money and jewels, simply asked what it was in which that person took the greatest interest. Upon receiving an answer, the robber repeated it until he had learned it by heart and then went to the next house. As so many of the citizens were confined in prisons, which the robbers easily entered, they transacted the business in much less time than they would otherwise have required.

The Hermit's Pupil was very active, climbing into and out of houses with great agility. He obtained his answers quite as easily as did the others, but whenever he left a house there was a shade of disappointment upon his features. Among the last places that he visited was a room in which two boys were sleeping. He awoke them and asked the usual question. While they were trembling in their bed, not knowing what to answer, the Pupil drew his sword and exclaimed, "Come, now, no prevarication; you know it's fishing tackle. Speak out!" Each of the boys then promptly declared it was fishing tackle, and the Pupil left, greatly gratified. "I was very much afraid," he said to himself, "that not a person in my district would say fishing tackle; and I am glad to think that there were two boys who had sense enough to like something that is really interesting."

It was nearly daylight when the work was finished; and then the band gathered together in an appointed place on the outside of the city, where the Stranger awaited them. Each of the men had an excellent memory, which was necessary in their profession, and they repeated to the Stranger all the objects and subjects that had been mentioned to them, and he wrote them down upon tablets.

The next night, accompanied by the band, he proceeded to the castle of the magician, the great gate of which was silently opened for them by the Weirds. When they were ushered into the magician's room, Alfrarmedj took the tablets from the Stranger and examined them carefully.

"All these things should make a very complete collection," he said, "and I think I have specimens of the various objects in my interminable vaults." He then called his Weirds, and giving one of them the tablets, told him to go with his companions into the vaults and gather enough of the things therein mentioned to fill a large museum. In half an hour the Weirds returned and announced that the articles were ready in the great courtyard.

"Go, then," said the magician, "and assist these men to carry them to the Queen's museum."

The Stranger then heartily thanked Alfrarmedj for the assistance he had given; and the band, accompanied by a number of Weirds, proceeded to carry the objects of interest to the Queen's museum. It was a strange procession. Half a dozen Weirds carried a stuffed mammoth, followed by others bearing the skeleton of a whale, while the robbers and the rest of their queer helpers were loaded with every thing relating to history, science, and art which ought to be in a really good museum. When the whole collection had been put in place upon the floors, the shelves, and in the cases, it was nearly morning. The robbers, with the Hermit's Pupil, retired to the cave; the Weirds disappeared; while the Stranger betook himself to the Queen's palace, where, as soon as the proper hour arrived, he requested an audience.

When he saw the Queen, he perceived that she was very pale and that her cheeks bore traces of recent tears. "You are back in good time," she said to him, "but it makes very little difference whether you have succeeded in your mission or not. There is no longer any museum. There has been a great robbery, and the thieves have carried off the whole of the vast and valuable collection which I have been so long in making."

"I know of that affair," said the Stranger, "and I have already placed in your museum building the collection which I have obtained. If your Majesty pleases, I shall be glad to have you look at it. It may, in some degree, compensate for that which has been stolen."

"Compensate!" cried the Queen. "Nothing can compensate for it; I do not even wish to see what you have brought."

"Be that as your Majesty pleases," said the Stranger; "but I will be so bold as to say that I have great hopes that the collection which I have obtained will interest the people. Will your Majesty graciously allow them to see it?"

"I have no objection to that," said the Queen, "and indeed I shall be very glad if they can be made to be interested in the museum. I will give orders that the prisons be opened, so that everybody can go to see what you have brought; and those who shall be interested in it may return to their homes. I did not release my obstinate subjects when the museum was robbed, because their fault then was just as great as it was before; and it would not be right that they should profit by my loss."

The Queen's proclamation was made, and for several days the museum was crowded with people moving from morning till night through the vast collection of stuffed animals, birds, and fishes; rare and brilliant insects; mineral and vegetable curiosities; beautiful works of art; and all the strange, valuable, and instructive objects which had been brought from the interminable vaults of the magician Alfrarmedj. The Queen's officers, who had been sent to observe whether or not the people were interested, were in no doubt upon this point. Every eye sparkled with delight, for everyone found something which was the very thing he wished to see; and in the throng was the Hermit's Pupil, standing in rapt ecstasy before a large case containing all sorts of fishing tackle, from the smallest hooks for little minnows to the great irons and spears used in capturing whales.

No one went back to prison, and the city was full of reunited households and happy homes. On the morning of the fourth day a grand procession of citizens came to the palace to express to the Queen their delight and appreciation of her museum. The great happiness of her subjects could not but please the Queen. She called the Stranger to her and said to him, "Tell me how you came to know what it was that would interest my people."

"I asked them," said the Stranger. "That is to say, I arranged that they should be asked."

"That was well done," said the Queen; "but it is a great pity that my long labors in their behalf should have been lost. For many years I have been a collector of buttonholes; and there was nothing valuable or rare in the line of my studies of which I had not an original specimen or a facsimile. My agents brought me from foreign lands, even from the most distant islands of the sea, buttonholes of every kind—in silk, in wool, in cloth of gold, in every imaginable material—and of those which could not be obtained careful copies were made. There was not a duplicate specimen in the whole collection; only one of each kind; nothing repeated. Never before was there such a museum. With all my power I strove to educate my people up to an appreciation of buttonholes; but, with the exception of a few tailors and seamstresses, nobody took the slightest interest in what I had provided for their benefit. I am glad that my people are happy, but I cannot restrain a sigh for the failure of my efforts."

"The longer your Majesty lives," said the Stranger, "the better you will understand that we cannot make other people like a thing simply because we like it ourselves."

"Stranger," said the Queen, gazing upon him with admiration, "are you a king in disguise?"

"I am," he replied.

"I thought I perceived it," said the Queen, "and I wish to add that I believe you are far better able to govern this kingdom than I am. If you choose I will resign it to you."

"Not so, your Majesty," said the other. "I would not deprive you of your royal position, but I should be happy to share it with you."

"That will answer very well," said the Queen. And turning to an attendant, she gave orders that preparations should be made for their marriage on the following day.

After the royal wedding, which was celebrated with great pomp and grandeur, the Queen paid a visit to the museum, and much to her surprise, was greatly delighted and interested. The King then informed her that he happened to know where the robbers had stored her collection, which they could not sell or make use of, and if she wished, he would regain the collection and erect a building for its reception.

"We will not do that at present," said the Queen. "When I have thoroughly examined and studied all these objects, most of which are entirely new to me, we will decide about the button-holes."

The Hermit's Pupil did not return to his cave. He was greatly delighted with the spice and dash of a robber's life, so different from that of a hermit; and he determined, if possible, to change his business and enter the band. He had a conversation with the Captain on the subject, and that individual encouraged him in his purpose.

"I am tired," the Captain said, "of a robber's life. I have stolen so much that I cannot use what I have. I take no further interest in accumulating spoils. The quiet of a hermit's life attracts me; and, if you like, we will change places. I will become the pupil of your old master, and you shall be the captain of my band."

The change was made. The Captain retired to the cave of the Hermit's Pupil, while the latter, with the hearty consent of all the men, took command of the band of robbers.

When the King heard of this change, he was not at all pleased, and he sent for the ex-Pupil.

"I am willing to reward you," he said, "for assisting me in my recent undertaking; but I cannot allow you to lead a band of robbers in my dominions."

A dark shade of disappointment passed over the ex-Pupil's features, and his face lengthened visibly.

"It is too bad," he said, "to be thus cut short at the very outset of a brilliant career. I'll tell you what I'll do," he added suddenly, his face brightening. "If you'll let me keep on in my new profession, I'll promise to do nothing but rob robbers."

"Very well," said the King, "if you will confine yourself to that, you may retain your position."

The members of the band were perfectly willing to rob in the new way, for it seemed quite novel and exciting to them. The first place they robbed was their own cave, and as they all had excellent memories, they knew from whom the various goods had been stolen, and everything was returned to its proper owner. The ex-Pupil then led his band against the other dens of robbers in the kingdom, and his movements were conducted with such dash and vigor that the various hordes scattered in every direction, while the treasures in their dens were returned to the owners, or, if these could not be found, were given to the poor. In a short time every robber, except those led by the ex-Pupil, had gone into some other business; and the victorious youth led his band into other kingdoms to continue the great work of robbing robbers.

The Queen never sent for the collection of curiosities which the robbers had stolen from her. She was so much interested in the new museum that she continually postponed the reestablishment of her old one; and, as far as can be known, the buttonholes are still in the cave where the robbers shut them up.

This here one's guilty of piracy.

Prince Hassak's March

IN THE SPRING OF a certain year, long since passed away, Prince Hassak of Itoby determined to visit his uncle, the King of Yan.

"Whenever my uncle visited us," said the Prince, "or when my late father went to see him, the journey was always made by sea; and, in order to do this, it was necessary to go in a very round-about way between Itoby and Yan. Now, I shall do nothing of this kind. It is beneath the dignity of a prince to go out of his way on account of capes, peninsulas, and promontories. I shall march from my palace to that of my uncle in a straight line. I shall go across the country, and no obstacle shall cause me to deviate from my course. Mountains and hills shall be tunneled, rivers shall be bridged, houses shall be leveled; a road shall be cut through forests; and when I have finished my march, the course over which I have passed shall be a mathematically straight line. Thus will I show to the world that, when a prince desires to travel, it is not necessary for him to go out of his way on account of obstacles."

As soon as possible after the Prince had determined upon this march, he made his preparations, and set out. He took with him a few courtiers, and a large body of miners, rock-splitters, bridge-builders, and workmen of that class, whose services would very probably be needed. Besides these, he had an officer whose duty it was to point out the direct course to be taken, and another who was to draw a map of the march, showing the towns, mountains, and the various places it passed through. There were no compasses in those days, but the course-marker had an instrument which he would set in a proper direction by means of the stars, and then he could march by it all day. Besides these persons,

Prince Hassak selected from the schools of his city five boys and five girls and took them with him. He wished to show them how, when a thing was to be done, the best way was to go straight ahead and do it, turning aside for nothing.

"When they grow up, they will teach these things to their children," said he; "and thus I shall instill good principles into my people."

The first day Prince Hassak and his party marched over a level country, with no further trouble than that occasioned by the tearing down of fences and walls, and the destruction of a few cottages and barns. After encamping for the night, they set out the next morning, but had not marched many miles before they came to a rocky hill, on the top of which was a handsome house, inhabited by a Jolly-cum-pop.

"Your Highness," said the course-marker, "in order to go in a direct line we must make a tunnel through this hill, immediately under the house. This may cause the building to fall in, but the rubbish can be easily removed."

"Let the men go to work," said the Prince. "I will dismount from my horse and watch the proceedings."

When the Jolly-cum-pop saw the party halt before his house, he hurried out to pay his respects to the Prince. When he was informed of what was to be done, the Jolly-cum-pop could not refrain from laughing aloud.

"I never heard," he said, "of such a capital idea. It is so odd and original. It will be very funny, I am sure, to see a tunnel cut right under my house."

The miners and rock-splitters now began to work at the base of the hill, and then the Jolly-cum-pop made a proposition to the Prince.

"It will take your men some time," he said, "to cut this tunnel, and it is a pity your Highness should not be amused in the meanwhile. It is a fine day; suppose we go into the forest and hunt."

This suited the Prince very well, for he did not care about sitting under a tree and watching his workmen, and the Jolly-cum-pop having sent for his horse and some bows and arrows, the whole party, with the exception of the laborers, rode toward the forest, a short distance away.

"What shall we find to hunt?" asked the Prince of the Jolly-cum-pop.

"I really do not know," exclaimed the latter, "but we'll hunt whatever we happen to see—deer, small birds, rabbits, griffins, rhinoceroses, anything that comes along. I feel as gay as a skipping grasshopper. My spirits rise like a soaring bird. What a joyful thing it is to have such a hunt on such a glorious day!"

The gay and happy spirits of the Jolly-cum-pop affected the whole party, and they rode merrily through the forest; but they found no game, and after an hour or two, they emerged into the open country again. At a distance, on a slight elevation, stood a large and massive building.

"I am hungry and thirsty," said the Prince, "and perhaps we can get some refreshments at yonder house. So far, this has not been a very fine hunt."

"No," cried the Jolly-cum-pop, "not yet. But what a joyful thing to see a hospitable mansion just at the moment when we begin to feel a little tired and hungry!"

The building they were approaching belonged to a potentate, who lived at a great distance. In some of his travels he had seen this massive house and thought it would make a good prison. He accordingly bought it, fitted it up as a jail, and appointed a jailer and three myrmidons to take charge of it. This had occurred years before, but no prisoners had ever been sent to this jail.

A few days preceding the Jolly-cum-pop's hunt, the Potentate had journeyed this way and had stopped at his jail. After inquiring into its condition, he had said to the jailer, "It is now fourteen years since I appointed you to this place, and in all that time there have been no prisoners, and you and your men have been drawing your wages without doing anything. I shall return this way in a few days, and if I still find you idle, I shall discharge you all and close the jail."

This filled the jailer with great dismay, for he did not wish to lose his good situation. When he saw the Prince and his party approaching, the thought struck him that perhaps he might make prisoners of them, and so not be found idle when the Potentate returned. He came out to meet the hunters, and when they asked if they could here find refreshment, he gave them a most cordial welcome. His men took their horses, and inviting them to enter, he showed each member of the party into a small bedroom, of which there seemed to be a great many.

"Here are water and towels," he said to each one, "and when you have washed your face and hands, your refreshments will be ready." Then, going out, he locked the door on the outside.

The party numbered seventeen: the Prince, three courtiers, five boys, five girls, the course-marker, the map-maker, and the Jolly-cum-pop. The heart of the jailer was joyful; seventeen inmates was something to be proud of. He ordered his myrmidons to give the prisoners a meal of bread and water through the holes in their cell doors, and then he sat down to make out his report to the Potentate.

"They must all be guilty of crimes," he said to himself, "which are punished by long imprisonment. I don't want any of them executed."

So he numbered his prisoners from one to seventeen, according to the cell each happened to be in, and he wrote a crime opposite each number. The first was highway robbery, the next forgery, and after that followed treason, smuggling, barn-burning, bribery, poaching, usury, piracy, witchcraft, assault and battery, using false weights and measures, burglary, counterfeiting, robbing hen roosts, conspiracy, and poisoning his grandmother by proxy.

This report was scarcely finished when the Potentate returned. He was very much surprised to find that seventeen prisoners had come in since his previous visit, and he read the report with interest.

"Here is one who ought to be executed," he said, referring to Number Seventeen. "And how did he poison his grandmother by proxy? Did he get another woman to be poisoned in her stead? Or did he employ someone to act in his place as the poisoner?"

"I have not yet been fully informed, my lord," said the jailer, fearful that he should lose a prisoner; "but this is his first offense, and his grandmother, who did not die, has testified to his general good character."

"Very well," said the Potentate; "but if he ever does it again, let him be executed; and, by the way, I should like to see the prisoners."

Thereupon the jailer conducted the Potentate along the corridors and let him look through the holes in the doors at the prisoners within.

"What is this little girl in for?" he asked.

The jailer looked at the number over the door and then at his report.

"Piracy," he answered.

"A strange offense for such a child," said the Potentate.

"They often begin that sort of thing very early in life," said the jailer.

"And this fine gentleman," said the Potentate, looking in at the Prince, "what did he do?"

The jailer glanced at the number and the report.

"Robbed hen roosts," he said.

"He must have done a good deal of it to afford to dress so well," said the Potentate, passing on and looking into other cells. "It seems to me that many of your prisoners are very young."

"It is best to take them young, my lord," said the jailer. "They are very hard to catch when they grow up."

The Potentate then looked in at the Jolly-cum-pop and asked what was his offense.

"Conspiracy," was the answer.

"And where are the other conspirators?"

"There was only one," said the jailer.

Number Seventeen was the oldest of the courtiers.

"He appears to be an elderly man to have a grandmother," said the Potentate. "She must be very aged, and that makes it all the worse for him. I think he should be executed."

"Oh, no, my lord," cried the jailer. "I am assured that his crime was quite unintentional."

"Then he should be set free," said the Potentate.

"I mean to say," said the jailer, "that it was just intentional enough to cause him to be imprisoned here for a long time but not enough to deserve execution."

"Very well," said the Potentate, turning to leave; "take good care of your prisoners, and send me a report every month."

"That will I do, my lord," said the jailer, bowing very low.

The Prince and his party had been very much surprised and incensed when they found that they could not get out of their rooms, and they had kicked and banged and shouted until they were tired, but the jailer had informed them that they were to be confined there for years; and when the Potentate arrived, they had resigned themselves to despair. The Jolly-cum-pop, however, was affected in a different way. It seemed to him the most amusing joke in the world that a person should deliberately walk into a prison cell and be locked up for several years; and he lay down on his little bed and laughed himself to sleep.

That night one of the boys sat at his iron-barred window, wide awake. He was a truant and had never yet been in any place from which he could not run away. He felt that his schoolfellows depended upon him to run away and bring them assistance, and he knew that his reputation as a truant was at stake. His responsibility was so heavy that he could not sleep, and he sat at the window, trying to think of a way to get out. After some hours the moon arose, and by its light he saw upon the grass, not far from his window, a number of little creatures, which at first he took for birds or small squirrels; but on looking more attentively he perceived that they were pigwidgeons. They were standing around a flat stone and seemed to be making calculations on it with a piece of chalk. At this sight, the heart of the Truant jumped for joy. "Pigwidgeons can do anything," he said to himself, "and these certainly can get us out." He now tried in various ways to attract the attention of the pigwidgeons; but as he was afraid to call or whistle very loud, for fear of arousing the jailer, he did not succeed. Happily, he thought of a peashooter which he had in his pocket, and taking this out, he blew a pea into the midst of the little group with such force that it knocked the chalk from the hand of the pigwidgeon who was using it. The little fellows looked up in astonishment and perceived the Truant beckoning to them from his window. At first they stood angrily regarding him; but on his urging them in a loud whisper to come to his relief, they approached the prison, and clambering up a vine, soon reached his windowsill. The Truant now told his mournful tale, to which the pigwidgeons listened very attentively; and then, after a little consultation among themselves, one of them said, "We will get you out if you will tell us how to divide five-sevenths by six."

The poor Truant was silent for an instant, and then he said, "That is not the kind of thing I am good at, but I expect some of the other fellows could tell you easily enough. Our windows must be all in a row, and you can climb up and ask some of them; and if anyone tells you, will you get us all out?"

"Yes," said the pigwidgeon who had spoken before. "We will do that, for we are very anxious to know how to divide five-sevenths by six. We have been working at it for four or five days, and there won't be anything worth dividing if we wait much longer."

The pigwidgeons now began to descend the vine; but one of them lingering a little, the Truant, who had a great deal of curiosity, asked him what it was they had to divide.

"There were eight of us," the pigwidgeon answered, "who helped a farmer's wife, and she gave us a pound of butter. She did not count us properly, and divided the butter into seven parts. We did not notice this at first, and two of the party, who were obliged to go away to a distance, took their portions and departed, and now we can not divide among six the five-sevenths that remain."

"That is a pretty hard thing," said the Truant, "but I am sure some of the boys can tell you how to do it."

The pigwidgeons visited the next four cells, which were occupied by four boys, but not one of them could tell how to divide five-sevenths by six. The Prince was questioned, but he did not know; and neither did the course-marker, nor the map-maker. It was not until they came to the cell of the oldest girl that they received an answer. She was good at mental arithmetic; and after a minute's thought, she said, "It would be five forty-seconds."

"Good!" cried the pigwidgeons. "We will divide the butter into forty-two parts, and each take five. And now let us go to work and cut these bars."

Three of the six pigwidgeons were workers in iron, and they had their little files and saws in pouches by their sides. They went to work manfully, and the others helped them, and before morning one bar was cut in each of the seventeen windows. The cells were all on the ground floor, and it was quite easy for the prisoners to clamber out. That is, it was easy for all but the Jolly-cum-pop. He had laughed so much in his life that he had grown quite fat, and he found it impossible to squeeze himself through the opening made by the removal of one iron bar. The sixteen other prisoners had all departed; the pigwidgeons had hurried away to divide their butter into forty-two parts; and the Jolly-cum-pop still remained in his cell, convulsed with laughter at the idea of being caught in such a curious predicament.

"It is the most ridiculous thing in the world," he said. "I suppose I must stay here and cry until I get thin." And the idea so tickled him that he laughed himself to sleep.

The Prince and his party kept together and hurried from the prison as fast as they could. When the day broke, they had gone several miles, and then they stopped to rest. "Where is that Jolly-cum-pop?" said the Prince. "I suppose he has gone home. He is a pretty fellow to lead us into this trouble and then desert us! How are we to find the way back to his house? Course-marker, can you tell us the direction in which we should go?"

"Not until tonight, your Highness," answered the course-marker, "when I can set my instrument by the stars."

The Prince's party was now in a doleful plight. Every one was very hungry; they were in an open plain, no house was visible, and they knew not which way to go. They wandered about for some time, looking for a brook or a spring where they might quench their thirst; and then a rabbit sprang out from some bushes. The whole party immediately started off in pursuit of the rabbit. They chased it here, there, backward and forward, through hollows and over hills, until it ran quite away and disappeared. Then they were more tired, thirsty, and hungry than before; and to add to their miseries, when night came on, the sky was cloudy, and the course-marker could not set his instrument by the stars. It would be difficult to find sixteen more miserable people than the Prince and his companions when they awoke the next morning from their troubled sleep on the hard ground. Nearly starved, they gazed at one another with feelings of despair.

"I feel," said the Prince, in a weak voice, "that there is nothing I would not do to obtain food. I would willingly become a slave if my master would give me a good breakfast."

"So would I," ejaculated each of the others.

About an hour after this, as they were all sitting disconsolately upon the ground, they saw, slowly approaching, a large cart drawn by a pair of oxen. On the front of the cart, which seemed to be heavily loaded, sat a man with a red beard, reading a book. The boys, when they saw the cart, set up a feeble shout, and the man, lifting his eyes from his book, drove directly toward the group on the ground. Dismounting, he approached Prince

Hassak, who immediately told him his troubles and implored relief. "We will do anything," said the Prince, "to obtain food."

Standing for a minute in a reflective mood, the man with the red beard addressed the Prince in a slow, meditative manner: "How would you like," he said, "to form a nucleus?"

"Can we get anything to eat by it?" eagerly asked the Prince.

"Yes," replied the man, "you can."

"We'll do it!" immediately cried the whole sixteen, without waiting for further information.

"Which will you do first," said the man—"listen to my explanations or eat?"

"Eat!" cried the entire sixteen in chorus.

The man now produced from his cart of quantity of bread, meat, wine, and other provisions, which he distributed generously but judiciously to the hungry Prince and his followers. Everyone had enough but no one too much. And soon, revived and strengthened, they felt like new beings.

"Now," said the Prince, "we are ready to form a nucleus, as we promised. How is it done?"

"I will explain the matter to you in a few words," said the man with the red beard. "For a long time I have been desirous to found a city. In order to do this, one must begin by forming a nucleus. Every great city is started from a nucleus. A few persons settle down in some particular spot and live there. Then they are a nucleus. Then other people come there and gather around this nucleus, and then more people come and more, until in course of time there is a great city. I have loaded this cart with provisions, tools, and other things that are necessary for my purpose and have set out to find some people who would be willing to form a nucleus. I am very glad to have found you and that you are willing to enter into my plan; and this seems a good spot for us to settle upon."

"What is the first thing to be done?" said the Prince.

"We must all go to work," said the man with the red beard, "to build dwellings and also a schoolhouse for these young people. Then we must till some ground in the suburbs and lay the foundations, at least, of a few public buildings."

"All this will take a good while, will it not?" said the Prince.

"Yes," said the man, "it will take a good while; and the sooner we set about it, the better."

Thereupon tools were distributed among the party, and Prince, courtiers, boys, girls, and all went to work to build houses and form the nucleus of a city.

When the jailer looked into his cells in the morning and found that all but one of his prisoners had escaped, he was utterly astounded, and his face, when the Jolly-cum-pop saw him, made that individual roar with laughter. The jailer, however, was a man accustomed to deal with emergencies. "You need not laugh," he said. "Everything shall go on as before, and I shall take no notice of the absence of your companions. You are now numbered one to seventeen, inclusive, and you stand charged with highway robbery, forgery, treason, smuggling, barn-burning, bribery, poaching, usury, piracy, witchcraft, assault and battery, using false weights and measures, burglary, counterfeiting, robbing hen roosts, conspiracy, and poisoning your grandmother by proxy. I intended today to dress the convicts in prison garb, and you shall immediately be so clothed."

"I shall require seventeen suits," said the Jolly-cum-pop.

"Yes," said the jailer, "they shall be furnished."

"And seventeen rations a day," said the Jolly-cum-pop.

"Certainly," replied the jailer.

"This is luxury," roared the Jolly-cum-pop. "I shall spend my whole time in eating and putting on clean clothes."

Seventeen large prison suits were now brought to the Jolly-cum-pop. He put one on and hung up the rest in his cell. These suits were half bright yellow and half bright green, with spots of bright red as big as saucers.

The jailer now had doors cut from one cell to another. "If the

Potentate comes here and wants to look at the prisoners," he said to the Jolly-cum-pop, "you must appear in cell number one, so that he can look through the hole in the door and see you; then, as he walks along the corridor, you must walk through the cells, and whenever he looks into a cell, you must be there."

"He will think," merrily replied the Jolly-cum-pop, "that all your prisoners are very fat and that the little girls have grown up into big men."

"I will endeavor to explain that," said the jailer.

For several days the Jolly-cum-pop was highly amused at the idea of being seventeen criminals, and he would sit first in one cell and then in another, trying to look like a ferocious pirate, a hard-hearted usurer, or a mean-spirited chicken thief, and laughing heartily at his failures. But after a time he began to tire of this and to have a strong desire to see what sort of a tunnel the Prince's miners and rock-splitters were making under his house. "I had hoped," he said to himself, "that I should pine away in confinement and so be able to get through the window bars; but with nothing to do and seventeen rations a day, I see no chance of that. But I must get out of this jail, and as there seems no other way, I will revolt." Thereupon he shouted to the jailer through the hole in the door of his cell: "We have revolted! We have risen in a body and have determined to resist your authority and break jail!"

When the jailer heard this, he was greatly troubled. "Do not proceed to violence," he said; "let us parley."

"Very well," replied the Jolly-cum-pop, "but you must open the cell door. We cannot parley through a hole."

The jailer thereupon opened the cell door, and the Jolly-cum-pop, having wrapped sixteen suits of clothes around his left arm as a shield, and holding in his right hand the iron bar which had been cut from his window, stepped boldly into the corridor and confronted the jailer and his myrmidons.

"It will be useless for you to resist," he said. "You are but four, and we are seventeen. If you had been wise you would have made us all cheating shopkeepers, chicken thieves, or usurers. Then you might have been able to control us; but when you see before you a desperate highwayman, a daring smuggler, a bloodthirsty pirate, a wily poacher, a powerful ruffian, a reckless burglar, a bold conspirator, and a murderer by proxy, you well may tremble!"

The jailer and his myrmidons looked at each other in dismay.

"We sigh for no blood," continued the Jolly-cum-pop, "and will readily agree to terms. We will give you your choice: will you allow us to honorably surrender and peacefully disperse to our homes, or shall we rush upon you in a body, and after overpowering you by numbers, set fire to the jail and escape through the crackling timbers of the burning pile?"

The jailer reflected for a minute. "It would be better, perhaps," he said, "that you should surrender and disperse to your homes."

The Jolly-cum-pop agreed to these terms, and the great gate being opened, he marched out in good order. "Now," said he to himself, "the thing for me to do is to get home as fast as I can, or that jailer may change his mind." But being in a great hurry, he turned the wrong way and walked rapidly into a country unknown to him. His walk was a very merry one. "By this time," he said to himself, "the Prince and his followers have returned to my house, and are tired of watching the rock-splitters and miners. How amused they will be when they see me come back in this gay suit of green and yellow with red spots and with sixteen similar suits upon my arm! How my own dogs will bark at me! And how my own servants will not know me! It is the funniest thing I ever knew of!" And his gay laugh echoed far and wide. But when he had gone several miles without seeing any signs of his habitation, his gaiety abated. "It would have been much better," he said, as he sat down to rest under the shade of a tree, "if I had brought with me sixteen rations instead of these sixteen suits of clothes."

The Jolly-cum-pop soon set out again, but he walked a long

distance without seeing any person or any house. Toward the close of the afternoon he stopped, and looking back, he saw coming toward him a large party of foot travelers. In a few moments, he perceived that the person in advance was the jailer. At this the Jolly-cum-pop could not restrain his merriment. "How comically it has all turned out!" he exclaimed. "Here I've taken all this trouble and tired myself out and have nearly starved myself, and the jailer comes now, with a crowd of people, and takes me back. I might as well have stayed where I was. Ha ha!"

The jailer now left his party and came running toward the Jolly-cum-pop. "I pray you, sir," he said, bowing very low, "do not cast us off."

"Who are you all?" asked the Jolly-cum-pop, looking with much surprise at the jailer's companions, who were now quite near.

"We are myself, my three myrmidons, and our wives and children. Our situations were such good ones that we married long ago, and our families lived in the upper stories of the prison. But when all the convicts had left, we were afraid to remain, for should the Potentate again visit the prison, he would be disappointed and enraged at finding no prisoners and would probably punish us grievously. So we determined to follow you and to ask you to let us go with you, wherever you are going. I wrote a report, which I fastened to the great gate, and in it I stated that sixteen of the convicts escaped by the aid of outside confederates and that seventeen of them mutinied in a body and broke jail."

"That report," laughed the Jolly-cum-pop, "your Potentate will not readily understand."

"If I were there," said the jailer, "I could explain it to him; but, as it is, he must work it out for himself."

"Have you anything to eat with you?" asked the Jolly-cum-pop.

"Oh, yes," said the jailer, "we brought provisions."

"Well, then, I gladly take you under my protection. Let us

have supper. I have had nothing to eat since morning, and the weight of sixteen extra suits of clothes does not help to refresh one."

The Jolly-cum-pop and his companions slept that night under some trees and started off early the next morning. "If I could only get myself turned in the proper direction," said he, "I believe we should soon reach my house."

The Prince, his courtiers, the boys and girls, the course-marker, and the map-maker worked industriously for several days at the foundation of their city. They dug the ground, they carried stones, they cut down trees. This work was very hard for all of them, for they were not used to it. After a few days' labor, the Prince said to the man with the red beard, who was reading his book, "I think we have now formed a nucleus. Anyone can see that this is intended to be a city."

"No," said the man with the red beard, "nothing is truly a nucleus until something is gathered around it. Proceed with your work, while I continue my studies upon civil government."

Toward the close of that day, the red-bearded man raised his eyes from his book and beheld the Jolly-cum-pop and his party approaching. "Hurrah!" he cried, "we are already attracting settlers!" And he went forth to meet them.

When the Prince and the courtiers saw the Jolly-cum-pop in his bright and variegated dress, they did not know him; but the boys and girls soon recognized his jovial face, and tired as they were, they set up a hearty laugh, in which they were loudly joined by their merry friend. While the Jolly-cum-pop was listening to the adventures of the Prince and his companions and telling what had happened to himself, the man with the red beard was talking to the jailer and his party and urging them to gather around the nucleus which had been here formed and help to build a city.

"Nothing will suit us better," exclaimed the jailer, "and the sooner we build a town wall so as to keep off the Potentate if he should come this way, the better shall we be satisfied."

The next morning the Prince said to the red-bearded man, "Others have gathered around us. We have formed a nucleus and thus have done all that we promised to do. We shall now depart."

The man objected strongly to this, but the Prince paid no attention to his words. "What troubles me most," he said to the Jolly-cum-pop, "is the disgraceful condition of our clothes. They have been so torn and soiled during our unaccustomed work that they are not fit to be seen."

"As for that," said the Jolly-cum-pop, "I have sixteen suits with me, in which you can all dress, if you like. They are of unusual patterns, but they are new and clean."

"It is better," said the Prince, "for persons in my station to appear inordinately gay.than to be seen in rags and dirt. We will accept your clothes."

Thereupon the Prince and each of the others put on a prison dress of bright green and yellow with large red spots. There were some garments left over, for each boy wore only a pair of trousers with the waistband tied around his neck and holes cut for his arms; while the large jackets, with the sleeves tucked, made very good dresses for the girls. The Prince and his party, accompanied by the Jolly-cum-pop, now left the red-bearded man and his new settlers to continue the building of the city, and set off on their journey. The course-marker had not been informed the night before that they were to go away that morning and consequently did not set his instrument by the stars.

"As we do not know in which way we should go," said the Prince, "one way will be as good as another, and if we can find a road, let us take it; it will be easier walking."

In an hour or two they found a road and they took it. After journeying the greater part of the day, they reached the top of a low hill, over which the road ran, and saw before them a glittering sea and the spires and houses of a city.

"It is the city of Yan," said the course-marker.

"That is true," said the Prince; "and as we are so near, we may as well go there."

The astonishment of the people of Yan when this party, dressed in bright green and yellow with red spots, passed through their streets was so great that the Jolly-cum-pop roared with laughter. This set the boys and girls and all the people laughing, and the sounds of merriment became so uproarious that when they reached the palace the King came out to see what was the matter. What he thought when he saw his nephew in his fantastic guise, accompanied by a party apparently composed of sixteen other lunatics, cannot now be known; but after hearing the Prince's story, he took him into an inner apartment and thus addressed him: "My dear Hassak, the next time you pay me a visit, I beg for your sake and my own, that you will come in the ordinary way. You have sufficiently shown to the world that when a prince desires to travel it is often necessary for him to go out of his way on account of obstacles."

"My dear uncle," replied Hassak, "your words shall not be forgotten."

After a pleasant visit of a few weeks, the Prince and his party (in new clothes) returned (by sea) to Itoby, whence the Jolly-cum-pop soon repaired to his home. There he found the miners and rock-splitters still at work at the tunnel, which had now penetrated halfway through the hill on which stood his house. "You may go home," he said, "for the Prince has changed his plans. I will put a door to this tunnel, and it will make an excellent cellar in which to keep my wine and provisions."

The day after the Prince's return his map-maker said to him, "Your Highness, according to your commands, I made each day a map of your progress to the city of Yan. Here it is."

The Prince glanced at it, and then he cast his eyes upon the floor. "Leave me," he said. "I would be alone."

On the way he encountered a kindly Sphinx.

The Banished King

THERE WAS ONCE a kingdom in which everything seemed to go wrong. Everybody knew this, and everybody talked about it, especially the King. The bad state of affairs troubled him more than it did anyone else, but he could think of no way to make them better.

"I cannot bear to see things going on so badly," he said to the Queen and his chief councilors. "I wish I knew how other kingdoms were governed."

One of his councilors offered to go to some other countries and see how they were governed and come back and tell him all about it, but this did not suit his majesty.

"You would simply return," he said, "and give me your ideas about things. I want my own ideas."

The Queen then suggested that he should take a vacation and visit other kingdoms and see for himself how things were managed in them.

This did not suit the King. "A vacation would not answer," he said. "I should not be gone a week before something would happen here which would make it necessary for me to come back."

The Queen then suggested that he be banished for a certain time, say a year. In that case he could not come back and would be at full liberty to visit foreign kingdoms and find out how they were governed.

This plan pleased the King. "If it were made impossible for me to come back," he said, "of course I could not do it. The scheme is a good one. Let me be banished." And he gave orders that his council should pass a law banishing him for one year.

Preparations were immediately begun to carry out this plan,

and in a day or two the King bade farewell to the Queen and left his kingdom, a banished man. He went away on foot, entirely unattended. But as he did not wish to cut off all communication between himself and his kingdom, he made an arrangement which he thought a very good one. At easy shouting distance behind him walked one of the officers of the court, and at shouting distance behind him walked another, and so on at distances of about a hundred yards from each other. In this way there would always be a line of men extending from the King to his palace. Whenever the King had walked a hundred yards, the line moved on after him, and another officer was put in the gap between the last man and the palace door. Thus, as the King walked on, his line of followers lengthened and was never broken. Whenever he had any message to send to the Queen or any other person in the palace, he shouted it to the officer next to him, who shouted it to the one next to him, and it was so passed on until it reached the palace. If he needed food, clothes, or any other necessary thing, the order for it was shouted along the line, and the article was passed to him from man to man, each one carrying it forward to his neighbor and then retiring to his proper place.

In this way the King walked on day by day until he had passed entirely out of his own kingdom. At night he stopped at some convenient house on the road, and if any of his followers did not find himself near a house or cottage when the King shouted back the order to halt, he laid himself down to sleep wherever he might be. By this time the increasing line of followers had used up all the officers of the court, and it became necessary to draw upon some of the under government officers in order to keep the line perfect.

The King had not gone very far outside the limits of his dominions when he met a sphinx. He had often heard of these creatures, although he had never seen one before. But when he saw the winged body of a lion with a woman's head, he knew instantly what it was. He knew, also, that the chief business of a sphinx was that of asking people questions, and then getting them into trouble if the right answers were not given. He therefore determined that he would not be caught by any such tricks as these and that he would be on his guard if the Sphinx spoke to him. The creature was lying down when the King first saw it, but when he approached nearer, it rose to its feet. There was nothing savage about its look, and the King was not at all afraid.

"Where are you going?" said the Sphinx to him, in a pleasant voice.

"Give it up," replied the King.

"What do you mean by that?" said the other, with an air of surprise.

"I give that up, too," said the King.

The Sphinx then looked at him quite astonished.

"I don't mind telling you," said the King, "of my own free will and not in answer to any questions that I do not know where I am going. I am a king, as you may have noticed, and I have been banished from my kingdom for a year. I am now going to look into the government of other countries in order that I may find out what it is that is wrong in my own kingdom. Everything goes badly, and there is something very faulty at the bottom of it all. What this is, I want to discover."

"I am much interested in puzzles and matters of that kind," said the Sphinx, "and if you like I will go with you and help to find out what is wrong in your kingdom."

"All right," said the King. "I shall be glad of your company."

"What is the meaning of this long line of people following you at regular distances?" asked the Sphinx.

"Give it up," said the King.

The Sphinx laughed.

"I don't mind telling you," said the King, "of my own free will and not in answer to any question that these men form a line of communication between me and my kingdom, where matters, I fear, must be going on worse than ever in my absence."

The two now traveled on together until they came to a high

hill, from which they could see, not very far away, a large city.

"That city," said the Sphinx, "is the capital of an extensive country. It is governed by a king of mingled sentiments. Suppose we go there. I think you will find a government that is rather peculiar."

The King consented, and they walked down the hill toward the city.

"How did the king get his sentiments mingled?" asked the King.

"I really don't know how it began," said the Sphinx, "but the king, when a young man, had so many sentiments of different kinds and he mingled them up so much that no one could ever tell exactly what he thought on any particular subject. Of course, his people gradually got into the same frame of mind, and you never can know in this kingdom exactly what people think or what they are going to do. You will find all sorts of people here: giants, dwarfs, fairies, gnomes, and personages of that kind, who have been drawn here by the mingled sentiments of the people. I, myself, came into these parts because the people every now and then take a great fancy to puzzles and riddles."

On entering the city, the King was cordially welcomed by his brother sovereign, to whom he told his story; and he was lodged in a room in the palace. Such of his followers as came within the limits of the city were entertained by the persons near to whose houses they found themselves when the line halted.

Every day the Sphinx went with him to see the sights of this strange city. They took long walks through the streets and sometimes into the surrounding country—always going one way and returning another, the Sphinx being very careful never to bring the King back by the same road or street by which they went. In this way the King's line of followers, which, of course, lengthened out every time he took a walk, came to be arranged in long loops through many parts of the city and suburbs.

Many of the things the King saw showed plainly the mingled

sentiments of the people. For instance, he would one day visit a great smith's shop, where heavy masses of iron were being forged, the whole place resounding with tremendous blows from heavy hammers and the clank and din of iron on the anvils; while the next day he would find the place transformed into a studio, where the former blacksmith was painting dainty little pictures on the delicate surface of eggshells. The king of the country, in his treatment of his visitor, showed his peculiar nature very plainly. Sometimes he would receive him with enthusiastic delight, while at others he would upbraid him with having left his dominions to go wandering around the earth in this senseless way. One day his host invited him to attend a royal dinner, but when he went to the grand dining hall, pleased with anticipations of a splendid feast, he found that the sentiments of his majesty had become mingled and that he had determined, instead of having a dinner, to conduct the funeral services of one of his servants who had died the day before. All the guests were obliged by politeness to remain during the ceremonies, which our King, not having been acquainted with the deceased servant, had not found at all interesting.

"Now," said the King to the Sphinx, "I am in favor of moving on. I am tired of this place, where every sentiment is so mingled with others that you can never tell what anybody really thinks or feels. I don't believe anyone in this country was ever truly glad or sorry. They mix one sentiment so quickly with another that they never can discover the actual ingredients of any of their impulses."

"When this king first began to mingle his sentiments," said the Sphinx, "it was because he always desired to think and feel exactly right. He did not wish his feelings to run too much one way or the other."

"And so he is never either right or wrong," said the King. "I don't like that at all. I want to be one thing or the other."

"I have wasted a good deal of time at this place," remarked the

King, as they walked on, "and I have seen and heard nothing which I wish to teach my people. But I must find out some way to prevent everything going wrong in my kingdom. I have tried plan after plan and sometimes two or three together and have kept this up year after year, and yet nothing seems to do my kingdom any good."

"Have you heard how things are going on there now?" asked the Sphinx.

"Give it up," said the King. "But I don't mind saying of my own accord and not as an answer to any question that I have sent a good many communications to my Queen but have never received any from her. So I do not know how things are going on in my kingdom."

They then traveled on, the long line of followers coming after, keeping their relative positions a hundred yards apart and passing over all the ground the King had traversed in his circuitous walks about the city. Thus the line crept along like an enormous snake in straight lines, loops, and coils; and every time the King walked a hundred yards a fresh man from his capital city was obliged to take his place at the tail of the procession.

"By the way," said the Sphinx, after they had walked an hour or more, "if you want to see a kingdom where there really is something to learn, you ought to go to the country of the Gaumers, which we are now approaching."

"All right," said the King. "Let us go there."

In the course of the afternoon they reached the edge of a high bluff. "On the level ground, beneath this precipice," said the Sphinx, "is the country of the dwarfs called Gaumers. You can sit on the edge of the bluff and look down upon it."

The King and the Sphinx then sat down and looked out from the edge over the country of the little people. The officer of the court who had formed the head of the line wished very much to see what they were looking at; but when the line halted, he was not near enough.

"You will notice," said the Sphinx, "that the little houses and huts are gathered together in clusters. Each one of these clusters is under a separate king."

"Why don't they all live under one ruler?" asked the King. "That is the proper way."

"They do not think so," said the Sphinx. "In each of these clusters live the Gaumers who are best suited to each other; and if any Gaumer finds he cannot get along in one cluster, he goes to another. The kings are chosen from among the very best of them, and each one is always very anxious to please his subjects. He knows that everything that he and his queen and his children eat or drink or wear or have must be given to him by his subjects, and if it were not for them he could not be their ruler. And so he does everything that he can to make them happy and contented, for he knows if he does not please them and govern them well, they will gradually drop off from him and go to other clusters, and he will be left without any people or any kingdom."

"That is a very queer way of ruling," said the King. "I think the people ought to try to please their sovereign."

"He is only one, and they are a great many," said the Sphinx. "Consequently, they are much more important. No subject is ever allowed to look down upon a king simply because he helps to feed and clothe him and send his children to school. If anyone does a thing of this kind, he is banished until he learns better."

"All that may be very well for Gaumers," said the King, "but I can learn nothing from a government like that, where everything seems to be working in an opposite direction from what everybody knows is right and proper. A king anxious to deserve the good opinion of his subjects! What nonsense! It ought to be just the other way. The ideas of this people are as dwarfish as their bodies."

The King now arose and took up the line of march, turning away from the country of the Gaumers. But he had not gone more than two or three hundred yards before he received a message from the Queen. It came to him very rapidly, every man in the line seeming anxious to shout it to the man ahead of him as quickly as possible. The message was to the effect that he must either stop where he was or come home: his constantly lengthening line of communication had used up all the chief officers of the government, all the clerks in the departments, and all the officials of every grade, excepting the few who were actually needed to carry on the government, and if any more men went into the line it would be necessary to call upon the laborers and other persons who could not be spared.

"I think," said the Sphinx, "that you have made your line long enough."

"And I think," said the King, "that you made it a great deal longer than it need have been by taking me about in such winding ways."

"It may be so," said the Sphinx with its mystic smile.

"Well, I am not going to stop here," said the King, "and so I might as well go back as soon as I can." And he shouted to the head man of the line to pass on the order that his edict of banishment be revoked.

In a very short time the news came that the edict was revoked. The King then commanded that the procession return home, tail end foremost. The march was at once begun, each man, as he reached the city, going immediately to his home and family.

The King and the greater part of the line had a long and weary journey as they followed each other through the country and over the devious ways in which the Sphinx had led them in the City of Mingled Sentiments. The King was obliged to pursue all these complicated turnings or be separated from his officers and so break up his communication with his palace. The Sphinx accompanied him.

When at last he reached his palace, his line of former followers having apparently melted entirely away, he hurried upstairs to the Queen, leaving the Sphinx in the courtyard.

The King found, when he had time to look into the affairs of

It was clear that she could govern the country without him.

his dominions, that everything was in the most admirable condition. The Queen had retained a few of the best officials to carry on the government and had ordered the rest to fall, one by one, into the line of communication. The King set himself to work to think about the matter. It was not long before he came to the conclusion that the main thing which had been wrong in his kingdom was himself. He was so greatly impressed with this idea that he went down to the courtyard to speak to the Sphinx about it.

"I dare say you are right," said the Sphinx, "and I don't wonder that what you learned when you were away and what you have seen since you came back have made you feel certain that you were the cause of everything going wrong in this kingdom. And now, what do you intend to do about your government?"

"Give it up," promptly replied the King.

"That is exactly what I should advise," said the Sphinx.

The King did give up his kingdom. He was convinced that being a king was exactly the thing he was not suited for and that he would get on much better in some other business or profession. He determined to be a traveler and explorer, and to go abroad into other countries to find out things that might be useful to his own nation. His Queen had shown that she could govern the country most excellently, and it was not at all necessary for him to stay at home. She had ordered all the men who had made up his line to follow the King's example and to go into some good business, in order that not being bothered with so many officers, she would be able to get along quite easily.

The King was very successful in his new pursuit, and although he did not this time have a line of followers connecting him with the palace, he frequently sent home messages which were of use and value to his nation.

"I may as well retire," said the Sphinx to itself. "As the King has found his vocation and everything is going all right, it is not necessary that I should remain where I may be looked upon as a questionable personage."

The Griffin and the Minor Canon

OVER THE GREAT door of an old, old church, which stood in a quiet
town of a faraway land, there was carved in stone the figure of a
large griffin. The old-time sculptor had done his work with great
care, but the image he had made was not a pleasant one to look at.
It had a large head with enormous open mouth and savage teeth;
from its back arose great wings, armed with sharp hooks and
prongs; it had stout legs in front with projecting claws; but there
were no legs behind—the body running out into a long and powerful tail, finished off at the end with a barbed point. This tail was
coiled up under him, the end sticking up just back of his wings.

The sculptor, or the people who had ordered this stone figure,
had evidently been very much pleased with it, for little copies of
it, also in stone, had been placed here and there along the sides of
the church, not very far from the ground, so that people could
easily look at them and ponder on their curious form. There were
a great many other sculptures on the outside of this church—
saints, martyrs, grotesque heads of men, beasts, and birds, as well
as those of other creatures which cannot be named because nobody knows exactly what they were—but none were so curious
and interesting as the great griffin over the door and the little
griffins on the sides of the church.

A long, long distance from the town, in the midst of dreadful
wilds scarcely known to man, there dwelt the Griffin whose image
had been put up over the church door. In some way or other, the
old-time sculptor had seen him and afterward, to the best of his
memory, had copied his figure in stone. The Griffin had never
known this, until, hundreds of years afterward, he heard from a
bird, from a wild animal, or in some manner, which it is not now

"*. . . in the midst of dreadful wilds scarcely known to man, . . .*"

easy to find out, that there was a likeness of him on the old church in the distant town. Now, this Griffin had no idea how he looked. He had never seen a mirror, and the streams where he lived were so turbulent and violent that a quiet piece of water, which would reflect the image of anything looking into it, could not be found. Being, as far as could be ascertained, the very last of his race, he had never seen another griffin. Therefore it was, that, when he heard of this stone image of himself, he became very anxious to know what he looked like, and at last he determined to go to the old church and see for himself what manner of being he was. So he started off from the dreadful wilds and flew on and on until he came to the countries inhabited by men, where his appearance in the air created great consternation; but he alighted nowhere, keeping up a steady flight until he reached the suburbs of the town which had his image on its church. Here, late in the afternoon, he alighted in a green meadow by the side of a brook and stretched himself on the grass to rest. His great wings were tired, for he had not made such a long flight in a century or more.

The news of his coming spread quickly over the town, and the people, frightened nearly out of their wits by the arrival of so extraordinary a visitor, fled into their houses and shut themselves up. The Griffin called loudly for someone to come to him, but the more he called, the more afraid the people were to show themselves. At length he saw two laborers hurrying to their homes through the fields, and in a terrible voice he commanded them to stop. Not daring to disobey, the men stood, trembling.

"What is the matter with you all?" cried the Griffin. "Is there not a man in your town who is brave enough to speak to me?"

"I think," said one of the laborers, his voice shaking so that his words could hardly be understood, "that—perhaps—the Minor Canon—would come."

"Go call him, then!" said the Griffin. "I want to see him."

The Minor Canon, who filled a subordinate position in the old church, had just finished the afternoon services and was coming out of a side door with three aged women who had formed the weekday congregation. He was a young man of a kind disposition and very anxious to do good to the people of the town. Apart from his duties in the church, where he conducted services every weekday, he visited the sick and the poor, counseled and assisted persons who were in trouble, and taught a school composed entirely of the bad children in the town with whom nobody else would have anything to do. Whenever the people wanted something difficult done for them, they always went to the Minor Canon. Thus it was that the laborer thought of the young priest when he found that someone must come and speak to the Griffin.

The Minor Canon had not heard of the strange event, which was known to the whole town except himself and the three old women, and when he was informed of it and was told that the Griffin had asked to see him, he was greatly amazed and frightened.

"Me!" he exclaimed. "He has never heard of me! What should he want with *me*?"

"Oh, you must go instantly!" cried the two men. "He is very angry now because he has been kept waiting so long; and nobody knows what may happen if you don't hurry to him."

The poor Minor Canon would rather have had his hand cut off than go out to meet an angry griffin; but he felt that it was his duty to go, for it would be a woeful thing if injury should come to the people of the town because he was not brave enough to obey the summons of the Griffin. So, pale and frightened, he started off.

"Well," said the Griffin, as soon as the young man came near, "I am glad to see that there is someone who has the courage to come to me."

The Minor Canon did not feel very courageous, but he bowed his head.

"Is this the town," said the Griffin, "where there is a church with a likeness of myself over one of the doors?"

The Minor Canon looked at the frightful creature before him and saw that it was, without doubt, exactly like the stone image on the church. "Yes," he said. "You are right."

"Well, then," said the Griffin, "will you take me to it? I wish very much to see it."

The Minor Canon instantly thought that if the Griffin entered the town without the people knowing what he came for, some of them would probably be frightened to death, and so he sought to gain time to prepare their minds.

"It is growing dark now," he said, very much afraid, as he spoke, that his words might enrage the Griffin, "and objects on the front of the church cannot be seen clearly. It will be better to wait until morning if you wish to get a good view of the stone image of yourself."

"That will suit me very well," said the Griffin. "I see you are a man of good sense. I am tired, and I will take a nap here on this soft grass, while I cool my tail in the little stream that runs near me. The end of my tail gets red-hot when I am angry or excited, and it is quite warm now. So you may go, but be sure and come early tomorrow morning and show me the way to the church."

The Minor Canon was glad enough to take his leave and hurried into the town. In front of the church he found a great many people assembled to hear his report of his interview with the Griffin. When they found that he had not come to spread ruin and devastation but simply to see his stony likeness on the church, they showed neither relief nor gratification but began to upbraid the Minor Canon for consenting to conduct the creature into the town.

"What could I do?" cried the young man. "If I should not bring him, he would come himself and perhaps end by setting fire to the town with his red-hot tail."

Still the people were not satisfied, and a great many plans were proposed to prevent the Griffin from coming into the town. Some elderly persons urged that the young men should go out and kill him; but the young men scoffed at such a ridiculous idea. Then someone said that it would be a good thing to destroy the stone image so that the Griffin would have no excuse for entering the town; and this proposal was received with such favor that many of the people ran for hammers, chisels, and crowbars with which to tear down and break up the stone griffin. But the Minor Canon resisted this plan with all the strength of his mind and body. He assured the people that this action would enrage the Griffin beyond measure, for it would be impossible to conceal from him that his image had been destroyed during the night. But the people were so determined to break up the stone griffin that the Minor Canon saw that there was nothing for him to do but to stay there and protect it. All night he walked up and down in front of the church door, keeping away the men who brought ladders, by which they might mount to the great stone griffin and knock it to pieces with their hammers and crowbars. After many hours the people were obliged to give up their attempts and went home to sleep; but the Minor Canon remained at his post till early morning, and then he hurried away to the field where he had left the Griffin.

The monster had just awakened, and rising to his forelegs and shaking himself, he said that he was ready to go into the town. The Minor Canon, therefore, walked back, the Griffin flying slowly through the air, at a short distance above the head of his guide. Not a person was to be seen in the streets, and they proceeded directly to the front of the church, where the Minor Canon pointed out the stone griffin.

The real Griffin settled down in the little square before the church and gazed earnestly at his sculptured likeness. For a long time he looked at it. First he put his head on one side, and then he put it on the other; then he shut his right eye and gazed with his left, after which he shut his left eye and gazed with his right. Then he moved a little to one side and looked at the image, then he moved the other way.

After a while, he said to the Minor Canon, who had been standing by all this time, "It is, it must be, an excellent likeness! That breadth between the eyes, that expansive forehead, those massive jaws! I feel that it must resemble me. If there is any fault to find with it, it is that the neck seems a little stiff. But that is nothing. It is an admirable likeness—admirable!"

The Griffin sat looking at his image all the morning and all the afternoon. The Minor Canon had been afraid to go away and leave him and had hoped all through the day that he would soon be satisfied with his inspection and fly away home. But by evening the poor young man was utterly exhausted and felt that he must eat and sleep. He frankly admitted this fact to the Griffin and asked him if he would not like something to eat. He said this because he felt obliged in politeness to do so, but as soon as he had spoken the words, he was seized with dread lest the monster should demand half a dozen babies or some tempting repast of that kind.

"Oh, no," said the Griffin. "I never eat between the equinoxes. At the vernal and at the autumnal equinox I take a good meal, and that lasts me for half a year. I am extremely regular in my habits and do not think it healthful to eat at odd times. But if you need food, go and get it, and I will return to the soft grass where I slept last night and take another nap."

The next day the Griffin came again to the little square before the church, and remained there until evening, steadfastly regarding the stone griffin over the door. The Minor Canon came once or twice to look at him, and the Griffin seemed very glad to see him; but the young clergyman could not stay as he had done before, for he had many duties to perform. Nobody went to the church, but the people came to the Minor Canon's house and anxiously asked him how long the Griffin was going to stay.

"I do not know," he answered, "but I think he will soon be satisfied with regarding his stone likeness, and then he will go away."

But the Griffin did not go away. Morning after morning he came to the church, but after a time he did not stay there all day.

He seemed to have taken a great fancy to the Minor Canon and followed him about as he pursued his various avocations. He would wait for him at the side door of the church, for the Minor Canon held services every day, morning and evening, though nobody came now. "If anyone should come," he said to himself, "I must be found at my post." When the young man came out, the Griffin would accompany him in his visits to the sick and the poor and would often look into the windows of the schoolhouse where the Minor Canon was teaching his unruly scholars. All the other schools were closed, but the parents of the Minor Canon's scholars forced them to go to school, because they were so bad they could not endure them all day at home—griffin or no griffin. But it must be said they generally behaved very well when that great monster sat up on his tail and looked in at the schoolroom window.

When it was perceived that the Griffin showed no sign of going away, all the people who were able to do so left the town. The canons and the higher officers of the church had fled away during the first day of the Griffin's visit, leaving behind only the Minor Canon and some of the men who opened the doors and swept the church. All the citizens who could afford it shut up their houses and traveled to distant parts, and only the working people and the poor were left behind. After some days, these ventured to go about and attend to their business, for if they did not work they would starve. They were getting a little used to seeing the Griffin, and having been told that he did not eat between equinoxes, they did not feel so much afraid of him as before.

Day by day the Griffin became more and more attached to the Minor Canon. He kept near him a great part of the time and often spent the night in front of the little house where the young clergyman lived alone. This strange companionship was often burdensome to the Minor Canon; but on the other hand, he could not deny that he derived a great deal of benefit and instruction from it. The Griffin had lived for hundreds of years and had seen much, and he told the Minor Canon many wonderful things.

"It is like reading an old book," said the young clergyman to himself; "but how many books I would have had to read before I would have found out what the Griffin has told me about the earth, the air, the water, about minerals and metals and growing things and all the wonders of the world!"

Thus the summer went on and drew toward its close. And now the people of the town began to be very much troubled again.

"It will not be long," they said, "before the autumnal equinox is here, and then that monster will want to eat. He will be dreadfully hungry, for he has taken so much exercise since his last meal. He will devour our children. Without doubt, he will eat them all. What is to be done?"

To this question no one could give an answer, but all agreed that the Griffin must not be allowed to remain until the approaching equinox. After talking over the matter a great deal, a crowd of the people went to the Minor Canon, at a time when the Griffin was not with him.

"It is all your fault," they said, "that that monster is among us. You brought him here, and you ought to see that he goes away. It is only on your account that he stays here at all, for although he visits his image every day, he is with you the greater part of the time. If you were not here, he would not stay. It is your duty to go away, and then he will follow you, and we shall be free from the dreadful danger which hangs over us."

"Go away!" cried the Minor Canon, greatly grieved at being spoken to in such a way. "Where shall I go? If I go to some other town, shall I not take this trouble there? Have I a right to do that?"

"No," said the people, "you must not go to any other town. There is no town far enough away. You must go to the dreadful wilds where the Griffin lives; and then he will follow you and stay there."

They did not say whether or not they expected the Minor Canon to stay there also, and he did not ask them anything about it. He bowed his head and went into his house to think. The more he thought, the more clear it became to his mind that it was his duty to go away and thus free the town from the presence of the Griffin.

That evening he packed a leathern bag full of bread and meat, and early the next morning he set out on his journey to the dreadful wilds. It was a long, weary, and doleful journey, especially after he had gone beyond the habitations of men, but the Minor Canon kept on bravely and never faltered. The way was longer than he had expected, and his provisions soon grew so scanty that he was obliged to eat but a little every day; but he kept up his courage and pressed on, and after many days of toilsome travel, he reached the dreadful wilds.

When the Griffin found that the Minor Canon had left the town, he seemed sorry but showed no disposition to go and look for him. After a few days had passed, he became much annoyed and asked some of the people where the Minor Canon had gone. But although the citizens had been so anxious that the young clergyman should go to the dreadful wilds, thinking that the Griffin would immediately follow him, they were now afraid to mention the Minor Canon's destination, for the monster seemed angry already, and if he should suspect their trick, he would doubtless become very much enraged. So everyone said he did not know, and the Griffin wandered about disconsolate. One morning he looked into the Minor Canon's schoolhouse, which was always empty now, and thought that it was a shame that everything should suffer on account of the young man's absence.

"It does not matter so much about the church," he said, "for nobody went there; but it is a pity about the school. I think I will teach it myself until he returns."

It was the hour for opening the school, and the Griffin went inside and pulled the rope which rang the school bell. Some of the children who heard the bell ran in to see what was the matter, supposing it to be a joke of one of their companions; but when they saw the Griffin, they stood astonished and scared.

"Go tell the other scholars," said the monster, "that school is about to open, and that if they are not all here in ten minutes, I shall come after them."

In seven minutes every scholar was in place.

Never was seen such an orderly school. Not a boy or girl moved or uttered a whisper. The Griffin climbed into the master's seat, his wide wings spread on each side of him, because he could not lean back in his chair while they stuck out behind, and his great tail coiled around in front of the desk, the barbed end sticking up, ready to tap any boy or girl who might misbehave. The Griffin now addressed the scholars, telling them that he intended to teach them while their master was away. In speaking he endeavored to imitate, as far as possible, the mild and gentle tones of the Minor Canon, but it must be admitted that in this he was not very successful. He had paid a good deal of attention to the studies of the school, and he determined not to attempt to teach them anything new but to review them in what they had been studying; so he called up the various classes and questioned them upon their previous lessons. The children racked their brains to remember what they had learned. They were so afraid of the Griffin's displeasure that they recited as they had never recited before. One of the boys, far down in his class, answered so well that the Griffin was astonished.

"I should think you would be at the head," said he. "I am sure you have never been in the habit of reciting so well. Why is this?"

"Because I did not choose to take the trouble," said the boy, trembling in his boots. He felt obliged to speak the truth, for all the children thought that the great eyes of the Griffin could see right through them and that he would know when they told a falsehood.

"You ought to be ashamed of yourself," said the Griffin. "Go down to the very tail of the class, and if you are not at the head in two days, I shall know the reason why."

The next afternoon this boy was number one.

It was astonishing how much these children now learned of what they had been studying. It was as if they had been educated over again. The Griffin used no severity toward them, but there was a look about him which made them unwilling to go to bed until they were sure they knew their lessons for the next day.

The Griffin now thought that he ought to visit the sick and the poor; and he began to go about the town for this purpose. The effect upon the sick was miraculous. All except those who were very ill indeed jumped from their beds when they heard he was coming and declared themselves quite well. To those who could not get up, he gave herbs and roots, which none of them had ever before thought of as medicines but which the Griffin had seen used in various parts of the world; and most of them recovered. But for all that, they afterward said that no matter what happened to them, they hoped that they should never again have such a doctor coming to their bedsides, feeling their pulses and looking at their tongues.

As for the poor, they seemed to have utterly disappeared. All those who had depended upon charity for their daily bread were now at work in some way or other, many of them offering to do odd jobs for their neighbors just for the sake of their meals—a thing which before had been seldom heard of in the town. The Griffin could find no one who needed his assistance.

The summer had now passed, and the autumnal equinox was rapidly approaching. The citizens were in a state of great alarm and anxiety. The Griffin showed no signs of going away but seemed to have settled himself permanently among them. In a short time the day for his semiannual meal would arrive, and then what would happen? The monster would certainly be very hungry and would devour all their children.

Now they greatly regretted and lamented that they had sent away the Minor Canon; he was the only one on whom they could have depended in this trouble, for he could talk freely with the Griffin and so find out what could be done. But it would not do to be inactive. Some step must be taken immediately. A meeting of the citizens was called, and two old men were appointed to go and talk to the Griffin. They were instructed to offer to prepare a splendid dinner for him on equinox day—one which would entirely satisfy his hunger. They would offer him the fattest mutton, the most tender beef, fish, and game of various sorts, and anything of the kind that he might fancy. If none of these suited, they were to mention that there was an orphan asylum in the next town.

"Anything would be better," said the citizens, "than to have our dear children devoured."

The old men went to the Griffin, but their propositions were not received with favor.

"From what I have seen of the people of this town," said the monster, "I do not think I could relish anything which was prepared by them. They appear to be all cowards, and therefore mean and selfish. As for eating one of them, old or young, I could not think of it for a moment. In fact, there was only one creature in the whole place for whom I could have had any appetite and that is the Minor Canon, who has gone away. He was brave and good and honest, and I think I should have relished him."

"Ah!" said one of the old men very politely. "In that case I wish we had not sent him to the dreadful wilds!"

"What!" cried the Griffin. "What do you mean? Explain instantly what you are talking about!"

The old man, terribly frightened at what he had said, was obliged to tell how the Minor Canon had been sent away by the people, in the hope that the Griffin might be induced to follow him.

When the monster heard this, he became furiously angry. He dashed away from the old men, and spreading his wings, flew backward and forward over the town. He was so much excited that his tail became red-hot and glowed like a meteor against the evening sky. When at last he settled down in the little field where he usually rested and thrust his tail into the brook, the steam arose like a cloud, and the water of the stream ran hot through the town. The citizens were greatly frightened and bitterly blamed the old man for telling about the Minor Canon.

"It is plain," they said, "that the Griffin intended at last to go and look for him, and we should have been saved. Now who can tell what misery you have brought upon us."

The Griffin did not remain long in the little field. As soon as his tail was cool he flew to the town hall and rang the bell. The citizens knew that they were expected to come there, and although they were afraid to go, they were still more afraid to stay away; and they crowded into the hall. The Griffin was on the platform at one end, flapping his wings and walking up and down, and the end of his tail was still so warm that it slightly scorched the boards as he dragged it after him.

When everybody who was able to come was there, the Griffin stood still and addressed the meeting.

"I have had a contemptible opinion of you," he said, "ever since I discovered what cowards you are, but I had no idea that you were so ungrateful, selfish, and cruel as I now find you to be. Here was your Minor Canon, who labored day and night for your good and thought of nothing else but how he might benefit you and make you happy; and as soon as you imagine yourselves threatened with a danger—for well I know you are dreadfully afraid of me—you send him off, caring not whether he returns or perishes, hoping thereby to save yourselves. Now, I had conceived a great liking for that young man and had intended, in a day or two, to go and look him up. But I have changed my mind about him. I shall go and find him, but I shall send him back here to live among you, and I intend that he shall enjoy the reward of his labor and his sacrifices. Go, some of you, to the officers of the church, who so cowardly ran away when I first came here, and tell them never to return to this town under penalty of death. And if, when your Minor Canon comes back to you, you do not bow yourselves before him, put him in the highest place among you, and serve and honor him all his life, beware of my terrible vengeance! There were only two good things in this town: the Minor Canon and the stone image of myself over your church door. One of these you have sent away, and the other I shall carry away myself."

With these words he dismissed the meeting, and it was time, for the end of his tail had become so hot that there was danger of its setting fire to the building.

The next morning the Griffin came to the church, and tearing the stone image of himself from its fastenings over the great door, he grasped it with his powerful forelegs and flew up into the air. Then, after hovering over the town for a moment, he gave his tail an angry shake and took up his flight to the dreadful wilds. When he reached this desolate region, he set the stone griffin upon a ledge of a rock which rose in front of the dismal cave he called his home. There the image occupied a position somewhat similar to that it had had over the church door; and the Griffin, panting with the exertion of carrying such an enormous load to so great a distance, lay down upon the ground and regarded it with much satisfaction. When he felt somewhat rested, he went to look for the Minor Canon. He found the young man, weak and half starved, lying under the shadow of a rock. After picking him up and carrying him to his cave, the Griffin flew away to a distant marsh where he procured some roots and herbs which he well knew were strengthening and beneficial to man, although he had never tasted them himself. After eating these, the Minor Canon was greatly revived and sat up and listened while the Griffin told him what had happened in the town.

"Do you know," said the monster, when he had finished, "that I have had, and still have, a great liking for you?"

"I am very glad to hear it," said the Minor Canon, with his usual politeness.

"I am not at all sure that you would be," said the Griffin, "if you thoroughly understood the state of the case, but we will not consider that now. If some things were different, other things would be otherwise. I have been so enraged by discovering the manner in which you have been treated that I have determined that you shall at last enjoy the rewards and honors to which you are entitled. Lie down and have a good sleep, and then I will take you back to the town."

As he heard these words, a look of trouble came over the young man's face.

"You need not give yourself any anxiety," said the Griffin, "about my return to the town. I shall not remain there. Now that I have that admirable likeness of myself in front of my cave, where I can sit at my leisure and gaze upon its noble features and magnificent proportions, I have no wish to see that abode of cowardly and selfish people."

The Minor Canon, relieved from his fears, lay back and dropped into a doze; and when he was sound asleep, the Griffin took him up and carried him back to the town. He arrived just before daybreak, and putting the young man gently on the grass in the little field where he himself used to rest, the monster, without having been seen by any of the people, flew back to his home.

When the Minor Canon made his appearance in the morning among the citizens, the enthusiasm and cordiality with which he was received were truly wonderful. He was taken to a house which had been occupied by one of the banished high officers of the place, and everyone was anxious to do all that could be done for his health and comfort. The people crowded into the church when he held services, so that the three old women who used to be his weekday congregation could not get to the best seats, which they had always been in the habit of taking; and the parents of the bad children determined to reform them at home, in order that he might be spared the trouble of keeping up his former school. The Minor Canon was appointed to the highest office of the old church, and before he died, he became a bishop.

During the first years after his return from the dreadful wilds, the people of the town looked up to him as a man to whom they were bound to honor and reverence; but they often also looked up to the sky to see if there were any signs of the Griffin coming back. However, in the course of time, they learned to

honor and reverence their former Minor Canon without the fear
of being punished if they did not do so.

But they need never have been afraid of the Griffin. The
autumnal equinox day came around, and the monster ate nothing.
If he could not have the Minor Canon, he did not care for anything. So, lying down, with his eyes fixed upon the great stone
griffin, he gradually declined and died. It was a good thing for
some of the people of the town that they did not know this.

If you should ever visit the old town, you would still see the little griffins on the sides of the church; but the great stone griffin
that was over the door is gone.

The Accommodating Circumstance

IT WAS ON A BRIGHT afternoon, many, many years ago, that a young baron stood on the stone steps that led down from the door of his ancestral home. That great castle was closed and untenanted, and the baron was taking leave of it forever. His father, who was now dead, had been very unfortunate, and had been obliged to sell his castle and his lands. But he had made it a condition that the nobleman who bought the estate should allow the young baron to occupy it until he was twenty-one years of age.

This period had now arrived, and although the purchaser, who did not need the castle, had told the baron that he might remain there as long as he chose, the young man was too high-spirited to depend upon the charity of anyone, and he determined to go forth and seek a fortune for himself. His purpose was to go to the town of the Prince of Zisk, a journey of a few days, and to offer to join an army which the prince intended to lead against a formidable band of robbers who had set up a stronghold in his dominions. If he should distinguish himself in this army, the young baron hoped that he might rise to an honorable position. At any rate, he would earn a livelihood for himself and be dependent upon no one.

But it was a very sad thing for him to leave this home where he was born and where he had spent most of his life. His parents were dead, he had no relatives, and now he was to leave the house which had been so dear to him. He stood with one foot upon the ground and the other upon the bottom step and looked up to the great hall door, which he had shut and locked behind him, as if he were unwilling to make the movement which would finally separate him from the old place.

As he stood thus, he heard someone approaching, and turning,

The castle was closed and he was leaving it forever.

he saw an old woman and a young girl coming toward the castle. Each carried a small bundle, and besides these, the young girl had a little leathern bag, which was fastened securely to her belt.

"Good sir," said the old woman, "can you tell me if we can rest for the night in this castle? My granddaughter and I have walked since early morning, and I am very tired. It is a long time since we have passed a house, and I fear we might not come to another one today."

The baron hesitated for a moment. It was true that there was no other house for several miles, and the old woman looked as if she was not able to walk any farther. The castle was shut up and deserted, for he had discharged his few servants that morning and he was just about to leave it himself; but for all that, he could not find it in his heart to say that there was no refuge there for these two weary travelers. His family had always been generous and hospitable, and although there was very little that he could offer now, he felt that he must do what he could and not send away an old woman and a young girl to perish on the road in the cold winter night which was approaching.

"The castle is a bare and empty place," he said, "but you can rest here for the night." And so saying, he went up the steps, opened the door, and invited the travelers to enter.

Of course if they stayed there that night, he must do so also, for he could not leave the castle in the care of strangers, although these appeared to be very inoffensive people. And thus he very unexpectedly re-entered the home he thought he had left forever.

There was some wood by the fireplace in the great hall, and the baron made a fire. He had left no provisions in the house, having given everything of the kind to the servants, but he had packed into his wallet a goodly store of bread, meat, and cheese, and with these he spread a meal for the wayfarers. When they had been strengthened by the food and warmed by the fire, the old woman told her story.

"You must not think, kind sir," she said, "that we are poor outcasts and wanderers. I have a very pleasant little home of my own, where my granddaughter and myself have lived very happily ever since she was a little baby, and now, as you see, she is quite grown up. But Litza—that is her name—has a godmother who is a very peculiar person, whom we are all obliged to obey; and she came to us yesterday and gave Litza a little iron box, which is in that leathern bag she carries, and charged her to start with me the next morning and take it to its destination."

In order to account for the condition of his house, the baron then told his story. Litza and her grandmother were grieved to hear the account of the young nobleman's ill fortune, and the old woman said if they prevented his journey they might yet try to go on.

"Oh, no," said the baron. "I was starting too late anyway, for it had taken me so long to bid good-bye to my old home. It will be just as well for me to go tomorrow. So you and your grand-daughter shall have a room here tonight, and all will be well."

The next morning, after a breakfast which quite finished the baron's provisions, the three set out together, as their roads lay in the same direction. About noon the old woman became very tired and hungry. There was no house in sight, and the road seemed quite deserted.

"If I had known it would be so far," she said to herself, "we would not have come. I am too old to walk for two days. If I could only remember the meaning of the words, I would surely try them now. But I cannot remember—I cannot remember."

When this old woman was a little girl, she had lived with Litza's godmother, who was the daughter of a magician and was now over a hundred years old. From this person she had learned five magical words, which, when repeated, would each bring up a different kind of goblin or spirit. In her youth Litza's grandmother had never used these words, for she was a timid girl; and now for years, although she remembered the words, she had entirely forgotten what sort of creature each one would call forth. Some of these beings were good, and some she knew were very bad, and so, for fear of repeating the wrong word, she had never used any one of them. But now she felt that if ever she needed the help of goblin or fairy, she needed it this day.

"I can walk no farther," she said, "and that young man cannot carry me. If I do not use my words, I must perish here. I will try one of them, come what may." And so, with fear and trembling, she repeated aloud the third word.

Instantly there appeared before her a strange being. He was of a pale pea-green color, with great black eyes, and long arms and legs which seemed continually in motion. He jumped into the air, he snapped his fingers over his head, and suddenly taking from his pockets two empty bottles and an earthen jar, he began tossing them in the air, catching them dexterously as they fell.

"Who on earth are you?" said the old woman, much astonished.

"I am the Green Goblin of the Third Word," replied the other, still tossing up his jar and bottles; "but I am generally known as the Accommodating Circumstance."

"I don't know exactly what that may be," said the old woman, "but I wish that instead of a juggler with empty bottles and jars you were a pastrycook with a basket full of something to eat."

Instantly the goblin changed into a pastrycook carrying a large basket filled with hot meat pies and buns. The old woman jumped to her feet with delight and beckoned to the others, who had just turned around to see where she was.

"Come here," she cried. "Here is a pastrycook who has arrived just in the nick of time."

The party now made a good meal, for which the old woman would not allow the baron to pay anything, as it was a repast to which she had invited him. And then they moved on again, the pastrycook following. But although the grandmother was re-

"Now I can travel with ease and comfort."

freshed by the food, she was still very tired. She fell back a little and walked by the side of the pastrycook.

"I wish," she said, "that you were a man with a chair on your back. Then you might carry me."

Instantly the pastrycook changed into a stout man in a blue blouse, with a wooden armchair strapped to his back. He stooped down, and the old woman got into the chair. He then walked on and soon overtook the baron and Litza.

"Ah!" cried the old woman. "See what good fortune has befallen me! The pastrycook has gone, and this man with his chair has just arrived. Now I can travel with ease and comfort."

"What wonderful good fortune!" cried Litza.

"Wonderful good fortune, indeed!" exclaimed the baron, equally pleased.

The four now pursued their way, the old woman comfortably nodding in the chair, to which the baron had secured her with his belt. In about an hour the road branched, and the baron asked the chair man which way led to the town of Zisk. But the man, who was a dull, heavy fellow, did not know, and the baron took the road to the right. After walking two or three miles, they came to a wide river, at the edge of which the road stopped. On a post was a signboard on which was painted "Blow ye horn for ye ferryman." Below this hung a large horn, with a small pair of bellows attached to the mouthpiece.

"That is a good idea," said the baron. "One ought to be able to blow a horn very well with a pair of bellows." And so saying, he seized the handle of the bellows and blew a blast upon the horn that made Litza and her grandmother clap their hands to their ears. "I think that will bring the ferryman," said the baron, as he helped the old woman to get out of her chair.

In a few minutes they heard the sound of oars, and a boat made its appearance from behind a point of land to the right. To their surprise it was rowed by a boy about fourteen years old. When the boat touched the shore, they all got in.

"I am afraid you cannot row so heavy a load," said the baron to the boy; "but perhaps this good man will help you."

The boy, who was well dressed and of a grave demeanor, looked sternly at the baron. "Order must be kept in the boat," he said. "Sit down, all of you, and I will attend to the rowing." And he began to pull slowly but steadily from the shore. But instead of rowing directly across the river, he rounded the high point to the right and then headed toward an island in the stream.

"Where are you taking us?" asked the baron.

"This is the place to land," replied the boy gruffly. And in a few strokes he ran the boat ashore at the island.

A large house stood not far away from the water, and the baron thought he would go there and make some inquiries, for he did not like the manner of the boy in the boat. He accordingly stepped ashore and, followed by the rest of his party, approached the house. When they reached it, they saw over the door, in large black letters, the words "School for Men." Two boys, well dressed and sedate, came out to meet them and ushered them in.

"What is this place?" asked the baron, looking about him.

"It is a school," was the reply, "established by boys for the proper instruction and education of men. We have found that there are no human beings who need to be taught so much as men; and it is to supply this long-felt want that we have set up our school. By diverting the ferry from its original course we have obtained a good many scholars who would not otherwise have entered."

"What do you teach men?" asked the baron.

"The principal thing we try to teach them," said the other, "is the proper treatment of boys. But you will know all about this in good time."

"What I wish most now to know," said the baron, smiling, "is whether or not we can all obtain lodging here tonight. It is already growing dark."

"Did these two ladies come with you?" asked the boy.

"Yes," answered the baron.

"It was very good of them," said the boy. "Of course they can stay here all night. We always try to accommodate friends who come with scholars."

It was past suppertime at the school, but the baron and his party were provided with a good meal, and Litza and her grand-mother were shown to a guest chamber on the ground floor. One boy then took charge of the chair-carrier, while another con-ducted the baron to a small chamber upstairs, where he found everything very comfortable and convenient.

"You can sit up and read for an hour or two," said the boy. "We don't put our scholars all into one great room like a barrack and make them put out their lights and go to bed just at the time when other people begin to enjoy the evening."

When the baron arose the next morning, he was informed that the principal wished to see him, and he was taken downstairs into a room where there was a very solemn-looking boy sitting in an armchair before a fire. This was the principal, and he arose and gravely shook hands with the baron.

"I am glad to welcome you to our school," he said, "and I hope you will do honor to it."

"I have no intention of remaining here," said the baron.

The principal regarded him with a look of great severity. "Si-lence, sir!" he said. "It pains me to think of the sorrow which would fill the hearts of your children or your young relatives if they could hear you deliberately declare that you did not wish to avail yourself of the extraordinary educational opportunities which are offered to you here."

The principal then rang a bell, and two of the largest scholars, who acted as monitors, entered the room. "Take this new pupil," he said to them, "to the schoolroom and have him entered in the lowest class. He has much to learn."

The baron saw that it would be useless to resist these two tall fellows, who conducted him from the room, and he peacefully followed them to the large schoolroom where he was put in a class and given a lesson to learn.

The subject of the lesson was the folly of supposing that boys ought not to be trusted with horses, battleaxes, and all the arms used in war and hunting. There were twelve reasons proving that men were very wrong in denying these privileges to boys, and the baron was obliged to learn them all by heart.

At the other end of the room he saw the chair-carrier, who was hard at work over a lesson on the wickedness of whipping boys. On the wall, at one end of the room, was the legend, in large letters, "The Boy: Know Him, and You Are Educated." At the other end were the words "Respect Your Youngers."

In the afternoon the baron studied sixteen rules which proved that boys ought to be consulted in regard to the schools they were sent to, the number of their holidays, the style of their new clothes, and many other things which concerned them more than anyone else. At the end of the afternoon session the principal made a short address to the school, in which he said that in four days it would be Christmas, at which time the scholars would have a month's holiday.

"We believe," he said, "that scholars ought to have at least that much time at Christmas; and besides, your instructors need relaxation. But," said he, with a severe look at the baron, "disaffected newcomers must not suppose that they will be allowed this privilege. Such pupils will remain here during the holidays."

After this speech, school was dismissed, and the scholars were allowed three hours to play.

The baron was disturbed when he found that he would not be permitted to leave. He had heard that the Prince of Zisk intended to start on his expedition immediately after Christmas; and if he did not get to the town very soon, he could not join his army. So he determined to escape.

Walking about, he met Litza and her grandmother. The old

woman was much troubled. She had been told that she could leave whenever she chose, but she felt she could not go away without the chair-carrier, and he was detained as a pupil. She would not explain her trouble to her granddaughter, for she did not wish her to know anything about the magical nature of the assistance she had received. In a few moments the chair-carrier also made his appearance, and then the baron, seeing that none of the boys were in sight, proposed that they should go down to the beach and escape in a ferryboat.

The boat was found there, with the oars, and they all jumped in. The baron and the chair-carrier then each seized an oar and pushed off. They were not a dozen yards from the shore when several of the boys, accompanied by some of the larger pupils, came running down to the beach. The baron could not help smiling when he saw them, and resting on his oar, he made a little speech.

"My young friends," he said, "you seem to have forgotten, when you set up your school, that men, when they become scholars, are as likely to play truant as if they were boys."

To these remarks the boy teachers made no answer, but the big scholars on shore looked at each other and grinned. Then they all stooped down and took hold of a long chain that lay coiled in the shallow water. They began to pull, and the baron soon perceived that the other end of the chain was attached to the boat. He and the chair man pulled as hard as they could at the oars, but in spite of their efforts they were steadily drawn to shore. Litza and her grandmother were then sent to their room, while the baron and the chair man were put to bed without their suppers.

The next day the old grandmother walked about by herself, more troubled than ever, for she was very anxious that Litza should fulfill her mission and that they should get back home before Christmas. And yet she would not go away and leave her magical companion. Just then she saw the chair-carrier looking out of a second-story window, with a blanket wrapped around him.

"Come down here," she said.

"I can't," he answered. "They say I am to stay in bed all day, and they have taken away my clothes."

"You might as well be back with your goblin companions," said the old woman, "for all the use you are to me. I wish you were somebody who could set things straight here."

Instantly there stood by her side a school trustee. He was a boy of grave and pompous demeanor, handsomely dressed, and carrying a large gold-headed cane.

"My good woman," he said, in a stately voice, "is there anything I can do to serve you?"

"Yes, sir," she replied. "My granddaughter and I"—she pointed to Litza, who just then came up—"wish to leave this place as soon as possible and to pursue our journey."

"Of course you may do so," said he. "This is not a school for women."

"But, Grandma," said Litza, "it would be a shame to go away without the poor baron, who is as anxious to get on as we are."

"There is a gentleman here, sir," said the old woman, "who does not wish to stay."

"Did you bring him?" asked the trustee.

"Yes, sir; he came with us."

"And you wish to take him away again?" said he.

"Yes, sir; we do," said Litza.

"Very well, then," said the trustee, severely; "he shall be dismissed. We will have no pupils here whose children or guardians desire their removal. I will give orders in regard to the matter."

In a few moments the baron's clothes were brought to him, and he was told that he might get out of bed and leave the establishment. When he came down and joined Litza and her grandmother, he looked about him and said, "Where is the chair-carrier? I cannot consent to go away and leave him here."

"Do not trouble yourself about that man," said the grandmother; "he has already taken himself away."

The party, accompanied by the trustee, proceeded to the boat, where the boy ferryman was waiting for them. To the surprise of the baron the trustee got in with them, and they were all rowed to the other side of the river, where they found the road that led to Zisk. The school trustee walked with them, delivering his opinions in regard to the education of men. The baron grew very tired of hearing this talk.

"I am much obliged to this person," he thought, "for having enabled me to get away from that queer school; but he certainly is a dreadful bore. I wish he were going on some other road."

Litza and her grandmother agreed with the baron, and the old woman would gladly have changed the trustee into a chair-carrier again, but she had no opportunity of doing so, for the pompous little fellow never fell back behind the rest of the party, where he could be transformed unobserved. So they all walked on together until they reached the middle of a great plain, when suddenly a large body of horsemen appeared from behind a clump of trees at no great distance.

"It is a band of robbers!" said the baron, stopping and drawing his sword. "I know their flag. And they are coming directly toward us."

The grandmother and Litza were terribly frightened, and the baron turned very pale, for what could his one sword do against all those savage horsemen? As for the school trustee, he was glad to fall back now, and he crouched behind the baron, nearly scared out of his wits. He even pushed the old woman aside, so as to better conceal himself.

"You wretched coward!" she exclaimed. "I wish you were somebody able to defend us against these robbers."

Instantly there was a great clank of steel, and in the place of the trustee there stood an immense man, fully eight feet high, clothed in mail, and armed to the teeth. At his left side he carried a great sword, and on the other a heavy mace. In his hand he held a strong bow, higher than himself. His belt was filled with daggers and arrows, and at his back was an immense shield.

"Hold this in front of your party," he said to the baron, setting the shield down before him, "and I will attend to these rascals."

Quickly fitting a long arrow to his bow, he sent it directly through the foremost horseman and killed a man behind him. Arrow after arrow flew through the air, until half the robbers lay dead on the field. The rest turned to fly, but the armed giant sprang in among them, his sword in one hand and his mace in the other, and in less than five minutes he had slain every one of them.

"Now, then," said he, returning and taking up his bow and shield, "I think we may proceed without further fear."

The baron and Litza were no less delighted at their deliverance than surprised at the appearance of this defender, and the old woman was obliged to explain the whole matter to them. "I did not want you to know anything about it," she said to Litza, "for a young girl's head should not be filled with notions of magic; but the case was very urgent, and I could not hesitate."

"I am very glad you did not hesitate," said the baron, "for in a few minutes we should all have been killed. There was certainly never anything so useful as your Accommodating Circumstance."

The armed giant was a quiet and obliging fellow, and he offered to carry the old woman on his shoulder, which she found a very comfortable seat.

Toward evening they arrived in sight of the town of Zisk, and the baron said to the grandmother, "I am very much afraid you will lose your giant, for when the prince sees such a splendid soldier he will certainly enlist him into his army."

"Oh, dear!" cried the old woman, slipping down from the giant's shoulder. "I wish this great fellow was somebody who could not possibly be of any use to the prince as a soldier."

Instantly there toddled toward her a little baby about a year old. She had a white cap on her funny little head and was very round and plump. She had scarcely taken three steps when she stumbled and sat down very suddenly, and then she began to try to pull off one of her little shoes. They all burst out laughing at this queer little creature, and Litza rushed toward the baby and snatched her up in her arms.

"You dear little thing!" she said. "The prince will never take you for a soldier."

"No," said the baron, laughing, "and she can never grow up into one."

It was too late for the baron to see the Prince of Zisk that day, and the party stopped for the night at a little inn in the town. The next morning, as the baron was about to go to the palace, he asked Litza what was her business in Zisk and if he could help her.

"All my godmother told me to do," said the young girl, "was to give this box to the noblest man in Zisk, and of course he is the prince."

"Yes," said the baron; "and as I am on my way to the palace, I may help you to see him."

"Go you with the baron," said the grandmother to Litza, "and I will stay here and take care of this baby. And as soon as you come back I will change her into a long-legged man with two chairs on his back, and we will get home to my cottage as fast as we can."

When the baron and the young girl reached the palace they found the prince in his audience chamber, surrounded by officers and courtiers. Litza stood by the door, while the baron approached the prince and respectfully told him why he had come.

"You are the very man we want!" cried the prince. "I have conceived a most admirable plan of conquering my robber foes, and you shall carry it out. The day after tomorrow is Christmas, and these highwaymen always keep this festival as if they were decent people and good Christians. They gather together all their wives and children and their old parents, and they sing carols and make merry all day long. At this time they never think of attacking anybody or of being attacked, and if we fall upon them then, we can easily destroy them all, young and old, and thus be rid of the wretches forever. I have a strong body of soldiers ready to send, but they must be led by a man of rank, and all my officers of high degree wish to remain here with their families to celebrate Christmas. Now, you are a stranger and have nothing to keep you here, and you are the very man to lead my soldiers. Destroy that colony of robbers, and you shall have a good share of the booty that you find there."

"Oh, Prince!" exclaimed the baron. "Would you have me, on holy Christmas Day, when these families are assembled together to celebrate the blessed festival, rush upon them with an armed band and slay them, old and young, women and children, at the very foot of the Christmas tree? No man needs occupation more than I, but this is a thing I cannot do."

"Impudent upstart!" cried the prince in a rage. "If you cannot do this, there is nothing for you here. Begone!"

Without an answer the baron turned and left the hall. Litza, who still stood by the door, did not now approach the prince but ran after the baron, who was walking rapidly away. "This is yours," she said, taking the iron box from her little bag. "You are the noblest man."

The baron, surprised, objected to receiving the box, but Litza was firm. "I was told," she said, "to give it to the noblest man in Zisk, and I have done so."

When the baron found that he must keep the box, he asked Litza what was in it.

"I do not know," said Litza; "but the key is fastened to the handle."

They sat down under a tree in a quiet corner of the palace grounds and opened the box. Something inside was covered with a piece of velvet, on top of which lay a golden locket. The baron opened it and beheld a portrait of the beautiful Litza. "Why, you have given me yourself!" he cried, delighted.

"So it appears," said Litza, looking down upon the ground.

"And will you marry me?" he cried.

"If you wish it," said Litza. So that matter was settled.

The two then went to the inn and told the grandmother what had occurred. She looked quite pleased when she heard this story, and then she asked what else was in the box.

"I found so much," said the baron, "that I did not think of looking for anything more." He then opened the box, and lifting the piece of velvet, found it filled with sparkling diamonds.

"That is Litza's dowry," cried the old woman. "It was a wise thing in her godmother to send her out to look for a noble husband, for one would never have come to my little cottage to look for her. But it seems to me that the box might as well have been given to you at your castle. It would have saved us a weary journey."

"But if we had not taken that journey," said Litza, "we should not have become so well acquainted, and I would not have known he was the noblest man."

"It is all right," said the grandmother, "and your dowry will enable the baron to buy his castle again and to live there as his ancestors did before him."

The grandmother desired to leave Zisk immediately, but the baron objected. "There is something I wish to do today," he said; "and if we start early tomorrow morning on horseback, we can reach my castle before dark."

The old woman agreed to this, and the baron continued: "I would like you to lend me the baby for the rest of the day; and when the sundial in the courtyard shall mark three hours after noon, you will please open this piece of paper and wish what I have written upon it."

The grandmother took the folded piece of paper and let him have the baby. She and Litza wondered much what he was going to do, but they asked no questions.

The baron had learned that it was a three hours' walk from the town to the stronghold of the robbers, and just at noon he set out for that place, carrying the baby in his arms. Before he had gone a mile he wished that the baby had been changed into somebody who could walk, but it was too late now.

At three hours after noon the grandmother was about to open the paper when Litza exclaimed, "Before you wish anything, dear Grandmother, let me read what the baron has written."

Litza then took the paper and read it. "It is just what I expected," she cried. "He has gone out to fight the robbers, and he wants you to change the baby into that great armed giant to help him. But don't you do it, for the baron will certainly be killed, there are so many robbers in that place. Please change the baby into a very strong, fleet man who knows the country and who will take the baron in his arms and bring him back here just as fast as he can."

"I will wish that," said the grandmother. And she did so.

The baron had just arrived in sight of the robbers' stronghold when he was very much surprised to find that, instead of carrying a baby in his arms, he himself was in the grasp of a tall, powerful man who was carrying him at the top of his speed toward the town. The baron kicked and struggled much worse than the baby had, but the man paid no attention to his violent remonstrances and soon set him down in the courtyard of the inn.

"This is your doing," he said to Litza. "I wished to show the prince that it was not fear that kept me from fighting the robbers, and you have prevented me."

"You have proved that you are brave," said Litza, "and that is enough. The prince is a bad man; let him fight his own robbers."

The baron could not be angry at this proof of Litza's prudent affection. And the next morning the party left the town on three horses, which the baron bought with one of his diamonds. The tall, fleet man who knew the country acted as guide and led them by a byroad which did not pass near the School for Men. They arrived at the castle early on Christmas Eve, and the baron sent for his servants, his friends, and a priest, and he and Litza were married amid great rejoicing, for everybody was glad to see him come to his own again.

The next day Litza and the baron asked the grandmother to show them her magical servant in his original form. The old woman called the tall, fleet guide and transformed him into the Green Goblin of the Third Word. This strange creature wildly danced and skipped before them, and taking a watermelon and three pumpkins from his pocket, he tossed them up, keeping two of them always in the air.

The baron and his wife were very much amused by the antics of the goblin, and Litza exclaimed, "Oh, Grandmother, if I were you I would keep him this way always. He would be wonderfully amusing, and I am sure he could carry you about and scare away robbers, and do ever so many things."

"A merry green goblin might suit you," said the old woman, shaking her head, "but it would not suit me. I want to return to my own little home, and what I now wish is a suitable companion."

Instantly the goblin changed into a healthy middle-aged woman of agreeable manners and willing to make herself useful. With this "suitable companion" the old grandmother returned after the holidays to her much-loved cottage, where she was often visited by the young baron and his wife; but although they sometimes asked it, she never let them see the green goblin again.

"When a circumstance is just as accommodating as you want it to be," she said, "the less you meddle with it the better."

When he had crossed the bridge and gone a short distance
he sat down to rest.

Old Pipes and the Dryad

A MOUNTAIN BROOK ran through a little village. Over the brook there was a narrow bridge, and from the bridge a footpath led out from the village and up the hillside to the cottage of Old Pipes and his mother. For many, many years Old Pipes had been employed by the villagers to pipe the cattle down from the hills. Every afternoon, an hour before sunset, he would sit on a rock in front of his cottage and play on his pipes. Then all the flocks and herds that were grazing on the mountains would hear him, wherever they might happen to be, and would come down to the village—the cows by the easiest paths, the sheep by those not quite so easy, and the goats by the steep and rocky ways that were hardest of all.

But now, for a year or more, Old Pipes had not piped the cattle home. It is true that every afternoon he sat upon the rock and played upon his familiar instrument; but the cattle did not hear him. He had grown old, and his breath was feeble. The echoes of his cheerful notes, which used to come from the rocky hill on the other side of the valley, were heard no more; and twenty yards from Old Pipes one could scarcely tell what tune he was playing. He had become somewhat deaf and did not know that the sound of his pipes was so thin and weak and that the cattle did not hear him. The cows, the sheep, and the goats came down every afternoon as before, but this was because two boys and a girl were sent up after them. The villagers did not wish the good old man to know that his piping was no longer of any use, so they paid him his little salary every month and said nothing about the two boys and the girl.

Old Pipes's mother was, of course, a great deal older than he was and as deaf as a gate—posts, latch, hinges, and all—and she never knew that the sound of her son's pipe did not spread over all the mountainside and echo back strong and clear from the opposite hills. She was very fond of Old Pipes and proud of his piping; and as he was so much younger than she was, she never thought of him as being very old. She cooked for him and made his bed and mended his clothes; and they lived very comfortably on his little salary.

One afternoon, at the end of the month, when Old Pipes had finished his piping, he took his stout staff and went down the hill to the village to receive the money for his month's work. The path seemed a great deal steeper and more difficult than it used to be; and Old Pipes thought that it must have been washed by the rains and greatly damaged. He remembered it as a path that was quite easy to traverse either up or down. But Old Pipes had been a very active man, and as his mother was so much older than he was, he never thought of himself as aged and infirm.

When the Chief Villager had paid him and he had talked a little with some of his friends, Old Pipes started to go home. But when he had crossed the bridge over the brook and gone a short distance up the hillside, he became very tired and sat down upon a stone. He had not been sitting there half a minute when along came two boys and a girl.

"Children," said Old Pipes, "I'm very tired tonight, and I don't believe I can climb up this steep path to my home. I think I shall have to ask you to help me."

"We will do that," said the boys and the girl, quite cheerfully; and one boy took him by the right hand and the other by the left, while the girl pushed him in the back. In this way he went up the hill quite easily and soon reached his cottage door. Old Pipes gave each of the three children a copper coin, and then they sat down for a few minutes' rest before starting back to the village.

"I'm sorry that I tired you so much," said Old Pipes.

"Oh, that would not have tired us," said one of the boys, "if we had not been so far today after the cows, the sheep, and the goats. They rambled high up on the mountain, and we never before had such a time in finding them."

"Had to go after the cows, the sheep, and the goats!" exclaimed Old Pipes. "What do you mean by that?"

The girl, who stood behind the old man, shook her head, put her hand on her mouth, and made all sorts of signs to the boy to stop talking on this subject; but he did not notice her and promptly answered Old Pipes.

"Why, you see, good sir," said he, "that as the cattle can't hear your pipes now, somebody has to go after them every evening to drive them down from the mountain, and the Chief Villager has hired us three to do it. Generally it is not very hard work, but tonight the cattle had wandered far."

"How long have you been doing this?" asked the old man.

The girl shook her head and clapped her hand on her mouth more vigorously than before, but the boy went on.

"I think it is about a year now," he said, "since the people first felt sure that the cattle could not hear your pipes; and from that time we've been driving them down. But we are rested now and will go home. Good night, sir."

The three children then went down the hill, the girl scolding the boy all the way home. Old Pipes stood silent a few moments, and then he went into his cottage.

"Mother," he shouted, "did you hear what those children said?"

"Children!" exclaimed the old woman. "I did not hear them. I did not know there were any children here."

Then Old Pipes told his mother, shouting very loudly to make her hear, how the two boys and the girl had helped him up the hill and what he had heard about his piping and the cattle.

"They can't hear you?" cried his mother. "Why, what's the matter with the cattle?"

"Ah, me!" said Old Pipes. "I don't believe there's anything the matter with the cattle. It must be with me and my pipes that there is something the matter. But one thing is certain: if I do not earn the wages the Chief Villager pays me, I shall not take them. I shall go straight down to the village and give back the money I received today."

"Nonsense!" cried his mother. "I'm sure you've piped as well as you could, and no more can be expected. And what are we to do without the money?"

"I don't know," said Old Pipes; "but I'm going down to the village to pay it back."

The sun had now set, but the moon was shining very brightly on the hillside, and Old Pipes could see his way very well. He did not take the same path by which he had gone before, but followed another, which led among the trees upon the hillside, and although longer, was not so steep.

When he had gone about halfway, the old man sat down to rest, leaning his back against a great oak tree. As he did so, he heard a sound like knocking inside the tree, and then a voice distinctly said, "Let me out! Let me out!"

Old Pipes instantly forgot that he was tired and sprang to his feet. "This must be a dryad tree!" he exclaimed. "If it is, I'll let her out."

Old Pipes had never, to his knowledge, seen a dryad tree, but he knew there were such trees on the hillsides and the mountains and that dryads lived in them. He knew, too, that in the summertime, on those days when the moon rose before the sun went down, a dryad could come out of her tree if anyone could find the key which locked her in and turn it. Old Pipes closely examined the trunk of the tree, which stood in the full moonlight. "If I see that key," he said, "I shall surely turn it." Before long, he perceived a piece of bark standing out from the tree, which appeared to him very much like the handle of a key. He took hold of it and found he could turn it quite around. As he did so, a large part of the side of the tree was pushed open, and a beautiful dryad stepped quickly out.

For a moment she stood motionless, gazing on the scene before her—the tranquil valley, the hills, the forest, and the mountainside, all lying in the soft, clear light of the moon. "Oh, lovely! lovely!" she exclaimed. "How long it is since I have seen anything like this!" And then, turning to Old Pipes, she said, "How good of you to let me out! I am so happy and so thankful that I must kiss you, you dear old man!" And she threw her arms around the neck of Old Pipes and kissed him on both cheeks. "You don't know," she then went on to say, "how doleful it is to be shut up so long in a tree. I don't mind it in the winter, for then I am glad to be sheltered, but in summer it is a rueful thing not to be able to see all the beauties of the world. And it's ever so long since I've been let out. People so seldom come this way; and when they do come at the right time they either don't hear me, or they are frightened and run away. But you, you dear old man, you were not frightened, and you looked and looked for the key, and you let me out, and now I shall not have to go back till winter has come and the air grows cold. Oh, it is glorious! What can I do for you, to show you how grateful I am?"

"I am very glad," said Old Pipes, "that I let you out, since I see that it makes you so happy; but I must admit that I tried to find the key because I had a great desire to see a dryad. But if you wish to do something for me, you can, if you happen to be going down toward the village."

"To the village!" exclaimed the Dryad. "I will go anywhere for you, my kind old benefactor."

"Well, then," said Old Pipes, "I wish you would take this little bag of money to the Chief Villager and tell him that Old Pipes cannot receive pay for the services which he does not perform. It is now more than a year that I have not been able to make the cattle hear me when I piped to call them home. I did not know this until tonight; but now that I know it, I cannot keep the money, and so I send it back." And handing the little bag to the Dryad, he bade her good night and turned toward his cottage.

"Good night," said the Dryad. "And I thank you over and over and over again, you good old man!"

Old Pipes walked toward his home, very glad to be saved the fatigue of going all the way down to the village and back again. "To be sure," he said to himself, "this path does not seem at all steep, and I can walk along it very easily; but it would have tired me dreadfully to come up all the way from the village, especially as I could not have expected those children to help me again." When he reached home, his mother was surprised to see him returning so soon.

"What!" she exclaimed. "Have you already come back? What did the Chief Villager say? Did he take the money?"

Old Pipes was just about to tell her that he had sent the money to the village by a dryad when he suddenly reflected that his mother would be sure to disapprove such a proceeding, and so he merely said he had sent it by a person whom he had met.

"And how do you know that the person will ever take it to the Chief Villager?" cried his mother. "You will lose it, and the villagers will never get it. Oh, Pipes! Pipes! When will you be old enough to have ordinary common sense?"

Old Pipes considered that as he was already seventy years of age he could scarcely expect to grow any wiser, but he made no remark on this subject; and saying that he doubted not that the money would go safely to its destination, he sat down to his supper. His mother scolded him roundly, but he did not mind it; and after supper he went out and sat on a rustic chair in front of the cottage to look at the moonlit village and to wonder whether or not the Chief Villager really received the money. While he was doing these two things, he went fast asleep.

When Old Pipes left the Dryad, she did not go down to the village with the little bag of money. She held it in her hand and thought about what she had heard. "This is a good and honest old man," she said; "and it is a shame that he should lose this money. He looked as if he needed it, and I don't believe the people in the village will take it from one who has served them so long. Often, when in my tree, have I heard the sweet notes of his pipes. I am going to take the money back to him." She did not start immediately, because there were so many beautiful things to look at; but after a while she went up to the cottage, and finding Old Pipes asleep in his chair, she slipped the little bag into his coat pocket and silently sped away.

The next day Old Pipes told his mother that he would go up the mountain and cut some wood. He had a right to get wood from the mountain, but for a long time he had been content to pick up the dead branches which lay about his cottage. Today, however, he felt so strong and vigorous that he thought he would go and cut some fuel that would be better than this. He worked all the morning, and when he came back he did not feel at all tired, and he had a very good appetite for his dinner.

Now, Old Pipes knew a good deal about dryads, but there was one thing which, although he had heard, he had forgotten. This was that a kiss from a dryad made a person ten years younger. The people of the village knew this, and they were very careful not to let any child of ten years or younger go into the woods where the dryads were supposed to be; for if they should chance to be kissed by one of these tree nymphs, they would be set back so far that they would cease to exist. A story was told in the village that a very bad boy of eleven once ran away into the woods and had an adventure of this kind; and when his mother found him, he was a little baby of one year old. Taking advantage of her opportunity, she brought him up more carefully than she had done before, and he grew to be a very good boy indeed.

Now, Old Pipes had been kissed twice by the Dryad, once on each cheek, and he therefore felt as vigorous and active as when he was a hale man of fifty. His mother noticed how much work he was doing and told him that he need not try in that way to make up for the loss of his piping wages; for he would only tire himself out and get sick. But her son answered that he had not felt so well for years and that he was quite able to work. In the course of the afternoon Old Pipes, for the first time that day, put his hand in his coat pocket, and there, to his amazement, he found the little bag of money. "Well, well!" he exclaimed, "I am stupid, indeed! I really thought that I had seen a dryad; but when I sat down by that big oak tree, I must have gone to sleep and dreamed it all; and then I came home thinking I had given the money to a dryad, when it was in my pocket all the time. But the Chief Villager shall have the money. I shall not take it to him today, but tomorrow I wish to go to the village to see some of my old friends; and then I shall give up the money."

Toward the close of the afternoon Old Pipes, as had been his custom for so many years, took his pipes from the shelf on which they lay and went out to the rock in front of the cottage.

"What are you going to do?" cried his mother. "If you will not consent to be paid, why do you pipe?"

"I am going to pipe for my own pleasure," said her son. "I am used to it, and I do not wish to give it up. It does not matter now whether the cattle hear me or not, and I am sure that my piping will injure no one."

When the good man began to play upon his favorite instrument, he was astonished at the sound that came from it. The beautiful notes of the pipes sounded clear and strong down into the valley and spread over the hills and up the sides of the mountain beyond, while, after a little interval, an echo came back from the rocky hill on the other side of the valley.

"Ha ha!" he cried. "What has happened to my pipes? They must have been stopped up of late, but now they are as clear and good as ever."

Again the merry notes went sounding far and wide. The cattle on the mountain heard them, and those that were old enough remembered how these notes had called them from their pastures every evening, and so they started down the mountainside, the others following.

The merry notes were heard in the village below, and the people were much astonished thereby. "Why, who can be blowing the pipes of Old Pipes?" they said. But as they were all very busy, no one went up to see. One thing, however, was plain enough: the cattle were coming down the mountain. And so the two boys and the girl did not have to go after them and had an hour for play, for which they were very glad.

The next morning Old Pipes started down to the village with his money, and on the way he met the Dryad. "Oh, ho!" he cried. "Is that you? Why, I thought my letting you out of the tree was nothing but a dream."

"A dream!" cried the Dryad. "If you only knew how happy you have made me, you would not think it merely a dream. And has it not benefited you? Do you not feel happier? Yesterday I heard you playing beautifully on your pipes."

"Yes, yes," cried he. "I did not understand it before, but I see it all now. I have really grown younger. I thank you, I thank you, good Dryad, from the bottom of my heart. It was the finding of the money in my pocket that made me think it was a dream."

"Oh, I put it in when you were asleep," she said, laughing, "because I thought you ought to keep it. Good-bye, kind, honest man. May you live long and be as happy as I am now."

Old Pipes was greatly delighted when he understood that he was really a younger man; but that made no difference about the money, and he kept on his way to the village. As soon as he reached it, he was eagerly questioned as to who had been playing his pipes the evening before, and when the people heard that it was himself, they were very much surprised. Thereupon, Old Pipes told what had happened to him, and then there was greater wonder, with hearty congratulations and handshakes; for Old Pipes was liked by everyone. The Chief Villager refused to take his money, and although Old Pipes said that he had not earned it, everyone present insisted that, as he would now play on his pipes as before, he should lose nothing because for a time he was unable to perform his duty.

So Old Pipes was obliged to keep his money, and after an hour or two spent in conversation with his friends, he returned to his cottage.

There was one individual, however, who was not at all pleased with what had happened to Old Pipes. This was an echo-dwarf, who lived on the hills on the other side of the valley, and whose duty it was to echo back the notes of the pipes whenever they could be heard. There were a great many other echo-dwarfs on these hills, some of whom echoed back the songs of maidens, some the shouts of children, and others the music that was often heard in the village. But there was only one who could send back the strong notes of the pipes of Old Pipes, and this had been his sole duty for many years. But when the old man grew feeble and the notes of his pipes could not be heard on the opposite hills, this Echo-dwarf had nothing to do, and he spent his time in delightful idleness; and he slept so much and grew so fat that it made his companions laugh to see him walk.

On the afternoon on which, after so long an interval, the sound of the pipes was heard on the echo hills, this dwarf was fast asleep behind a rock. As soon as the first notes reached them, some of his companions ran to wake him. Rolling to his feet, he echoed back the merry tune of Old Pipes. Naturally, he was very much annoyed and indignant at being thus obliged to give up his life of comfortable leisure, and he hoped very much that this pipe-playing would not occur again. The next afternoon he was awake and listening, and, sure enough, at the usual hour, along came the notes of the pipes as clear and strong as they ever had been; and he was obliged to work as long as Old Pipes played. The Echo-dwarf was very angry. He had supposed, of course, that the pipe-playing had ceased forever, and he felt that he had a right to be indignant at being thus deceived. He was so much disturbed that he made up his mind to go and try to find out whether this was to be a temporary matter or not. He had plenty of time, as the pipes were played but once a day, and he set off early in the morning for the hill on which Old Pipes lived. It was hard work for the fat little fellow, and when he had crossed the valley and had gone some distance into the woods on the hillside, he stopped to rest, and in a few minutes the Dryad came tripping along.

"Ho, ho!" exclaimed the dwarf. "What are you doing here, and how did you get out of your tree?"

"Doing!" cried the Dryad. "I am being happy; that's what I am doing. And I was let out of my tree by the good old man who plays the pipes to call the cattle down from the mountain. And it makes me happier to think that I have been of service to him. I gave him two kisses of gratitude, and now he is young enough to play his pipes as well as ever."

The Echo-dwarf stepped forward, his face pale with passion. "Am I to believe," he said, "that you are the cause of this great evil that has come upon me and that you are the wicked creature who has again started this old man upon his career of pipe-playing? What have I ever done to you that you should have condemned me for years and years to echo back the notes of those wretched pipes?"

At this the Dryad laughed loudly.

"What a funny little fellow you are!" she said. "Anyone would think you had been condemned to toil from morning till night; while what you really have to do is merely to imitate for half an hour every day the merry notes of Old Pipes's piping. Fie upon you, Echo-dwarf! You are lazy and selfish; and that is what is the matter with you. Instead of grumbling at being obliged to do a little wholesome work, which is less, I am sure, than that of any other echo-dwarf upon the rocky hillside, you should rejoice at the good fortune of the old man who has regained so much of his strength and vigor. Go home and learn to be just and generous; and then perhaps you may be happy. Good-bye."

"Insolent creature!" shouted the dwarf, as he shook his fat little fist at her. "I'll make you suffer for this. You shall find out what it is to heap injury and insult upon one like me and to snatch from him the repose that he has earned by long years of toil." And shaking his head savagely, he hurried back to the rocky hillside.

Every afternoon the merry notes of the pipes of Old Pipes sounded down into the valley and over the hills and up the mountainside; and every afternoon, when he had echoed them back, the little dwarf grew more and more angry with the Dryad. Each day, from early morning till it was time for him to go back to his duties upon the rocky hillside, he searched the woods for her. He intended, if he met her, to pretend to be very sorry for what he had said, and he thought he might be able to play a trick upon her which would avenge him well. One day, while thus wandering among the trees, he met Old Pipes. The Echo-dwarf did not generally care to see or speak to ordinary people; but now he was so anxious to find the object of his search that he stopped and asked Old Pipes if he had seen the Dryad. The piper had not noticed the little fellow, and he looked down on him with some surprise.

"No," he said, "I have not seen her, and I have been looking everywhere for her."

"You!" cried the dwarf. "What do you wish with her?"

Old Pipes then sat down on a stone, so that he should be nearer the ear of his small companion, and he told what the Dryad had done for him.

When the Echo-dwarf heard that this was the man whose pipes he was obliged to echo back every day, he would have slain him on the spot had he been able; but as he was not able, he merely ground his teeth and listened to the rest of the story.

"I am looking for the Dryad now," Old Pipes continued, "on account of my aged mother. When I was old myself, I did not notice how very old my mother was; but now it shocks me to see how feeble and decrepit her years have caused her to become; and I am looking for the Dryad to ask her to make my mother younger, as she made me."

The eyes of the Echo-dwarf glistened. Here was a man who might help him in his plans.

"Your idea is a good one," he said to Old Pipes, "and it does you honor. But you should know that a dryad can make no person younger but one who lets her out of her tree. However, you can manage the affair very easily. All you need do is to find the Dryad, tell her what you want, and request her to step into her tree and be shut up for a short time. Then you will go and bring your mother to the tree; she will open it, and everything will be as you wish. Is not this a good plan?"

"Excellent!" cried Old Pipes; "and I will go instantly and search more diligently for the Dryad."

"Take me with you," said the Echo-dwarf. "You can easily carry me on your strong shoulders; and I shall be glad to help you in any way that I can."

"Now, then," said the little fellow to himself, as Old Pipes carried him rapidly along, "if he persuades the Dryad to get into a tree—and she is quite foolish enough to do it—and then goes away to bring his mother, I shall take a stone or a club, and I will break off the key to that tree, so that nobody can ever turn it again. Then Mistress Dryad will see what she has brought upon herself by her behavior to me."

Before long they came to the great oak tree in which the Dryad had lived, and at a distance they saw that beautiful creature herself coming toward them.

"How excellently well everything happens!" said the dwarf. "Put me down, and I will go. Your business with the Dryad is more important than mine; and you need not say anything about my having suggested your plan to you. I am willing that you should have all the credit of it yourself."

Old Pipes put the Echo-dwarf upon the ground, but the little rogue did not go away. He concealed himself between some low, mossy rocks, and he was so much of their color that you would not have noticed him if you had been looking straight at him.

When the Dryad came up, Old Pipes lost no time in telling her about his mother and what he wished her to do. At first the Dryad answered nothing but stood looking very sadly at Old Pipes.

"Do you really wish me to go into my tree again?" she said. "I should dreadfully dislike to do it, for I don't know what might happen. It is not at all necessary, for I could make your mother younger at any time if she would give me the opportunity. I had already thought of making you still happier in this way; and several times I have waited about your cottage, hoping to meet your aged mother, but she never comes outside, and you know a dryad cannot enter a house. I cannot imagine what put this idea into your head. Did you think of it yourself?"

"No, I cannot say that I did," answered Old Pipes. "A little dwarf whom I met in the woods proposed it to me."

"Oh!" cried the Dryad. "Now I see through it all. It is the scheme of that vile Echo-dwarf—your enemy and mine. Where is he? I should like to see him."

"I think he has gone away," said Old Pipes.

"No, he has not," said the Dryad, whose quick eyes perceived the Echo-dwarf among the rocks. "There he is. Seize him and drag him out, I beg of you."

Old Pipes perceived the dwarf as soon as he was pointed out to him, and running to the rocks, he caught the little fellow by the arm and pulled him out.

"Now, then," cried the Dryad, who had opened the door of the great oak, "just stick him in there, and we will shut him up. Then I shall be safe from his mischief for the rest of the time I am free."

Old Pipes thrust the Echo-dwarf into the tree; the Dryad pushed the door shut; there was a clicking sound of bark and wood, and no one would have noticed that the big oak had ever had an opening in it.

"There," said the Dryad; "now we need not be afraid of him. And I assure you, my good piper, that I shall be very glad to make your mother younger as soon as I can. Will you not ask her to come out and meet me?"

"Of course I will," cried Old Pipes; "and I will do it without delay."

And then, the Dryad by his side, he hurried to his cottage. But when he mentioned the matter to his mother, the old woman became very angry indeed. She did not believe in dryads; and if they really did exist, she knew they must be witches and sorceresses, and she would have nothing to do with them. If her son had ever allowed himself to be kissed by one of them, he ought to be ashamed of himself. As to its doing him the least bit of good, she did not believe a word of it. He felt better than he used to feel, but that was very common. She had sometimes felt that way herself, and she forbade him ever to mention a dryad to her again.

That afternoon Old Pipes, feeling very sad that his plan in regard to his mother had failed, sat down upon the rock and played upon his pipes. The pleasant sounds went down the valley and up the hills and mountain, but to the great surprise of some persons who happened to notice the fact, the notes were not echoed back from the rocky hillside but from the woods on the side of the valley on which Old Pipes lived. The next day many of the villagers stopped in their work to listen to the echo of the pipes coming from the woods. The sound was not as clear and strong as it used to be when it was sent back from the rocky hillside, but it certainly came from among the trees. Such a thing as an echo changing its place in this way had never been heard of before, and nobody was able to explain how it could have happened. Old Pipes, however, knew very well that the sound came from the Echo-dwarf shut up in the great oak tree. The sides of the tree were thin, and the sound of the pipes could be heard through them, and the dwarf was obliged by the laws of his being to echo back those notes whenever they came to him. But Old Pipes thought he might get the Dryad in trouble if he let anyone know that the Echo-dwarf was shut up in the tree, and so he wisely said nothing about it.

One day the two boys and the girl who had helped Old Pipes up the hill were playing in the woods. Stopping near the great oak tree, they heard a sound of knocking within it, and then a voice plainly said, "Let me out! Let me out!"

For a moment the children stood still in astonishment, and then one of the boys exclaimed, "Oh, it is a dryad, like the one Old Pipes found! Let's let her out!"

"What are you thinking of?" cried the girl. "I am the oldest of all, and I am only thirteen. Do you wish to be turned into crawling babies? Run! Run! Run!"

And the two boys and the girl dashed down into the valley as fast as their legs could carry them. There was no desire in their youthful hearts to be made younger than they were. And for fear that their parents might think it well that they should commence their careers anew, they never said a word about finding the dryad tree.

As the summer days went on, Old Pipes's mother grew feebler and feebler. One day when her son was away—for he now frequently went into the woods to hunt or fish or down into the valley to work—she arose from her knitting to prepare the simple dinner. But she felt so weak and tired that she was not able to do the work to which she had been so long accustomed. "Alas! Alas!" she said. "The time has come when I am too old to work. My son will have to hire someone to come here and cook his meals, make his bed, and mend his clothes. Alas! Alas! I had hoped that as long as I lived I should be able to do these things. But it is not so. I have grown utterly worthless, and someone else must prepare the dinner for my son. I wonder where he is." And tottering to the door, she went outside to look for him. She did not feel able to stand, and reaching the rustic chair, she sank into it, quite exhausted, and soon fell asleep.

The Dryad, who had often come to the cottage to see if she could find an opportunity of carrying out Old Pipes's affectionate design, now happened by; and seeing that the much desired occasion had come, she stepped up quietly behind the old woman and gently kissed her on each cheek and then as quietly disappeared.

In a few minutes the mother of Old Pipes awoke, and looking up at the sun, she exclaimed, "Why, it is almost dinner time! My son will be here directly, and I am not ready for him." And rising to her feet, she hurried into the house, made the fire, set the meat and vegetables to cook, laid the cloth; and by the time her son arrived, the meal was on the table.

"How a little sleep does refresh one," she said to herself as she was bustling about. She was a woman of very vigorous constitution and at seventy had been a great deal stronger and more active than her son was at that age. The moment Old Pipes saw his mother, he knew that the Dryad had been there; but, while he felt as happy as a king, he was too wise to say anything about her.

"It is astonishing how well I feel today," said his mother; "and either my hearing has improved or you speak much more plainly than you have done of late."

The summer days went on and passed away, the leaves were falling from the trees, and the air was becoming cold.

"Nature has ceased to be lovely," said the Dryad, "and the night winds chill me. It is time for me to go back into my comfortable quarters in the great oak. But first I must pay another visit to the cottage of Old Pipes."

She found the piper and his mother sitting side by side on the rock in front of the door. The cattle were not to go to the mountain any more that season, and he was piping them down for the last time. Loud and merrily sounded the pipes of Old Pipes, and down the mountainside came the cattle—the cows by the easiest paths, the sheep by those not quite so easy, and the goats by the most difficult ones among the rocks—while from the great oak tree were heard the echoes of the cheerful music.

"How happy they look, sitting there together," said the Dryad; "and I don't believe it will do them a bit of harm to be still younger." And moving quietly up behind them, she first kissed Old Pipes on his cheek and then his mother.

Old Pipes, who had stopped playing, knew what it was, but he did not move, and said nothing. His mother, thinking that her son had kissed her, turned to him with a smile and kissed him in return. And then she arose and went into the cottage, a vigorous woman of sixty, followed by her son, erect and happy and twenty years younger than herself.

The Dryad sped away to the woods, shrugging her shoulders as she felt the cool evening wind.

When she reached the great oak, she turned the key and opened the door. "Come out," she said to the Echo-dwarf, who sat blinking within. "Winter is coming on, and I want the comfortable shelter of my tree for myself. The cattle have come down from the mountain for the last time this year, the pipes will no longer sound, and you can go to your rocks and have a holiday until next spring."

Upon hearing these words, the dwarf skipped quickly out, and the Dryad entered the tree and pulled the door shut after her. "Now, then," she said to herself, "he can break off the key if he likes. It does not matter to me. Another will grow out next spring. And although the good piper made me no promise, I know that when the warm days arrive next year, he will come and let me out again."

The Echo-dwarf did not stop to break the key of the tree. He was too happy to be released to think of anything else, and he hastened as fast as he could to his home on the rocky hillside.

The Dryad was not mistaken when she trusted in the piper. When the warm days came again, he went to the oak tree to let her out. But to his sorrow and surprise he found the great tree lying upon the ground. A winter storm had blown it down, and it lay with its trunk shattered and split. And what became of the Dryad, no one ever knew.

"The Philosophy of Relative Existences"

IN A CERTAIN SUMMER, not long ago, my friend Bentley and I found ourselves in a little hamlet which overlooked a placid valley, through which a river gently moved, winding its way through green stretches until it turned the end of a line of low hills and was lost to view. Beyond this river, far away but visible from the door of the cottage where we dwelt, there lay a city. Through the mists which floated over the valley we could see the outlines of steeples and tall roofs; and buildings of a character which indicated thrift and business stretched themselves down to the opposite edge of the river. The more distant parts of the city, evidently a small one, lost themselves in the hazy summer atmosphere.

Bentley was young, fair-haired, and a poet; I was a philosopher, or trying to be one. We were good friends and had come down into this peaceful region to work together. Although we had fled from the bustle and distractions of the town, the appearance in this rural region of a city, which, so far as we could observe, exerted no influence on the quiet character of the valley in which it lay, aroused our interest. No craft plied up and down the river; there were no bridges from shore to shore; there were none of those scattered and half-squalid habitations which generally are found on the outskirts of a city; there came to us no distant sound of bells; and not the smallest wreath of smoke rose from any of the buildings.

In answer to our inquiries our landlord told us that the city over the river had been built by one man, who was a visionary and who had a great deal more money than common sense. "It is not as big a town as you would think, sirs," he said, "because the general mistiness of things in this valley makes them look larger than they are. Those hills, for instance, when you get to them are not as high as they look to be from here. But the town is big enough and a good deal too big; for it ruined its builder and owner, who, when he came to die, had not money enough left to put up a decent tombstone at the head of his grave. He had a queer idea that he would like to have his town all finished before anybody lived in it, and so he kept on working and spending money year after year and year after year until the city was done and he had not a cent left. During all the time that the place was building, hundreds of people came to him to buy houses or to hire them, but he would not listen to anything of the kind. No one must live in his town until it was all done. Even his workmen were obliged to go away at night to lodge. It is a town, sirs, I am told, in which nobody has slept for even a night. There are streets there and places of business and churches and public halls and everything that a town full of inhabitants could need; but it is all empty and deserted and has been so as far back as I can remember, and I came to this region when I was a little boy."

"And is there no one to guard the place?" we asked. "No one to protect it from wandering vagrants who might choose to take possession of the buildings?"

"There are not many vagrants in this part of the country," he said, "and if there were, they would not go over to that city. It is haunted."

"By what?" we asked.

"Well, sirs, I scarcely can tell you—queer beings that are not flesh and blood, and that is all I know about it. A good many people living hereabouts have visited that place once in their lives, but I know of no one who has gone there a second time."

"And travelers," I said, "are they not excited by curiosity to explore that strange uninhabited city?"

"Oh, yes," our host replied; "almost all visitors to the valley go over to that queer city—generally in small parties, for it is not a place in which one wishes to walk about alone. Sometimes they see things and sometimes they don't. But I never knew any man or woman to show a fancy for living there, although it is a very good town."

This was said at suppertime, and as it was the period of full moon, Bentley and I decided that we would visit the haunted city that evening. Our host endeavored to dissuade us, saying that no one ever went over there at night; but as we were not to be deterred, he told us where we would find his small boat tied to a stake on the riverbank. We soon crossed the river and landed at a broad but low stone pier, at the land end of which a line of tall grasses waved in the gentle night wind as if they were sentinels warning us from entering the silent city. We pushed through these and walked up a street fairly wide and so well paved that we noticed none of the weeds and other growths which generally denote desertion or little use. By the bright light of the moon we could see that the architecture was simple and of a character highly gratifying to the eye. All the buildings were of stone and of good size. We were greatly excited and interested and proposed to continue our walks until the moon should set and to return on the following morning—"to live here, perhaps," said Bentley. "What could be so romantic and yet so real? What could conduce better to the marriage of verse and philosophy?" But as he said this, we saw around the corner of a cross-street some forms as of people hurrying away.

"The spectres," said my companion, laying his hand on my arm.

"Vagrants, more likely," I answered, "who have taken advantage of the superstition of the region to appropriate this comfort and beauty to themselves."

"If that be so," said Bentley, "we must have a care for our lives."

We proceeded cautiously and soon saw other forms fleeing before us and disappearing, as we supposed, around corners and into houses. And now, suddenly finding ourselves upon the edge of a wide, open public square, we saw in the dim light—for a tall steeple obscured the moon—the forms of vehicles, horses, and men moving here and there. But before, in our astonishment, we could say a word one to the other, the moon moved past the steeple, and in its bright light we could see none of the signs of life and traffic which had just astonished us.

Timidly, with hearts beating fast, but with not one thought of turning back nor any fear of vagrants—for we were now sure that what we had seen was not flesh and blood, and therefore harmless—we crossed the open space and entered a street down which the moon shone clearly. Here and there we saw dim figures, which quickly disappeared; but approaching a low stone balcony in front of one of the houses, we were surprised to see, sitting thereon and leaning over a book which lay open upon the top of the carved parapet, the figure of a woman who did not appear to notice us.

"That is a real person," whispered Bentley, "and she does not see us."

"No," I replied; "it is like the others. Let us go near it."

We drew near to the balcony and stood before it. At this the figure raised its head and looked at us. It was beautiful, it was young; but its substance seemed to be of an ethereal quality which we had never seen or known of. With its full, soft eyes fixed upon us, it spoke.

"Why are you here?" it asked. "I have said to myself that the next time I saw any of you I would ask you why you come to trouble us. Cannot you live content in your own realms and spheres, knowing, as you must know, how timid we are, and how you frighten us and make us unhappy? In all the city there is, I believe, not one of us except myself who does not flee and hide from you whenever you cruelly come here. Even I would do that, had not I declared to myself that I would see you and speak to you and endeavor to prevail upon you to leave us in peace."

"—we crossed the open space and entered a street down which

the moon shone clearly."

The clear, frank tones of the speaker gave me courage. "We are two men," I answered, "strangers in this region and living for the time in the beautiful country on the other side of the river. Having heard of this quiet city, we have come to see it for ourselves. We had supposed it to be uninhabited, but now that we find that this is not the case, we would assure you from our hearts that we do not wish to disturb or annoy anyone who lives here. We simply came as honest travelers to view the city."

The figure now seated herself again, and as her countenance was nearer to us, we could see that it was filled with pensive thought. For a moment she looked at us without speaking. "Men!" she said. "And so I have been right. For a long time I have believed that the beings who sometimes come here, filling us with dread and awe, are men."

"And you," I exclaimed, "who are you, and who are these forms that we have seen, these strange inhabitants of this city?"

She gently smiled as she answered, "We are the ghosts of the future. We are the people who are to live in this city generations hence. But all of us do not know that, principally because we do not think about it and study about it enough to know it. And it is generally believed that the men and women who sometimes come here are ghosts who haunt the place."

"And that is why you are terrified and flee from us?" I exclaimed. "You think we are ghosts from another world?"

"Yes," she replied; "that is what is thought and what I used to think."

"And you," I asked, "are spirits of human beings yet to be?"

"Yes," she answered; "but not for a long time. Generations of men—I know not how many—must pass away before we are men and women."

"Heavens!" exclaimed Bentley, clasping his hands and raising his eyes to the sky. "I shall be a spirit before you are a woman."

"Perhaps," she said again, with a sweet smile upon her face, "you may live to be very, very old."

But Bentley shook his head. This did not console him. For some minutes I stood in contemplation, gazing upon the stone pavement beneath my feet. "And this," I ejaculated, "is a city inhabited by the ghosts of the future, who believe men and women to be phantoms and spectres?"

She bowed her head.

"But how is it," I asked, "that you discovered that you are spirits and we mortal men?"

"There are so few of us who think of such things," she answered, "so few who study, ponder, and reflect. I am fond of study, and I love philosophy; and from the reading of many books I have learned much. From the book which I have here I have learned most; and from its teachings I have gradually come to the belief, which you tell me is the true one, that we are spirits and you men."

"And what book is that?" I asked.

"It is *The Philosophy of Relative Existences*, by Rupert Vance."

"Ye gods!" I exclaimed, springing upon the balcony, "that is my book, and I am Rupert Vance." I stepped toward the volume to seize it, but she raised her hand.

"You cannot touch it," she said. "It is the ghost of a book. And did you write it?"

"Write it? No," I said, "I am writing it. It is not yet finished."

"But here it is," she said, turning over the last pages. "As a spirit book it is finished. It is very successful; it is held in high estimation by intelligent thinkers; it is a standard work."

I stood trembling with emotion. "High estimation!" I said. "A standard work!"

"Oh yes," she replied, with animation; "and it well deserves its great success, especially in its conclusion. I have read it twice."

"But let me see these concluding pages," I exclaimed. "Let me look upon what I am to write."

She smiled and shook her head and closed the book. "I would

like to do that," she said, "but if you are really a man, you must not know what you are going to do."

"Oh, tell me, tell me," cried Bentley from below, "do you know a book called *Stellar Studies* by Arthur Bentley? It is a book of poems."

The figure gazed at him. "No," it said presently, "I never heard of it."

I stood trembling. Had the youthful figure before me been flesh and blood, had the book been a real one, I would have torn it from her.

"O wise and lovely being!" I exclaimed, falling on my knees before her, "be also benign and generous. Let me but see the last page of my book. If I had been of benefit to your world; more than all, if I have been of benefit to you, let me see, I implore you —let me see how it is that I have done it."

She rose with the book in her hand. "You have only to wait until you have done it," she said, "and then you will know all that you could see here." I started to my feet and stood alone upon the balcony.

"I am sorry," said Bentley, as we walked toward the pier where we had left our boat, "that we talked only to the ghost girl and that the other spirits were all afraid of us. Persons whose souls are choked up with philosophy are not apt to care much for poetry; and even if my book is to be widely known, it is easy to see that she may not have heard of it."

I walked triumphant. The moon, almost touching the horizon, beamed like red gold. "My dear friend," said I, "I have always told you that you should put more philosophy into your poetry. That would make it live."

"And I have always told you," said he, "that you should not put so much poetry into your philosophy. It misleads people."

"It didn't mislead that ghost girl," said I.

"How do you know?" said Bentley. "Perhaps she is wrong and the other inhabitants of the city are right, and we may be the ghosts after all. Such things, you know, are only relative. Anyway," he continued, after a little pause, "I wish I knew that those ghosts were now reading the poem which I am going to begin to-morrow."

The Transferred Ghost

THE COUNTRY RESIDENCE of Mr. John Hinckman was a delightful place to me, for many reasons. It was the abode of a genial, though somewhat impulsive, hospitality. It had broad, smooth-shaven lawns and towering oaks and elms; there were bosky shades at several points, and not far from the house there was a little rill spanned by a rustic bridge with the bark on; there were fruits and flowers, pleasant people, chess, billiards, rides, walks, and fishing. These were great attractions, but none of them, nor all of them together, would have been sufficient to hold me to the place very long. I had been invited for the trout season but should probably have finished my visit early in the summer had it not been that upon fair days, when the grass was dry and the sun was not too hot and there was but little wind, there strolled beneath the lofty elms, or passed lightly through the bosky shades, the form of my Madeline.

This lady was not, in very truth, my Madeline. She had never given herself to me, nor had I, in any way, acquired possession of her. But as I considered her possession the only sufficient reason for the continuance of my existence, I called her, in my reveries, mine. It may have been that I would not have been obliged to confine the use of this possessive pronoun to my reveries had I confessed the state of my feelings to the lady.

But this was an unusually difficult thing to do. Not only did I dread, as almost all lovers dread, taking the step which would in an instant put an end to that delightful season which may be termed the ante-interrogatory period of love and which might at the same time terminate all intercourse or connection with the object of my passion, but I was also dreadfully afraid of John

Hinckman. This gentleman was a good friend of mine, but it would have required a bolder man than I was at that time to ask him for the gift of his niece, who was the head of his household, and according to his own frequent statement, the main prop of his declining years. Had Madeline acquiesced in my general views on the subject, I might have felt encouraged to open the matter to Mr. Hinckman; but as I said before, I had never asked her whether or not she would be mine. I thought of these things at all hours of the day and night, particularly the latter.

I was lying awake one night, in the great bed in my spacious chamber, when by the dim light of the new moon, which partially filled the room, I saw John Hinckman standing by a large chair near the door. I was very much surprised at this for two reasons: in the first place, my host had never before come into my room, and in the second place, he had gone from home that morning and had not expected to return for several days. Therefore it was that I had been able that evening to sit much later than usual with Madeline on the moonlit porch. The figure was certainly that of John Hinckman in his ordinary dress, but there was a vagueness and indistinctness about it which presently assured me that it was a ghost. Had the good old man been murdered, and had his spirit come to tell me of the deed and to confide to me the protection of his dear—? My heart fluttered, but I felt that I must speak. "Sir," said I.

"Do you know," interrupted the figure, with a countenance that indicated anxiety, "whether or not Mr. Hinckman will return tonight?"

I thought it well to maintain a calm exterior, and I answered, "We do not expect him."

"I am glad of that," said he, sinking into the chair by which he stood. "During the two years and a half that I have inhabited this house, that man has never before been away for a single night. You can't imagine the relief it gives me."

As he spoke, he stretched out his legs and leaned back in the chair. His form became less vague and the colors of his garments more distinct and evident, while an expression of gratified relief succeeded to the anxiety of his countenance.

"Two years and a half!" I exclaimed. "I don't understand you."

"It is fully that length of time," said the ghost, "since I first came here. Mine is not an ordinary case. But before I say anything more about it, let me ask you again if you are sure Mr. Hinckman will not return tonight."

"I am as sure of it as I can be of anything," I answered. "He left today for Bristol, two hundred miles away."

"Then I will go on," said the ghost, "for I am glad to have the opportunity of talking to someone who will listen to me. But if John Hinckman should come in and catch me here, I should be frightened out of my wits."

"This is all very strange," I said, greatly puzzled by what I had heard. "Are you the ghost of Mr. Hinckman?"

This was a bold question, but my mind was so full of other emotions that there seemed to be no room for that of fear.

"Yes, I am his ghost," my companion replied, "and yet I have no right to be. And this is what makes me so uneasy and so much afraid of him. It is a strange story, and, I truly believe, without precedent. Two years and a half ago John Hinckman was dangerously ill in this very room. At one time he was so far gone that he was really believed to be dead. It was in consequence of too precipitate a report in regard to this matter that I was at that time appointed to be his ghost. Imagine my surprise and horror, sir, when after I had accepted the position and assumed its responsibilities, that old man revived, became convalescent, and eventually regained his usual health. My situation was now one of extreme delicacy and embarrassment. I had no power to return to my original unembodiment, and I had no right to be the ghost of a man who was not dead. I was advised by my friends to quietly maintain my position and was assured that, as John Hinckman was an elderly man, it could not be long before I could rightfully assume the position for which I had been selected. But I tell you, sir," he continued with animation, "the old fellow seems as vigorous as ever, and I have no idea how much longer this annoying state of things will continue. I spend my time trying to get out of that old man's way. I must not leave this house, and he seems to follow me everywhere. I tell you, sir, he haunts me."

"That is truly a queer state of things," I remarked. "But why are you afraid of him? He couldn't hurt you."

"Of course he couldn't," said the ghost. "But his very presence is a shock and terror to me. Imagine, sir, how you would feel if my case were yours."

I could not imagine such a thing at all. I simply shuddered.

"And if one must be a wrongful ghost at all," the apparition continued, "it would be much pleasanter to be the ghost of some man other than John Hinckman. There is in him an irascibility of temper, accompanied by a facility of invective, which is seldom met with; and what would happen if he were to see me and find out, as I am sure he would, how long and why I had inhabited his house, I can scarcely conceive. I have seen him in his bursts of passion, and although he did not hurt the people he stormed at any more than he would hurt me, they seemed to shrink before him."

All this I knew to be very true. Had it not been for this peculiarity of Mr. Hinckman, I might have been more willing to talk to him about his niece.

"I feel sorry for you," I said, for I really began to have a sympathetic feeling toward this unfortunate apparition. "Your case is indeed a hard one. It reminds me of those persons who have had doubles; and I suppose a man would often be very angry indeed when he found that there was another being who was personating himself."

"Oh, the cases are not similar at all," said the ghost. "A double, or doppelgänger, lives on the earth with a man, and being exactly like him, he makes all sorts of trouble, of course. It is very different with me. I am not here to live with Mr. Hinckman. I am here to take his place. Now, it would make John Hinckman very angry if he knew that. Don't you know it would?"

I assented promptly.

"Now that he is away, I can be easy for a little while," continued the ghost, "and I am so glad to have an opportunity of talking to you. I have frequently come into your room and watched you while you slept but did not dare to speak to you for fear that if you talked with me Mr. Hinckman would hear you and come into the room to know why you were talking to yourself."

"But would he not hear you?" I asked.

"Oh, no!" said the other. "There are times when anyone may see me, but no one hears me except the person to whom I address myself."

"But why did you wish to speak to me?" I asked.

"Because," replied the ghost, "I like occasionally to talk to people and especially to someone like yourself, whose mind is so troubled and perturbed that you are not likely to be frightened by a visit from one of us. But I particularly want to ask you to do me a favor. There is every probability, so far as I can see, that John Hinckman will live a long time, and my situation is becoming insupportable. My great object at present is to get myself transferred, and I think that you may, perhaps, be of use to me."

"Transferred!" I exclaimed. "What do you mean by that?"

"What I mean," said the other, "is this: now that I have started on my career, I have got to be the ghost of somebody, and I want to be the ghost of a man who is really dead."

"I should think that would be easy enough," I said. "Opportunities must continually occur."

"Not at all! not at all!" said my companion, quickly. "You have no idea what a rush and pressure there is for situations of this kind. Whenever a vacancy occurs, if I may express myself in that way, there are crowds of applications for the ghostship."

"I had no idea that such a state of things existed," I said, becoming quite interested in the matter. "There ought to be some regular system, or order of precedence, by which you could all take your turns, like customers in a barber's shop."

"Oh, dear, that would never do at all!" said the other. "Some of us would have to wait forever. There is always a great rush whenever a good ghostship offers itself—while, as you know, there are some positions that no one would care for. It was in consequence of my being in too great a hurry on an occasion of this kind that I got myself into my present disagreeable predicament, and I have thought that it might be possible that you would help me out of it. You might know of a case where an opportunity for a ghostship was not generally expected but which might present itself at any moment. If you would give me a short notice, I know I could arrange for a transfer."

"What do you mean?" I exclaimed. "Do you want me to commit suicide or to undertake a murder for your benefit?"

"Oh, no, no, no!" said the other, with a vapory smile. "I mean nothing of that kind. To be sure, there are lovers who are watched with considerable interest, such persons having been known, in moments of depression, to offer very desirable ghostships, but I did not think of anything of that kind in connection with you. You were the only person I cared to speak to, and I hoped that you might give me some information that would be of use; and, in return, I shall be very glad to help you in your love affair."

"You seem to know that I have such an affair," I said.

"Oh, yes!" replied the other, with a little yawn. "I could not be here so much as I have been without knowing all about that."

There was something horrible in the idea of Madeline and myself having been watched by a ghost, even, perhaps, when we wandered together in the most delightful and bosky places. But, then, this was quite an exceptional ghost, and I could not have the objections to him which would ordinarily arise in regard to beings of his class.

"I must go now," said the ghost, rising, "but I will see you somewhere tomorrow night; and remember—you help me, and I'll help you."

I had doubts the next morning as to the propriety of telling Madeline anything about this interview and soon convinced myself that I must keep silent on the subject. If she knew there was a ghost about the house, she would probably leave the place instantly. I did not mention the matter and so regulated my demeanor that I am quite sure Madeline never suspected what had taken place.

For some time I had wished that Mr. Hinckman would absent himself, for a day at least, from the premises. In such case I thought I might more easily nerve myself up to the point of speaking to Madeline on the subject of our future collateral existence. But now that the opportunity for such speech had really occurred, I did not feel ready to avail myself of it. What would become of me if she refused me?

I had an idea, however, that the lady thought that if I were going to speak at all, this was the time. She must have known that certain sentiments were afloat within me, and she was not unreasonable in her wish to see the matter settled one way or the other. But I did not feel like taking a bold step in the dark. If she wished me to ask her to give herself to me, she ought to offer me some reason to suppose that she would make the gift. If I saw no probability of such generosity, I would prefer that things should remain as they were.

That evening I was sitting with Madeline on the moonlit porch. It was nearly ten o'clock, and ever since suppertime I had been working myself up to the point of making an avowal of my sentiments. I had not positively determined to do this but wished gradually to reach the proper point when, if the prospect looked bright, I might speak. My companion appeared to understand the situation—at least, I imagined that the nearer I came to a proposal the more she seemed to expect it. It was certainly a very critical and important epoch in my life. If I spoke, I should make myself happy or miserable forever; and if I did not speak, I had every reason to believe that the lady would not give me another chance to do so.

Sitting thus with Madeline, talking a little and thinking very hard over these momentous matters, I looked up and saw the ghost, not a dozen feet away from us. He was sitting on the railing of the porch, one leg thrown up before him, the other dangling down as he leaned against a post. He was behind Madeline but almost in front of me, as I sat facing the lady. It was fortunate that Madeline was looking out over the landscape, for I must have appeared very much startled. The ghost had told me that he would see me sometime this night, but I did not think he would make his appearance when I was in the company of Madeline. If she should see the spirit of her uncle, I could not answer for the consequences. I made no exclamation, but the ghost evidently saw that I was troubled.

"Don't be afraid," he said; "I shall not let her see me, and she cannot hear me speak unless I address myself to her, which I do not intend to do."

I suppose I looked grateful.

"So you need not trouble yourself about that," the ghost continued. "But it seems to me that you are not getting along very well with your affair. If I were you, I should speak out without waiting any longer. You will never have a better chance. You are not likely to be interrupted, and so far as I can judge, the lady seems disposed to listen to you favorably—that is, if she ever intends to do so. There is no knowing when John Hinckman will go away again; certainly not this summer. If I were in your place, I should never dare to make love to Hinckman's niece if he were anywhere about the place. If he should catch anyone offering himself to Miss Madeline, he would then be a terrible man to encounter."

I agreed perfectly to all this.

"I cannot bear to think of him!" I ejaculated aloud.

"Think of whom?" asked Madeline, turning quickly toward me.

Here was an awkward situation. The long speech of the ghost, to which Madeline paid no attention but which I heard with perfect distinctness, had made me forget myself.

It was necessary to explain quickly. Of course, it would not do to admit that it was of her dear uncle that I was speaking, and so I mentioned hastily the first name I thought of.

"Mr. Vilars," I said.

This statement was entirely correct, for I never could bear to think of Mr. Vilars, who was a gentleman who had, at various times, paid much attention to Madeline.

"It is wrong for you to speak in that way of Mr. Vilars," she said. "He is a remarkably well educated and sensible young man and has very pleasant manners. He expects to be elected to the legislature this fall, and I should not be surprised if he made his mark. He will do well in a legislative body, for whenever Mr. Vilars has anything to say, he knows just how and when to say it."

This was spoken very quietly, and without any show of resentment, which was all very natural, for if Madeline thought at all favorably of me she could not feel displeased that I should have disagreeable emotions in regard to a possible rival. The concluding words contained a hint which I was not slow to understand. I felt very sure that if Mr. Vilars were in my present position he would speak quickly enough.

"I know it is wrong to have such ideas about a person," I said, "but I cannot help it."

The lady did not chide me, and after this she seemed even in a softer mood. As for me, I felt considerably annoyed, for I had not wished to admit that any thought of Mr. Vilars had ever occupied my mind.

"You should not speak aloud that way," said the ghost, "or you may get yourself into trouble. I want to see everything go well with you, because then you may be disposed to help me, especially if I should chance to be of any assistance to you, which I hope I shall be."

I longed to tell him that there was no way in which he could help me so much as by taking his instant departure. To make love to a young lady with a ghost sitting on the railing near by, and that ghost the apparition of a much-dreaded uncle, the very idea of whom in such a position and at such a time made me tremble, was a difficult, if not an impossible, thing to do. But I forbore to speak, although I may have looked my mind.

"I suppose," continued the ghost, "that you have not heard anything that might be of advantage to me. Of course, I am very anxious to hear, but if you have anything to tell me, I can wait until you are alone. I will come to you tonight in your room, or I will stay here until the lady goes away."

"You need not wait here," I said; "I have nothing at all to say to you."

Madeline sprang to her feet, her face flushed and her eyes ablaze.

"Wait here!" she cried. "What do you suppose I am waiting for? Nothing to say to me, indeed! I should think so! What should you have to say to me?"

"Madeline," I exclaimed, stepping toward her, "let me explain."

But she had gone.

Here was the end of the world for me! I turned fiercely to the ghost.

"Wretched existence!" I cried, "you have ruined everything. You have blackened my whole life! Had it not been for you—"

But here my voice faltered. I could say no more.

"You wrong me," said the ghost. "I have not injured you. I have tried only to encourage and assist you, and it is your own folly that has done this mischief. But do not despair. Such mistakes as these can be explained. Keep up a brave heart. Goodbye."

And he vanished from the railing like a bursting soap bubble.

I went gloomily to bed, but I saw no apparitions that night except those of despair and misery, which my wretched thoughts called up. The words I had uttered had sounded to Madeline like the basest insult. Of course, there was only one interpretation she could put upon them.

As to explaining my ejaculations, that was impossible. I thought the matter over and over again as I lay awake that night, and I determined that I would never tell Madeline the facts of the case. It would be better for me to suffer all my life than for her to know that the ghost of her uncle haunted the house. Mr. Hinckman was away, and if she knew of his ghost she could not be made to believe that he was not dead. She might not survive the shock! No, my heart might bleed, but I would never tell her.

The next day was fine, neither too cool nor too warm. The breezes were gentle, and nature smiled. But there were no walks or rides with Madeline. She seemed to be much engaged during the day, and I saw but little of her. When we met at meals she was polite but very quiet and reserved. She had evidently determined on a course of conduct and had resolved to assume that, although I had been very rude to her, she did not understand the import of my words. It would be quite proper, of course, for her not to know what I meant by my expressions of the night before.

I was downcast and wretched and said but little, and the only bright streak across the black horizon of my woe was the fact that she did not appear to be happy, although she affected an air of unconcern. The moonlit porch was deserted that evening, but wandering about the house, I found Madeline in the library alone. She was reading, but I went in and sat down near her. I felt that, although I could not do so fully, I must in a measure explain my conduct of the night before. She listened quietly to a somewhat labored apology I made for the words I had used.

"I have not the slightest idea what you meant," she said, "but you were very rude."

I earnestly disclaimed any intention of rudeness and assured her, with a warmth of speech that must have made some impression upon her, that rudeness to her would be an action impossible to me. I said a great deal upon the subject, and implored her to believe that if it were not for a certain obstacle I could speak to her so plainly that she would understand everything.

She was silent for a time, and then she said, rather more kindly, I thought, than she had spoken before, "Is that obstacle in any way connected with my uncle?"

"Yes," I answered, after a little hesitation, "it is, in a measure, connected with him."

She made no answer to this and sat looking at her book but not reading. From the expression of her face, I thought she was somewhat softened toward me. She knew her uncle as well as I did, and she may have been thinking that if he were the obstacle that prevented my speaking (and there were many ways in which he might be that obstacle), my position would be such a hard one that it would excuse some wildness of speech and eccentricity of manner. I saw, too, that the warmth of my partial explanations had had some effect on her, and I began to believe that it might be a good thing for me to speak my mind without delay. No matter how she should receive my proposition, my relations with her could not be worse than they had been the previous night and day, and there was something in her face which encouraged me to hope that she might forget my foolish exclamations of the evening before if I began to tell her my tale of love.

I drew my chair a little nearer to her, and as I did so, the ghost burst into the room from the doorway behind her. I say burst, although no door flew open and he made no noise. He was wildly excited and waved his arms above his head. The moment I saw him, my heart fell within me. With the entrance of that impertinent apparition, every hope fled from me. I could not speak while he was in the room.

I must have turned pale, and I gazed steadfastly at the ghost, almost without seeing Madeline, who sat between us.

"Do you know," he cried, "that John Hinckman is coming up the hill? He will be here in fifteen minutes, and if you are doing anything in the way of lovemaking, you had better hurry it up. But this is not what I came to tell you. I have glorious news! At last I am transferred! Not forty minutes ago a Russian nobleman was murdered by the Nihilists. Nobody ever thought of him in connection with an immediate ghostship. My friends instantly applied for the situation for me and obtained my transfer. I am off before that horrid Hinckman comes up the hill. The moment I reach my new position, I shall put off this hated semblance. Goodbye! You can't imagine how glad I am to be, at last, the real ghost of somebody."

"Oh!" I cried, rising to my feet and stretching out my arms in utter wretchedness, "I would to Heaven you were mine!"

"I *am* yours," said Madeline, raising to me her tearful eyes.

Our Story

I BECAME ACQUAINTED with Miss Bessie Vancouver at a reception given by an eminent literary gentleman in New York. The circumstances were a little peculiar. Miss Vancouver and I had each written and recently published a book, and we were introduced to each other as young authors whose works had made us known to the public and who, consequently, should know each other. The peculiarity of the situation lay in the fact that I had not read Miss Vancouver's book, nor had she read mine. Consequently, although each felt bound to speak of the work of the other, neither of us could do it except in the most general and cautious way. I was quite sure that her book was a novel, but that was all that I knew about it, except that I had heard it well spoken of. But she supposed my book was of a scientific character, whereas, in reality, it also was a novel, although its title did not indicate the fact. There was, therefore, an air of restraint and stiffness about our first interview, which it might not have had if we had frankly acknowledged our shortcomings. But as the general conversation led her to believe that she was the only person in the room who had not read my book and me to believe that I was the only one who had not read hers, we were naturally loath to confess the truth to each other.

I next met Miss Vancouver in Paris, at the house of a lady whose parlors are the frequent rendezvous of Americans, especially those given to art or literature. This time we met on different ground. I had read her book and she mine, and as soon as we had shaken hands, we began to talk of each other's work, not as if it had been the beginning of a new conversation but rather as the continuation of one broken off. Each liked the book of the other extremely, and we were free to say so.

"But I am not satisfied with my novel," said Miss Vancouver. "There is too much oneness about it, by which I mean that it is not diversified enough. It is all, or nearly all, about two people, who, of course, have but one object in life, and it seems to me now that their story might have been finished a great deal sooner, though, of course, in that case it would not have been long enough to make a book."

To this I politely answered that I did not agree with her, for the story was interesting to the very end. But, of course, if she had put more characters into it and they had been as good in their way as those she already had, the book would have been that much the better. "As for me," I continued, "my trouble is entirely the other way. I have no oneness whatever. My tendency is much more to fifteenness or twentyness. I carry a story a little way in one direction, and then I stop and go off in another. It is sometimes difficult to make it understood why a character should have been brought into the story at all, and I have had a good deal of trouble in making some of them do something toward the end to show that they are connected with the general plot."

She said she had noticed that there was a wideness of scope in my book, but what she would have said further I do not know, for our hostess now came down upon us and carried off Miss Vancouver to introduce her to an old lady who had successfully steered about fifty barks across that sea on which Miss Vancouver had just set out.

Our next meeting was in a town on the Mediterranean, in the south of France. I had secured board at a large pension there and was delighted to find that Miss Bessie Vancouver and her mother were already inmates of the house. As soon as I had the opportunity, I broached to her an idea which had frequently possessed my mind since our conversation in Paris. I proposed that we should write a story together, something like Erckmann-Chatrian or Mark Twain and Mr. Warner in *The Gilded Age*. Since she had too much unity of purpose and traveled in too narrow a path while I branched off too much and had too great a tendency to variety, our styles, if properly blended, would possess all the qualities needed in a good story. So there was no reason why we should not, writing thus together, achieve a success greater, perhaps, than either of us could expect writing alone. I had thought so much on this subject that I was able to say a great deal and to say it pretty well, too, so far as I could judge. Miss Vancouver listened with great attention, and the more I said, the better the idea pleased her. She said she would take the afternoon to consider the matter, and in the evening she told me in the parlor that she had made up her mind, if I still thought well of the plan, to assist me in writing a story—this being the polite way in which she chose to put it—but that she thought it would be better for us to begin with a short story and not with a book, for in this way we could sooner see how we would be likely to succeed. Of course I agreed to this proposition, and we arranged that we should meet the next morning in the garden and lay out a plan for our story.

The garden attached to the house in which we lived was a very quaint and pleasant one. It had been made a hundred years ago or more by an Italian nobleman, whose mansion, now greatly altered, had become our present pension. The garden was laid out in a series of terraces on the side of a hill, and abounded in walks shaded by orange and lemon trees, arbors, and vine-covered trellises, fountains half concealed by overhanging ivy, and suddenly discovered stairways, wide and shadowy, leading up into regions of greater quaintness and seclusion. Flowers were here, and palm trees, and great cactus bushes, with their red fruit half hollowed out by the nibbling birds. From the upper terraces we could see the blue Mediterranean spreading far away on one side, while the snow-covered tops of the Maritime Alps stood bright against the sky. The garden was little frequented, and altogether it was a good place in which to plan a story.

We consulted together for several days before we actually began to work. At first we sat in an arbor on one of the lower terraces, where there were a little iron table and some chairs; but now and then a person would come there for a morning stroll, and so we moved up higher to a seat under a palm tree and the next day to another terrace, where there was a secluded corner overshadowed by huge cacti. But the place which suited us best of all was the top of an old tower at one end of the garden. This tower had been built many, many hundred years before the garden was thought of, and its broad, flat roof was level with one of the higher terraces. Here we could work and consult in quiet, with little fear of being disturbed.

We shared an interest in the development of character.

Not finding it easy to plan out the whole story at once, we determined to begin by preparing backgrounds. We concluded that as this was to be a short story, it would be sufficient to have descriptions of two natural scenes in which the two principal incidents should occur; and as we wished to do all our work from natural models, we thought it best to describe the scene which lay around us, than which nothing could be more beautiful or more suitable. One scene was to be on the seashore, with a mellow light upon the rippling waves and the sails of fishing vessels in the distance. This Miss Vancouver was to do, while I was to take a scene among the hills and mountains at the back of the town. I walked over there one afternoon when Miss Vancouver had gone out with her mother. I got on a high point and worked up a very satisfactory description of the frowning mountains behind me, the old monasteries on the hills, and the town stretching out below, with a little river rushing along between two rows of picturesque washerwomen to the sea.

We read our backgrounds to each other and were both very well satisfied. Our styles were as different as the scenes we described. Hers was clear and smooth and mine forcible and somewhat abrupt, and thus the strong points of each scene were better brought out; but in order that our styles might be unified, so to speak, by being judiciously blended, I suggested some strong and effective points to be introduced into her description, while she toned down some of my phrases and added a word here and there, which gave a color and beauty to the description that it had not possesssed before.

Our backgrounds being thus satisfactory—and it took a good deal of consultation to make them so—our next work was to provide characters for the story. These were to be drawn from life, for it would be perfectly ridiculous to create imaginary characters when there were so many original and interesting personages around us. We soon agreed upon an individual who would serve as a model for our hero. I forgot whether it was I or Miss Vancouver who first suggested him. He was a young man, but not so very young either, who lived in the house with us and about whom there was a mystery. Nobody knew exactly who he was or where he came from or why he was here. It was evident he did not come for society, for he kept very much to himself. And the attractions of the town could not have brought him here, for he seemed to care very little about them. We seldom saw him, except at the table and occasionally in the garden. When we met him in the latter place, he always seemed anxious to avoid observation, and as we did not wish to hurt his feelings by letting him suppose that he was an object of curiosity to us, we endeavored, as far as possible, to make it apparent that we were not looking at him or thinking of him. But still, whenever we had a good chance, we studied him. Of course, we could not make out his mystery, but that was not necessary, nor did we, indeed, think it would be proper. We could draw him as we saw him and then make the mystery what we pleased, its character depending a good deal upon the plot we devised.

Miss Vancouver undertook to draw the hero, and she went to work upon him immediately. In personal appearance she altered the model a good deal. She darkened his hair and took off his whiskers, leaving him only a mustache. She thought, too, that he ought to be a little taller and asked me my height, which is five feet nine. She considered that a very good height and brought the hero up to it. She also made him some years younger but endeavored, as far as seemed suitable to the story, to draw him exactly as he was.

I was to do the heroine but found it very hard to choose a model. As I said before, we determined to draw all our characters from life; but I could think of no one, in the somewhat extensive company by which we were surrounded, who would answer my purpose. Nor could I fix my mind upon any person in other parts of the world, whom I knew or had known, who resembled the idea I had formed of our heroine. After thinking this matter over a good deal, I told Miss Vancouver that I believed the best thing I could do would be to take her for my model. I was with her a good deal and thus could study out and work up certain points as I wrote, which would be a great advantage. She objected to this because, as she said, the author of a story should not be drawn as its heroine. But I asserted that this would not be the case. She would merely suggest the heroine to me, and I would so do my work that the heroine would not suggest her to anybody else. This, I thought, was the way in which a model ought to be used. After we had talked the subject over a good deal, she agreed to my plan, and I went to work with much satisfaction. I gave no definite description of the lady but endeavored to indicate the impression which her person and character produced upon me. As such impressions are seldom the same in any two cases, there was no danger that my description could be referred back to her.

When I read to her the sketch I had written, she objected to parts of it as not being correct. But as I asserted that it was not intended as an exact copy of the model, she could not say it was not a true picture, and so, with some slight modifications, we let it stand. I thought myself that it was a very good piece of work. To me it seemed very lifelike and piquant, and I believed that other people would think it so.

We were now ready for the incidents and the plot. But at this point we were somewhat interrupted by Mrs. Vancouver. She came to me one morning when I was waiting to go with her daughter to our study in the garden and told me that she was very sorry to notice that Miss Vancouver and I had attracted attention to ourselves by being so much together, and while she understood the nature of the literary labor on which we were engaged, she did not wish her daughter to become the object of general attention and remark in a foreign pension. I was very angry when I heard that people had been directing upon us their impertinent curiosity, and I discoursed warmly upon the subject.

"Where is the good," I said, "of a person or persons devoting himself or themselves, with enthusiasm and earnestness, to his or their life work, if he or they are to be interfered with by the impertinent babble of the multitude?"

Mrs. Vancouver was not prepared to give an exact answer to this question, but she considered the babble of the multitude a very serious thing. She had been talking to her daughter on the subject and thought it right to speak to me.

That morning we worked separately in our rooms, but we accomplished little or nothing. It was, of course, impossible to do anything of importance in a work of this kind without consultation and cooperation. The next day, however, I devised a plan which would enable us, I thought, to pursue our labors without attracting attention, and Mrs. Vancouver, who was a kindhearted woman and took a great interest in her daughter's literary career, told me if I could successfully carry out anything of the kind I might do so. She did not inquire into particulars, nor did I explain them to Miss Bessie, but I told the latter that we would not go out together into the garden, but that I would go first, and she should join me about ten minutes afterwards on the tower, but she was not to come if she saw anyone about.

Near the top of the hill, above the garden, once stood an ancient mansion, of which nothing now remained but the remnants of some massive masonry. A courtyard, however, of this old edifice was still surrounded by a high wall, which formed the upper boundary of our garden. From a point near the tower a flight of twisting stone steps, flanked by blank walls, which turned themselves in various directions to suit the angles of the stairway, led to a green door in this wall. Through this door Miss Vancouver and myself, and doubtless many other persons, had often wished to pass, but it was locked, and on inquiry we found that there was no key to be had. The day previous, however, when wandering by myself, I had examined this door and found that it was fastened merely by a snap lock, which had no handle but was opened by a key. I had a knife with a long, strong blade, and pushing this into the hasp, I easily forced back the bolt. I then opened the door and walked into the old courtyard.

When Miss Vancouver appeared on the tower, I was standing at the top of the stone steps just mentioned, with the green door slightly ajar. Calling to her in a low tone, she ran up the steps, and, to her amazement, I ushered her into the courtyard and closed the door behind us.

"There," I exultingly exclaimed, "is our study, where we can write our story without interruption. We will come and go away separately. The people of the pension will not know that we are here or have been here, and there will be no occasion for that impertinent attention to which your mother so properly objects."

Miss Vancouver was delighted, and we walked about and surveyed the courtyard with much satisfaction. I had already selected the spot for our work. It was in the shade of an olive tree, the only tree in the enclosure, beneath which there was a rude seat. I spread a rug upon the grass, and Miss Bessie sat upon the seat and put her feet upon the rug, leaving room for me to sit thereon. We now took out our little blank books and our stylograph pens and were ready for work. I explained that I had done nothing the day before, and Miss Vancouver said that had also been the case with her. She had not wished to do anything important without consultation but supposing that, of course, the hero was to fall in love with the heroine, she thought she might as well make him begin, but she found she could not do it as she wished. She wanted him to indicate to the lady that he was in love with her without exactly saying so. Could I not suggest some good form for giving expression to this state of things? After a little reflection, I thought I could.

"I will speak," said I, "as if I were the hero, and then you can see how it will suit."

"Yes," said she, "but you must not forget that what you say should be very gradual."

I tried to be as gradual as I could and to indicate by slow degrees the state of mind in which we wished our hero to be. As the indication became stronger and stronger, I thought it right to take Miss Vancouver's hand; but to this she objected because, as she said, it was more than indication, and, besides, it prevented her from writing down what I said. We argued this point a little while without altering our position, and I asserted that the hand-holding only gave point and earnestness to the hero's remarks, which otherwise would not be so natural and true to life, and if she wanted to use her right hand, her left hand would do to hold. We made this change, and I proceeded with the hero's remarks.

There was in our pension a young German girl named Margarita. She was a handsome, plump maiden, and spoke English very well. There was another young lady, also a German, named Gretzel. She was a little creature and the fast friend of Margarita. These two had a companion whose name I did not know. She was a little older than the others, and was, I think, a Pole. She also understood English.

As I was warming up toward the peroration of our hero's indication, I raised my eyes and saw, on the brow of the hill not a stone's throw from us, these three girls. They were talking earnestly and walking directly toward us. The place where they were was used as a public pleasure ground and was separated from the old courtyard by a picket fence. Although the girls could not come to us, there was nothing to prevent their seeing us if they chose to look our way, for they were on ground which was higher than the top of the fence.

When I saw these girls I was horror-stricken, and my knees, on which I rested, trembled beneath me. I did not dare to rise nor to change my position, for fear the motion should attract attention, nor did I cease my remarks, for had I suddenly done so, my companion would have looked around to see what was the matter and would certainly have jumped up or have done something which would have brought the eyes of those girls upon us. But my voice dropped very low, and I wondered if there was any way of my gently rolling out of sight.

But at this moment our young man with a mystery suddenly appeared on the other side of the fence, walking rapidly toward the girls. There was something on the ocean, probably a ship, to which he directed their attention, and then he actually led them off, pointing, as it appeared, to a spot from which the distant object could be more plainly seen. They all walked away and disappeared behind the brow of the hill. With a great feeling of relief, I arose and recounted what had happened. Miss Vancouver sprang to her feet, shut up her blank book, and put the stopper on her stylograph.

"This place will not do at all to work in," she said. "I will not have those girls staring at us."

I was obliged to admit that this particular spot would not do. I had not thought of anyone walking in the grounds immediately above us, especially in the morning, which was our working time.

"They may return," she said, "and we must go away immediately and separately."

But I could not agree thus to give up our new-found study. The enclosure was quite extensive with ruins at the other end, near which we might find some spot entirely protected from observation. So I went to look for such a place, leaving Miss Vancouver under the olive tree, where, if she were seen alone, it would not matter. I found a spot which might answer, and returning to the tree, sent her to look at it. While we were thus engaged, we heard the report of the noon cannon. This startled us both. The hour for *déjeuner à la fourchette* at the pension was twelve o'clock, and people were generally very prompt at that meal. It would not do for us to be late. Snatching up our effects, we hurried to the green door, but when I tried to open it as before, I found it impossible—a projecting strip of wood on the inside of the doorway preventing my reaching the bolt with my knife blade. I tried to tear away the strip, but it was too firmly fastened. We both became very nervous and troubled. It was impossible to get out of the enclosure except through that door, for the wall was quite high and the top covered with broken glass embedded in the mortar. The party on the hill had had time to go down and around through the town to the pension. Our places at the table would be the only ones empty. What could attract more attention than this? And what would Mrs. Vancouver think and say? At this moment we heard some one working at the lock on the other side. The door opened, and there stood our hero.

"I heard someone at this door," he said, "and supposing it had been accidentally closed, I came up and opened it."

"Thank you; thank you very much!" cried Miss Vancouver.

Away she ran to the house. If only I were late it did not matter at all. I followed with our hero and endeavored to make some explanation of the predicament of myself and the young lady. He took it all as a matter of course, as if the old courtyard were a place of general resort.

"When persons stroll through that door," he said, "they should put a piece of stick or of stone against the jamb, so that if the door is blown shut by the wind the latch may not catch."

And then he called my attention to a beautiful plant of the aloe kind, which had just begun to blossom.

Miss Vancouver reached the breakfast table in good time, but she told me afterwards she would work in the old courtyard no more; the perils were too many.

For some days after this, our story made little progress, for opportunities for consultation did not occur. I was particularly sorry for this, because I wanted very much to know how Miss Vancouver liked my indicative speech and what she had made of it.

Early one afternoon about this time, our hero, between whom and myself a slight acquaintance had sprung up, came to me and said, "The sea is so perfectly smooth and quiet today that I thought it would be pleasant to take a row, and I have hired a boat. How would you like to go with me?"

I was pleased with his friendly proposition, and I am very fond of rowing, but yet I hesitated about accepting the invitation, for I had hoped that afternoon to find some opportunity for consultation in regard to the work on which I was engaged.

"The boat is rather large for two persons," he remarked. "Have you any friends you would like to ask to go with us?"

This put a different phase upon affairs. I instantly said that I thought a row would be charming that afternoon and suggested that Mrs. Vancouver and her daughter might like to take advantage of the opportunity.

The ladies were quite willing to go, and in twenty minutes we set off, two fishermen in red liberty caps pushing us from the pebbly beach. Our hero took one oar and I another, and we pulled together very well. The ladies sat in the stern and enjoyed the smooth sea and the lovely day. We rowed across the little bay and around a high promontory, where there was a larger bay with a small town in the distance. The hero suggested that we should land here, as we could get some good views from the rocks. To this we all agreed, and when we had climbed up a little distance, Mrs. Vancouver found some wild flowers which interested her very much. She was, in a certain way, a floraphile, and took an especial delight in finding in foreign countries blossoms which were the same as or similar to flowers she was familiar with in New England. Our hero also had a fancy for wild flowers, and it was not long before he showed Mrs. Vancouver a little blossom which she was very sure she had seen either at East Gresham or Milton Centre. Leaving these two to their floral researches, Miss Vancouver and I climbed higher up the rocks, where the view would be better. We found a pleasant ledge, and although we could not see what was going on below us and the view was quite cut off in the direction of the town, we had an admirable outlook over the sea, on which, in the far distance, we could see the sails of a little vessel.

"This will be an admirable place to do a little work on our story," I said. "I have brought my blank book and stylograph."

"And so have I," said she.

I then told her that I had been thinking over the matter a good deal and that I believed in a short story two long speeches would be enough for the hero to make and proposed that we should now go on with the second one. She thought well of that and took a seat upon a rocky projection, while I sat upon another quite near.

"This second speech," said I, "ought to be more than indicative and should express the definite purpose of the hero's sentiments, and I think there should be corresponding expressions from the heroine and would be glad to have you suggest such as you think she would make." I then began to say what I thought a hero ought to say under the circumstances. I soon warmed up to my task wonderfully and expressed with much earnestness and ardor the sentiments I thought proper for the occasion. I first held one of Miss Vancouver's hands and then both of them, she trusting to her memory in regard to memoranda. Her remarks in the character of the heroine were, however, much briefer than mine, but they were enough. If necessary, they could be worked up and amplified.

I think we had said all or very nearly all there was to say when we heard a shout from below. It was our hero calling us. We could not see him, but I knew his voice. He shouted again, and then I arose from the rock on which Bessie was sitting and answered him. He now made his appearance some distance below us and said that Mrs. Vancouver did not care to come up any higher to get the views and that she thought it would be better to reach home before the sun should set.

That evening, in the salon, Bessie spoke to me apart. "Our hero," she said, "is more than a hero. He is a guardian angel. You must fathom his mystery. I am sure that it is far better than anything we can invent for him."

I set myself to work to discover, if possible, not only the mystery which had first interested us in our hero but also the reason and purpose of his guardian-angelship. He was an American, and now that I had come to know him better, I found him a very agreeable talker.

Our hero was the first person whom I told of my engagement to Bessie. Mrs. Vancouver was very particular that this state of affairs should be made known. "If you are engaged," she said, "of course you can be together as much as you please. It is the custom in America, and nobody need make any remarks."

In talking to our hero, I told him of many little things that had happened at various times, and endeavored by these friendly confidences to make him speak of his own affairs. It must not be supposed that I was actuated by prying curiosity, but certainly I had a right to know something of a person to whom I had told so much. But he always seemed a great deal more interested in us than in himself, and I took so much interest in his interest, which was very kindly expressed, that his affairs never came into our conversation.

But just as he was going away—he left the little town a few days before we did—he told me that he was a writer and that for some time past he had been engaged upon a story.

Our story was never finished. His was. This is it.

She knew behind which door crouched the tiger.

The Lady or the Tiger?

IN THE VERY OLDEN time, there lived a semi-barbaric king, whose ideas, although somewhat polished and sharpened by the progressiveness of distant Latin neighbors, were still large, florid, and untrammeled, as became the half of him which was barbaric. He was a man of exuberant fancy and, withal, of an authority so irresistible that, at his will, he turned his varied fancies into facts. He was greatly given to self-communing, and when he and himself agreed upon anything, the thing was done. When every member of his domestic and political systems moved smoothly in its appointed course, his nature was bland and genial; but whenever there was a little hitch and some of his orbs got out of their orbits, he was blander and more genial still, for nothing pleased him so much as to make the crooked straight and crush down uneven places.

Among the borrowed notions by which his barbarism had become semified was that of the public arena, in which, by exhibitions of manly and beastly valor, the minds of his subjects were refined and cultured.

But even here the exuberant and barbaric fancy asserted itself. The arena of the king was built, not to give the people an opportunity of hearing the rhapsodies of dying gladiators, nor to enable them to view the inevitable conclusion of a conflict between religious opinions and hungry jaws, but for purposes far better adapted to widen and develop the mental energies of the people. This vast amphitheater, with its encircling galleries, its mysterious vaults, and its unseen passages, was an agent of poetic justice, in which crime was punished or virtue rewarded by the decrees of an impartial and incorruptible chance.

When a subject was accused of a crime of sufficient importance to interest the king, public notice was given that on an appointed day the fate of the accused person would be decided in the king's arena—a structure which well deserved its name, for although its form and plan were borrowed from afar, its purpose emanated solely from the brain of this man, who, every barleycorn a king, knew no tradition to which he owed more allegiance than pleased his fancy and who ingrafted on every adopted form of human thought and action the rich growth of his barbaric idealism.

When all the people had assembled in the galleries and the king, surrounded by his court, sat high up on his throne of royal state on one side of the arena, he gave a signal, a door beneath him opened, and the accused subject stepped out into the amphitheater. Directly opposite him, on the other side of the enclosed space, were two doors, exactly alike and side by side. It was the duty and the privilege of the person on trial to walk directly to these doors and open one of them. He could open either door he pleased. He was subject to no guidance or influence but that of the aforementioned impartial and incorruptible chance. If he opened the one, there came out of it a hungry tiger, the fiercest and most cruel that could be procured, which immediately sprang upon him and tore him to pieces, as a punishment for his guilt. The moment that the case of the criminal was thus decided, doleful iron bells were clanged, great wails went up from the hired mourners posted on the outer rim of the arena, and the vast audience, with bowed heads and downcast hearts, wended slowly their homeward way, mourning greatly that one so young and fair, or so old and respected, should have merited so dire a fate.

But if the accused person opened the other door, there came forth from it a lady, the most suitable to his years and station that his Majesty could select among his fair subjects; and to this lady he was immediately married, as a reward of his innocence. It mattered not that he might already possess a wife and family or that his affections might be engaged upon an object of his own selection. The king allowed no such subordinate arrangements to interfere with his great scheme of retribution and reward. The exercises, as in the other instance, took place immediately and in the arena. Another door opened beneath the king, and a priest, followed by a band of choristers and dancing maidens blowing joyous airs on golden horns and treading an epithalamic measure, advanced to where the pair stood side by side, and the wedding was properly and cheerily solemnized. Then the gay brass bells rang forth their merry peals, the people shouted glad hurrahs, and the innocent man, preceded by children strewing flowers on his path, led his bride to his home.

This was the king's semi-barbaric method of administering justice. Its perfect fairness is obvious. The criminal could not know out of which door would come the lady. He opened either he pleased, without having the slightest idea whether, in the next instant, he was to be devoured or married. On some occasions the tiger came out of one door, and on some out of the other. The decisions of this tribunal were not only fair—they were positively determinate. The accused person was instantly punished if he found himself guilty, and if innocent he was rewarded on the spot, whether he liked it or not. There was no escape from the judgments of the king's arena.

The institution was a very popular one. When the people gathered together on one of the great trial days, they never knew whether they were to witness a bloody slaughter or a hilarious wedding. This element of uncertainty lent an interest to the occasion which it could not otherwise have attained. Thus the masses were entertained and pleased, and the thinking part of the community could bring no charge of unfairness against this plan; for did not the accused person have the whole matter in his own hands?

This semi-barbaric king had a daughter as blooming as his most florid fancies and with a soul as fervent and imperious as his own. As is usual in such cases, she was the apple of his eye and was loved by him above all humanity. Among his courtiers was a young man of that fineness of blood and lowness of station common to the conventional heroes of romance who love royal maidens. This royal maiden was well satisfied with her lover, for he was handsome and brave to a degree unsurpassed in all this kingdom, and she loved him with an ardor that had enough of barbarism in it to make it exceedingly warm and strong. This love affair moved on happily for many months, until one day the king happened to discover its existence. He did not hesitate nor waver in regard to his duty in the premises. The youth was immediately cast into prison, and a day was appointed for his trial in the king's arena. This, of course, was an especially important occasion, and his Majesty, as well as all the people, was greatly interested in the workings and development of this trial. Never before had such a case occurred—never before had a subject dared to love the daughter of a king. In after years such things became commonplace enough, but then they were, in no slight degree, novel and startling.

The tiger cages of the kingdom were searched for the most savage and relentless beasts, from which the fiercest monsters might be selected for the arena, and the ranks of maiden youth and beauty throughout the land were carefully surveyed by competent judges, in order that the young man might have a fitting bride in case fate did not determine for him a different destiny. Of course, everybody knew that the deed with which the accused was charged had been done. He had loved the princess, and neither he, she, nor anyone else thought of denying the fact. But the king would not think of allowing any fact of this kind to interfere with the workings of the tribunal, in which he took such great delight and satisfaction. No matter how the affair turned out, the youth would be disposed of, and the king would take an æsthetic pleasure in watching the course of events which would determine whether or not the young man had done wrong in allowing himself to love the princess.

The appointed day arrived. From far and near the people gathered and thronged the great galleries of the arena, while crowds, unable to gain admittance, massed themselves against its outside walls. The king and his court were in their places, opposite the twin doors—those fateful portals, so terrible in their similarity!

All was ready. The signal was given. A door beneath the royal party opened, and the lover of the princess walked into the arena. Tall, beautiful, fair, his appearance was greeted with a low hum of admiration and anxiety. Half the audience had not known so grand a youth had lived among them. No wonder the princess loved him! What a terrible thing for him to be there!

As the youth advanced into the arena, he turned, as the custom was, to bow to the king. But he did not think at all of that royal personage; his eyes were fixed upon the princess, who sat to the right of her father. Had it not been for the moiety of barbarism in her nature, it is probable that lady would not have been there. But her intense and fervid soul would not allow her to be absent on an occasion in which she was so terribly interested. From the moment that the decree had gone forth that her lover should decide his fate in the king's arena, she had thought of nothing night or day but this great event and the various subjects connected with it. Possessed of more power, influence, and force of character than anyone who had ever before been interested in such a case, she had done what no other person had done—she had possessed herself of the secret of the doors. She knew in which of the two rooms behind those doors stood the cage of the tiger, with its open front, and in which waited the lady. Through these thick doors, heavily curtained with skins on the inside, it was impossible that any noise or suggestion should come from within to the person who should approach to raise the latch of one of them. But gold and the power of a woman's will had brought the secret to the princess.

Not only did she know in which room stood the lady, ready to emerge all blushing and radiant should her door be opened, but she knew who the lady was. It was one of the fairest and loveliest of the damsels of the court who had been selected as the reward of the accused youth, should he be proved innocent of the crime of aspiring to one so far above him; and the princess hated her. Often had she seen, or imagined that she had seen, this fair creature throwing glances of admiration upon the person of her lover, and sometimes she thought these glances were perceived and even returned. Now and then she had seen them talking together. It was but for a moment or two, but much can be said in a brief space. It may have been on most unimportant topics, but how could she know that? The girl was lovely, but she had dared to raise her eyes to the loved one of the princess, and with all the intensity of the savage blood transmitted to her through long lines of wholly barbaric ancestors, she hated the woman who blushed and trembled behind that silent door.

When her lover turned and looked at her and his eye met hers as she sat there paler and whiter than anyone in the vast ocean of anxious faces about her, he saw, by that power of quick perception which is given to those whose souls are one, that she knew behind which door crouched the tiger and behind which stood the lady. He had expected her to know it. He understood her nature, and his soul was assured that she would never rest until she had made plain to herself this thing, hidden to all other lookers-on, even to the king. The only hope for the youth in which there was any element of certainty was based upon the success of the princess in discovering this mystery, and the moment he looked upon her, he saw she had succeeded.

Then it was that his quick and anxious glance asked the question, "Which?" It was as plain to her as if he shouted it from where he stood. There was not an instant to be lost. The question was asked in a flash; it must be answered in another.

Her right arm lay on the cushioned parapet before her. She raised her hand and made a slight, quick movement toward the right. No one but her lover saw her. Every eye but his was fixed on the man in the arena.

He turned, and with a firm and rapid step he walked across the empty space. Every heart stopped beating, every breath was held, every eye was fixed immovably upon that man. Without the slightest hesitation, he went to the door on the right and opened it.

Now, the point of the story is this: did the tiger come out of that door or did the lady?

The more we reflect upon this question, the harder it is to answer. It involves a study of the human heart which leads us through devious mazes of passion, out of which it is difficult to find our way. Think of it, fair reader, not as if the decision of the question depended upon yourself, but upon that hot-blooded, semi-barbaric princess, her soul at a white heat beneath the combined fires of despair and jealousy. She had lost him, but who should have him?

How often in her waking hours and in her dreams had she started in wild horror and covered her face with her hands as she thought of her lover opening the door on the other side of which waited the cruel fangs of the tiger!

But how much oftener had she seen him at the other door! How in her grievous reveries had she gnashed her teeth and torn her hair when she saw his start of rapturous delight as he opened the door of the lady! How her soul had burned in agony when she had seen him rush to meet that woman, with her flushing cheek and sparkling eye of triumph; when she had seen him lead her forth, his whole frame kindled with the joy of recovered life; when she had heard the glad shouts from the multitude and the wild ringing of the happy bells; when she had seen the priest, with his joyous followers, advance to the couple and make them man and wife before her very eyes; and when she had seen them walk away together upon their path of flowers, followed by the tremendous shouts of the hilarious multitude, in which her one despairing shriek was lost and drowned!

Would it not be better for him to die at once and go to wait for her in the blessed regions of semi-barbaric futurity?

And yet that awful tiger, those shrieks, that blood!

Her decision had been indicated in an instant, but it had been made after days and nights of anguished deliberation. She had known she would be asked, she had decided what she would answer, and without the slightest hesitation, she had moved her hand to the right.

The question of her decision is one not to be lightly considered, and it is not for me to presume to set up myself as the one person able to answer it. So I leave it with all of you: which came out of the opened door—the lady or the tiger?

"My income was at an end, and want . . . stared me in the face."

"His Wife's Deceased Sister"

IT IS NOW FIVE years since an event occurred which so colored my life, or rather so changed some of its original colors, that I have thought it well to write an account of it, deeming that its lessons may be of advantage to persons whose situations in life are similar to my own.

When I was quite a young man, I adopted literature as a profession, and having passed through the necessary preparatory grades, I found myself, after a good many years of hard and often unremunerative work, in possession of what might be called a fair literary practice. My articles—grave, gay, practical, or fanciful—had come to be considered with favor by the editors of the various periodicals for which I wrote, on which I found in time I could rely with a very comfortable certainty. My productions created no enthusiasm in the reading public; they gave me no great reputation or very valuable pecuniary return; but they were always accepted, and my receipts from them, at the time to which I have referred, were as regular and reliable as a salary and quite sufficient to give me more than a comfortable support.

It was at this time I married. I had been engaged for more than a year but had not been willing to assume the support of a wife until I felt that my pecuniary position was so assured that I could do so with full satisfaction to my own conscience. There was now no doubt in regard to this position, either in my mind or in that of my wife. I worked with great steadiness and regularity; I knew exactly where to place the productions of my pen and could calculate, with a fair degree of accuracy, the sums I should receive for them. We were by no means rich, but we had enough and were thoroughly satisfied and content.

Those of my readers who are married will have no difficulty in remembering the peculiar ecstasy of the first weeks of their wedded life. It is then that the flowers of this world bloom brightest; that its sun is the most genial; that its clouds are the scarcest; that its fruit is the most delicious; that the air is the most balmy; that its cigars are of the highest flavor; that the warmth and radiance of early matrimonial felicity so rarefy the intellectual atmosphere that the soul mounts higher and enjoys a wider prospect than ever before.

These experiences were mine. The plain claret of my mind was changed to sparkling champagne, and at the very height of its effervescence I wrote a story. The happy thought that then struck me for a tale was of a very peculiar character, and it interested me so much that I went to work at it with great delight and enthusiasm and finished it in a comparatively short time. The title of the story was "His Wife's Deceased Sister," and when I read it to Hypatia, she was delighted with it and at times was so affected by its pathos that her uncontrollable emotion caused a sympathetic dimness in my eyes which prevented my seeing the words I had written. When the reading was ended and my wife had dried her eyes, she turned to me and said, "This story will make your fortune. There has been nothing so pathetic since Lamartine's 'History of a Servant Girl.' "

As soon as possible the next day, I sent my story to the editor of the periodical for which I wrote most frequently and in which my best productions generally appeared. In a few days I had a letter from the editor, in which he praised my story as he had never before praised anything from my pen. It had interested and charmed, he said, not only himself, but all his associates in the office. Even old Gibson, who never cared to read anything until it was in proof and who never praised anything which had not a joke in it, was induced by the example of the others to read this manuscript and shed, as he asserted, the first tears that had come from his eyes since his final paternal castigation some forty years before. The story would appear, the editor assured me, as soon as he could possibly find room for it.

If anything could make our skies more genial, our flowers brighter, and the flavor of our fruit and cigars more delicious, it was a letter like this. And when, in a very short time, the story was published, we found that the reading public was inclined to receive it with as much sympathetic interest and favor as had been shown to it by the editors. My personal friends soon began to express enthusiastic opinions upon it. It was highly praised in many of the leading newspapers, and altogether it was a great literary success. I am not inclined to be vain of my writings, and in general, my wife tells me, I think too little of them. But I did feel a good deal of pride and satisfaction in the success of "His Wife's Deceased Sister." If it did not make my fortune, as my wife asserted it would, it certainly would help me very much in my literary career.

In less than a month from the writing of this story, something very unusual and unexpected happened to me. A manuscript was returned by the editor of the periodical in which "His Wife's Deceased Sister" had appeared.

"It is a good story," he wrote, "but not equal to what you have just done. You have made a great hit, and it would not do to interfere with the reputation you have gained by publishing anything inferior to 'His Wife's Deceased Sister,' which has had such a deserved success."

I was so unaccustomed to having my work thrown back on my hands that I think I must have turned a little pale when I read the letter. I said nothing of the matter to my wife, for it would be foolish to drop such grains of sand as this into the smoothly oiled machinery of our domestic felicity, but I immediately sent the story to another editor. I am not able to express the astonishment I felt when, in the course of a week, it was sent back to me. The tone of the note accompanying it indicated a somewhat injured feeling on the part of the editor.

"I am reluctant," he said, "to decline a manuscript from you; but you know very well that if you sent me anything like 'His Wife's Deceased Sister' it would be most promptly accepted."

I now felt obliged to speak of the affair to my wife, who was quite as much surprised, although perhaps not quite as much shocked, as I had been.

"Let us read the story again," she said, "and see what is the matter with it."

When we had finished its perusal, Hypatia remarked, "It is quite as good as many of the stories you have had printed, and I think it very interesting, although, of course, it is not equal to 'His Wife's Deceased Sister.' "

"Of course not," said I. "That was an inspiration that I cannot expect every day. But there must be something wrong about this last story which we do not perceive. Perhaps my recent success may have made me a little careless in writing it."

"I don't believe that," said Hypatia.

"At any rate," I continued, "I will lay it aside and will go to work on a new one."

In due course of time I had another manuscript finished, and I sent it to my favorite periodical. It was retained some weeks and then came back to me.

"It will never do," the editor wrote, quite warmly, "for you to go backward. The demand for the number containing 'His Wife's Deceased Sister' still continues, and we do not intend to let you disappoint that great body of readers who would be so eager to see another number containing one of your stories."

I sent this manuscript to four other periodicals, and from each of them it was returned with remarks to the effect that, although it was not a bad story in itself, it was not what they would expect from the author of "His Wife's Deceased Sister."

The editor of a Western magazine wrote to me for a story to be published in a special number, which he would issue for the holidays. I wrote him one of the character and length he desired and sent it to him. By return mail it came back to me.

"I had hoped," the editor wrote, "when I asked for a story from your pen, to receive something like 'His Wife's Deceased Sister,' and I must own that I am very much disappointed."

I was so filled with anger when I read this note that I openly objurgated "His Wife's Deceased Sister." "You must excuse me," I said to my astonished wife, "for expressing myself thus in your presence, but that confounded story will be the ruin of me yet. Until it is forgotten, nobody will ever take anything I write."

"And you cannot expect it ever to be forgotten," said Hypatia, with tears in her eyes.

It is needless for me to detail my literary efforts in the course of the next few months. The ideas of the editors, with whom my principal business had been done, in regard to my literary ability, had been so raised by my unfortunate story of "His Wife's Deceased Sister" that I found it was of no use to send them anything of lesser merit. And as to the other journals I tried, they evidently considered it an insult for me to send them matter inferior to that by which my reputation had lately risen. The fact was that my successful story had ruined me. My income was at an end, and want actually stared me in the face; and I must admit that I did not like the expression of its countenance. It was of no use for me to try to write another story like "His Wife's Deceased Sister." I could not get married every time I began a new manuscript, and it was the exaltation of mind caused by my wedded felicity which produced that story.

"It's perfectly dreadful!" said my wife. "If I had had a sister and she had died, I would have thought it was my fault."

"It could not be your fault," I answered, "and I do not think it was mine. I had no intention of deceiving anybody into the belief that I could do that sort of thing every time, and it ought not to be expected of me. Suppose Raphael's patrons had tried to keep him screwed up to the pitch of the Sistine Madonna and had refused to buy anything which was not as good as that. In that case I think he would have occupied a much earlier and narrower grave than the one on which Mr. Morris Moore hangs his funeral decorations."

"But, my dear," said Hypatia, who was posted on such subjects, "the Sistine Madonna was one of his latest paintings."

"Very true," said I. "But if he had married as I did, he would have painted it earlier."

I was walking homeward one afternoon about this time when I met Barbel, a man I had known well in my early literary career. He was now about fifty years of age but looked older. His hair and beard were quite gray, and his clothes, which were of the same general hue, gave me the idea that they, like his hair, had originally been black. Age is very hard on a man's external appointments. Barbel had an air of having been to let for a long time and quite out of repair. But there was a kindly gleam in his eye, and he welcomed me cordially.

"Why, what is the matter, old fellow?" said he. "I never saw you look so woebegone."

I had no reason to conceal anything from Barbel. In my younger days he had been of great use to me, and he had a right to know the state of my affairs. I laid the whole case plainly before him.

"Look here," he said, when I had finished; "come with me to my room; I have something I would like to say to you there."

I followed Barbel to his room. It was at the top of a very dirty and well-worn house, which stood in a narrow and lumpy street

into which few vehicles ever penetrated, except the ash and gar-
bage carts and the rickety wagons of the venders of stale vegetables.

"This is not exactly a fashionable promenade," said Barbel, as
we approached the house, "but in some respects it reminds me of
the streets in Italian towns, where the palaces lean over toward
each other in such a friendly way."

Barbel's room was, to my mind, rather more doleful than the
street. It was dark, it was dusty, and cobwebs hung from every
corner. The few chairs upon the floor and the books upon a greasy
table seemed to be afflicted with some dorsal epidemic, for their
backs were either gone or broken. A little bedstead in the corner
was covered with a spread made of New York *Heralds* with their
edges pasted together.

"There is nothing better," said Barbel, noticing my glance toward this novel counterpane, "for a bed-covering than newspapers; they keep you as warm as a blanket and are much lighter.
I used to use *Tribunes*, but they rattled too much."

The only part of the room which was well lighted was one end
near the solitary window. Here, upon a table with a spliced leg,
stood a little grindstone.

"At the other end of the room," said Barbel, "is my cookstove,
which you can't see unless I light the candle in the bottle which
stands by it. But if you don't care particularly to examine it, I
won't go to the expense of lighting up. You might pick up a
good many odd pieces of bric-a-brac around here, if you chose to
strike a match and investigate. But I would not advise you to do
so. It would pay better to throw the things out of the window than
to carry them downstairs. The particular piece of indoor decoration to which I wish to call your attention is this." And he led me
to a little wooden frame, which hung against the wall near the
window. Behind a dusty piece of glass it held what appeared to be
a leaf from a small magazine or journal. "There," said he, "you
see a page from the *Grasshopper*, a humorous paper which

flourished in this city some half-dozen years ago. I used to write regularly for that paper, as you may remember."

"Oh, yes, indeed!" I exclaimed. "And I shall never forget your 'Conundrum of the Anvil' which appeared in it. How often have I laughed at that most wonderful conceit, and how often have I put it to my friends!"

Barbel gazed at me silently for a moment, and then he pointed to the frame. "That printed page," he said solemnly, "contains the 'Conundrum of the Anvil.' I hang it there so that I can see it while I work. That conundrum ruined me. It was the last thing I wrote for the *Grasshopper*. How I ever came to imagine it, I cannot tell. It is one of those things which occur to a man but once in a lifetime. After the wild shout of delight with which the public greeted that conundrum, my subsequent efforts met with hoots of derision. The *Grasshopper* turned its hind legs upon me. I sank from bad to worse—much worse—until at last I found myself reduced to my present occupation, which is that of grinding points on pins. By this I procure my bread, coffee, and tobacco, and sometimes potatoes and meat. One day while I was hard at work, an organ-grinder came into the street below. He played the serenade from *Trovatore*, and the familiar notes brought back visions of old days and old delights, when the successful writer wore good clothes and sat at operas, when he looked into sweet eyes and talked of Italian airs, when his future appeared all a succession of bright scenery and joyous acts, without any provision for a drop curtain. And as my ear listened and my mind wandered in this happy retrospect, my every faculty seemed exalted, and without any thought upon the matter, I ground points upon my pins so fine, so regular, and so smooth that they would have pierced with ease the leather of a boot or slipped, without abrasion, among the finest threads of rare old lace. When the organ stopped and I fell back into my real world of cobwebs and mustiness, I gazed upon the pins I had just ground, and without a moment's hesitation, I threw them into the street and reported the lot as spoiled. This cost me a little money, but it saved me my livelihood."

After a few moments of silence, Barbel resumed: "I have no more to say to you, my young friend. All I want you to do is to look upon that framed conundrum, then upon his grindstone, and then to go home and reflect. As for me, I have a gross of pins to grind before the sun goes down."

I cannot say that my depression of mind was at all relieved by what I had seen and heard. I had lost sight of Barbel for some years, and I had supposed him still floating on the sun-sparkling stream of prosperity where I had last seen him. It was a great shock to me to find him in such a condition of poverty and squalor and to see a man who had originated the "Conundrum of the Anvil" reduced to the soul-depressing occupation of grinding pin-points. As I walked and thought, the dreadful picture of a totally eclipsed future arose before my mind. The moral of Barbel sank deep into my heart.

When I reached home, I told my wife the story of my friend Barbel. She listened with a sad and eager interest.

"I am afraid," she said, "if our fortunes do not quickly mend, that we shall have to buy two little grindstones. You know I could help you at that sort of thing."

For a long time we sat together and talked and devised many plans for the future. I did not think it necessary yet for me to look out for a pin contract; but I must find some way of making money, or we should starve to death. Of course, the first thing that suggested itself was the possibility of finding some other business. But apart from the difficulty of immediately obtaining remunerative work in occupations to which I had not been trained, I felt a great and natural reluctance to give up a profession for which I had carefully prepared myself and which I had adopted as my life work. It would be very hard for me to lay down my pen forever and to close the top of my inkstand upon all the bright and happy fancies which I had seen mirrored in its tranquil pool. We talked and pondered the rest of that day and a good deal of the night, but we came to no conclusion as to what it would be best for us to do.

The next day I determined to go and call upon the editor of the journal for which, in happier days, before the blight of "His Wife's Deceased Sister" rested upon me, I used most frequently to write, and having frankly explained my condition to him, to ask his advice. The editor was a good man and had always been my friend. He listened with great attention to what I told him and evidently sympathized with me in my trouble.

"As we have written to you," he said, "the only reason why we did not accept the manuscripts you sent us was that they would have disappointed the high hopes that the public had formed in regard to you. We have had letter after letter asking when we were going to publish another story like 'His Wife's Deceased Sister.' We felt, and we still feel, that it would be wrong to allow you to destroy the fair fabric which you yourself have raised. But," he added, with a kind smile, "I see very plainly that your well-deserved reputation will be of little advantage to you if you should starve at the moment that its genial beams are, so to speak, lighting you up."

"Its beams are not genial," I answered. "They have scorched and withered me."

"How would you like," said the editor, after a short reflection, "to allow us to publish the stories you have recently written under some other name than your own? That would satisfy us and the public, would put money in your pocket, and would not interfere with your reputation."

Joyfully I seized the noble fellow by the hand and instantly accepted his proposition. "Of course," said I, "a reputation is a very good thing; but no reputation can take the place of food, clothes, and a house to live in, and I gladly agree to sink my over-illumined name into oblivion and to appear before the public as a new and unknown writer."

"I hope that need not be for long," he said, "for I feel sure that you will yet write stories as good as 'His Wife's Deceased Sister.' "

All the manuscripts I had on hand I now sent to my good friend the editor, and in due and proper order they appeared in his journal under the name of John Darmstadt, which I had selected as a substitute for my own, permanently disabled. I made a similar arrangement with other editors, and John Darmstadt received the credit of everything that proceeded from my pen. Our circumstances now became very comfortable, and occasionally we even allowed ourselves to indulge in little dreams of prosperity.

Time passed on very pleasantly. One year, another, and then a little son was born to us. It is often difficult, I believe, for thoughtful persons to decide whether the beginning of their conjugal career, or the earliest weeks in the life of their firstborn, be the happiest and proudest period of their existence. For myself I can only say that the same exaltation of mind, the same rarefication of idea and invention, which succeeded upon my wedding day came upon me now. As then, my ecstatic emotions crystallized themselves into a motive for a story, and without delay I set myself to work upon it. My boy was about six weeks old when the manuscript was finished, and one evening, as we sat before a comfortable fire in our sitting room, with the curtains drawn and the soft lamp lighted and the baby sleeping soundly in the adjoining chamber, I read the story to my wife.

When I had finished, my wife arose and threw herself into my arms. "I was never so proud of you," she said, her glad eyes sparkling, "as I am at this moment. That is a wonderful story! It is, indeed I am sure it is, just as good as 'His Wife's Deceased Sister.' "

As she spoke these words, a sudden and chilling sensation crept over us both. All her warmth and fervor, and the proud and happy glow engendered within me by this praise and appreciation from one I loved, vanished in an instant. We stepped apart and gazed upon each other with pallid faces. In the same moment the terrible truth had flashed upon us both. This story *was* as good as "His Wife's Deceased Sister"!

We stood silent. The exceptional lot of Barbel's super-pointed pins seemed to pierce our very souls. A dreadful vision rose before me of an impending fall and crash, in which our domestic happiness should vanish and our prospects for our boy be wrecked, just as we had begun to build them up.

My wife approached me and took my hand in hers, which was as cold as ice. "Be strong and firm," she said. "A great danger threatens us, but you must brace yourself against it. Be strong and firm."

I pressed her hand, and we said no more that night.

The next day I took the manuscript I had just written and carefully infolded it in stout wrapping paper. Then I went to a neighboring grocery store and bought a small, strong, tin box, originally intended for biscuit, with a cover that fitted tightly. In this I placed my manuscript, and then I took the box to a tinsmith and had the top fastened on with hard solder. When I went home I ascended into the garret and brought down to my study a ship's cashbox, which had once belonged to one of my family who was a sea captain. This box was very heavy and firmly bound with iron and was secured by two massive locks. Calling my wife, I told her of the contents of the tin case, which I then placed in the box, and having shut down the heavy lid, I doubly locked it.

"This key," said I, putting it in my pocket, "I shall throw into the river when I go out this afternoon."

My wife watched me eagerly, with a pallid and firm-set countenance but upon which I could see the faint glimmer of returning happiness.

"Wouldn't it be well," she said, "to secure it still further by sealing wax and pieces of tape?"

"No," said I. "I do not believe that anyone will attempt to tamper with our prosperity. And now, my dear," I continued in an impressive voice, "no one but you, and, in the course of time, our son, shall know that this manuscript exists. When I am dead, those who survive me may, if they see fit, cause this box to be split open and the story published. The reputation it may give my name cannot harm me then."

I skipped up the mountainside.

A Tale of Negative Gravity

MY WIFE AND I were staying at a small town in northern Italy; and on a certain pleasant afternoon in spring we had taken a walk of six or seven miles to see the sun set behind some low mountains to the west of the town. Most of our walk had been along a hard, smooth highway, and then we turned into a series of narrower roads, sometimes bordered by walls and sometimes by light fences of reed or cane. Nearing the mountain, to a low spur of which we intended to ascend, we easily scaled a wall about four feet high and found ourselves upon pasture land, which led, sometimes by gradual ascents and sometimes by bits of rough climbing, to the spot we wished to reach. We were afraid we were a little late and therefore hurried on, running up the grassy hills and bounding briskly over the rough and rocky places. I carried a knapsack strapped firmly to my shoulders, and under my wife's arm was a large, soft basket of a kind much used by tourists. Her arm was passed through the handles and around the bottom of the basket, which she pressed closely to her side. This was the way she always carried it. The basket contained two bottles of wine, one sweet for my wife and another a little acid for myself. Sweet wines give me a headache.

When we reached the grassy bluff, well known thereabouts to lovers of sunset views, I stepped immediately to the edge to gaze upon the scene, but my wife sat down to take a sip of wine, for she was very thirsty; and then, leaving her basket, she came to my side. The scene was indeed one of great beauty. Beneath us stretched a wide valley of many shades of green, with a little river running through it and red-tiled houses here and there. Beyond rose a range of mountains, pink, pale green, and purple where their tips caught the reflection of the setting sun, and of a rich gray-green in shadows. Beyond all was the blue Italian sky, illumined by an especially fine sunset.

My wife and I are Americans, and at the time of this story were middle-aged people and very fond of seeing in each other's company whatever there was of interest or beauty around us. We had a son about twenty-two years old, of whom we were also very fond, but he was not with us, being at that time a student in Germany. Although we had good health, we were not very robust people, and under ordinary circumstances, not much given to long country tramps. I was of medium size, without much muscular development, while my wife was quite stout and growing stouter.

The reader may, perhaps, be somewhat surprised that a middle-aged couple, not very strong or very good walkers, the lady loaded with a basket containing two bottles of wine and a metal drinking cup, and the gentleman carrying a heavy knapsack, filled with all sorts of odds and ends, strapped to his shoulders, should set off on a seven-mile walk, jump over a wall, run up a hillside, and yet feel in very good trim to enjoy a sunset view. This peculiar state of things I will proceed to explain.

I had been a professional man, but some years before had retired upon a very comfortable income. I had always been very fond of scientific pursuits and now made these the occupation and pleasure of much of my leisure time. Our home was in a small town; and in a corner of my grounds I built a laboratory, where I carried on my work and my experiments. I had long been anxious to discover the means, not only of producing, but of retaining and controlling, a natural force, really the same as centrifugal force, but which I called negative gravity. This name I adopted because it indicated better than any other the action of the force in question as I produced it. Positive gravity attracts everything toward the center of the earth. Negative gravity, therefore, would be that power which repels everything from the center of the earth, just as the negative pole of a magnet repels the needle while the positive pole attracts it. My object was, in fact, to store centrifugal force and to render it constant, controllable, and available for use. The advantages of such a discovery could scarcely be described. In a word, it would lighten the burdens of the world.

I will not touch upon the labors and disappointments of several years. It is enough to say that at last I discovered a method of producing, storing, and controlling negative gravity.

The mechanism of my invention was rather complicated, but the method of operating it was very simple. A strong metallic case, about eight inches long and half as wide, contained the machinery for producing the force; and this was put into action by means of the pressure of a screw worked from the outside. As soon as this pressure was produced, negative gravity began to be evolved and stored, and the greater the pressure the greater the force. As the screw was moved outward and the pressure diminished, the force decreased, and when the screw was withdrawn to its fullest extent, the action of negative gravity entirely ceased. Thus this force could be produced or dissipated at will to such degrees as might be desired, and its action, so long as the requisite pressure was maintained, was constant.

When this little apparatus worked to my satisfaction, I called my wife into my laboratory and explained to her my invention and its value. She had known that I had been at work with an important object, but I had never told her what it was. I had said that if I succeeded I would tell her all, but if I failed she need not be troubled with the matter at all. Being a very sensible woman, this satisfied her perfectly. Now I explained everything to her, the construction of the machine and the wonderful uses to which this invention could be applied. I told her that it could diminish, or entirely dissipate, the weight of objects of any kind. A heavily loaded wagon, with two of these instruments fastened to its sides and each screwed to a proper force, would be so lifted and supported that it would press upon the ground as lightly as an empty cart, and a small horse could draw it with ease. A bale of cotton, with one of these machines attached, could be handled and carried by a boy. A car, with a number of these machines, could be made to rise in the air like a balloon. Everything, in fact, that was heavy could be made light; and as a great part of labor all over the world is caused by the attraction of gravitation, so this repellent force, wherever applied, would make weight less and work easier. I told her of many, many ways in which the invention might be used and would have told her of many more if she had not suddenly burst into tears.

"The world has gained something wonderful," she exclaimed, between her sobs, "but I have lost a husband!"

"What do you mean by that?" I asked, in surprise.

"I haven't minded it so far," she said, "because it gave you something to do, and it pleased you, and it never interfered with our home pleasures and our home life. But now that is all over. You will never be your own master again. It will succeed, I am sure, and you may make a great deal of money, but we don't need money. What we need is the happiness which we have always had until now. Now there will be companies and patents and lawsuits and experiments and people calling you a humbug and other people saying they discovered it long ago and all sorts of persons coming to see you, and you'll be obliged to go to all sorts of places, and you will be an altered man, and we shall never be happy again. Millions of money will not repay us for the happiness we have lost."

These words of my wife struck me with much force. Before I had called her my mind had begun to be filled and perplexed with ideas of what I ought to do now that the great invention was perfected. Until now the matter had not troubled me at all. Sometimes I had gone backward and sometimes forward, but on the whole I had always felt encouraged. I had taken great pleasure in the work, but I had never allowed myself to be too much absorbed by it. But now everything was different. I began to feel that it was due to myself and to my fellow beings that I should properly put this invention before the world. And how should I set about it? What steps should I take? I must make no mistakes. When the matter should become known, hundreds of scientific people might set themselves to work; how could I tell but that they might discover other methods of producing the same effect? I must guard myself against a great many things. I must get patents in all parts of the world. Already, as I have said, my mind began to be troubled and perplexed with these things. A turmoil of this sort did not suit my age or disposition. I could not but agree with my wife that the joys of a quiet and contented life were now about to be broken into.

"My dear," said I, "I believe, with you, that the thing will do us more harm than good. If it were not for depriving the world of the invention, I would throw the whole thing to the winds. And yet," I added, regretfully, "I had expected a great deal of personal gratification from the use of this invention."

"Now, listen," said my wife eagerly, "don't you think it would be best to do this: use the thing as much as you please for your own amusement and satisfaction, but let the world wait. It has waited a long time, and let it wait a little longer. When we are dead, let Herbert have the invention. He will then be old enough to judge for himself whether it will be better to take advantage of it for his own profit or simply to give it to the public for nothing. It would be cheating him if we were to do the latter, but it would also be doing him a great wrong if we were, at his age, to load him with such a heavy responsibility. Besides, if he took it up, you could not help going into it, too."

I took my wife's advice. I wrote a careful and complete account of the invention, and sealing it up, I gave it to my lawyers to be handed to my son after my death. If he died first, I would make other arrangements. Then I determined to get all the good and fun out of the thing that was possible without telling anyone anything about it. Even Herbert, who was away from home, was not to be told of the invention.

The first thing I did was to buy a strong leathern knapsack, and inside of this I fastened my little machine, with a screw so arranged that it could be worked from the outside. Strapping this firmly to my shoulders, my wife gently turned the screw at the back until the upward tendency of the knapsack began to lift and sustain me. When I felt myself so gently supported and upheld that I seemed to weigh about thirty or forty pounds, I would set out for a walk. The knapsack did not raise me from the ground, but it gave me a very buoyant step. It was no labor at all to walk; it was a delight, an ecstasy. With the strength of a man and the weight of a child, I gaily strode along. The first day I walked half a dozen miles at a very brisk pace and came back without feeling in the least degree tired. These walks now became one of the greatest joys of my life. When nobody was looking, I would bound over a fence, sometimes just touching it with one hand and sometimes not touching it at all. I delighted in rough places. I sprang over streams. I jumped and I ran. I felt like Mercury himself.

I now set about making another machine so that my wife could accompany me in my walks; but when it was finished, she positively refused to use it. "I can't wear a knapsack," she said, "and there is no other good way of fastening it to me. Besides, everybody about here knows I am no walker, and it would only set them talking."

I occasionally made use of this second machine, but I will only give one instance of its application. Some repairs were needed to the foundation walls of my barn, and a two-horse wagon, loaded with building stone, had been brought into my yard and left there. In the evening, when the men had gone away, I took my two machines and fastened them with strong chains, one on each side of the loaded wagon. Then, gradually turning the screws, the wagon was so lifted that its weight became very greatly diminished. We had an old donkey, which used to belong to Herbert and which was now occasionally used with a small cart to bring packages from the station. I went into the barn and put the harness on the little fellow, and bringing him out to the wagon, I attached him to it. In this position he looked very funny, with a long pole sticking out in front of him and the great wagon behind him. When all was ready, I touched him up; and to my great delight, he moved off with the two-horse load of stone as easily as if he were drawing his own cart. I led him out into the public road, along which he proceeded without difficulty. He was an opinionated little beast and sometimes stopped, not liking the peculiar manner in which he was harnessed; but a touch of the switch made him move on, and I soon turned him and brought the wagon back into the yard. This determined the success of my invention in one of its most important uses, and with a satisfied heart I put the donkey into the stable and went into the house.

Our trip to Europe was made a few months after this and was mainly on our son Herbert's account. He, poor fellow, was in great trouble, and so, therefore, were we. He had become engaged, with our full consent, to a young lady in our town, the daughter of a gentleman whom we esteemed very highly. Herbert was young to be engaged to be married, but as we felt that he would never find a girl to make him so good a wife, we were entirely satisfied, especially as it was agreed on all hands that the marriage was not to take place for some time. It seemed to us that in marrying Janet Gilbert, Herbert would secure for himself, in the very beginning of his career, the most important element of a happy life. But suddenly, without any reason that seemed to us justifiable, Mr. Gilbert, the only surviving parent of Janet, broke off the match; and he and his daughter soon after left the town for a trip to the West.

This blow nearly broke poor Herbert's heart. He gave up his professional studies and came home to us, and for a time we thought he would be seriously ill. Then we took him to Europe, and after a Continental tour of a month or two we left him, at his own request, in Göttingen, where he thought it would do him good to go to work again. Then we went down to the little town in Italy where my story first finds us. My wife had suffered much in mind and body on her son's account, and for this reason I was anxious that she should take outdoor exercise and enjoy as much as possible the bracing air of the country. I had brought with me both my little machines. One was still in my knapsack, and the other I had fastened to the inside of an enormous family trunk. As one is obliged to pay for nearly every pound of his baggage on the Continent, this saved me a great deal of money. Everything heavy was packed into this great trunk—books, papers, the bronze, iron, and marble relics we had picked up, and all the articles that usually weigh down a tourist's baggage. I screwed up the negative gravity apparatus until the trunk could be handled with great ease by an ordinary porter. I could have made it weigh nothing at all, but this, of course, I did not wish to do. The lightness of my baggage, however, had occasioned some comment, and I had overheard remarks which were not altogether complimentary about people traveling around with empty trunks; but this only amused me.

Desirous that my wife should have the advantage of negative gravity while taking our walks, I had removed the machine from the trunk and fastened it inside of the basket, which she could carry under her arm. This assisted her wonderfully. When one arm was tired she put the basket under the other, and thus, with one hand on my arm, she could easily keep up with the free and buoyant steps my knapsack enabled me to take. She did not object to long tramps here, because nobody knew that she was not a walker, and she always carried some wine or other refreshment in the basket, not only because it was pleasant to have it with us, but because it seemed ridiculous to go about carrying an empty basket.

There were English-speaking people stopping at the hotel where we were, but they seemed more fond of driving than walking, and none of them offered to accompany us on our rambles, for which we were very glad. There was one man there, however, who was a great walker. He was an Englishman, a member of an Alpine Club, and generally went about dressed in a knickerbocker suit, with gray woolen stockings covering an enormous pair of calves. One evening this gentleman was talking to me and some others about the ascent of the Matterhorn, and I took occasion to deliver in pretty strong language my opinion upon such exploits. I declared them to be useless, foolhardy, and, if the climber had anyone who loved him, wicked.

"Even if the weather should permit a view," I said, "what is that compared to the terrible risk to life? Under certain circumstances," I added (thinking of a kind of waistcoat I had some idea of making, which, set about with little negative gravity machines, all connected with a conveniently handled screw, would enable the wearer at times to dispense with his weight altogether), "such ascents might be divested of danger and be quite admissible; but ordinarily they should be frowned upon by the intelligent public."

The Alpine Club man looked at me, especially regarding my somewhat slight figure and thinnish legs.

"It's all very well for you to talk that way," he said, "because it is easy to see that you are not up to that sort of thing."

"In conversations of this kind," I replied, "I never make personal allusions; but since you have chosen to do so, I feel inclined to invite you to walk with me tomorrow to the top of the mountain to the north of this town."

"I'll do it," he said, "at any time you choose to name." And as I left the room soon afterward, I heard him laugh.

The next afternoon, about two o'clock, the Alpine Club man and myself set out for the mountain.

"What have you got in your knapsack?" he said.

"A hammer to use if I come across geological specimens, a field glass, a flask of wine, and some other things."

"I wouldn't carry any weight, if I were you," he said.

"Oh, I don't mind it," I answered, and off we started.

The mountain to which we were bound was about two miles from the town. Its nearest side was steep and in places almost precipitous, but it sloped away more gradually toward the north, and up that side a road led by devious windings to a village near the summit. It was not a very high mountain, but it would do for an afternoon's climb.

"I suppose you want to go up by the road," said my companion.

"Oh, no," I answered, "we won't go so far around as that. There is a path up this side, along which I have seen men driving their goats. I prefer to take that."

"All right, if you say so," he answered, with a smile; "but you'll find it pretty tough."

After a time he remarked, "I wouldn't walk so fast, if I were you."

"Oh, I like to step along briskly," I said. And briskly on we went.

My wife had screwed up the machine in the knapsack more than usual, and walking seemed scarcely any effort at all. I carried a long alpenstock, and when we reached the mountain and began the ascent, I found that with the help of this and my knapsack I could go uphill at a wonderful rate. My companion had taken the lead, so as to show me how to climb. Making a detour over some rocks, I quickly passed him and went ahead. After that it was impossible for him to keep up with me. I ran up steep places, I cut off the windings of the path by lightly clambering over rocks, and even when I followed the beaten track, my step was as rapid as if I had been walking on level ground.

"Look here!" shouted the Alpine Club man from below. "You'll kill yourself if you go at that rate! That's no way to climb mountains."

"It's my way!" I cried. And on I skipped.

Twenty minutes after I arrived at the summit, my companion

joined me, puffing and wiping his red face with his handkerchief.

"Confound it!" he cried. "I never came up a mountain so fast in my life."

"You need not have hurried," I said coolly.

"I was afraid something would happen to you," he growled, "and I wanted to stop you. I never saw a person climb in such an utterly absurd way."

"I don't see why you should call it absurd," I said, smiling with an air of superiority. "I arrived here in a perfectly comfortable condition, neither heated nor wearied."

He made no answer but walked off to a little distance, fanning himself with his hat and growling words which I did not catch. After a time I proposed to descend.

"You must be careful as you go down," he said. "It is much more dangerous to go down steep places than to climb up."

"I am always prudent," I answered, and started in advance. I found the descent of the mountain much more pleasant than the ascent. It was positively exhilarating. I jumped from rocks and bluffs eight and ten feet in height and touched the ground as gently as if I had stepped down but two feet. I ran down steep paths, and with the aid of my alpenstock stopped myself in an instant. I was careful to avoid dangerous places, but the runs and jumps I made were such as no man had ever made before upon that mountainside. Once only I heard my companion's voice.

"You'll break your————neck!" he yelled.

"Never fear!" I called back and soon left him far above.

When I reached the bottom, I would have waited for him, but my activity had warmed me up, and as a cool evening breeze was beginning to blow, I thought it better not to stop and take cold. Half an hour after my arrival at the hotel I came down to the court, cool, fresh, and dressed for dinner, and just in time to meet the Alpine man as he entered, hot, dusty, and growling.

"Excuse me for not waiting for you," I said; but without stopping to hear my reason, he muttered something about waiting in a place where no one would care to stay and passed into the house.

There was no doubt that what I had done gratified my pique and tickled my vanity.

"I think now," I said, when I related the matter to my wife, "that he will scarcely say that I am not up to that sort of thing."

"I am not sure," she answered, "that it was exactly fair. He did not know how you were assisted."

"It was fair enough," I said. "He is enabled to climb well by the inherited vigor of his constitution and by his training. He did not tell me what methods of exercise he used to get those great muscles upon his legs. I am enabled to climb by the exercise of my intellect. My method is my business and his method is his business. It is all perfectly fair."

Still she persisted: "He *thought* that you climbed with your legs and not with your head."

And now, after this long digression, necessary to explain how a middle-aged couple of slight pedestrian ability and loaded with a heavy knapsack and basket should have started out on a rough walk and climb, fourteen miles in all, we will return to ourselves, standing on the little bluff and gazing out upon the sunset view. When the sky began to fade a little, we turned from it and prepared to go back to the town.

"Where is the basket?" I said.

"I left it right here," answered my wife. "I unscrewed the machine and it lay perfectly flat."

"Did you afterward take out the bottles?" I asked, seeing them lying on the grass.

"Yes, I believe I did. I had to take out yours in order to get at mine."

"Then," said I, after looking all about the grassy patch on which we stood, "I am afraid you did not entirely unscrew the instrument and that when the weight of the bottles was removed, the basket gently rose into the air."

"It may be so," she said lugubriously. "The basket was behind me as I drank my wine."

"I believe that is just what has happened," I said. "Look up there! I vow that is our basket!"

I pulled out my field glass and directed it at a little speck high above our heads. It was the basket floating high in the air. I gave the glass to my wife to look, but she did not want to use it.

"What shall I do?" she cried. "I can't walk home without that basket. It's perfectly dreadful!" And she looked as if she was going to cry.

"Do not distress yourself," I said, although I was a good deal disturbed myself. "We shall get home very well. You shall put your hand on my shoulder, while I put my arm around you. Then you can screw up my machine a good deal higher, and it will support us both. In this way I am sure that we shall get on very well."

We carried out this plan and managed to walk on with moderate comfort. To be sure, with the knapsack pulling me upward and the weight of my wife pulling me down, the straps hurt me somewhat, which they had not done before. We did not spring lightly over the wall into the road, but still clinging to each other, we clambered awkwardly over it. The road for the most part declined gently toward the town, and with moderate ease we made our way along it. But we walked much more slowly than we had done before, and it was quite dark when we reached our hotel. If it had not been for the light inside the court, it would have been difficult for us to find it. A traveling carriage was standing before the entrance and against the light. It was necessary to pass around it, and my wife went first. I attempted to follow her, but strange to say, there was nothing under my feet. I stepped vigorously but only wagged my legs in the air. To my horror I found that I was rising in the air! I soon saw, by the light below me, that I was some fifteen feet from the ground. The carriage drove away, and in the darkness I was not noticed. Of course I knew what had happened. The instrument in my knapsack had been screwed up to such an intensity, in order to support both myself and my wife, that when her weight was removed, the force of the negative gravity was sufficient to raise me from the ground. But I was glad to find that when I had risen to the height I have mentioned, I did not go up any higher but hung in the air, about on a level with the second tier of windows of the hotel.

I now began to try to reach the screw in my knapsack in order to reduce the force of the negative gravity; but, do what I would, I could not get my hand to it. The machine in the knapsack had been placed so as to support me in a well-balanced and comfortable way; and in doing this it had been impossible to set the screw so that I could reach it. But in a temporary arrangement of the kind this had not been considered necessary, as my wife always turned the screw for me until sufficient lifting power had been attained. I had intended, as I have said before, to construct a negative gravity waistcoat, in which the screw should be in front and entirely under the wearer's control; but this was a thing of the future.

When I found that I could not turn the screw, I began to be much alarmed. Here I was, dangling in the air, without any means of reaching the ground. I could not expect my wife to return to look for me, as she would naturally suppose I had stopped to speak to someone. I thought of loosening myself from the knapsack, but this would not do, for I should fall heavily and either kill myself or break some of my bones. I did not dare to call for assistance, for if any of the simpleminded inhabitants of the town had discovered me floating in the air, they would have taken me for a demon and would probably have shot at me. A moderate breeze was blowing, and it wafted me gently down the street. If it had blown me against a tree, I would have seized it and have endeavored, so to speak, to climb down it; but there were no trees. There was a dim street lamp here and there, but reflectors above them threw their light upon the pavement and none up to me. On many accounts I was glad that the night was so dark, for much as I desired to get down, I wanted no one to see me in my strange position, which, to anyone but myself and wife, would be utterly unaccountable. If I could rise as high as the roofs, I might get on one of them, and tearing off an armful of tiles, so load myself that I would be heavy enough to descend. But I did not rise to the eaves of any of the houses. If there had been a telegraph pole, or anything of the kind that I could have clung to, I would have taken off the knapsack and would have endeavored to scramble down as well as I could. But there was nothing I could cling to. Even the waterspouts, if I could have reached the face of the houses, were imbedded in the walls. At an open window, near which I was slowly blown, I saw two little boys going to bed by the light of a dim candle. I was dreadfully afraid that they would see me and raise an alarm. I actually came so near to the window that I threw out one foot and pushed against the wall with such force that I went nearly across the street. I thought I caught sight of a frightened look on the face of one of the boys; but of this I am not sure, and I heard no cries. I still floated, dangling, down the street. What was to be done? Should I call out? In that case, if I were not shot or stoned, my strange predicament and the secret of my invention would be exposed to the world. If I did not do this, I must either let myself drop and be killed or mangled, or hang there and die. When, during the course of the night, the air became more rarefied, I might rise higher and higher, perhaps to an altitude of one or two hundred feet. It would then be impossible for the people to reach me and get me down, even if they were convinced that I was not a demon. I should then expire, and when the birds of the air had eaten all of me that they could devour, I should forever hang above the unlucky town, a dangling skeleton with a knapsack on its back.

Such thoughts were not reassuring, and I determined that if I could find no means of getting down without assistance, I would call out and run all risks; but so long as I could endure the tension of the straps I would hold out and hope for a tree or a pole. Perhaps it might rain, and my wet clothes would then become so heavy that I would descend as low as the top of a lamppost.

As this thought was passing through my mind, I saw a spark of light upon the street approaching me. I rightly imagined that it came from a tobacco pipe, and presently I heard a voice. It was that of the Alpine Club man. Of all people in the world I did not want him to discover me, and I hung as motionless as possible. The man was speaking to another person who was walking with him.

"He is crazy beyond a doubt," said the Alpine man. "Nobody but a maniac could have gone up and down that mountain as he did! He hasn't any muscles, and one need only look at him to know that he couldn't do any climbing in a natural way. It is only the excitement of insanity that gives him strength."

The two now stopped almost under me, and the speaker continued: "Such things are very common with maniacs. At times they acquire an unnatural strength which is perfectly wonderful. I have seen a little fellow struggle and fight so that four strong men could not hold him."

Then the other person spoke: "I am afraid what you say is too true," he remarked. "Indeed, I have known it for some time."

At these words my breath almost stopped. It was the voice of Mr. Gilbert, my townsman, and the father of Janet. It must have been he who had arrived in the traveling carriage. He was acquainted with the Alpine Club man, and they were talking of me. Proper or improper, I listened with all my ears.

"It is a very sad case," Mr. Gilbert continued. "My daughter was engaged to marry his son, but I broke off the match. I could not have her marry the son of a lunatic, and there could be no doubt of his condition. He has been seen—a man of his age, and the head of a family—to load himself up with a heavy knapsack, which there was no earthly necessity for him to carry, and go

BERNARDA
BRYSON

skipping along the road for miles, vaulting over fences and jumping over rocks and ditches like a young calf or a colt. I myself saw a most heartrending instance of how a kindly man's nature can be changed by the derangement of his intellect. It was at some distance from his house, but I plainly saw him harness a little donkey which he owns to a large two-horse wagon loaded with stone and beat and lash the poor little beast until it drew the heavy load some distance along the public road. I would have remonstrated with him on this horrible cruelty, but he had the wagon back in his yard before I could reach him."

"Oh, there can be no doubt of his insanity," said the Alpine Club man, "and he oughtn't to be allowed to travel about in this way. Someday he will pitch his wife over a precipice just for the fun of seeing her shoot through the air."

"I am sorry he is here," said Mr. Gilbert, "for it would be very painful to meet him. My daughter and I will retire very soon and go away as early tomorrow morning as possible, so as to avoid seeing him."

And then they walked back to the hotel.

For a few moments I hung, utterly forgetful of my condition and absorbed in the consideration of these revelations. One idea now filled my mind. Everything must be explained to Mr. Gilbert, even if it should be necessary to have him called to me and for me to speak to him from the upper air.

Just then I saw something white approaching me along the road. My eyes had become accustomed to the darkness, and I perceived that it was an upturned face. I recognized the hurried gait, the form; it was my wife. As she came near me, I called her name and in the same breath entreated her not to scream. It must have been an effort for her to restrain herself, but she did it.

"You must help me to get down," I said, "without anybody seeing us."

"What shall I do?" she whispered.

"Try to catch hold of this string."

Taking a piece of twine from my pocket, I lowered one end to her. But it was too short; she could not reach it. I then tied my handkerchief to it, but still it was not long enough.

"I can get more string or handkerchiefs," she whispered hurriedly.

"No," I said, "you could not get them up to me. But leaning against the hotel wall on this side, in the corner, just inside of the garden gate, are some fishing poles. I have seen them there every day. You can easily find them in the dark. Go, please, and bring me one of those."

The hotel was not far away, and in a few minutes my wife returned with a fishing pole. She stood on tiptoe and reached it high in air; but all she could do was to strike my feet and legs with it. My most frantic exertions did not enable me to get my hands low enough to touch it.

"Wait a minute," she said; and the rod was withdrawn.

I knew what she was doing. There was a hook and line attached to the pole, and with womanly dexterity she was fastening the hook to the extreme end of the rod. Soon she reached up and gently struck at my legs. After a few attempts the hook caught in my trousers, a little below my right knee. Then there was a slight pull, a long scratch down my leg, and the hook was stopped by the top of my boot. Then came a steady downward pull, and I felt myself descending. Gently and firmly the rod was drawn down; carefully the lower end was kept free from the ground; and in a few moments my ankle was seized with a vigorous grasp. Then someone seemed to climb up me, my feet touched the ground, an arm was thrown around my neck, the hand of another arm was busy at the back of my knapsack, and I soon stood firmly in the road, entirely divested of negative gravity.

"Oh, that I should have forgotten," sobbed my wife, "and that I should have dropped your arms and let you go up into the air! At first I thought that you had stopped below, and it was only a little while ago that the truth flashed upon me. Then I rushed out and began looking up for you. I knew that you had wax matches in your pocket and hoped that you would keep on striking them, so that you would be seen."

"But I did not wish to be seen," I said, as we hurried to the hotel; "and I can never be sufficiently thankful that it was you who found me and brought me down. Do you know that it is Mr. Gilbert and his daughter who have just arrived? I must see him instantly. I will explain it all to you when I come upstairs."

I took off my knapsack and gave it to my wife, who carried it to our room, while I went to look for Mr. Gilbert. Fortunately I found him just as he was about to go up to his chamber. He took my offered hand but looked at me sadly and gravely.

"Mr. Gilbert," I said, "I must speak to you in private. Let us step into this room. There is no one here."

"My friend," said Mr. Gilbert, "it will be much better to avoid discussing this subject. It is very painful to both of us, and no good can come from talking of it."

"You can not now comprehend what it is I want to say to you," I replied. "Come in here, and in a few minutes you will be very glad that you listened to me."

My manner was so earnest and impressive that Mr. Gilbert was constrained to follow me, and went into a small room called the smoking room, but in which people seldom smoked, and closed the door. I immediately began my statement. I told my old friend that I had discovered, by means that I need not explain at present, that he had considered me crazy and that now the most important object of my life was to set myself right in his eyes. I thereupon gave him the whole history of my invention and explained the reason of the actions that had appeared to him those of a lunatic. I said nothing about the little incident of that evening. That was a mere accident, and I did not care now to speak of it.

Mr. Gilbert listened to me very attentively.

"Your wife is here?" he asked, when I had finished.

"Yes," I said; "and she will corroborate my story in every item, and no one could ever suspect her of being crazy. I will go and bring her to you."

In a few minutes my wife was in the room, had shaken hands with Mr. Gilbert, and had been told of my suspected madness. She turned pale but smiled.

"He did act like a crazy man," she said, "but I never supposed that anybody would think him one." And tears came into her eyes.

"And now, my dear," said I, "perhaps you will tell Mr. Gilbert how I did all this."

And then she told him the story that I had told.

Mr. Gilbert looked from the one to the other of us with a troubled air.

"Of course I do not doubt either of you, or rather I do not doubt that you believe what you say. All would be right if I could bring myself to credit that such a force as that you speak of can possibly exist."

"That is a matter," said I, "which I can easily prove to you by actual demonstration. If you can wait a short time, until my wife and I have had something to eat—for I am nearly famished, and I am sure she must be—I will set your mind at rest upon that point."

"I will wait here," said Mr. Gilbert, "and smoke a cigar. Don't hurry yourselves. I shall be glad to have some time to think about what you have told me."

When we had finished the dinner, which had been set aside for us, I went upstairs and got my knapsack, and we both joined Mr. Gilbert in the smoking room. I showed him the little machine and explained, very briefly, the principle of its construction. I did not give any practical demonstration of its action, because there were people walking about the corridor who might at any moment come into the room; but looking out of the window, I saw that the night was much clearer. The wind had dissipated the clouds, and the stars were shining brightly.

"If you will come up the street with me," said I to Mr. Gilbert, "I will show you how this thing works."

"That is just what I want to see," he answered.

"I will go with you," said my wife, throwing a shawl over her head. And we started up the street.

When we were outside the little town, I found the starlight was quite sufficient for my purpose. The white roadway, the low walls, and objects about us could easily be distinguished.

"Now," said I to Mr. Gilbert, "I want to put this knapsack on you and let you see how it feels and how it will help you to walk." To this he assented with some eagerness, and I strapped it firmly on him. "I will now turn this screw," said I, "until you shall become lighter and lighter."

"Be very careful not to turn it too much," said my wife earnestly.

"Oh, you may depend on me for that," said I, turning the screw very gradually.

Mr. Gilbert was a stout man, and I was obliged to give the screw a good many turns.

"There seems to be considerable hoist in it," he said directly. And then I put my arms around him, and found that I could raise him from the ground. "Are you lifting me?" he exclaimed in surprise.

"Yes; I did it with ease," I answered.

"Upon—my—word!" ejaculated Mr. Gilbert.

I then gave the screw a half turn more and told him to walk and run. He started off, at first slowly; then he made long strides; then he began to run, and then to skip and jump. It had been many years since Mr. Gilbert had skipped and jumped. No one was in sight, and he was free to gambol as much as he pleased. "Could you give it another turn?" said he, bounding up to me. "I want to try that wall." I put on a little more negative gravity, and he vaulted over a five-foot wall with great ease. In an instant he had leaped back into the road and in two bounds was at my side. "I came down as light as a cat," he said. "There was never anything like it." And away he went up the road, taking steps at least eight feet long, leaving my wife and me laughing heartily at the preternatural agility of our stout friend. In a few minutes he was with us again. "Take it off," he said. "If I wear it any longer I shall want one myself, and then I shall be taken for a crazy man and perhaps clapped into an asylum."

"Now," said I, as I turned back the screw before unstrapping the knapsack, "do you understand how I took long walks and leaped and jumped, how I ran uphill and downhill, and how the little donkey drew the loaded wagon?"

"I understand it all," cried he. "I take back all I ever said or thought about you, my friend."

"And Herbert may marry Janet?" cried my wife.

"*May* marry her!" cried Mr. Gilbert. "Indeed he *shall* marry her, if I have anything to say about it! My poor girl has been drooping ever since I told her it could not be."

My wife rushed at him, but whether she embraced him or only shook his hands I cannot say; for I had the knapsack in one hand, and was rubbing my eyes with the other.

"But, my dear fellow," said Mr. Gilbert directly, "if you still consider it to your interest to keep your invention a secret, I wish you had never made it. No one having a machine like that can help using it, and it is often quite as bad to be considered a maniac as to be one."

"My friend," I cried, with some excitement, "I have made up my mind on this subject. The little machine in this knapsack, which is the only one I now possess, has been a great pleasure to me. But I now know it has also been of the greatest injury indirectly to me and mine, not to mention some direct inconvenience and danger, which I will speak of another time. The secret lies with us three, and we will keep it. But the invention itself is too full of temptation and danger for any of us."

As I said this I held the knapsack with one hand while I quickly turned the screw with the other. In a few moments it was high above my head, while I with difficulty held it down by the straps. "Look!" I cried. And then I released my hold, and the knapsack shot into the air and disappeared into the upper gloom.

I was about to make a remark but had no chance, for my wife threw herself upon my bosom, sobbing with joy.

"Oh, I am so glad—so glad!" she said. "And you will never make another?"

"Never another!" I answered.

"And now let us hurry in and see Janet," said my wife.

"You don't know how heavy and clumsy I feel," said Mr. Gilbert, striving to keep up with us as we walked back. "If I had worn that thing much longer, I should never have been willing to take it off!"

Janet had retired, but my wife went up to her room.

"I think she has felt it as much as our boy," she said, when she rejoined me. "But I tell you, my dear, I left a very happy girl in that little bedchamber over the garden."

And there were three very happy elderly people talking together until quite late that evening. "I shall write to Herbert tonight," I said, when we separated, "and tell him to meet us all in Geneva. It will do the young man no harm if we interrupt his studies just now."

"You must let me add a postscript to the letter," said Mr. Gilbert, "and I am sure it will require no knapsack with a screw in the back to bring him quickly to us."

And it did not.

There is a wonderful pleasure in tripping over the earth like a winged Mercury and in feeling one's self relieved of much of that attraction of gravitation which drags us down to earth and gradually makes the movement of our bodies but weariness and labor. But this pleasure is not to be compared, I think, to that given by the buoyancy and lightness of two young and loving hearts, reunited after a separation which they had supposed would last forever.

What became of the basket and the knapsack, or whether they ever met in upper air, I do not know. If they but float away and stay away from ken of mortal man, I shall be satisfied.

And whether or not the world will ever know more of the power of negative gravity depends entirely upon the disposition of my son Herbert, when—after a good many years, I hope—he shall open the packet my lawyers have in keeping.

[NOTE: It would be quite useless for any one to interview my wife on this subject, for she has entirely forgotten how my machine was made. And as for Mr. Gilbert, he never knew.]

*"It was half past one by the clock in the office
of the Registrar of Woes."*

The Remarkable Wreck of the
Thomas Hyke

IT WAS HALF PAST one by the clock in the office of the Registrar of
Woes. The room was empty, for it was Wednesday, and the
Registrar always went home early on Wednesday afternoons. He
had made that arrangement when he accepted the office. He was
willing to serve his fellow citizens in any suitable position to which
he might be called, but he had private interests which could not be
neglected. He belonged to his country, but there was a house in
the country which belonged to him; and there were a great many
things appertaining to that house which needed attention, especially in pleasant summer weather. It is true he was often absent
on afternoons which did not fall on the Wednesday, but the fact
of his having appointed a particular time for the furtherance of
his outside interests so emphasized their importance that his associates in the office had no difficulty in understanding that affairs
of such moment could not always be attended to in a single afternoon of the week.

But although the large room devoted to the especial use of the
Registrar was unoccupied, there were other rooms connected with
it which were not in that condition. With the suite of offices to the
left we have nothing to do but will confine our attention to a
moderate-sized room to the right of the Registrar's office and connected by a door, now closed, with that large and handsomely furnished chamber. This was the office of the Clerk of Shipwrecks,
and it was at present occupied by five persons. One of these was
the Clerk himself, a man of goodly appearance, somewhere between twenty-five and forty-five years of age, and of a demeanor
such as might be supposed to belong to one who had occupied a
high position in state affairs but who, by the cabals of his enemies,

had been forced to resign the great operations of statesmanship which he had been directing and who now stood, with a quite resigned air, pointing out to the populace the futile and disastrous efforts of the incompetent one who was endeavoring to fill his place. The Clerk of Shipwrecks had never fallen from such a position, having never occupied one, but he had acquired the demeanor referred to without going through the preliminary exercises.

Another occupant was a very young man, the personal clerk of the Registrar of Woes, who always closed all the doors of the office of that functionary on Wednesday afternoons and at other times when outside interests demanded his principal's absence, after which he betook himself to the room of his friend the Shipwreck Clerk.

Then there was a middle-aged man named Mathers, also a friend of the Clerk, and who was one of the eight who had made application for a sub-position in this department, which was now filled by a man who was expected to resign when a friend of his, a gentleman of influence in an interior county, should succeed in procuring the nomination as congressional representative of his district of an influential politician, whose election was considered assured in case certain expected action on the part of the administration should bring his party into power. The person now occupying the sub-position hoped then to get something better, and Mathers, consequently, was very willing, while waiting for the place, to visit the offices of the department and acquaint himself with its duties.

A fourth person was J. George Watts, a juryman by profession, who had brought with him his brother-in-law, a stranger in the city.

The Shipwreck Clerk had taken off his good coat, which he had worn to luncheon, and had replaced it by a lighter garment of linen, much bespattered with ink; and he now produced a cigar box, containing six cigars.

"Gents," said he, "here is the fag end of a box of cigars. It's not like having the pick of the box, but they are all I have left."

Mr. Mathers, J. George Watts, and the brother-in-law each took a cigar with that careless yet deferential manner which always distinguishes the treatee from the treator; and then the box was protruded in an offhand way toward Harry Covare, the personal clerk of the Registrar; but this young man declined, saying that he preferred cigarettes, a package of which he drew from his pocket. He had very often seen that cigar box with a Havana brand, which he himself had brought from the other room after the Registrar had emptied it, passed around with six cigars, no more nor less, and he was wise enough to know that the Shipwreck Clerk did not expect to supply him with smoking material. If that gentleman had offered to the friends who generally dropped in on him on Wednesday afternoon the paper bag of cigars sold at five cents each when bought singly but half a dozen for a quarter of a dollar they would have been quite as thankfully received; but it better pleased his deprecative soul to put them in an empty cigar box and thus throw around them the halo of the presumption that ninety-four of their imported companions had been smoked.

The Shipwreck Clerk, having lighted a cigar for himself, sat down in his revolving chair, turned his back to his desk, and threw himself into an easy cross-legged attitude, which showed that he was perfectly at home in that office. Harry Covare mounted a high stool, while the visitors seated themselves in three wooden armchairs. But few words had been said, and each man had scarcely tossed his first tobacco ashes on the floor when someone wearing heavy boots was heard opening an outside door and entering the Registrar's room. Harry Covare jumped down from his stool, laid his half-smoked cigarette thereon, and bounced into the next room, closing the door after him. In about a minute he returned, and the Shipwreck Clerk looked at him inquiringly.

"An old cock in a pea jacket," said Mr. Covare, taking up his cigarette and mounting his stool. "I told him the Registrar would be here in the morning. He said he had something to report about a shipwreck; and I told him the Registrar would be here in the morning. Had to tell him that three times, and then he went."

"School don't keep Wednesday afternoons," said Mr. J. George Watts, with a knowing smile.

"No, sir," said the Shipwreck Clerk, emphatically, changing the crossing of his legs. "A man can't keep grinding on day in and out without breaking down. Outsiders may say what they please about it, but it can't be done. We've got to let up sometimes. People who do the work need the rest just as much as those who do the looking on."

"And more, too, I should say," observed Mr. Mathers.

"Our little letup on Wednesday afternoons," modestly observed Harry Covare, "is like death; it is sure to come, while the letups we get other days are more like the diseases which prevail in certain areas; you can't be sure whether you're going to get them or not."

The Shipwreck Clerk smiled benignantly at this remark, and the rest laughed. Mr. Mathers had heard it before, but he would not impair the pleasantness of his relations with a future colleague by hinting that he remembered it.

"He gets such ideas from his beastly statistics," said the Shipwreck Clerk.

"Which come pretty heavy on him sometimes, I expect," observed Mr. Mathers.

"They needn't," said the Shipwreck Clerk, "if things were managed here as they ought to be. If John J. Laylor," meaning thereby the Registrar, "was the right kind of a man, you'd see things very different here from what they are now. There'd be a larger force."

"That's so," said Mr. Mathers.

"And not only that, but there'd be better buildings, and more accommodations. Were any of you ever up to Anster? Well, take a run up there some day, and see what sort of buildings the department has there. William Q. Green is a very different man from John J. Laylor. You don't see him sitting in his chair and picking his teeth the whole winter, while the representative from his district never says a word about his department from one end of a session of Congress to the other. Now if I had charge of things here, I'd make such changes that you wouldn't know the place. I'd throw two rooms off here and a corridor and entrance door at that end of the building. I'd close up this door," pointing toward the Registrar's room, "and if John J. Laylor wanted to come in here, he might go around to the end door like other people."

The thought struck Harry Covare that in that case there would be no John J. Laylor, but he would not interrupt.

"And what is more," continued the Shipwreck Clerk, "I'd close up this whole department at twelve o'clock on Saturdays. The way things are managed now, a man has no time to attend to his own private business. Suppose I think of buying a piece of land and want to go out and look at it, or suppose any one of you gentlemen were here and thought of buying a piece of land and wanted to go out and look at it, what are you going to do about it? You don't want to go on Sunday, and when are you going to go?"

Not one of the other gentlemen had ever thought of buying a piece of land, nor had they any reason to suppose that they ever would purchase an inch of soil unless they bought it in a flowerpot; but they all agreed that the way things were managed now there was no time for a man to attend to his own business.

"But you can't expect John J. Laylor to do anything," said the Shipwreck Clerk.

However, there was one thing which that gentleman always expected John J. Laylor to do. When the Clerk was surrounded by a number of persons in hours of business and when he had succeeded in impressing them with the importance of his functions and the necessity of paying deferential attention to himself if they wished their business attended to, John J. Laylor would be sure to walk into the office and address the Shipwreck Clerk in such a manner as to let the people present know that he was a clerk and nothing else and that he, the Registrar, was the head of that department. These humiliations the Shipwreck Clerk never forgot.

There was a little pause here, and then Mr. Mathers remarked, "I should think you'd be awfully bored with the long stories of shipwrecks that the people come and tell you."

He hoped to change the conversation, because although he wished to remain on good terms with the subordinate officers, it was not desirable that he should be led to say much against John J. Laylor.

"No, sir," said the Shipwreck Clerk, "I am not bored. I did not come here to be bored, and as long as I have charge of this office I don't intend to be. The long-winded old salts who come here to report their wrecks never spin out their prosy yarns to me. The first thing I do is to let them know just what I want of them; and not an inch beyond that does a man of them go, at least while I am managing the business. There are times when John J. Laylor comes in and puts in his oar and wants to hear the whole story, which is pure stuff and nonsense, for John J. Laylor doesn't know anything more about a shipwreck than he does about—"

"The endemies in the Lake George area," suggested Harry Covare.

"Yes; or any other part of his business," said the Shipwreck Clerk; "and when he takes it into his head to interfere, all business stops till some second mate of a coal schooner has told his whole story, from his sighting land on the morning of one day to his getting ashore on it on the afternoon of the next. Now I don't put up with any such nonsense. There's no man living that can tell me anything about shipwrecks. I've never been to sea myself, but that's not necessary; and if I had gone, it's not likely I'd been wrecked. But I've read about every kind of shipwreck that ever happened. When I first came here, I took care to post myself upon these matters, because I knew it would save trouble. I have read *Robinson Crusoe, The Wreck of the* Grosvenor, *The Sinking of the* Royal George, and wrecks by waterspouts, tidal waves, and every other thing which would knock a ship into a cocked hat, and I've classified every sort of wreck under its proper head; and when I've found out to what class a wreck belongs, I know all about it. Now, when a man comes here to report a wreck, the first thing he has to do is just to shut down on his story and to stand up square and answer a few questions that I put to him. In two minutes I know just what kind of shipwreck he's had; and then, when he gives me the name of his vessel, and one or two other points, he may go. I know all about that wreck, and I make a much better report of the business than he could have done if he'd stood here talking three days and three nights. The amount of money that's been saved to our taxpayers by the way I've systematized the business of this office is not to be calculated in figures."

The brother-in-law of J. George Watts knocked the ashes from the remnant of his cigar, looked contemplatively at the coal for a moment, and then remarked, "I think you said there's no kind of shipwreck you don't know about?"

"That's what I said," replied the Shipwreck Clerk.

"I think," said the other, "I could tell you of a shipwreck, in which I was concerned, that wouldn't go into any of your classes."

The Shipwreck Clerk threw away the end of his cigar, put both his hands into his trouser pockets, stretched out his legs, and looked steadfastly at the man who had made this unwarrantable remark. Then a pitying smile stole over his countenance, and he said, "Well, sir, I'd like to hear your account of it; and before you get a quarter through, I can stop you just where you are and go ahead and tell the rest of the story myself."

"That's so," said Harry Covare. "You'll see him do it just as sure pop as a spread rail bounces the engine."

"Well, then," said the brother-in-law of J. George Watts, "I'll tell it." And he began: "It was just two years ago, the first of this month, that I sailed for South America in the *Thomas Hyke*."

At this point the Shipwreck Clerk turned and opened a large book at the letter **T**.

"That wreck wasn't reported here," said the other, "and you won't find it in your book."

"At Anster, perhaps?" said the Shipwreck Clerk, closing the volume and turning around again.

"Can't say about that," replied the other. "I've never been to Anster and haven't looked over their books."

"Well, you needn't want to," said the clerk. "They've got good accommodations at Anster, and the Registrar has some ideas of the duties of his post, but they have no such system of wreck reports as we have here."

"Very like," said the brother-in-law. And he went on with his story. "The *Thomas Hyke* was a small iron steamer of six hundred tons, and she sailed from Ulford for Valparaiso with a cargo principally of pig iron."

"Pig iron for Valparaiso?" remarked the Shipwreck Clerk. And then he knitted his brows thoughtfully and said, "Go on."

"She was a new vessel," continued the narrator, "and built with watertight compartments; rather uncommon for a vessel of her class, but so she was. I am not a sailor and don't know anything about ships. I went as passenger, and there was another one named William Anderson, and his son Sam, a boy about fifteen years old. We were all going to Valparaiso on business. I don't remember just how many days we were out nor do I know just where we were, but it was somewhere off the coast of South America when one dark night, with a fog besides, for aught I know, for I was asleep, we ran into a steamer coming north. How we managed to do this, with room enough on both sides for all the ships in the world to pass, I don't know; but so it was. When I got on deck, the other vessel had gone on, and we never saw anything more of her. Whether she sunk or got home is something I can't tell. But we pretty soon found that the *Thomas Hyke* had some of the plates in her bow badly smashed, and she took in water like a thirsty dog. The captain had the forward watertight bulkhead shut tight and the pumps set to work, but it was no use. That forward compartment just filled up with water, and the *Thomas Hyke* settled down with her bow clean under. Her deck was slanting forward like the side of a hill, and the propeller was lifted up so that it wouldn't have worked even if the engine had been kept going. The captain had the masts cut away, thinking this might bring her up some, but it didn't help much. There was a pretty heavy sea on, and the waves came rolling up the slant of the deck like the surf on the seashore. The captain gave orders to have all the hatches battened down so that water couldn't get in, and the only way by which anybody could go below was by the cabin door, which was far aft. This work of stopping up all openings in the deck was a dangerous business, for the decks sloped right down into the water, and if anybody had slipped, away he'd have gone into the ocean, with nothing to stop him; but the men made a line fast to themselves and worked away with a good will and soon got the deck and the house over the engine as tight as a bottle. The smokestack, which was well forward, had been broken down by a spar when the masts had been cut, and as the waves washed into the hole that it left, the captain had this plugged up with old sails, well fastened down. It was a dreadful thing to see the ship a-lying with her bows clean underwater and her stern sticking up. If it hadn't been for her watertight compartments that were left uninjured, she would have gone down to the bottom as slick as a whistle. On the afternoon of the day after the collision the wind fell, and the sea soon became pretty smooth. The captain was quite sure that there would be no trouble about keeping afloat until some ship came along and took us off. Our flag was flying, upside down, from a pole in the stern; and if anybody saw a ship making such a guy of herself as the *Thomas Hyke* was then doing, they'd be sure to come to see what was the matter with

her, even if she had no flag of distress flying. We tried to make
ourselves as comfortable as we could, but this wasn't easy with
everything on such a dreadful slant. But that night we heard a
rumbling and grinding noise down in the hold, and the slant
seemed to get worse. Pretty soon the captain roused all hands and
told us that the cargo of pig iron was shifting and sliding down to
the bow and that it wouldn't be long before it would break
through all the bulkheads, and then we'd fill and go to the bottom
like a shot. He said we must all take to the boats and get away as
quick as we could. It was an easy matter launching the boats.
They didn't lower them outside from the davits, but they just let
'em down on deck and slid 'em along forward into the water and
then held 'em there with a rope till everything was ready to start.
They launched three boats, put plenty of provisions and water in
'em, and then everybody began to get aboard. But William
Anderson and me and his son Sam couldn't make up our minds to
get into those boats and row out on the dark, wide ocean. They
were the biggest boats we had, but still they were little things
enough. The ship seemed to us to be a good deal safer and more
likely to be seen when day broke than those three boats, which
might be blown off if the wind rose, nobody knew where. It seemed
to us that the cargo had done all the shifting it intended to, for
the noise below had stopped; and, altogether, we agreed that we'd
rather stick to the ship than go off in those boats. The captain, he
tried to make us go, but we wouldn't do it; and he told us if we
chose to stay behind and be drowned it was our affair, and he
couldn't help it; and then he said there was a small boat aft, and
we'd better launch her and have her ready in case things should
get worse and we should make up our minds to leave the vessel. He
and the rest then rowed off so as not to be caught in the vortex if
the steamer went down, and we three stayed aboard. We launched
the small boat in the way we'd seen the other launched, being
careful to have ropes tied to us while we were doing it; and we put
things aboard that we thought we should want. Then we went into

the cabin, and waited for morning. It was a queer kind of a cabin, with a floor inclined like the roof of a house, but we sat down in the corners and were glad to be there. The swinging lamp was burning, and it was a good deal more cheerful in there than it was outside. But about daybreak the grinding and rumbling down below began again, and the bow of the *Thomas Hyke* kept going down more and more; and it wasn't long before the forward bulk-head of the cabin, which was what you might call its front wall when everything was all right, was under our feet, as level as a floor, and the lamp was lying close against the ceiling that it was hanging from. You may be sure that we thought it was time to get out of that. There were benches with arms to them fastened to the floor, and by these we climbed up to the foot of the cabin stairs, which, being turned bottom upward, we went down in order to get out. When we reached the cabin door, we saw part of the deck below us, standing up like the side of a house that is built in the water, as they say the houses in Venice are. We had made our boat fast to the cabin door by a long line, and now we saw her floating quietly on the water, which was very smooth, and about twenty feet below us. We drew her up as close under us as we could, and then we let the boy Sam down by a rope, and after some kicking and swinging, he got into her; and then he took the oars and kept her right under us while we scrambled down by the ropes which we had used in getting her ready. As soon as we were in the boat, we cut her rope and pulled away as hard as we could; and when we got to what we thought was a safe distance, we stopped to look at the *Thomas Hyke*. You never saw such a ship in all your born days. Two-thirds of the hull was sunk in the water, and she was standing straight up and down with the stern in the air, her rudder up as high as the topsail ought to be, and the screw pro-peller looking like the wheel on the top of one of these windmills that they have in the country for pumping up water. Her cargo had shifted so far forward that it had turned her right upon end, but she couldn't sink, owing to the air in the compartments that the water hadn't got into; and on the top of the whole thing was the distress flag flying from the pole, which stuck out over the stern. It was broad daylight, but not a thing did we see of the other boats. We'd supposed that they wouldn't row very far but would lay off at a safe distance until daylight; but they must have been scared and rowed farther than they intended. Well, sir, we stayed in that boat all day and watched the *Thomas Hyke;* but she just kept as she was and didn't seem to sink an inch. There was no use of rowing away, for we had no place to row to; and besides, we thought that passing ships would be much more likely to see that stern sticking high in the air than our little boat. We had enough to eat, and at night two of us slept while the other watched, dividing off the time and taking turns to do this. In the morning there was the *Thomas Hyke* standing stern up just as before. There was a long swell on the ocean now, and she'd rise and lean over a little on each wave, but she'd come up again just as straight as before. That night passed as the last one had, and in the morning we found we'd drifted a good deal farther from the *Thomas Hyke*, but she was floating just as she had been, like a big buoy that's moored over a sand bar. We couldn't see a sign of the boats, and we about gave them up. We had our breakfast, which was a pretty poor meal, being nothing but hardtack and what was left of a piece of boiled beef. After we'd sat for a while doing nothing but feeling mighty uncomfortable, William Anderson said, 'Look here, do you know that I think we would be three fools to keep on shivering all night and living on hardtack in the daytime, when there's plenty on that vessel for us to eat and to keep us warm. If she's floated that way for two days and two nights, there's no knowing how much longer she'll float, and we might as well go on board and get the things we want as not.' 'All right,' said I, for I was tired doing nothing, and Sam was as willing as anybody. So we rowed up to the steamer and stopped close to the deck, which, as I said before, was standing straight up out of the water like the wall of a house. The cabin door, which was the only opening into her, was about twenty feet above us, and the ropes which we had tied to the rails of the stairs inside were still hanging down. Sam was an active youngster, and he managed to climb up one of these ropes; but when he got to the door, he drew it up and tied knots in it about a foot apart, and then he let it down to us, for neither William Anderson nor me could go up a rope hand over hand without knots or something to hold on to. As it was, we had a lot of bother getting up, but we did it at last, and then we walked up the stairs, treading on the front part of each step instead of the top of it, as we would have done if the stairs had been in their proper position. When we got to the floor of the cabin, which was now perpendicular like a wall, we had to clamber down by means of the furniture, which was screwed fast, until we reached the bulkhead, which was now the floor of the cabin. Close to this bulkhead was a small room, which was the steward's pantry, and here we found lots of things to eat but all jumbled up in a way that made us laugh. The boxes of biscuits and the tin cans and a lot of bottles in wicker covers were piled up on one end of the room, and everything in the lockers and drawers was jumbled together. William Anderson and me set to work to get out what we thought we'd want, and we told Sam to climb up into some of the staterooms, of which there were four on each side of the cabin, and get some blankets to keep us warm, as well as a few sheets, which we thought we could rig up for an awning to the boat; for the days were just as hot as the nights were cool. When we'd collected what we wanted, William Anderson and me climbed into our own rooms, thinking we'd each pack a valise with what we most wanted to save of our clothes and things; and while we were doing this, Sam called out to us that it was raining. He was sitting at the cabin door looking out. I first thought to tell him to shut the door so's to keep the rain from coming in; but when I thought how things really were, I laughed at the idea. There was a sort of little house built over the entrance to the cabin, and in one end of it was the door; and in the way the ship now was, the open doorway was underneath the little house, and of course no rain could come in. Pretty soon we heard the rain pouring down, beating on the stern of the vessel like hail. We got to the stairs and looked out. The rain was falling in perfect sheets, in a way you never see except round about the tropics. 'It's a good thing we're inside,' said William Anderson, 'for if we'd been out in this rain we'd been drowned in the boat.' I agreed with him, and we made up our minds to stay where we were until the rain was over. Well, it rained about four hours; and when it stopped and we looked out, we saw our little boat nearly full of water and sunk so deep that if one of us had stepped on her she'd have gone down, sure. 'Here's a pretty kettle of fish,' and William Anderson; 'there's nothing for us to do now but to stay where we are.' I believe in his heart he was glad of that, for if ever a man was tired of a little boat, William Anderson was tired of that one we'd been in for two days and two nights. At any rate there was no use talking about it, and we set to work to make ourselves comfortable. We got some mattresses and pillows out of the staterooms, and when it began to get dark, we lighted the lamp, which we had filled with sweet oil from a flask in the pantry, not finding any other kind, and we hung it from the railing of the stairs. We had a good night's rest, and the only thing that disturbed me was William Anderson lifting up his head every time he turned over, and saying how much better this was than that blasted little boat. The next morning we had a good breakfast, even making some tea with a spirit lamp we found, using brandy instead of alcohol. William Anderson and I wanted to get into the captain's room, which was near the stern and pretty high up, so as to see if there was anything there that we ought to get ready to save when a vessel should come along and pick us up; but we were not good at climbing, like Sam, and we didn't see how we could get up there. Sam said he was sure he had once seen a ladder in the compartment just forward of the bulkhead, and as William was very anxious to get up to the captain's room, we let the boy go and look for it. There was a sliding door in the bulkhead under our feet, and we opened this far enough to let Sam get through; and he scrambled down like a monkey into the next compartment, which was light enough, although the lower half of it, which was next to the engine room, was under the water line. Sam actually found a ladder with hooks at one end of it, and while he was handing it up to us, which was very hard to do for he had to climb up on all sorts of things, he let it topple over, and the end with the iron hooks fell against the round glass of one of the portholes. The glass was very thick and strong, but the ladder came down very heavy and shivered it. As bad luck would have it, this window was below the water line, and the water came rushing in in a big spout. We chucked blankets down to Sam for him to stop up the hole, but 'twas of no use; for it was hard for him to get at the window, and when he did, the water came in with such force that he couldn't get a blanket into the hole. We were afraid he'd be drowned down there and told him to come out as quick as he could. He put up the ladder again and hooked it on to the door in the bulkhead, and we held it while he climbed up. Looking down through the doorway, we saw, by the way the water was pouring in at the opening, that it wouldn't be long before that compartment was filled up; so we shoved the door to and made it all tight, and then said William Anderson, 'The ship'll sink deeper and deeper as that fills up, and the water may get up to the cabin door, and we must go and make that as tight as we can.' Sam had pulled the ladder up after him, and this we found of great use in getting to the foot of the cabin stairs. We shut the cabin door and locked and bolted it; and as it fitted pretty tight, we didn't think it would let in much water if the ship sunk that far. But over the top of the cabin stairs were a couple of folding doors, which shut down horizontally when the ship was in its proper position and which were only used in very bad, cold weather. These we pulled to and fastened tight, thus having a double protection against the water. Well, we didn't get this done any too soon, for the water did come up to the cabin door, and a little trickled in from the outside door and through the cracks in the inner one. But we went to work and stopped these up with strips from the sheets, which we crammed well in with our pocket knives. Then we sat down on the steps and waited to see what would happen next. The doors of all the staterooms were open, and we could see through the thick plate-glass windows in them, which were all shut tight, that the ship was sinking more and more as the water came in. Sam climbed up into one of the after staterooms and said the outside water was nearly up to the stern; and pretty soon we looked up to the two portholes in the stern and saw that they were covered with water; and as more and more water could be seen there, and as the light came through less easily, we knew that we were sinking under the surface of the ocean. 'It's a mighty good thing,' said William Anderson, 'that no water can get in here.' William had a hopeful kind of mind and always looked on the bright side of things; but I must say that I was dreadfully scared when I looked through those stern windows and saw water instead of sky. It began to get duskier and duskier as we sank lower and lower, but still we could see pretty well, for it's astonishing how much light comes down through water. After a little while we noticed that the light remained about the same; and then William Anderson, he sings out, 'Hooray, we've stopped sinking!' 'What difference does that make?' says I. 'We must be thirty or forty feet underwater and more yet for aught I know.' 'Yes, that may be,' said he; 'but it is clear that all the water has got into that compartment that can get in, and we have sunk just as far down as we are going.' 'But that don't help matters,' said I; 'thirty or forty feet underwater is just as bad as a thousand as to drowning a man.' 'Drowning!' said William. 'How are you going to be drowned? No water can get in here.' 'Nor no air, either,' said I; 'and people are drowned for want of air, as I take it.' 'It would be a queer sort of thing,' said William, 'to be drowned in the ocean and yet stay as dry as a chip. But it's no use being worried about air. We've got air enough here to last us for ever so long. This stern compartment is the biggest in the ship, and it's got lots of air in it. Just think of that hold! It must be nearly full of air. The stern compartment of the hold has got nothing in it but sewing machines. I saw 'em loading her. The pig iron was mostly amidships or at least forward of this compartment. Now, there's no kind of a cargo that'll accommodate as much air as sewing machines. They're packed in wooden frames, not boxes, and don't fill up half the room they take. There's air all through and around 'em. It's a very comforting thing to think the hold isn't filled up solid with bales of cotton or wheat in bulk.' It might be comforting, but I couldn't get much good out of it. And now Sam, who'd been scrambling all over the cabin to see how things were going on, sung out that the water was leaking in a little again at the cabin door and around some of the iron frames of the windows. 'It's a lucky thing,' said William Anderson, 'that we didn't sink any deeper, or the pressure of the water would have burst in those heavy glasses. And what we've got to do now is to stop up all the cracks. The more we work, the livelier we'll feel.' We tore off more strips of sheets and went all round, stopping up cracks wherever we found them. 'It's fortunate,' said William Anderson, 'that Sam found that ladder, for we would have had hard work getting to the windows of the stern staterooms without it; but by resting it on the bottom step of the stairs, which now happens to be the top one, we can get to any part of the cabin.' I couldn't help thinking that if Sam hadn't found the ladder it would have been a good deal better for us; but I didn't want to damp William's spirits, and I said nothing.

"And now I beg your pardon, sir," said the narrator, addressing the Shipwreck Clerk, "but I forgot that you said you'd finish this story yourself. Perhaps you'd like to take it up just here?"

The Shipwreck Clerk seemed surprised and had apparently forgotten his previous offer. "Oh, no," said he, "tell your own story. This is not a matter of business."

"Very well, then," said the brother-in-law of J. George Watts,

"I'll go on. We made everything as tight as we could, and then we got our supper, having forgotten all about dinner and being very hungry. We didn't make any tea, and we didn't light the lamp, for we knew that would use up air; but we made a better meal than three people sunk out of sight in the ocean had a right to expect. 'What troubles me most,' said William Anderson, as he turned in, 'is the fact that if we are forty feet underwater, our flagpole must be covered up. Now, if the flag was sticking out, up-side down, a ship sailing would see it and would know there was something wrong.' 'If that's all that troubles you,' said I, 'I guess you'll sleep easy. And if the ship was to see the flag, I wonder how they'd know we were down here and how they'd get us out if they did!' 'Oh, they'd manage it,' said William Anderson. 'Trust those sea captains for that.' And then he went to sleep. The next morn-ing the air began to get mighty disagreeable in the part of the cabin where we were, and then William Anderson, he says, 'What we've got to do is to climb up into the stern staterooms, where the air is purer. We can come down here to get our meals and then go up again to breathe comfortable.' 'And what are we going to do when the air up there gets foul?' says I to William, who seemed to be making arrangements for spending the summer in our present quarters. 'Oh, that'll be all right,' said he. 'It don't do to be ex-travagant with air any more than with anything else. When we've used up all there is in this cabin, we can bore holes through the floor to the hold and let in air from there. If we're economical, there'll be enough to last for dear knows how long.' We passed the night each in a stateroom, sleeping on the end wall instead of the berth, and it wasn't till the afternoon of the next day that the air of the cabin got so bad we thought we'd have some fresh; so we went down on the bulkhead, and with an auger that we found in the pantry we bored three holes, about a yard apart, in the cabin floor, which was now one of the walls of the room, just as the bulk-head was the floor, and the stern end, where the two round win-dows were, was the ceiling or roof. We each took a hole, and I tell you it was pleasant to breathe the air which came in from the hold. 'Isn't this jolly?' said William Anderson. 'And we ought to be mighty glad that that hold wasn't loaded with codfish or soap. But there's nothing that smells better than new sewing machines that haven't ever been used, and this air is pleasant enough for anybody.' By William's advice we made three plugs, by which we stopped up the holes when we thought we'd had air enough for the present. 'And now,' says he, 'we needn't climb up into those awkward staterooms any more. We can just stay down here and be comfortable and let in air when we want it.' 'And how long do you suppose that air in the hold is going to last?' said I. 'Oh, ever so long,' said he, 'using it so economically as we do; and when it stops coming out lively through these little holes, as I suppose it will after a while, we can saw a big hole in this flooring and go into the hold and do our breathing, if we want to.' That evening we did saw a hole about a foot square, so as to have plenty of air while we were asleep, but we didn't go into the hold, it being pretty well filled up with machines; though the next day Sam and I sometimes stuck our heads in for a good sniff of air, though William Anderson was opposed to this, being of the opinion that we ought to put ourselves on short rations of breathing so as to make the supply of air hold out as long as possible. 'But what's the good,' said I to William, 'of trying to make the air hold out if we've got to be suffocated in this place after all?' 'What's the good?' says he. 'Haven't you enough biscuits and canned meats and plenty of other things to eat and a barrel of water in that room opposite the pantry, not to speak of wine and brandy if you want to cheer yourself up a bit, and haven't we good mattresses to sleep on, and why shouldn't we try to live and be comfortable as long as we can?' 'What I want,' said I, 'is to get out of this box. The idea of being shut up in here down under the water is more than I can stand. I'd rather take my chances going up to the surface and swimming about till I found a piece of the wreck or something to float on.' 'You needn't think of anything of that sort,' said William, 'for if we were to open a door or a window to get out, the water'd rush in and drive us back and fill up this place in no time; and then the whole concern would go to the bottom. And what would you do if you did to get to the top of the water? It's not likely you'd find anything there to get on, and if you did, you wouldn't live very long floating about with nothing to eat. No, sir,' says he, 'what we've got to do is to be content with the comforts we have around us, and something will turn up to get us out of this; you see if it don't.' There was no use talking against William Anderson, and I didn't say any more about getting out. As for Sam, he spent his time at the windows of the staterooms a-looking out. We could see a good way into the water, further than you would think, and we sometimes saw fishes, especially porpoises, swimming about, most likely trying to find out what a ship was doing hanging bows down under the water. What troubled Sam was that a swordfish might come along and jab his sword through one of the windows. In that case it would be all up, or rather down, with us. Every now and then he'd sing out, 'Here comes one!' And then, just as I'd give a jump, he'd say, 'No, it isn't; it's a porpoise.' I thought from the first, and I think now, that it would have been a great deal better for us if that boy hadn't been along. That night there was a good deal of motion in the ship, and she swung about and rose up and down more than she had done since we'd been left in her. 'There must be a big sea running on top,' said William Anderson, 'and if we were up there we'd be tossed about dreadful. Now the motion down here is just as easy as a cradle, and, what's more, we can't be sunk very deep; for if we were, there wouldn't be any motion at all.' About noon the next day we felt a sudden tremble and shake run through the whole ship, and far down under us we heard a rumbling and grinding that nearly scared me out of my wits. I first thought we'd struck bottom, but William he said that couldn't be, for it was just as light in the cabin as it had been, and if we'd gone down it would have grown much darker, of course. The rumbling stopped after a little while, and then it seemed to grow lighter instead of darker; and Sam, who was looking up at the stern windows over our heads, he sung out, 'Sky!' And, sure enough, we could see the blue sky, as clear as daylight, through those windows! And then the ship, she turned herself on the slant, pretty much as she had been when her forward compartment first took in water, and we found ourselves standing on the cabin floor instead of the bulkhead. I was near one of the open staterooms, and as I looked in, there was the sunlight coming through the wet glass in the window and more cheerful than anything I ever saw before in this world. William Anderson, he just made one jump, and unscrewing one of the stateroom windows, he jerked it open. We had thought the air inside was good enough to last some time longer; but when that window was open and the fresh air came rushing in, it was a different sort of thing, I can tell you. William put his head out and looked up and down and all around. 'She's nearly all out of water!' he shouted, 'and we can open the cabin door.' Then we all three rushed at those stairs, which were nearly right side up now, and we had the cabin doors open in no time. When we looked out, we saw that the ship was truly floating pretty much as she had been when the captain and crew left her, though we all agreed that her deck didn't slant as much forward as it did then. 'Do you know what's happened?' sung out William Anderson, after he'd stood still for a minute to look around and think. 'That bobbing up and down that the vessel got last night shook up and settled down the pig iron inside of her, and the iron plates in the bow that were smashed and loosened by the collision have given way under the weight, and the whole cargo of pig iron has burst through and gone to the bottom. Then, of course, up we came. Didn't I tell you something would happen to make us all right?'

"Well, I won't make this story any longer than I can help. The next day after that we were taken off by a sugar ship bound north, and we were carried safe back to Ulford, where we found our captain and the crew, who had been picked up by a ship after they'd been three or four days in their boats. This ship had sailed our way to find us, which, of course, she couldn't do, as at that time we were underwater and out of sight.

"And now, sir," said the brother-in-law of J. George Watts to the Shipwreck Clerk, "to which of your classes does this wreck of mine belong?"

"Gents," said the Shipwreck Clerk, rising from his seat, "it's four o'clock, and at that hour this office closes."

The Water-Devil

A Marine Tale

IN THE VILLAGE of Riprock there was neither tavern nor inn, for it was but a small place through which few travelers passed; but it could not be said to be without a place of entertainment, for if by chance a stranger—or two or three of them, for that matter—wished to stop at Riprock for a meal, or to pass the night, there was the house of blacksmith Fryker, which was understood to be always open to decent travelers.

The blacksmith was a prominent man in the village, and his house was a large one, with several spare bedrooms, and it was said by those who had had an opportunity of judging that nobody in the village lived better than blacksmith Fryker and his family.

Into the village there came, late one autumn afternoon, a tall man, who was traveling on foot, with a small valise hanging from his shoulder. He had inquired for lodging for the night, had been directed to the blacksmith's house, had arranged to stop there, had had his supper, which greatly satisfied him, and was now sitting before the fire in the large living room, smoking blacksmith Fryker's biggest pipe. This stranger was a red-haired man, with a cheery expression and a pair of quick, bright eyes. He was slenderly but strongly built and was a good fellow, who would stand by, with his hands in the pockets of his short pea jacket, and right willingly tell one who was doing something how the thing ought to be done.

But the traveler did not sit alone before the crackling fire of logs, for the night being cool, a table was drawn near to one side of the fireplace, and by this sat Mistress Fryker and her daughter Joanna, both engaged in some sort of needlework. The blacksmith sat between the corner of the fireplace and this table, so that when he had finished smoking his after-supper pipe, he might put on his spectacles and read the weekly paper by the light of the big lamp. On the other side of the stranger, whose chair was in front of the middle of the fireplace, sat the schoolmaster, Andrew Cardly by name, a middle-aged man of sober and attentive aspect and very glad when chance threw in his way a book he had not read or a stranger who could reinforce his stock of information. At the other corner of the fireplace, in a cushioned chair, which was always given to him when he dropped in to spend an evening with the blacksmith, sat Mr. Harberry, an elderly man, a man of substance, and a man in whom all Riprock, not excluding himself, placed unqualified confidence as to his veracity, his financial soundness, and his deep insight into the causes, the influences, and the final issue of events and conditions.

"On a night like this," said the stranger, stretching his long legs toward the blaze, "there is nothing I like better than a fire of wood, except indeed it be the society of ladies who do not object to a little tobacco smoke." And he glanced with a smile toward the table with a lamp upon it.

Now blacksmith Fryker was a prudent man, and he did not consider that the privileges of his hearthstone—always freely granted to a decent stranger—included an acquaintance with his pretty daughter; and so without allowing his womenfolk a chance to enter into the conversation, he offered the stranger a different subject to hammer upon.

"In the lower country," said he, "they don't need fires as early in the season as we do. What calling do you follow, sir? Some kind of trade, perhaps?"

"No," said the traveler, "I follow no trade; I follow the sea."

At this the three men looked at him, as also the two women. His appearance no more suggested that he was a seaman than the appearance of Mr. Harberry suggested that he was what the village of Riprock believed him to be.

"I should not have taken you for a sailor," said the blacksmith.

"I am not a sailor," said the other; "I am a soldier, a sea soldier—in fact, a marine."

"I should say, sir," remarked the schoolmaster, in a manner intended rather to draw out information than to give it, "that the position of a soldier on a ship possessed advantages over that of a soldier on land. The former is not required to make long marches nor to carry heavy baggage. He remains at rest, in fact, while traversing great distances. Nor is he called on to resist the charges of cavalry nor to form hollow squares on the deadly battlefield."

The stranger smiled. "We often find it hard enough," said he, "to resist the charges made against us by our officers; the hollow squares form themselves in our stomachs when we are on short rations; and I have known many a man who would rather walk twenty miles than sail one, especially when the sea chops."

"I am very sure, sir," said schoolmaster Cardly, "that there is nothing to be said against the endurance and the courage of marines. We all remember how they presented arms and went down with the *Royal George*."

The marine smiled.

"I suppose," said the blacksmith, "that you never had to do anything of that sort?"

The stranger did not immediately answer but sat looking into the fire. Presently he said, "I have done things of nearly every sort, although not exactly that; but I have thought my ship was going down with all on board, and that's the next worst thing to going down, you know."

"And how was that?" inquired Fryker.

"Well," said the other, "it happened more times than I can tell you of or even remember. Yes," said he, meditatively, "more times than I can remember."

"I am sure," said the schoolmaster, "that we should all like to hear some of your experiences."

The marine shrugged his shoulders. "These things," said he, "come to a man, and then if he lives through them, they pass on, and he is ready for the next streak of luck, good or bad. That's the way with us followers of the sea, especially if we happen to be marines and have to bear, so to speak, the responsibility of two professions. But sometimes a mischance or a disaster does fix itself upon a man's mind so that he can tell about it if he is called upon; and just now there comes to my mind a very odd thing which once happened to me, and I can give you the points of that, if you like."

The three men assured him that they would very much like it, and the two women looked as if they were of the same opinion.

Before he began, the marine glanced about him, with a certain good-natured wistfulness which might have indicated, to those who understood the countenances of the seagoing classes, a desire to wet his whistle; but if this expression were so intended, it was thrown away, for blacksmith Fryker took no spirits himself nor furnished them to anybody else. Giving up all hope in this direction, the marine took a long pull at his pipe and began.

"It was in the winter of 1878 that I was on the Bay of Bengal, on my way to Calcutta, and about five hundred miles distant from that city. I was not on my own ship but was returning from a leave of absence on an American steamer from San Francisco to Calcutta, where my vessel, the United States frigate *Apache*, was then lying. My leave of absence would expire in three days; but although the *General Brooks*, the vessel I was aboard of, was more of a freight than a passenger vessel and was heavily laden, we would have been in port in good time if, two days before, something had not happened to the machinery. I am not a machinist myself and don't know exactly what it was that was out of order, but the engine stopped, and we had to proceed under sail. That sounds like a slow business; but the *Brooks* was a clipper-built vessel with three masts and a lot of sails—square sails, fore-and-aft sails, jib sails, and all that sort of thing. I am not a regular sailor myself and don't know the names of all the sails; but whatever sails she could have she did have, and although she was an iron vessel and heavily freighted, she was a good sailer. We had a strong, steady wind from the south, and the captain told me that at the rate we were going he didn't doubt that he would get me aboard my vessel before my leave ran out or at least so soon afterward that it wouldn't make any difference.

"Well, as I said, the wind blew strong and steady behind us, the sails were full, and the spray dashed up at our bow in a way calculated to tickle the soul of anyone anxious to get to the end of his voyage; and I was one of that sort, I can tell you.

"In the afternoon of the second day after our engine stopped, I was standing at the bow and looking over when suddenly I noticed that there wasn't any spray dashing up in front of the vessel. I thought we must have struck a sudden calm, but, glancing up, I saw the sails were full, and the wind blew fair in my face as I turned toward the stern. I walked aft to the skipper, and touching my cap, I said, 'Captain, how is it that when a ship is dashing along at this rate she doesn't throw up any spray with her cutwater?' He grinned a little and said, 'But she does, you know.' 'If you will come forward,' said I, 'I'll show you that she doesn't,' and then we walked forward, and I showed him that she didn't. I never saw a man so surprised. At first he thought that somebody had been squirting oil in front, but even if that had been the case, there would have been some sort of a ripple on each side of the bow, and there wasn't anything of the kind. The skipper took off his cap and scratched his head. Then he turned and sang out, 'Mr. Rogers, throw the log.'

"Now the log," said the marine, turning to Mrs. Fryker and her daughter, "is a little piece of wood with a long line to it that they throw out behind a vessel to see how fast she is going. I am not a regular Jack Tar myself and don't understand the principle of the thing, but it tells you exactly how many miles an hour the ship is going.

"In about two minutes Mr. Rogers stepped up, with his eyes like two auger holes, and said he, 'Captain, we're makin' no knots an hour. We're not sailing at all.'

" 'Get out,' roared the captain. 'Don't you see the sails? Don't you feel the wind? Throw that log again, sir.'

"Well, they threw the log again, the captain saw it done, and sure enough Mr. Rogers was right. The vessel wasn't moving. With a wind that ought to have carried her spinning along, miles and miles in an hour, she was standing stock-still. The skipper here let out one of the strongest imprecations used in navigation, and said he, 'Mr. Rogers, is it possible that there is a sand bar in the middle of the Bay of Bengal and that we've stuck on it? Cast the lead.'

"I will just state to the ladies," said the marine, turning toward the table, "that the lead is a heavy weight that is lowered to the bottom of a body of water to see how deep it is, and this operation is called sounding. Well, they sounded and they sounded, but everywhere—fore, aft, and midship—they found plenty of water; in fact, not having a line for deep-sea sounding they couldn't touch bottom at all.

"I can tell you, ladies and gentlemen," said the marine, looking from one to the other of the party, "that things now began to feel creepy. I am not afraid of storms nor fires at sea nor any of the common accidents of the ocean; but for a ship to stand still with plenty of water under her and a strong wind filling her sails has more of the uncanny about it than I fancy. Pretty near the whole of the crew was on deck by this time, and I could see that they felt very much as I did, but nobody seemed to know what to say about it.

"Suddenly the captain thought that some unknown current was setting against us and forcing the vessel back with the same power that the wind was forcing her forward, and he tried to put the ship about so as to have the wind on her starboard quarter; but as she hadn't any headway, or for some other reason, this didn't work. Then it struck him that perhaps one of the anchors had been accidentally dropped, but they were all in their places, and if one of them had dropped, its cable would not have been long enough to touch bottom.

"Now I could see that he began to look scared. 'Mr. Browser,' said he, to the chief engineer, 'for some reason or other this ship does not make headway undersail. You must go to work and get the engine running.' And for the rest of that day everybody on board who understood that sort of thing was down below, hard at work with the machinery, hammering and banging like good fellows.

"The chief officer ordered a good many of the sails to be taken in, for they were only uselessly straining the masts, but there were enough left to move her in case the power of the current, or whatever it was that stopped her, had slackened, and she steadily kept her position with the breeze abaft.

"All the crew who were not working below were crowded together on deck, talking about this strange thing. I joined them and soon found that they thought it was useless to waste time and labor on the machinery. They didn't believe it could be mended, and if it should be, how could an engine move a vessel that the wind couldn't stir?

"These men were of many nationalities—Dutch, Scandinavian, Spanish, Italian, South American, and a lot more. Like many other American vessels that sail from our ports, nearly all the officers and crew were foreigners. The captain was a Finlander, who spoke very good English. And the only man who called himself an American was the chief officer; and he was only half a one; for he was born in Germany, came to the United States when he was twenty years old, stayed there five years, which didn't count either way, and had now been naturalized for twenty years.

"The consequence of this variety in nationality was that the men had all sorts of ideas and notions regarding the thing that was happening. They had thrown over chips and bits of paper to see if the vessel had begun to move and had found that she didn't budge an inch, and now they seemed afraid to look over the sides.

"They were a superstitious lot, as might be expected, and they all believed that in some way or other the ship was bewitched; and in fact I felt like agreeing with them, although I did not say so.

"There was an old Portuguese sailor on board, an ugly-looking, weather-beaten little fellow, and when he had listened to everything the others had to say, he shuffled himself into the middle of the group. 'Look here, mates,' said he, in good enough English, 'it's no use talking no more about this. I know what's the matter; I've sailed these seas afore, and I've been along the coast of this bay all the way from Negapatam to Jellasore on the west coast and from Chittagong to Kraw on the other; and I have heard stories of the strange things that are in this Bay of Bengal and what they do, and the worst of them all is the Water-devil—and he's got us!'

"When the old rascal said this, there wasn't a man on deck who didn't look pale, in spite of his dirt and his sunburn. The chief officer tried to keep his knees stiff, but I could see him shaking. 'What's a Water-devil?' said he, trying to make believe he thought it all stuff and nonsense. The Portuguese touched his forelock. 'Do you remember, sir,' said he, 'what was the latitude and longitude when you took your observation today?' 'Yes,' said the other, 'it was 15° north and 90° east.' The Portuguese nodded his head. 'That's just about the spot, sir, just about. I can't say exactly where the spot is, but it's just about here, and we've struck it. There isn't a native seaman on any of these coasts that would sail over that point if he knowed it and could help it, for that's the spot where the Water-devil lives.'

"It made me jump to hear the grunt that went through the crowd when he said this, but nobody asked any questions, and he went on. 'This here Water-devil,' said he, 'is about as big as six whales and in shape very like an oyster without its shell, and he fastens himself to the rocks at the bottom with a million claws. Right out of the middle of him there grows up a long arm that reaches to the top of the water, and at the end of this arm is a fist about the size of a yawl boat, with fifty-two figures to it, with each one of them covered with little suckers that will stick fast to anything—iron, wood, stone, or flesh. All that this Water-devil gets to eat is what happens to come swimmin' or sailin' along where he can reach it, and it doesn't matter to him whether it's a shark or a porpoise or a shipful of people, and when he takes a grab of anything, that thing never gets away.'

"About this time there were five or six men on their knees saying their prayers, such as they were, and a good many others looked as if they were just about to drop.

" 'Now, when this Water-devil gets hold of a ship,' the old fellow went on, 'he don't generally pull her straight down to the bottom but holds on to it till he counts his claws and sees that they are all fastened to the rocks; for if a good many of them wasn't fastened, he might pull himself loose, instead of pulling the ship down, and then he'd be a goner, for he'd be towed away and like as not put in a museum. But when he is satisfied that he is moored fast and strong, then he hauls on his arm, and down comes the ship, no matter how big she is. As the ship is sinkin', he turns her over every now and then, keel uppermost, and gives her a shake, and when the people drop out, he sucks them into a sort of funnel, which is his mouth.'

" 'Does he count fast?' asked one of the men, this being the first question that had been asked.

" 'I've heard,' said the Portuguese, 'that he's a rapid calculator, and the minute he's got to his millionth claw and finds it's hooked tight and fast, he begins to haul down the ship.' "

At this point the marine stopped and glanced around at the little group. The blacksmith's wife and daughter had put down their work and were gazing at him with an air of horrified curiosity. The blacksmith held his pipe in his hand and regarded the narrator with the steadiness and impassiveness of an anvil. The schoolmaster was listening with the greatest eagerness. He was an enthusiast on natural history and mythology and had written an article for a weekly paper on the reconciliation of the beasts of tradition with the fauna of today. Mr. Harberry was not looking at the marine. His eyes were fixed upon the schoolmaster.

"Mr. Cardly," said he, "did you ever read of an animal like that?"

"I cannot say that I have," was his reply; "but it is certain that there are many strange creatures, especially in the sea, of which scientists are comparatively ignorant."

"Such as the sea serpent," added the marine quickly, "and a great many other monsters who are not in the books but who have a good time at the bottom of the sea, all the same. Well, to go on with my story, you must understand that, though this Portuguese spoke broken English, which I haven't tried to give you, he made himself perfectly plain to all of us, and I can assure you that when he got through talking, there was a shaky lot of men on that deck.

"The chief officer said he would go below and see how the captain was getting on, and the crew huddled together in the bow and began whispering among themselves, as if they were afraid the Water-devil would hear them. I turned to walk aft, feeling pretty queer, I can tell you, when I saw Miss Minturn just coming up from the cabin below.

"I haven't said anything about Miss Minturn, but she and her father, who was an elderly English gentleman and an invalid who had never left his berth since we took him up at Singapore, were our only passengers, except, of course, myself. She was a beautiful girl, with soft blue eyes and golden hair, and a little pale from constantly staying below to nurse her father.

"Of course I had had little or nothing to say to her, for her father was a good deal of a swell and I was only a marine; but now she saw me standing there by myself, and she came right up to me. 'Can you tell me, sir,' she said, 'if anything else has happened? They are making a great din in the engine room. I have been looking out of our port, and the vessel seems to me to be stationary.' She stopped at that and waited to hear what I had to say, but I assure you I would have liked to have had her go on talking for half an hour. Her voice was rich and sweet, like that of so many Englishwomen, although, I am happy to say, a great many of my countrywomen have just as good voices; and when I meet any of them for the first time, I generally give them the credit of talking in soft and musical notes, even though I have not had the pleasure of hearing them speak."

"Look here," said the blacksmith, "can't you skip the girl and get back to the devil?"

"No," said the marine, "I couldn't do that. The two are mixed together, so to speak, so that I have to tell of both of them."

"You don't mean to say," exclaimed Mrs. Fryker, speaking for the first time, and by no means in soft and musical tones, "that he swallowed her?"

"I'll go on with the story," said the marine; "that's the best way, and everything will come up in its place. Now, of course, I wasn't going to tell this charming young woman, with a sick father, anything about the Water-devil, though what reason to give her for our standing still here I couldn't imagine; but of course I had to speak, and I said, 'Don't be alarmed, miss, we have met with an unavoidable detention; that sort of thing often happens in navigation. I can't explain it to you, but you see the ship is perfectly safe and sound, and she is merely under sail instead of having her engines going.'

" 'I understood about that,' said she, 'and father and I were both perfectly satisfied; for he said that if we had a good breeze, we would not be long in reaching Calcutta; but we seem to have a breeze, and yet we don't go.' 'You'll notice,' said I, 'that the sails are not all set, and for some reason the wind does not serve. When the engines are mended, we shall probably go spinning along.' She looked as if she was trying to appear satisfied. 'Thank you, sir,' she said. 'I hope we may shortly proceed on our way, but in the meantime I shall not say anything to my father about this detention. I think he has not noticed it.' 'That would be very wise,' I replied, and as she turned toward the companionway, I was wild to say to her that it would be a lot better for her to stay on deck and get some good fresh air instead of cooping herself up in that close cabin; but I didn't know her well enough for that."

"Now that you are through with the girl," said the blacksmith, "what did the devil do?"

"I haven't got to him yet," said the marine, "but after Miss Minturn went below, I began to think of him, and the more I thought of him, the less I liked him. I think the chief officer must have told the men below about the Water-devil, for pretty soon the whole kit and boodle of them left their work and came on deck, skipper and all. They told me they had given up the engine as a bad job, and I thought to myself that most likely they were all too nervous to rightly know what they were about. The captain threw out the log again, but it floated alongside like a cork on a fishing line, and at this he turned pale and walked away from the ship's side, forgetting to pull it in again.

"It was now beginning to grow dark, and as nobody seemed to think about supper, I went below to look into that matter. It wouldn't do for Miss Minturn and her father to go without their regular meal, for that would be sure to scare them to death; and if I'm to have a big scare I like to take it on a good square meal, so I went below to see about it. But I wasn't needed, for Miss Minturn's maid, who was an elderly woman and pretty sharp set in her temper, was in the cook's galley superintending supper for her people, and after she got through, I superintended some for myself.

"After that I felt a good deal bolder, and I lighted a pipe and went on deck. There I found the whole ship's company, officers and crew, none of them doing anything, and most of them clustered together in little groups, whispering or grunting.

"I went up to the captain and asked him what he was going to do next. 'Do?' said he. 'There is nothing to do; I've done everything that I can do. I'm all upset; I don't know whether I am myself or some other man.' And then he walked away.

"I sat there and smoked and looked at them, and I can tell you the sight wasn't cheerful. There was the ship, just as good and sound, as far as anybody could see, as anything that floated on the ocean, and here were all her people, shivering and shaking and not speaking above their breath, looking for all the world, under the light of the stars and the ship's lamps, which some of them had had sense enough to light, as if they expected in the course of the next half-hour to be made to walk the plank; and, to tell the truth, what they were afraid of would come to pretty much the same thing."

"Mr. Cardly," here interrupted Mr. Harberry, "how long does it take to count a million?"

"That depends," said the schoolmaster, "on the rapidity of the calculator; some calculators count faster than others. An ordinary boy, counting two hundred a minute, would require nearly three days and a half to count a million."

"Very good," said Mr. Harberry; "please go on with your story, sir."

"Of course," said the marine, "there is a great difference between a boy and a Water-devil, and it is impossible for anybody to know how fast the latter can count, especially as he may be supposed to be used to it. Well, I couldn't stand it any longer on deck, and having nothing else to do, I turned in and went to sleep."

"To sleep! Went to sleep!" exclaimed Mrs. Fryker. "I don't see how you could have done that."

"Ah, madam," said the marine, "we soldiers of the sea are exposed to all sorts of dangers—combination dangers, you might call them—and in the course of time we get used to it; if we didn't, we couldn't do our duty.

"As the ship had been in its present predicament for six or seven hours and nothing had happened, there was no reason to suppose that things would not remain as they were for six or seven hours more, in which time I might get a good sleep and be better prepared for what might come. There's nothing like a good meal and a good sleep as a preparation for danger.

"It was daylight when I awakened, and rapidly glancing about me, I saw that everything appeared to be all right. Looking out of the porthole, I could see that the vessel was still motionless. I hurried on deck and was greatly surprised to find nobody there —no one on watch, no one at the wheel, no one anywhere. I ran down into the fo'c'sle, which is the sailors' quarters, but not a soul could I see. I called, I whistled, I searched everywhere, but no one answered; I could find no one. Then I dashed up on deck and glared around me. Every boat was gone.

"Now I knew what had happened: the cowardly rascals, from captain to cook, had deserted the ship in the night, and I had been left behind!

"For some minutes I stood motionless, wondering how men could be so unfeeling as to do such a thing. I soon became convinced, from what I had seen of the crew, that they had not all gone off together, that there had been no concerted action. A number of them had probably quietly lowered a boat and sneaked away; then another lot had gone off, hoping their mates would not hear them and therefore crowd into their boat. And so they had all departed, not one boatload thinking of anybody but themselves; or if they thought at all about others, quieting their consciences by supposing that there were enough boats on the vessel, and that the other people were as likely to get off as they were.

"Suddenly I thought of the other passengers. Had they been left behind? I ran down below, and I had scarcely reached the bot-

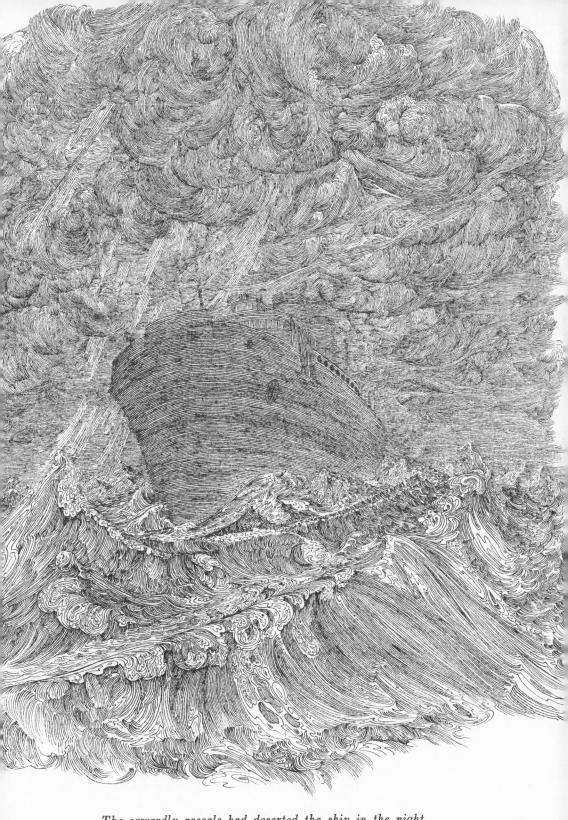

The cowardly rascals had deserted the ship in the night.

tom of the steps when I met Miss Minturn's maid. 'It seems to me,' she said sharply, 'that the people on this ship are neglecting their duty. There's nobody in the kitchen, and I want some gruel.' 'My good woman,' said I, 'who do you want it for?' 'Who!' she replied. 'Why, for Mr. Minturn, of course; and Miss Minturn may like some, too.'

"Then I knew that all the passengers had been left behind!

" 'If you want any gruel,' said I, 'you will have to go into the galley and make it yourself.' And then in a low tone I told her what had happened, for I knew that it would be much better for me to do this than for her to find it out for herself. Without a word she sat right down on the floor and covered her head with her apron. 'Now don't make a row,' said I, 'and frighten your master and mistress to death; we're all right so far, and all you've got to do is to take care of Mr. and Miss Minturn and cook their meals. The steamer is tight and sound, and it can't be long before some sort of a craft will come by and take us off.' I left her sniffling with her apron over her head, but when I came back, ten minutes afterward, she was in the galley making gruel.

"I don't think you will be surprised, my friends," continued the marine, "when I tell you that I now found myself in a terrible state of mind. Of course I hadn't felt very jovial since the steamer had been so wonderfully stopped; but when the captain and all the crew were aboard, I had that sort of confidence which comes from believing that when there are people about whose duty it is to do things, when the time comes to do the things, they will do them; but now, practically speaking, there was nobody but me. The others on board were not to be counted, except as encumbrances. In truth, I was alone—alone with the Water-devil!

"The moment I found no one to depend upon but myself and that I was deserted in the midst of this lonely mass of water, in that moment did my belief in the Water-devil begin to grow. When I first heard of the creature, I didn't consider that it was my business either to believe in it or not to believe in it, and I could let the whole thing drop out of my mind if I chose; but now it was a different matter. I was bound to think for myself, and the more I thought, the more I believed in the Water-devil.

"The fact was, there wasn't anything else to believe in. I had gone over the whole question, and the skipper had gone all over it, and everybody else had gone all over it, and no one could think of anything but a Water-devil that could stop a steamer in this way in the middle of the Bay of Bengal and hold her there hour after hour, in spite of wind and wave and tide. It could not be anything but the monster the Portuguese had told us of, and all I now could do was to wonder whether, when he was done counting his million claws, he would be able to pull down a vessel of a thousand tons, for that was about the size of the *General Brooks*.

"I think I should now have begun to lose my wits if it had not been for one thing, and that was the coming of Miss Minturn on deck. The moment I saw her lovely face I stiffened up wonderfully. 'Sir,' said she, 'I would like to see the captain.' 'I am representing the captain, miss,' I said, with a bow. 'What is it that I can do for you?' 'I want to speak to him about the steward,' she said; 'I think he is neglecting his duty.' 'I also represent the steward,' I replied; 'tell me what you wish of him.' She made no answer to this but looked about her in a startled way. 'Where are all the men?' she said. 'Miss Minturn,' said I, 'I represent the crew—in fact, I represent the whole ship's company except the cook, and his place must be taken by your maid.' 'What do you mean?' she asked, looking at me with her wide-opened, beautiful eyes.

"Then, as there was no help for it, I told her everything, except that I did not mention the Water-devil in connection with our marvelous stoppage. I only said that that was caused by something which nobody understood.

"She did not sit down and cover her head, nor did she scream or faint. She turned pale but looked steadily at me, and her voice did not shake as she asked me what was to be done. 'There is nothing to be done,' I answered, 'but to keep up good hearts, eat three meals a day, and wait until a ship comes along and takes us off.'

"She stood silent for about three minutes. 'I think,' she then said, 'that I will not yet tell my father what has happened'; and she went below.

"Now, strange to say, I walked up and down the deck with my hat cocked on one side and my hands in my pockets, feeling a great deal better. I did not like Water-devils any more than I did before, and I did not believe in this one any less than I did before, but, after all, there was some good about him. It seems odd, but the arm of this submarine monster, over a mile long for all that I knew, was a bond of union between the lovely Miss Minturn and me. She was a lady; I was a marine. So far as I knew anything about bonds of union, there wasn't one that could have tackled itself to us two, except this long, slippery arm of the Water-devil, with one end in the monstrous flob at the bottom and the other fast to our ship.

"There was no doubt about it, if it hadn't been for that Water-devil she would have been no more to me than the Queen of Madagascar was; but under the circumstances, if I wasn't everything to her, who could be anything—that is, if one looked at the matter from a practical point of view?"

The blacksmith made a little movement of impatience. "Suppose you cut all that," said he. "I don't care about the bond of union; I want to know what happened to the ship."

"It is likely," said the marine, "if I could have cut the bond of union that I spoke of, that is to say, the Water-devil's arm, that I would have done it, hoping that I might safely float off somewhere with Miss Minturn; but I couldn't cut it then, and I can't cut it now. That bond is part of my story, and it must all go on together.

"I now set myself to work to do what I thought ought to be done under the circumstances, but, of course, that wasn't very much. I hoisted a flag upside down, and after considering the matter, I concluded to take in all the sails that had been set. I thought that a steamer without smoke coming from her funnel and no sails set would be more likely to attract attention from distant vessels than if she appeared to be under sail.

"I am not a regular sailor, as I said before, but I got out on the yard and cut the square sail loose and let it drop on the deck, and I let the jib come down on a run, and managed to bundle it up some way on the bowsprit. This sort of thing took all the nautical gymnastics that I was master of and entirely occupied my mind, so that I found myself whistling while I worked. I hoped Miss Minturn heard me whistle, because it would not only give her courage but would let her see that I was not a man who couldn't keep up his spirits in a case like this.

"When that work was over, I began to wonder what I should do next, and then an idea struck me. 'Suppose,' thought I, 'that we are not stationary but that we are in some queer kind of a current and that the water, ship, and all are steadily moving on together, so that after a while we shall come in sight of land or into the track of vessels!'

"I instantly set about to find out if this was the case. It was about noon, and it so happened that on the day before, when the chief officer took his observation, I was seized with a desire to watch him and see how he did it. I don't see why I should have had this notion, but I had it, and I paid the strictest attention to the whole business, calculation part and all, and I found out exactly how it was done.

"Well, then, I went and got the quadrant—that's the thing they do it with—and I took an observation, and I found that we were in latitude 15° north, 90° east; exactly where we had been twenty-four hours before!

"When I found out this, I turned so faint that I wanted to sit down and cover up my head. The Water-devil had us; there was no mistake about it and no use trying to think of anything else. I staggered along the deck, went below, and cooked myself a meal.

In a case like this there's nothing like a square meal to keep a man up.

"I know you don't like to hear her mentioned," said the marine, turning to the blacksmith, "but I am bound to say that in the course of the afternoon Miss Minturn came on deck several times to ask if anything new had happened and if I had seen a vessel. I showed her all that I had done and told her I was going to hang out lights at night, and did everything I could to keep her on deck as long as possible; for it was easy to see that she needed fresh air, and I needed company. As long as I was talking to her, I didn't care a snap of my finger for the Water-devil. It is queer what an influence a beautiful woman has on a man, but it's so, and there's no use arguing about it. She said she had been puzzling her brains to find out what had stopped us, and she supposed it must be that we had run onto a shallow place and stuck fast in the mud but thought it wonderful that there should be such a place so far from land. I agreed with her that it was wonderful and added that that was probably the reason the captain and the crew had been seized with a panic. But sensible people like herself and her father, I said, ought not to be troubled by such an occurrence, especially as the vessel remained in a perfectly sound condition.

"She said that her father was busily engaged in writing his memoirs, and that his mind was so occupied, he had not concerned himself at all about our situation, that is, if he had noticed that we were not moving. 'If he wants to see the steward or anybody else,' I said, 'please call upon me. You know I represent the whole ship's company, and I shall be delighted to do anything for him or for you.' She thanked me very much and went below.

"She came up again, after this, but her maid came with her, and the two walked on deck for a while. I didn't have much to say to them that time; but just before dark Miss Minturn came on deck alone and walked forward, where I happened to be. 'Sir,' said she, and her voice trembled a little as she spoke, 'if anything should happen, will you promise me that you will try to save my father?' You can't imagine how these touching words from this beautiful woman affected me. 'My dear lady,' said I, and I hope she did not take offense at the warmth of my expression, 'I don't see how anything can happen; but I promise you, on the word of a sea soldier, that if danger should come upon us, I will save not only your father but yourself and your maid. Trust me for that.'

"The look she gave me when I said these words, and especially the flash of her eye when I spoke of my being a sea soldier, made me feel strong enough to tear that sea monster's arm in twain and to sail away with the lovely creature for whom my heart was beginning to throb."

"It's a pity," said the blacksmith, "that you hadn't jumped into the water while the fit was on you and done the tearing."

"A man often feels strong enough to do a thing," said the marine, "and yet doesn't care to try to do it, and that was my case at that time; but I vowed to myself that if the time came when there was any saving to be done, I'd attend to Miss Minturn, even if I had to neglect the rest of the family.

"She didn't make any answer, but she gave me her hand; and she couldn't have done anything I liked better than that. I held it as long as I could, which wasn't very long, and then she went down to her father."

"Glad of it," said the blacksmith.

"When I had had my supper and had smoked my pipe and everything was still and I knew I shouldn't see anybody anymore that night, I began to have the quakes and the shakes. If even I had had the maid to talk to, it would have been a comfort; but in the way of faithfully attending to her employers that woman was a trump. She cooked for them and did for them and stuck by them straight along, so she hadn't any time for chats with me.

"Being alone, I couldn't help all the time thinking about the Water-devil, and although it seems a foolish thing now that I look back on it, I set to work to calculate how long it would take him to count his feet. I made it about the same time as you did, sir," said the marine, nodding to the schoolmaster, "only I considered that if he counted twelve hours and slept and rested twelve hours, that would make it seven days, which would give me a good long time with Miss Minturn, and that would be the greatest of joys to me, no matter what happened afterward.

"But then nobody could be certain that the monster at the bottom of the bay needed rest or sleep. He might be able to count without stopping, and how did I know that he couldn't check off four hundred claws a minute? If that happened to be the case, our time must be nearly up.

"When that idea came into my head, I jumped up and began to walk about. What could I do? I certainly ought to be ready to do something when the time came. I thought of getting life preservers and strapping one on each of us, so that if the Water-devil turned over the vessel and shook us out, we shouldn't sink down to him but would float on the surface.

"But then the thought struck me that if he should find the vessel empty of live creatures and should see us floating around on the top, all he had to do was to let go of the ship and grab us, one at a time. When I thought of a fist as big as a yawl boat, clapping its fifty-two fingers on me, it sent a shiver through my bones. The fact was there wasn't anything to do, and so after a while I managed to get asleep, which was a great comfort."

"Mr. Cardly," said Mr. Harberry to the schoolmaster, "what reason can you assign why a sea monster, such as has been described to us, should neglect to seize upon several small boats filled with men who were escaping from a vessel which it held in custody?"

"I do not precisely see," answered Mr. Cardly, "why these men should have been allowed this immunity, but I—"

"Oh, that is easily explained," interrupted the marine, "for of course the Water-devil could not know that a lot more people were not left in the ship, and if he let go his hold on her, to try and grab a boat that was moving as fast as men could row it, the steamer might get out of his reach, and he mightn't have another chance for a hundred years to make fast to a vessel. No, sir, a creature like that isn't apt to take any wild chances, when he's got hold of a really good thing. Anyway, we were held tight and fast, for at twelve o'clock the next day I took another observation, and there we were, in the same latitude and longitude that we had been in for two days. I took the captain's glass, and I looked all over the water of that bay, which, as I think I have said before, was all the same as the ocean, being somewhere about a thousand miles wide. Not a sail, not a puff of smoke could I see. It must have been a slack season for navigation, or else we were out of the common track of vessels. I had never known the Bay of Bengal was so desperately lonely.

"It seems unnatural, and I can hardly believe it when I look back on it, but it's a fact, that I was beginning to get used to the situation. We had plenty to eat, the weather was fine—in fact, there was now only breeze enough to make things cool and comfortable. I was headman on that vessel, and Miss Minturn might come on deck at any moment, and as long as I could forget that there was a Water-devil fastened to the bottom of the vessel, there was no reason why I should not be perfectly satisfied with things as they were. And if things had stayed as they were, for two or three months, I should have been right well pleased, especially since Miss Minturn's maid, by order of her mistress, had begun to cook my meals, which she did in a manner truly first-class. I believed then, and I stand to it now, that there is no better proof of a woman's good feeling toward a man than for her to show an interest in his meals. That's the sort of sympathy that comes home to a man and tells on him, body and soul."

As the marine made this remark, he glanced at the blacksmith's daughter; but that young lady had taken up her sewing and appeared to be giving it her earnest attention. He then went on with his story.

"But things did not remain as they were. The next morning,

about half an hour after breakfast, I was walking up and down the upper deck, smoking my pipe and wondering when Miss Minturn would be coming up to talk to me about the state of affairs, when suddenly I felt the deck beneath me move with a quick, sharp jerk, something like, I imagine, a small shock of an earthquake.

"Never, in all my life, did the blood run so cold in my veins; my legs trembled so that I could scarcely stand. I knew what had happened—the Water-devil had begun to haul upon the ship!

"I was in such a state of collapse that I did not seem to have any power over my muscles; but for all that, I heard Miss Minturn's voice at the foot of the companionway, and knew that she was coming on deck. In spite of the dreadful awfulness of that moment, I felt it would never do for her to see me in the condition I was in, and so, shuffling and half tumbling, I got forward, went below, and made my way to the steward's room, where I had already discovered some spirits, and I took a good dram; for although I am not by any means an habitual drinker, being principled against that sort of thing, there are times when a man needs the support of some good brandy or whiskey.

"In a few minutes I felt more like myself and went on deck, and there was Miss Minturn, half scared to death. 'What is the meaning of that shock?' she said. 'Have we struck anything?' 'My dear lady,' said I, with as cheerful a front as I could put on, 'I do not think we have struck anything. There is nothing to strike.' She looked at me for a moment like an angel ready to cry, and clasping her hands, she said, 'Oh, tell me, sir, I pray you, sir, tell me what has happened. My father felt that shock. He sent me to inquire about it. His mind is disturbed.' At that moment, before I could make an answer, there was another jerk of the ship, and we both went down on our knees, and I felt as if I had been tripped. I was up in a moment, however, but she continued on her knees. I am sure she was praying, but very soon up she sprang. 'Oh, what is it, what is it?' she cried. 'I must go to my father.'

" 'I cannot tell you,' said I. 'I do not know, but don't be frightened. How can such a little shock hurt so big a ship?'

"It was all very well to tell her not to be frightened, but when she ran below she left on deck about as frightened a man as ever stood in shoes. There could be no doubt about it; that horrible beast was beginning to pull upon the ship. Whether or not it would be able to draw us down below was a question which must soon be solved.

"I had had a small opinion of the maid, who, when I told her the crew had deserted the ship, had sat down and covered her head; but now I did pretty much the same thing; I crouched on the deck and pulled my cap over my eyes. I felt that I did not wish to see, hear, or feel anything.

"I had sat in this way for about half an hour and had felt no more shocks, when a slight gurgling sound came to my ears. I listened for a moment, then sprang to my feet. Could we be moving? I ran to the side of the ship. The gurgle seemed to be coming from the stern. I hurried there and looked over. The wheel had been lashed fast, and the rudder stood straight out behind us. On each side of it there was a ripple in the quiet water. We were moving, and we were moving backward!

"Overpowered by horrible fascination, I stood grasping the rail and looking over at the water beneath me as the vessel moved slowly and steadily onward, stern foremost. In spite of the upset condition of my mind, I could not help wondering why the vessel should move in this way.

"There was only one explanation possible: the Water-devil was walking along the bottom and towing us after him! Why he should pull us along in this way, I could not imagine, unless he was making for his home in some dreadful cave at the bottom, into which he would sink, dragging us down after him.

"While my mind was occupied with these horrible subjects, someone touched me on the arm, and turning, I saw Miss Minturn. 'Are we not moving?' she said. 'Yes,' I answered, 'we certainly are.' 'Do you not think,' she then asked, 'that we may have been struck by a powerful current, which is now carrying us onward?' I did not believe this, for there was no reason to suppose that there were currents which wandered about, starting off vessels with a jerk, but I was glad to think that this idea had come into her head and said that it was possible that this might be the case. 'And now we are going somewhere,' she said, speaking almost cheerfully. 'Yes, we are,' I answered, and I had to try hard not to groan as I said the words. 'And where do you think we are going?' she asked. It was altogether out of my power to tell that sweet creature that in my private opinion she, at least, was going to heaven, and so I answered that I really did not know. 'Well,' she said, 'if we keep moving, we're bound at last to get near land or to some place where ships would pass near us.'

"There is nothing in this world," said the marine, "which does a man so much good in time of danger as to see a hopeful spirit in a woman—that is, a woman that he cares about. Some of her courage comes to him, and he is better and stronger for having her alongside of him."

Having made this remark, the speaker again glanced at the blacksmith's daughter. She had put down her work and was looking at him with an earnest brightness in her eyes.

"Yes," he continued, "it is astonishing what a change came over me as I stood by the side of that noble girl. She was a born lady, I was a marine, just the same as we had been before, but there didn't seem to be the difference between us that there had been. Her words, her spirits, everything about her, in fact, seemed to act on me, to elevate me, to fill my soul with noble sentiments, to make another man of me. Standing there beside her, I felt myself her equal. In life or death I would not be ashamed to say, 'Here I am, ready to stand by you, whatever happens.' "

Having concluded this sentiment, the marine again glanced toward the blacksmith's daughter. Her eyes were slightly moist, and her face was glowing with a certain enthusiasm.

"Look here," said the blacksmith, "I suppose that woman goes along with you into the very maw of the sunken devil, but I do wish you could take her more for granted and get on faster with the real part of the story."

"One part is as real as another," said the marine; "but on we go, and on we did go for the whole of the rest of that day, at the rate of about half a knot an hour, as near as I could guess at it. The weather changed, and a dirty sort of fog came down on us, so that we couldn't see far in any direction.

"Why that Water-devil should keep on towing us, and where he was going to take us, were things I didn't dare to think about. The fog did not prevent me from seeing the water about our stern, and I leaned over the rail, watching the ripples that flowed on each side of the rudder, which showed that we were still going at about the same uniform rate.

"But toward evening the gurgling beneath me ceased, and I could see that the rudder no longer parted the quiet water and that we had ceased to move. A flash of hope blazed up within me. Had the Water-devil found the ship too heavy a load, and had he given up the attempt to drag it to its under-ocean cave? I went below and had my supper; I was almost a happy man. When Miss Minturn came to ask me how we were getting along, I told her that I thought we were doing very well indeed. I did not mention that we had ceased to move, for she thought that a favorable symptom. She went back to her quarters greatly cheered up. Not so much, I think, from my words, as from my joyful aspect; for I did feel jolly, there was no doubt about it. If that Water-devil had let go of us, I was willing to take all the other chances that might befall a ship floating about loose on the Bay of Bengal.

"The fog was so thick that night that it was damp and unpleasant on deck, and so, having hung out and lighted a couple of lanterns, I went below for a comfortable smoke in the captain's room. I was puffing away here at my ease, with my mind filled with happy thoughts of two or three weeks with Miss Minturn on this floating paradise, where she was bound to see a good deal of me and couldn't help liking me better and depending on me more and more every day, when I felt a little jerking shock. It was the same thing that we had felt before. The Water-devil still had hold of us!

"I dropped my pipe, my chin fell upon my breast, I shivered all over. In a few moments I heard the maid calling to me, and then she ran into the room. 'Miss Minturn wants to know, sir,' she said, 'if you think that shock is a sudden twist in the current which is carrying us on?' I straightened myself up as well as I could, and in the dim light I do not think she noticed my condition. I answered that I thought it was something of that sort, and she went away.

"More likely, a twist of the devil's arm, I thought, as I sat there alone in my misery.

"In ten or fifteen minutes there came two shocks, not very far apart. This showed that the creature beneath us was at work in some way or another. Perhaps he had reached the opening of his den and was shortening up his arm before he plunged down into it with us after him. I couldn't stay any longer in that room alone. I looked for the maid, but she had put out the galley light and had probably turned in for the night.

"I went up and looked out on deck, but everything was horribly dark and sticky and miserable there. I noticed that my lanterns were not burning, and then I remembered that I had not filled them. But this did not trouble me. If a vessel came along and saw our lights she would probably keep away from us, and I would have been glad to have a vessel come to us, even if she ran into us. Our steamer would probably float long enough for us to get on board the other one, and almost anything would be better than being left alone in this dreadful place, at the mercy of the Water-devil.

"Before I left the deck I felt another shock. This took out of me whatever starch was left, and I shuffled below and got to my bunk, where I tumbled in and covered myself up, head and all. If there had been any man to talk to, it would have been different, but I don't know when I ever felt more deserted than I did at that time.

"I tried to forget the awful situation in which I was; I tried to think of other things, to imagine that I was drilling with the rest of my company, with Tom Rogers on one side of me and old Humphrey Peters on the other. You may say, perhaps, that this wasn't exactly the way of carrying out my promise of taking care of Miss Minturn and the others. But what was there to do? When the time came to do anything and I could see what to do, I was ready to do it; but there was no use of waking them up now and setting their minds on edge, when they were all comfortable in their beds, thinking that every jerk of the devil's arm was a little twist in the current that was carrying them to Calcutta or some other desirable port.

"I felt some shocks after I got into bed, but whether or not there were many in the night, I don't know, for I went to sleep. It was daylight when I awoke, and jumping out of my bunk, I dashed on deck. Everything seemed pretty much as it had been, and the fog was as thick as ever. I ran to the stern and looked over, and I could scarcely believe my eyes when I saw that we were moving again, still stern foremost, but a little faster than before. That beastly Water-devil had taken a rest for the night and had probably given us the shocks by turning over in his sleep, and now he was off again, making up for lost time.

"Pretty soon Miss Minturn came on deck and bade me good morning, and then she went and looked over the stern. 'We are still moving on,' she said, with a smile, 'and the fog doesn't seem to make any difference. It surely cannot be long before we get somewhere.' 'No, miss,' said I, 'it cannot be very long.' 'You look tired,' she said, 'and I don't wonder, for you must feel the heavy responsibility on you. I have told my maid to prepare breakfast for you in our cabin. I want my father to know you, and I think it is a shame that you, the only protector that we have, should be shut off so much by yourself; so after this we shall eat together.' 'After this,' I groaned to myself, 'we shall be eaten together.' At that moment I did not feel that I wanted to breakfast with Miss Minturn."

"Mr. Cardly," said Mr. Harberry to the schoolmaster, "have you ever read, in any of your scientific books, that the Bay of Bengal is subject to heavy fogs that last day after day?"

"I cannot say," answered the schoolmaster, "that my researches into the geographical distribution of fogs have resulted—"

"As to fogs," interrupted the marine, "you can't get rid of them, you know. If you had been in the habit of going to sea, you would know that you are likely to run into a fog at any time and in any weather; and as to lasting, they are just as likely to last for days as for hours. It wasn't the fog that surprised me. I did not consider that of any account at all. I had enough other things to occupy my mind." And having settled this little matter, he went on with his story.

"Well, my friends, I did not breakfast with Miss Minturn and her father. Before that meal was ready, and while I was standing alone at the stern, I saw coming out of the water, a long way off in the fog, which must have been growing thinner about this time, a dark and mysterious object, apparently without any shape or form. This sight made the teeth chatter in my head. I had expected to be pulled down to the Water-devil, but I had never imagined that he would come up to us!

"While my eyes were glued upon this apparition, I could see that we were approaching it. When I perceived this, I shut my eyes and turned my back—I could look upon it no longer. My mind seemed to forsake me; I did not even try to call out and give the alarm to the others. Why should I? What could they do?"

"If it had been me," said Mrs. Fryker, in a sort of gasping whisper, "I should have died right there." The marine turned his eyes in the direction of the blacksmith's daughter. She was engaged with her work and was not looking at him.

"I cannot say," he continued, "that, had Miss Minturn been there at that moment, I would not have declared that I was ready to die for her or with her; but there was no need of trying to keep up her courage; that was all right. She knew nothing of our danger. That terrible knowledge pressed on me alone. Is it wonderful that a human soul should sink a little under such an awful load?" Without turning to observe the effect of these last words, the marine went on. "Suddenly I heard behind me a most dreadful sound. 'Good Heavens,' I exclaimed, 'can a Water-devil bray?'

"The sound was repeated. Without knowing what I did, I turned. I heard what sounded like words; I saw in the fog the stern of a vessel, with a man above it, shouting to me through a speaking trumpet.

"I do not know what happened next; my mind must have become confused. When I regained my senses, Miss Minturn, old Mr. Minturn, and the maid were standing by me. The man had stopped shouting from his trumpet, and a boat was being lowered from the other ship. In about ten minutes there were half a dozen men on board of us, all in the uniform of the British Navy. I was stiff enough now and felt myself from top to toe a regular marine in the service of my country. I stepped up to the officer in command and touched my cap.

"He looked at me and my companions in surprise, and then glancing along the deck, said, 'What has happened to this vessel? Who is in command?' I informed him that, strictly speaking, no one was in command, but that I represented the captain, officers, and crew of this steamer, the *General Brooks*, from San Francisco to Calcutta, and I then proceeded to tell him the whole story of our misfortunes; and concluded by telling the officer that if we had not moved since his vessel had come in sight, it was probably because the Water-devil had let go of us and was preparing to make fast to the other ship; and therefore it would be advisable for us all to get on board his vessel and steam away as quickly as possible.

"The Englishmen looked at me in amazement. 'Drunk!' ejaculated the officer I had addressed. 'Cracked, I should say,' suggested another. 'Now,' spoke up Mr. Minturn, 'I do not understand what I have just heard,' he said. 'What is a Water-devil? I am astounded.' 'You never said a word of this to me!' exclaimed Miss Minturn. 'You never told me that we were in the grasp of a Water-devil and that that was the reason the captain and the crew ran away.' 'No,' said I, 'I never divulged the dreadful danger we were in. I allowed you to believe that we were in the influence of a current and that the shocks we felt were the sudden twists of that current. The terrible truth I kept to myself. Not for worlds would I have made known to a tenderly nurtured lady, to her invalid father, and devoted servant what might have crushed their souls, driven them to the borders of frenzy; in which case the relief which now has come to us would have been of no avail.'

"The officer stood and steadily stared at me. 'I declare,' he said, 'you do not look like a crazy man. At what time did this Water-devil begin to take you in tow?'

" 'Yesterday morning,' I answered. 'And he stopped during last night?' he asked. I replied that that was the case. Then he took off his cap, rubbed his head, and stood silent for a minute. 'We'll look into this matter!' he suddenly exclaimed, and turning, he and his party left us to ourselves. The boat was now sent back with a message to the English vessel, and the officers and men who remained scattered themselves over our steamer, examining the engine room, hold, and every part of her.

"I was very much opposed to all this delay; for although the Englishmen might doubt the existence of the Water-devil, I saw no reason to do so, and in any case I was very anxious to be on the safe side by getting away as soon as possible; but, of course, British officers would not be advised by me, and as I was getting very hungry, I went down to breakfast. I ate this meal alone, for my fellow passengers seemed to have no desire for food.

"I cannot tell all that happened during the next hour, for, to tell the truth, I did not understand everything that was done. The boat passed several times between the two vessels, bringing over a number of men—two of them scientific fellows, I think. Another was a diver, whose submarine suit and air-pumping machines came over with him. He was lowered over the side, and after he had been down about fifteen minutes he was hauled up again, and down below was the greatest hammering and hauling that ever you heard. The *General Brooks* was put in charge of an officer and some men; a sail was hoisted to keep her in hand, so that she wouldn't drift into the other ship; and in the midst of all the rowdy-dow we were told that if we liked we might go on board the English vessel immediately.

"Miss Minturn and her party instantly accepted this invitation, and although under ordinary circumstances I would have remained to see for myself what these people found out, I felt a relief in the thought of leaving that vessel which is impossible for me to express, and I got into the boat with the others.

"We were treated very handsomely on board the English vessel, which was a mail steamship, at that time in the employment of the English Government. I told my story at least half a dozen times, sometimes to the officers and sometimes to the men, and whether they believed me or not, I don't think anyone ever created a greater sensation with a story of the sea.

"In an hour or so the officer in charge of the operations on the *General Brooks* came aboard. As he passed me on his way to the captain, he said, 'We found your Water-devil, my man.' 'And he truly had us in tow?' I cried. 'Yes, you are perfectly correct,' he said and went on to make his report to the captain."

"Now, then," said the blacksmith, "I suppose we are going to get to the p'int. What did he report?"

"I didn't hear his report," said the marine, "but everybody

soon knew what had happened to our unlucky vessel, and I can give you the whole story of it. The *General Brooks* sailed from San Francisco to Calcutta, with a cargo of stored electricity, contained in large, strongly made boxes. This I knew nothing about, not being in the habit of inquiring into cargoes. Well, in some way or other, which I don't understand, not being a scientific man myself, a magnetic connection was formed between these boxes and also, if I got the story straight, between them and the iron hull of our vessel, so that it became, in fact, an enormous floating magnet, one of the biggest things of the kind on record. I have an idea that this magnetic condition was the cause of the trouble to our machinery; every separate part of it was probably turned to a magnet, and they all stuck together."

"Mr. Cardly," said Mr. Harberry to the schoolmaster, "I do not suppose you have given much attention to the study of commerce and therefore are not prepared to give us any information in regard to stored electricity as an article of export from this country; but perhaps you can tell us what stored electricity is and how it is put into boxes."

"In regard to the transportation," answered the schoolmaster, speaking a little slowly, "of encased electric potency, I cannot—"

"Oh, bless me!" interrupted the marine. "That is all simple enough; you can store electricity and send it all over the world, if you like; in places like Calcutta, I think it must be cheaper to buy it than to make it. They use it as a motive power for sewing machines, apple parers, and it can be used in a lot of ways, such as digging postholes and churning butter. When the stored electricity in a box is all used up, all you have to do is to connect a fresh box with your machinery, and there you are, ready to start again. There was nothing strange about our cargo. It was the electricity leaking out and uniting itself and the iron ship into a sort of conglomerate magnet that was out of the way."

"Mr. Cardly," said Mr. Harberry, "if an iron ship were magnetized in that manner, wouldn't it have a deranging effect upon the needle of the compass?"

The marine did not give the schoolmaster time to make answer. "Generally speaking," said he, "that sort of thing would interfere with keeping the vessel on its proper course, but with us it didn't make any difference at all. The greater part of the ship was in front of the binnacle where they keep the compass, and so the needle naturally pointed that way, and as we were going north before a south wind, it was all right.

"Being a floating magnet, of course, did not prevent our sailing, so we went along well enough until we came to longitude 90°, latitude 15° north. Now it so happened that a telegraphic cable, which had been laid down by the British Government to establish communication between Madras and Rangoon, had broken some time before, and not very far from this point.

"Now you can see for yourselves that when an enormous mass of magnetic iron, in the shape of the *General Brooks,* came sailing along there, the part of that cable which lay under us was so attracted by such a powerful and irresistible force that its broken end raised itself from the bottom of the bay and reached upward until it touched our ship, when it laid itself along our keel, to which it instantly became fastened as firmly as if it had been bolted and riveted there. Then, as the rest of this part of the cable was on the bottom of the bay all the way to Madras, of course we had to stop; that's simple enough. That's the way the Water-devil held us fast in one spot for two days.

"The British Government determined not to repair this broken cable, but to take it up and lay down a better one; so they chartered a large steamer and fitted her up with engines and a big drum that they used for that sort of thing and set her to work to wind up the Madras end of the broken cable. She had been at this business a good while before we were caught by the other end, and when they got near enough to us for their engines to be able to take up the slack from the bottom between us and them, then of course they pulled upon us, and we began to move. And when they lay to for the night and stopped the winding business, of course we stopped, and the stretch of cable between the two ships had no effect upon us, except when the big mail steamer happened to move this way or that, as they kept her head to the wind; and that's the way we lay quiet all night except when we got our shocks.

"When they set the drum going again in the morning, it wasn't long before they wound us near enough for them to see us, which they would have done sooner if my lights hadn't gone out so early in the evening."

"And that," said the blacksmith, with a somewhat severe expression on his face, "is all that you have to tell about your wonderful Water-devil!"

"All!" said the marine. "I should say it was quite enough, and nothing could be more wonderful than what really happened. A Water-devil is one of two things: he is real or he's not real. If he's not real, he's no more than an ordinary spook or ghost and is not to be practically considered. If he's real, then he's an alive animal and can be put in a class with other animals and described in books, because even if nobody sees him, the scientific men know how he must be constructed, and then he's no more than a great many other wonderful things, which we can see alive, stuffed, or in plaster casts.

"But if you want to put your mind upon something really wonderful, just think of a snakelike rope of wire, five or six hundred miles long, lying down at the very bottom of the great Bay of Bengal, with no more life in it than there is in a ten-penny nail.

"Then imagine that long, dead wire snake to be suddenly filled with life and to know that there was something far up above it, on the surface of the water, that it wants to reach up to and touch. Think of it lifting and flapping its broken end, and then imagine it raising yard after yard of itself up and up, through the solemn water, more and more of it lifting itself from the bottom, curling itself backward and forward as it rises higher and higher, until at last, with a sudden jump that must have ripped a mile or more of it from the bottom, it claps its end against the thing it wants to touch and which it can neither see nor hear nor smell, but which it knows is there. Could there be anything in this world more wonderful than that?

"And then, if that isn't enough of a wonder, think of the Rangoon end of that cable squirming and wriggling and stretching itself out toward our ship but not being able to reach us on account of a want of slack—just as alive as the Madras part of the cable, and just as savage and frantic to get up to us and lay hold of us—and then, after our vessel had been gradually pulled away from it, think of this other part getting weaker and weaker, minute by minute, until it falls flat on the bay, as dead as any other iron thing!"

The marine ceased to speak, and Mrs. Fryker heaved a sigh.

"It makes me shiver to think of all that down so deep," she said; "but I must say I am disappointed."

"In what way?" asked the marine.

"A Water-devil," said she, "as big as six whales and with a funnelly mouth to suck in people is different; but, of course, after all, it was better as it was."

"Look here," said the blacksmith, "what became of the girl? I wanted her finished up long ago, and you haven't done it yet."

"Miss Minturn, you mean," said the marine.

"Well, there is not much to say about her. Things happened in the usual way. When the danger was all over, when she had other people to depend upon besides me and we were on board a fine steamer, with a lot of handsomely dressed naval officers and going comfortably to Madras, of course she thought no more of the humble sea soldier who once stood between her and—nobody knew what. In fact, the only time she spoke to me after we got on board the English steamer, she made me feel, although she didn't say it in words, that she was not at all obliged to me for supposing that she would have been scared to death if I had told her about the Water-devil."

"I suppose," said the blacksmith, "by the time you got back to your ship you had overstayed your leave of absence a good while. Did your captain let you off when you told him this story of the new-fashioned Water-devil?"

The marine smiled. "I never went back to the *Apache*," he said. "When I arrived at Madras, I found that she had sailed from Calcutta. It was, of course, useless for me to endeavor to follow her, and I therefore concluded to give up the marine service for a time and go into another line of business, about which it is too late to tell you now."

"Mr. Cardly," said Mr. Harberry to the schoolmaster, "have you ever read that the British Government has a submarine cable from Madras to Rangoon?"

The marine took it upon himself to answer this question. "The cable of which I spoke to you," he said, "was taken up, as I told you, and I never heard that another one was laid. But it is getting late, and I think I will go to bed; I have a long walk before me tomorrow." So saying, he rose, put his pipe upon the mantelpiece, and bade the company good night. As he did so, he fixed his eyes on the blacksmith's daughter, but that young lady did not look at him; she was busily reading the weekly newspaper, which her father had left upon the table.

Mr. Harberry now rose, preparatory to going home; and as he buttoned up his coat, he looked from one to another of the little group, and remarked, "I have often heard that marines are a class of men who are considered as fit subjects to tell tough stories to, but it strikes me that the time has come when the tables are beginning to be turned."

The Casting Away of Mrs.
Lecks and Mrs. Aleshine

---

1. Mrs. *Lecks* and Mrs. *Aleshine*
Desert a *Sinking* Steamer

I WAS ON MY WAY from San Francisco to Yokohama, when in a very desultory and gradual manner, I became acquainted with Mrs. Lecks and Mrs. Aleshine. The steamer, on which I was making a moderately rapid passage toward the land of the legended fan and the lacquered box, carried a fair complement of passengers, most of whom were Americans; and among these my attention was attracted from the very first of the voyage to two middle-aged women who appeared to me very unlike the ordinary traveler or tourist. At first sight they might have been taken for farmers' wives who, for some unusual reason, had determined to make a voyage across the Pacific; but on closer observation one would have been more apt to suppose that they belonged to the families of prosperous tradesmen in some little country town, where, besides the arts of rural housewifery, there would be opportunities of becoming acquainted in some degree with the ways and manners of the outside world. They were not of that order of persons who generally take first-class passages on steamships, but the stateroom occupied by Mrs. Lecks and Mrs. Aleshine was one of the best in the vessel; and although they kept very much to themselves and showed no desire for the company or notice of the other passengers, they evidently considered themselves quite as good as anyone else and with as much right to voyage to any part of the world in any manner or style which pleased them.

Mrs. Lecks was a rather tall woman, large-boned and muscular, and her well-browned countenance gave indications of that conviction of superiority which gradually grows up in the minds of those who for a long time have had absolute control of the destinies of a state or the multifarious affairs of a country household. Mrs. Aleshine was somewhat younger than her friend, somewhat shorter, and a great deal fatter. She had the same air of reliance upon her individual worth that characterized Mrs. Lecks, but there was a certain geniality about her which indicated that she would have a good deal of forbearance for those who never had had the opportunity or the ability of becoming the thoroughly good housewife which she was herself.

These two worthy dames spent the greater part of their time on deck, where they always sat together in a place at the stern of the vessel which was well sheltered from wind and weather. As they sat thus, they were generally employed in knitting, although this occupation did not prevent them from keeping up what seemed to me, as I passed them in my walks about the deck, a continuous conversation. From a question which Mrs. Lecks once asked me about a distant sail, our acquaintance began. There was no one on board for whose society I particularly cared, and as there was something quaint and odd about these countrywomen on the ocean which interested me, I was glad to vary my solitary promenades by an occasional chat with them. They were not at all backward in giving me information about themselves. They were both widows, and Mrs. Aleshine was going out to Japan to visit a son who had a position there in a mercantile house. Mrs. Lecks had no children and was accompanying her friend because, as she said, she would not allow Mrs. Aleshine to make such a voyage as that by herself and because, being quite able to do so, she did not know why she should not see the world as well as other people.

These two friends were not educated women. They made frequent mistakes in their grammar, and a good deal of Middle States provincialism showed itself in their pronunciation and expressions. But although they brought many of their rural ideas to sea with them, they possessed a large share of that common sense which is available anywhere, and they frequently made use of it in a manner which was very amusing to me. I think, also, that they found in me a quarry of information concerning nautical matters, foreign countries, and my own affairs, the working of which helped to make us very good ship friends.

Our steamer touched at the Sandwich Islands; and it was a little more than two days after we left Honolulu that, about nine o'clock in the evening, we had the misfortune to come into collision with an eastern-bound vessel. The fault was entirely due to the other ship, the lookout on which, although the night was rather dark and foggy, could easily have seen our lights in time to avoid collision, if he had not been asleep or absent from his post. Be this as it may, this vessel, which appeared to be a small steamer, struck us with great force near our bows, and then, backing, disappeared into the fog, and we never saw or heard of her again. The general opinion was that she was injured very much more than we were and that she probably sank not very long after the accident; for when the fog cleared away, about an hour afterward, nothing could be seen of her lights.

As it usually happens on occasions of accidents at sea, the damage to our vessel was at first reported to be slight; but it was soon discovered that our injuries were serious and, indeed, disastrous. The hull of our steamer had been badly shattered on the port bow, and the water came in at a most alarming rate. For nearly two hours the crew and many of the passengers worked at the pumps, and everything possible was done to stop the enormous leak; but all labor to save the vessel was found to be utterly unavailing, and a little before midnight the captain announced that it was impossible to keep the steamer afloat and that we must all take to the boats. The night was now clear, the stars were bright, and as there was but little wind, the sea was comparatively smooth. With all these advantages, the captain assured us that there was no reason to apprehend danger, and he thought that by noon of the following day we could easily make a small inhabited island, where we could be sheltered and cared for until we should be taken off by some passing vessel.

There was plenty of time for all necessary preparations, and these were made with much order and subordination. Some of the ladies among the cabin passengers were greatly frightened and inclined to be hysterical. There were pale faces also among the gentlemen. But everybody obeyed the captain's orders, and all prepared themselves for the transfer to the boats. The first officer came among us and told each of us what boats we were to take and where we were to place ourselves on deck. I was assigned to a large boat which was to be principally occupied by steerage passengers; and as I came up from my stateroom, where I had gone to secure my money and some portable valuables, I met on the companion-way Mrs. Lecks and Mrs. Aleshine, who expressed considerable dissatisfaction when they found that I was not going in the boat with them. They, however, hurried below, and I went on deck, where in about ten minutes I was joined by Mrs. Lecks, who apparently had been looking for me. She told me she had something very particular to say to me and conducted me toward the stern of the vessel, where, behind one of the deckhouses, we found Mrs. Aleshine.

"Look here," said Mrs. Lecks, leading me to the rail and pointing downward. "Do you see that boat there? It has been let down, and there is nobody in it. The boat on the other side has just gone off, full to the brim. I never saw so many people crowded into a boat. The other ones will be just as packed, I expect. I don't see why we shouldn't take this empty boat, now we've got a chance, instead of squeezin' ourselves into those crowded ones. If any of the other people come afterward, why, we shall have our choice of seats, and that's considerable of a p'int, I should say, in a time like this."

"That's so," said Mrs. Aleshine; "and me and Mrs. Lecks would 'a' got right in when we saw the boat was empty, if we hadn't been afraid to be there without any man, for it might have floated off, and neither of us don't know nothin' about rowin'. And then Mrs. Lecks, she thought of you, supposin' a young man who knew so much about the sea would know how to row."

"Oh, yes," said I; "but I cannot imagine why this boat should have been left empty. I see a keg of water in it and the oars and some tin cans, and so I suppose it has been made ready for somebody. Will you wait here a minute until I run forward and see how things are going on there?"

Amidships and forward I saw that there was some confusion among the people who were not yet in their boats, and I found that there was to be rather more crowding than at first was expected. People who had supposed that they were to go in a certain boat found there no place and were hurrying to other boats. It now became plain to me that no time should be lost in getting into the small boat which Mrs. Lecks had pointed out and which was probably reserved for some favored persons, as the officers were keeping the people forward and amidships, the other stern boat having already departed. But as I acknowledged no reason why anyone should be regarded with more favor than myself and the two women who were waiting for me, I slipped quietly aft and joined Mrs. Lecks and Mrs. Aleshine.

"We must get in as soon as we can," said I, in a low voice, "for this boat may be discovered, and then there will be a rush for it. I suspect it may have been reserved for the captain and some of the officers, but we have as much right in it as they."

"And more too," replied Mrs. Lecks; "for we had nothin' to do with the steerin' and smashin'."

"But how are we goin' to get down there?" said Mrs. Aleshine. "There's no steps."

"That is true," said I. "I shouldn't wonder if this boat is to be taken forward when the others are filled. We must scramble down as well as we can by the tackle at the bow and stern. I'll get in first and keep her close to the ship's side."

"That's goin' to be a scratchy business," said Mrs. Lecks, "and

I'm of the opinion we ought to wait till the ship has sunk a little more, so we'll be nearer to the boat."

"It won't do to wait," said I, "or we shall not get in it at all."

"And goodness gracious!" exclaimed Mrs. Aleshine, "I can't stand here and feel the ship sinkin' cold-blooded under me till we've got where we can make an easy jump!"

"Very well, then," said Mrs. Lecks, "we won't wait. But the first thing to be done is for each one of us to put on one of these life preservers. Two of them I brought from Mrs. Aleshine's and my cabin, and the other one I got next door, where the people had gone off and left it on the floor. I thought if anythin' happened on the way to the island, these would give us a chance to look about us; but it seems to me we'll need 'em more gettin' down them ropes than anywhere else. I did intend puttin' on two myself to make up for Mrs. Aleshine's fat; but you must wear one of 'em, sir, now that you are goin' to join the party."

As I knew that two life preservers would not be needed by Mrs. Lecks and would greatly inconvenience her, I accepted the one offered me but declined to put it on until it should be necessary, as it would interfere with my movements.

"Very well," said Mrs. Lecks, "if you think you are safe in gettin' down without it. But Mrs. Aleshine and me will put ours on before we begin sailor-scramblin'. We know how to do it, for we tried 'em on soon after we started from San Francisco. And now, Barb'ry Aleshine, are you sure you've got everythin' you want? for it'll be no use thinkin' about anythin' you've forgot after the ship has sunk out of sight."

"There's nothin' else I can think of," said Mrs. Aleshine; "at least, nothin' I can carry; and so I suppose we may as well begin, for your talk of the ship sinkin' under our feet gives me a sort o' feelin' like an oyster creepin' up and down my back."

Mrs. Lecks looked over the side at the boat, into which I had already descended. "I'll go first, Barb'ry Aleshine," said she, "and show you how."

The sea was quiet, and the steamer had already sunk so much that Mrs. Lecks's voice sounded frightfully near me, although she spoke in a low tone.

"Watch me," said she to her companion. "I'm goin' to do just as he did, and you must follow in the same way."

So saying, she stepped on a bench by the rail; then, with one foot on the rail itself, she seized the ropes which hung from one of the davits to the bow of the boat. She looked down for a moment, and then she drew back.

"It's no use," she said. "We must wait until she sinks more, and I can get in easier."

This remark made me feel nervous. I did not know at what moment there might be a rush for this boat, nor when, indeed, the steamer might go down. The boat amidships on our side had rowed away some minutes before, and through the darkness I could distinguish another boat, near the bows, pushing off. It would be too late now for us to try to get into any other boat, and I did not feel that there was time enough for me to take this one to a place where the two women could more easily descend to her. Standing upright, I urged them not to delay.

"You see," said I, "I can reach you as soon as you swing yourself off the ropes, and I'll help you down."

"If you're sure you can keep us from comin' down too sudden, we'll try it," said Mrs. Lecks; "but I'd as soon be drowned as to get to an island with a broken leg. And as to Mrs. Aleshine, if she was to slip she'd go slam through that boat to the bottom of the sea. Now, then, be ready! I'm comin' down."

So saying, she swung herself off, and she was then so near me that I was able to seize her and make the rest of her descent comparatively easy. Mrs. Aleshine proved to be a more difficult subject. Even after I had a firm grasp of her capacious waist, she refused to let go the ropes, for fear that she might drop into the ocean instead of the boat. But the reproaches of Mrs. Lecks and the downward weight of myself made her loosen her nervous grip;

and although we came very near going overboard together, I safely placed her on one of the thwarts.

I now unhooked the tackle from the stern; but before casting off at the bow I hesitated, for I did not wish to desert any of those who might be expecting to embark in this boat. But I could hear no approaching footsteps, and from my position close to the side of the steamer, I could see nothing. Therefore I cast off, and taking the oars, I pushed away and rowed to a little distance, where I could get whatever view was possible of the deck of the steamer. Seeing no forms moving about, I called out, and receiving no answer, I shouted again at the top of my voice. I waited for nearly a minute, and hearing nothing and seeing nothing, I became convinced that no one was left on the vessel.

"They are all gone," said I, "and we will pull after them as fast as we can."

And I began to row toward the bow of the steamer, in the direction which the other boats had taken.

"It's a good thing you can row," said Mrs. Lecks, settling herself comfortably in the stern sheets, "for what Mrs. Aleshine and me would ha' done with them oars I am sure I don't know."

"I'd never have got into this boat," said Mrs. Aleshine, "if Mr. Craig hadn't been here."

"No, indeed," replied her friend. "You'd ha' gone to the bottom, hangin' for dear life to them ropes."

When I had rounded the bow of the steamer, which appeared to me to be rapidly settling in the water, I perceived at no great distance several lights, which of course belonged to the other boats, and I rowed as hard as I could, hoping to catch up with them, or at least to keep sufficiently near. It might be my duty to take off some of the people who had crowded into the other boats, probably supposing that this one had been loaded and gone. How such a mistake could have taken place I could not divine, and it was not my business to do so. Quite certain that no one was left on the sinking steamer, all I had to do was to row after the other boats and to overtake them as soon as possible. I thought it would not take me very long to do this, but after rowing for half an hour, Mrs. Aleshine remarked that the lights seemed as far off, if not farther, than when we first started after them. Turning, I saw that this was the case and was greatly surprised. With only two passengers I ought soon to have come up with those heavily laden boats. But after I had thought over it a little, I considered that as each of them was probably pulled by half a dozen stout sailors, it was not so very strange that they should make as good or better headway than I did.

It was not very long after this that Mrs. Lecks said that she thought that the lights on the other boats must be going out and that this, most probably, was due to the fact that the sailors had forgotten to fill their lanterns before they started. "That sort of thing often happens," she said, "when people leave a place in a hurry."

But when I turned around and peered over the dark waters, it was quite plain to me that it was not want of oil but increased distance which made those lights so dim. I could now perceive but three of them, and as the surface was agitated only by a gentle swell, I could not suppose that any of them were hidden from our view by waves. We were being left behind, that was certain, and all I could do was to row on as long and as well as I could in the direction which the other boats had taken. I had been used to rowing and thought I pulled a good oar, and I certainly did not expect to be left behind in this way.

"I don't believe this boat has been emptied out since the last rain," said Mrs. Aleshine, "for my feet are wet, though I didn't notice it before."

At this I shipped my oars and began to examine the boat. The bottom was covered with a movable floor of slats, and as I put my hand down, I could feel the water welling up between the slats. The flooring was in sections, and lifting the one beneath me, I felt under it and put my hand into six or eight inches of water.

The exact state of the case was now as plain to me as if it had been posted up on a bulletin board. This boat had been found to be unseaworthy, and its use had been forbidden, all the people having been crowded into the others. This had caused confusion at the last moment, and, of course, we were supposed to be on some one of the other boats.

And now here was I, in the middle of the Pacific Ocean, in a leaky boat, with two middle-aged women!

"Anythin' the matter with the floor?" asked Mrs. Lecks.

I let the section fall back into its place and looked aft. By the starlight I could see that my two companions had each fixed upon me a steadfast gaze. They evidently felt that something was the matter and wanted to know what it was. I did not hesitate for a moment to inform them. They appeared to me to be women whom it would be neither advisable nor possible to deceive in a case like this.

"This boat has a leak in it," I said. "There is a lot of water in her already, and that is the reason we have got along so slowly."

"And that is why," said Mrs. Aleshine, "it was left empty. We ought to have known better than to expect to have a whole boat just for three of us. It would have been much more sensible, I think, if we had tried to squeeze into one of the others."

"Now, Barb'ry Aleshine," said Mrs. Lecks, "don't you begin findin' fault with good fortune when it comes to you. Here we've got a comfortable boat, with room enough to set easy and stretch out if we want to. If the water is comin' in, what we've got to do is to get it out again just as fast as we can. What's the best way to do that, Mr. Craig?"

"We must bail her out, and lose no time about it," said I. "If I can find the leak, I may be able to stop it."

I now looked about for something to bail with, and the two women aided actively in the search. I found one leather scoop in the bow; but as it was well that we should all go to work, I took two tin cans that had been put in by someone who had begun to provision the boat and proceeded to cut the tops from them with my jackknife.

"Don't lose what's in 'em," said Mrs. Lecks; "that is, if it's anythin' we'd be likely to want to eat. If it's tomatoes, pour it into the sea, for nobody ought to eat tomatoes put up in tins."

I hastily passed the cans to Mrs. Lecks, and I saw her empty the contents of one into the sea and those of the other on a newspaper which she took from her pocket and placed in the stern.

I pulled up the movable floor and threw it overboard and then began to bail.

"I thought," said Mrs. Aleshine, "that they always had pumps for leaks."

"Now, Barb'ry Aleshine," said Mrs. Lecks, "just gether yourself up on one of them seats, and go to work. The less talkin' we do and the more scoopin', the better it'll be for us."

I soon perceived that it would have been difficult to find two more valuable assistants in the bailing of a boat than Mrs. Lecks and Mrs. Aleshine. They were evidently used to work, and were able to accommodate themselves to the unusual circumstances in which they were placed. We threw out the water very rapidly, and every little while I stopped bailing and felt about to see if I could discover where it came in. As these attempts met with no success, I gave them up after a time, and set about bailing with new vigor, believing that if we could get the boat nearly dry I should surely be able to find the leak.

But, after working half an hour more, I found that the job would be a long one; and if we all worked at once, we would all be tired out at once, and that might be disastrous. Therefore I proposed that we should take turns in resting, and Mrs. Aleshine was ordered to stop work for a time. After this Mrs. Lecks took a rest, and when she went to work, I stopped bailing and began again to search for the leak.

For about two hours we worked in this way, and then I concluded it was useless to continue any longer this vain exertion.

With three of us bailing we were able to keep the water at the level we first found it; but with only two at work, it slightly gained upon us, so that now there was more water in the boat than when we first discovered it. The boat was an iron one, and the leak in it I could neither find nor remedy. It had probably been caused by the warping of the metal under a hot sun, an accident which, I am told, frequently occurs to iron boats. The little craft, which would have been a lifeboat had its air boxes remained intact, was now probably leaking from stem to stern; and in searching for the leak without the protection of the flooring, my weight had doubtless assisted in opening the seams, for it was quite plain that the water was now coming in more rapidly than it did at first. We were very tired, and even Mrs. Lecks, who had all along counseled us to keep at work and not to waste one breath in talking, now admitted that it was of no use to try to get the water out of that boat.

It had been some hours since I had used the oars, but whether we had drifted or remained where we were when I stopped rowing, of course I could not know; but this mattered very little; our boat was slowly sinking beneath us, and it could make no difference whether we went down in one spot or another. I sat and racked my brain to think what could be done in this fearful emergency. To bail any longer was useless labor, and what else was there that we could do?

"When will it be time," asked Mrs. Lecks, "for us to put on the life preservers? When the water gets nearly to the seats?"

I answered that we should not wait any longer than that; but in my own mind I could not see any advantage in putting them on at all. Why should we wish to lengthen our lives by a few hours of helpless floating upon the ocean?

"Very good," said Mrs. Lecks; "I'll keep a watch on the water. One of them cans was filled with lobster, which would be more than likely to disagree with us, and I've throwed it out; but the other had baked beans in it, and the best thing we can do is to eat some of these right away. They are mighty nourishin' and will keep up strength as well as anythin', and then, as you said there's a keg of water in the boat, we can all take a drink of that, and it'll make us feel like new cre'tur's. You'll have to take the beans in your hands, for we've got no spoons nor forks."

Mrs. Lecks and Mrs. Aleshine were each curled up out of reach of the water, the first in the stern, and the other on the aft thwart. The day was now beginning to break, and we could see about us very distinctly. Before reaching out her hands to receive her beans, Mrs. Aleshine washed them in the water in the boat, remarking at the same time that she might as well make use of it since it was there. Having then wiped her hands on some part of her apparel, they were filled with beans from the newspaper held by Mrs. Lecks, and these were passed over to me. I was very hungry, and when I had finished my beans, I agreed with my companions that although they would have been a great deal better if heated up with butter, pepper, and salt, they were very comforting as they were. One of the empty cans was now passed to me, and after having been asked by Mrs. Lecks to rinse it out very carefully, we all satisfied our taste from the water in the keg.

"Cold baked beans and lukewarm water ain't exactly company vittles," said Mrs. Aleshine, "but there's many a poor wretch would be glad to get 'em."

I could not imagine any poor wretch who would be glad of the food together with the attending circumstances; but I did not say so.

"The water is just one finger from the bottom of the seat," said Mrs. Lecks, who had been stooping over to measure, "and it's time to put on the life preservers."

"Very good," said Mrs. Aleshine; "hand me mine."

Each of us now buckled on a life preserver, and as I did so, I stood up upon a thwart and looked about me. It was quite light now, and I could see for a long distance over the surface of the ocean, which was gently rolling in wide, smooth swells. As we rose upon the summit of one of these, I saw a dark spot upon the water, just on the edge of our near horizon. "Is that the steamer?" I thought. "And has she not yet sunk?"

At this there came to me a glimmering of courageous hope. If the steamer had remained afloat so long, it was probable that on account of watertight compartments, or for some other reason, her sinking had reached its limit, and that if we could get back to her, we might be saved. But, alas, how were we to get back to her? This boat would sink long, long before I could row that distance.

However, I soon proclaimed the news to my companions, whereupon Mrs. Aleshine prepared to stand upon a thwart and see for herself. But Mrs. Lecks restrained her.

"Don't make things worse, Barb'ry Aleshine," said she, "by tumblin' overboard. If we've got to go into the water, let us do it decently and in order. If that's the ship, Mr. Craig, don't you suppose we can float ourselves to it in some way?"

I replied that by the help of a life preserver a person who could swim might reach the ship.

"But neither of us can swim," said Mrs. Lecks, "for we've lived where the water was never more'n a foot deep, except in time of freshets, when there's no swimmin' for man or beast. But if we see you swim, perhaps we can follow, after a fashion. At any rate, we must do the best we can, and that's all there is to be done."

"The water now," remarked Mrs. Aleshine, "is so near to the bottom of my seat that I've got to stand up, tumble overboard or no."

"All right," remarked Mrs. Lecks; "we'd better all stand up and let the boat sink under us. That will save our jumpin' overboard or rollin' out any which way, which might be awkward."

"Goodness gracious me!" exclaimed Mrs. Aleshine. "You set the oysters creepin' over me again! First you talk of the ship sinkin' under us, and now it's the boat goin' to the bottom under our feet. Before any sinkin's to be done I'd ruther get out."

"Now, Barb'ry Aleshine," said Mrs. Lecks, "stand up straight, and don't talk so much. It'll be a great deal better to be let down gradual than to flop into the water all of a bunch."

"Very well," said Mrs. Aleshine; "it may be best to get used to it by degrees; but I must say I wish I was home."

As for me, I would have much preferred to jump overboard at once, instead of waiting in this cold-blooded manner; but as my companions had so far preserved their presence of mind, I did not wish to do anything which might throw them into a panic. I believed there would be no danger from the suction caused by the sinking of a small boat like this, and if we took care not to entangle ourselves with it in any way, we might as well follow Mrs. Lecks's advice as not. So we all stood up, Mrs. Lecks in the stern, I in the bow, and Mrs. Aleshine on a thwart between us. The last did not appear to have quite room enough for a steady footing, but, as she remarked, it did not matter very much, as the footing, broad or narrow, would not be there very long.

I am used to swimming and have never hesitated to take a plunge into river or ocean, but I must admit that it was very trying to my nerves to stand up this way and wait for a boat to sink beneath me. How the two women were affected I do not know. They said nothing, but their faces indicated that something disagreeable was about to happen and that the less that was said about it the better.

The boat had now sunk so much that the water was around Mrs. Aleshine's feet, her standing place being rather lower than ours. I made myself certain that there were no ropes nor any other means of entanglement near my companions or myself, and then I waited. There seemed to be a good deal of buoyancy in the bow and stern of the boat, and it was a frightfully long time in sinking. The suspense became so utterly unendurable that I was tempted to put one foot on the edge of the boat, and by tipping it, put an end to this nerve-rack; but I refrained, for I probably would throw the women off their balance, when they might fall against some part of the boat and do themselves a hurt. I had just relinquished this intention, when two little waves seemed to rise one on each side of Mrs. Aleshine, and gently flowing over the side of the boat, they flooded her feet with water.

"Hold your breaths!" I shouted. And now I experienced a sensation which must have been very like that which comes to a condemned criminal at the first indication of the pulling of the drop. Then there was a horrible sinking, a gurgle, and a swash, and the ocean over which I had been gazing appeared to rise up and envelop me.

In a moment, however, my head was out of the water, and looking hastily about me, I saw, close by, the heads and shoulders of Mrs. Lecks and Mrs. Aleshine. The latter was vigorously winking her eyes and blowing from her mouth some seawater that had got into it; but as soon as her eyes fell upon me, she exclaimed, "That was ever so much more suddint than I thought it was goin' to be!"

"Are you both all right?"

"I suppose I am," said Mrs. Aleshine, "but I never thought that a person with a life preserver on would go clean under the water."

"But since you've come up again, you ought to be satisfied," said Mrs. Lecks. "And now," she added, turning her face toward me, "which way ought we to try to swim? And have we got everythin' we want to take with us?"

"What we haven't got we can't get," remarked Mrs. Aleshine; "and as for swimmin', I expect I'm goin' to make a poor hand at it."

I had a hope, which was not quite strong enough to be a belief, that, supported by their life preservers, the two women might paddle themselves along; and that, by giving them in turn a helping hand, I might eventually get them to the steamer. There was a strong probability that I would not succeed, but I did not care to think of that.

I now swam in front of my companions and endeavored to instruct them in the best method of propelling themselves with their

*She plied the oar as if it
had been the handle of a broom.*

arms and their hands. If they succeeded in this, I thought I would give them some further lessons in striking out with their feet. After watching me attentively, Mrs. Lecks did manage to move herself slowly through the smooth water, but poor Mrs. Aleshine could do nothing but splash.

"If there was anythin' to take hold of," she said to me, "I might get along; but I can't get any grip on the water, though you seem to do it well enough. Look there!" she added in a higher voice. "Isn't that an oar floatin' over there? If you can get that for me, I believe I can row myself much better than I can swim."

This seemed an odd idea, but I swam over to the floating oar and brought it her. I was about to show her how she could best use it, but she declined my advice.

"If I do it at all," she said, "I must do it in my own way." And taking the oar in her strong hands, she began to ply it on the water very much in the way in which she would handle a broom. At first she dipped the blade too deeply, but, correcting this error, she soon began to paddle herself along at a slow but steady rate.

"Capital!" I cried. "You do that admirably!"

"Anybody who's swept as many rooms as I have," she said, "ought to be able to handle anythin' that can be used like a broom."

"Isn't there another oar?" cried Mrs. Lecks, who had now been left a little distance behind us. "If there is, I want one."

Looking about me, I soon discovered another floating oar and brought it to Mrs. Lecks, who, after holding it in various positions, so as to get "the hang of it," as she said, soon began to use it with as much skill as that shown by her friend. If either of them had been obliged to use an oar in the ordinary way, I fear they would have had a bad time of it; but, considering the implement in the light of a broom, its use immediately became familiar to them, and they got on remarkably well.

I now took a position a little in advance of my companions, and as I swam slowly, they were easily able to keep up with me. Mrs.

Aleshine, being so stout, floated much higher out of the water than either Mrs. Lecks or I, and this permitted her to use her oar with a great deal of freedom. Sometimes she would give such a vigorous brush to the water that she would turn herself almost entirely around, but after a little practice she learned to avoid undue efforts of this kind.

I was not positively sure that we were going in the right direction, for my position did not allow me to see very far over the water; but I remembered that when I was standing up in the boat and made my discovery, the sun was just about to rise in front of me, while the dark spot on the ocean lay to my left. Judging, therefore, from the present position of the sun, which was not very high, I concluded that we were moving toward the north and therefore in the right direction. How far off the steamer might be I had no idea, for I was not accustomed to judging distances at sea; but I believed that if we were careful of our strength and if the ocean continued as smooth as it now was, we might eventually reach the vessel, provided she were yet afloat.

"After you are fairly in the water," said Mrs. Aleshine, as she swept along, although without the velocity which that phrase usually implies, "it isn't half so bad as I thought it would be. For one thing, it don't feel a bit salt, although I must say it tasted horribly that way when I first went into it."

"You didn't expect to find pickle brine, did you?" said Mrs. Lecks. "Though, if it was, I suppose we could float on it settin'."

"And as to bein' cold," said Mrs. Aleshine, "the part of me that's in is actually more comfortable than that which is out."

"There's one thing I would have been afraid of," said Mrs. Lecks, "if we hadn't made preparations for it, and that's sharks."

"Preparations!" I exclaimed. "How in the world did you prepare for sharks?"

"Easy enough," said Mrs. Lecks. "When we went down into our room to get ready to go away in the boats, we both put on black stockin's. I've read that sharks never bite colored people, although if they see a white man in the water, they'll snap him up as quick as lightnin'; and black stockin's was the nearest we could come to it. You see, I thought as like as not we'd have some sort of an upset before we got through."

"It's a great comfort," remarked Mrs. Aleshine, "and I'm very glad you thought of it, Mrs. Lecks. After this I shall make it a rule: black stockin's for sharks."

"I suppose in your case," said Mrs. Lecks, addressing me, "dark trousers will do as well."

To which I answered that I sincerely hoped they would.

"Another thing I'm thankful for," said Mrs. Aleshine, "is that I thought to put on a flannel skeert."

"And what's the good of it," said Mrs. Lecks, "when it's soppin' wet?"

"Flannel's flannel," replied her friend, "whether it's wet or dry; and if you'd had the rheumatism as much as I have, you'd know it."

To this Mrs. Lecks replied with a sniff and asked me how soon I thought we would get sight of the ship; for if we were going the wrong way and had to turn round and go back, it would certainly be very provoking.

I should have been happy indeed to be able to give a satisfactory answer to this question. Every time that we rose upon a swell I threw a rapid glance around the whole circle of the horizon; and at last, not a quarter of an hour after Mrs. Lecks's question, I was rejoiced to see, almost in the direction in which I supposed it ought to be, the dark spot which I had before discovered. I shouted the glad news, and as we rose again, my companions strained their eyes in the direction to which I pointed. They both saw it and were greatly satisfied.

"Now, then," said Mrs. Aleshine, "it seems as if there was somethin' to work for." And she began to sweep her oar with great vigor.

"If you want to tire yourself out before you get there, Barb'ry Aleshine," said Mrs. Lecks, "you'd better go on in that way. Now what I advise is that we stop rowin' altogether and have somethin' to eat; for I'm sure we need it to keep up our strength."

"Eat!" I cried. "What are you going to eat? Do you expect to catch fish?"

"And eat 'em raw?" said Mrs. Lecks. "I should think not. But do you suppose, Mr. Craig, that Mrs. Aleshine and me would go off and leave that ship without takin' somethin' to eat by the way? Let's all gether here in a bunch and see what sort of a meal we can make. And now, Barb'ry Aleshine, if you lay your oar down there on the water, I recommend you to tie it to one of your bonnet strings, or it'll be floatin' away, and you won't get it again."

As she said this, Mrs. Lecks put her right hand down into the water and fumbled about, apparently in search of a pocket. I could not but smile as I thought of the condition of food when, for an hour or more, it had been a couple of feet under the surface of the ocean; but my ideas on the subject were entirely changed when I saw Mrs. Lecks hold up in the air two German sausages and shake the briny drops from their smooth and glittering surfaces.

"There's nothin'," she said, "like sausages for shipwreck and that kind o' thing. They're very sustainin', and bein' covered with a tight skin, water can't get at 'em, no matter how you carry 'em. I wouldn't bring these out in the boat, because, havin' the beans, we might as well eat them. Have you a knife about you, Mr. Craig?"

I produced a dripping jackknife, and after the open blade had been waved in the air to dry it a little, Mrs. Lecks proceeded to divide one of the sausages, handing the other to me to hold meanwhile.

"Now don't go eatin' sausages without bread, if you don't want 'em to give you dyspepsy," said Mrs. Aleshine, who was tugging at a submarine pocket.

"I'm very much afraid your bread is all soaked," said Mrs. Lecks.

To which her friend replied that that remained to be seen, and forthwith produced, with a splash, a glass preserve-jar with a metal top.

"I saw this nearly empty, as I looked into the ship's pantry, and I stuffed into it all the soft biscuits it would hold. There was some sort of jam left at the bottom, so that the one who gets the last biscuit will have somethin' of a little spread on it. And now, Mrs. Lecks," she continued triumphantly, as she unscrewed the top, "that rubber ring has kept 'em as dry as chips. I'm mighty glad of it, for I had trouble enough gettin' this jar into my pocket and gettin' it out, too, for that matter."

Floating thus, with our hands and shoulders above the water, we made a very good meal from the sausages and soft biscuit.

"Barb'ry Aleshine," said Mrs. Lecks, as her friend proceeded to cut the second sausage, "don't you lay that knife down, when you've done with it, as if't was an oar; for if you do, it'll sink, as like as not, about six miles. I've read that the ocean is as deep as that in some places."

"Goodness gracious me!" exclaimed Mrs. Aleshine, "I hope we are not over one of them deep spots."

"There's no knowin'," said Mrs. Lecks, "but if it's more comfortin' to think it's shallerer, we'll make up our minds that way. Now, then," she continued, "we'll finish off this meal with a little somethin' to drink. I'm not given to takin' spirits, but I never travel without a little whisky, ready mixed with water, to take if it should be needed."

So saying, she produced from one of her pockets a whisky flask tightly corked, and of its contents we each took a sip, Mrs. Aleshine remarking that, leaving out being chilled or colicky, we were never likely to need it more than now.

Thus refreshed and strengthened, Mrs. Lecks and Mrs. Aleshine took up their oars, while I swam slightly in advance, as before. When, with occasional intermissions of rest and a good deal of desultory conversation, we had swept and swam for about an hour, Mrs. Lecks suddenly exclaimed, "I can see that thing ever so much plainer now, and I don't believe it's a ship at all. To me it looks like bushes."

"You're mighty long-sighted without your specs," said Mrs. Aleshine, "and I'm not sure but what you're right."

For ten minutes or more I had been puzzling over the shape of the dark spot, which was now nearly all the time in sight. Its peculiar form had filled me with a dreadful fear that it was the steamer, bottom upward, although I knew enough about nautical matters to have no good reason to suppose that this could be the case. I am not farsighted, but when Mrs. Lecks suggested bushes, I gazed at the distant object with totally different ideas and soon began to believe that it was not a ship, either right side up or wrong side up, but that it might be an island. This belief I proclaimed to my companions, and for some time we all worked with increased energy in the desire to get near enough to make ourselves certain in regard to this point.

"As true as I'm standin' here," said Mrs. Lecks, who, although she could not read without spectacles, had remarkably good sight at long range, "them is trees and bushes that I see before me, though they do seem to be growin' right out of the water."

"There's an island under them; you may be sure of that!" I cried. "Isn't this ever so much better than a sinking ship?"

"I'm not so sure about that," said Mrs. Aleshine. "I'm used to the ship, and as long as it didn't sink, I'd prefer it. There's plenty to eat on board of it and good beds to sleep on, which is more than can be expected on a little bushy place like that ahead of us. But then the ship might sink all of a suddint, beds, vittles, and all."

"Do you suppose that is the island the other boats went to?" asked Mrs. Lecks.

This question I had already asked of myself. I had been told that the island to which the captain intended to take his boats lay about thirty miles south of the point where we left the steamer.

Now I knew very well that we had not come thirty miles and had reason to believe, moreover, that the greater part of the progress we had made had been toward the north. It was not at all probable that the position of this island was unknown to our captain; and it must, therefore, have been considered by him as an unsuitable place for the landing of his passengers. There might be many reasons for this unsuitableness: the island might be totally barren and desolate; it might be the abode of unpleasant natives; and, more important than anything else, it was, in all probability, a spot where steamers never touched.

But, whatever its disadvantages, I was most wildly desirous to reach it; more so, I believe, than either of my companions. I do not mean that they were not sensible of their danger and desirous to be freed from it; but they were women who had probably had a rough time of it during a great part of their lives, and on emerging from their little circle of rural experiences, accepted with equanimity and almost as a matter of course, the rough times which come to people in the great outside world.

"I do not believe," I said, in answer to Mrs. Lecks, "that that is the island to which the captain would have taken us; but, whatever it is, it is dry land, and we must get there as soon as we can."

"That's true," said Mrs. Aleshine, "for I'd like to have ground nearer to my feet than six miles; and if we don't find anything to eat and any place to sleep when we get there, it's no more than can be said of the place where we are now."

"You're too particular, Barb'ry Aleshine," said Mrs. Lecks, "about your comforts. If you find the ground too hard to sleep on when you get there, you can put on your life preserver and go to bed in the water."

"Very good," said Mrs. Aleshine; "and if these islands are made of coral, as I've heard they are, and if they're as full of small p'ints as some coral I've got at home, you'll be glad to take a berth by me, Mrs. Lecks."

I counseled my companions to follow me as rapidly as possible, and we all pushed vigorously forward. When we had approached near enough to the island to see what sort of place it really was, we perceived that it was a low-lying spot, apparently covered with verdure, and surrounded, as far as we could see as we rose on the swells, by a rocky reef, against which a tolerably high surf was running.

I knew enough of the formation of these coral islands to suppose that within this reef was a lagoon of smooth water, into which there were openings through the rocky barrier. It was necessary to try to find one of these, for it would be difficult and perhaps dangerous to attempt to land through the surf.

Before us we could see a continuous line of white-capped breakers, and so I led my little party to the right, hoping that we would soon see signs of an opening in the reef.

We swam and paddled, however, for a long time, and still the surf rolled menacingly on the rocks before us. We were now as close to the island as we could approach with safety, and I determined to circumnavigate it, if necessary, before I would attempt, with these two women, to land upon that jagged reef. At last we perceived, at no great distance before us, a spot where there seemed to be no breakers; and when we reached it, we found, to our unutterable delight, that here was smooth water flowing through a wide opening in the reef. The rocks were piled up quite high, and the reef, at this point at least, was a wide one, but as we neared the opening, we found that it narrowed very soon and made a turn to the left, so that from the outside we could not see into the lagoon.

I swam into this smooth water, followed closely by Mrs. Lecks and Mrs. Aleshine, who, however, soon became unable to use their oars, owing to the proximity of the rocks. Dropping these useful implements, they managed to paddle after me with their hands, and they were as much astonished as I was when, just after making the slight turn, we found stretched across the narrow passage a great iron bar about eight or ten inches above the water. A little farther on, two or three feet above the water, another iron bar extended from one rocky wall to the other. Without uttering a word I examined the lower bar and found one end of it fastened by means of a huge padlock to a great staple driven into the rock. The lock was securely wrapped in what appeared to be tarred canvas. A staple through an eyehole in the bar secured the other end of it to the rocks.

"These bars were put here," I exclaimed, "to keep out boats, whether at high or low water. You see they can only be thrown out of the way by taking off the padlocks."

"They won't keep us out," said Mrs. Lecks, "for we can duck under. I suppose whoever put 'em here didn't expect anybody to arrive on life preservers."

2. The *Ladies Manage* a *Desert Island* and a *Fellow Castaway*

ADOPTING MRS. LECKS's suggestion, I "ducked" my head under the bar and passed to the other side of it. Mrs. Lecks, with but little trouble, followed my example; but Mrs. Aleshine, who, by reason of her stoutness, floated so much higher out of the water than her friend and I, found it impossible to get herself under the bar. In whatever manner she made the attempt, her head or her shoulders were sure to bump and arrest her progress.

"Now, Barb'ry Aleshine," said Mrs. Lecks, who had been watching her, "if you ever want to get out of this salt water, you've got to make up your mind to take some of it into your mouth and into your eyes; that is, if you don't keep 'em shut. Get yourself as close to that bar as you can, and I'll come and put you under." So saying, Mrs. Lecks returned to the other side of the bar, and having made Mrs. Aleshine bow down her head and close her eyes and mouth, she placed both hands upon her companion's broad shoulders and threw as much weight as possible upon them. Mrs. Aleshine almost disappeared beneath the water, but she came up sputtering and blinking on the other side of the bar, where she was quickly joined by Mrs. Lecks.

"Merciful me!" exclaimed Mrs. Aleshine, wiping her wet face with her still wetter sleeve, "I never supposed the heathens would be up to such tricks as makin' us do that!"

I had waited to give any assistance that might be required, and while doing so, had discovered another bar under the water, which proved that entrance at almost any stage of the tide had been guarded against. Warning my companions not to strike their feet against this submerged bar, we paddled and pushed ourselves around the turn in the rocky passage and emerged into the open lagoon.

This smooth stretch of water, which separated the island from its encircling reef, was here about a hundred feet wide; and the first thing that arrested our attention as we gazed across it was a little wharf or landing stage, erected upon the narrow beach of the island, almost opposite to us.

"As sure as I stand here," exclaimed Mrs. Lecks, who never seemed to forget her upright position, "somebody lives in this place!"

"And it isn't a stickery coral island, either," cried Mrs. Aleshine, "for that sand's as smooth as any I ever saw."

"Whoever does live here," resumed Mrs. Lecks, "has got to take us in, whether they like or not, and the sooner we get over there, the better."

Mrs. Aleshine now regretted the loss of her oar, and suggested that some one of us who could get under bars easily should go back after it. But Mrs. Lecks would listen to no such proposition.

"Let the oars go," she said. "We won't want 'em again, for I'll never leave this place if I have to scoop myself out to sea with an oar."

I told the two women that I could easily tow them across this narrow piece of water; and instructing Mrs. Lecks to take hold of the tail of my coat, while Mrs. Aleshine grasped her companion's dress, I began to swim slowly toward the beach, towing my companions behind me.

"Goodness gracious me!" suddenly exclaimed Mrs. Aleshine, with a great bounce and a splash. "Look at the fishes!"

The water in the lagoon was so clear that it was almost transparent, and beneath us and around us we could see fish, some large and some small, swimming about as if they were floating in the air, while down below, the white sandy bottom seemed to sparkle in the sunlight.

"Now don't jerk my skeert off on account of the fishes," said Mrs. Lecks. "I expect there was just as many outside, though we couldn't see 'em. But I must say that this water looks as if it had been boiled and filtered."

If any inhabitant of the island had then been standing on the wharf, he would have beheld on the surface of the lagoon the peculiar spectacle of a man's head surmounted by a wet and misshapen straw hat and followed by two other heads, each wearing a dripping and bedraggled bonnet, while beneath, among the ripples of the clear water, would have been seen the figures belonging to these three heads, each dressed in the clothes ordinarily worn on land.

As I swam, I could see before me on the island nothing but a mass of low-growing, tropical vegetation, behind which rose some palms and other trees. I made for the little wharf, from which steps came down into the water, and as soon as we reached it, we all clambered rapidly up and stood dripping upon the narrow platform, stamping our feet and shaking our clothes.

"Do you see that house?" said Mrs. Lecks. "That's where they live, and I wonder which way we must go to get there."

From this somewhat elevated position I could plainly see, over the tops of the bushes and low trees, the upper part of the roof of a house. When I found the bars across the passage in the reef, I had easily come to the conclusion that the inhabitants of this island were not savages; and now since I had seen the wharf and the roof of this house, I felt quite convinced that we had reached the abode of civilized beings. They might be pirates or some other sort of sea miscreants, but they were certainly not savages or cannibals.

Leaving the wharf, we soon found a broad path through the bushes, and in a few moments reached a wide, open space, in which stood a handsome modern-built house. It was constructed after the fashion of tropical houses belonging to Europeans, with jalousied porches and shaded balconies; the grounds about it were neatly laid out, and behind it was a walled enclosure, probably a garden.

"Upon my word," exclaimed Mrs. Aleshine, "I'd like to be less drippin' before I make a call on genteel folks!"

"Genteel folks!" exclaimed Mrs. Lecks indignantly. "If you're too proud to go in as you are, Barb'ry Aleshine, you can go set in the sun till you're dry. As for me, I'm goin' to ask for the lady of the house, and if she don't like me she can lump me, so long as she gives me somethin' to eat and a dry bed to get into."

I was too much amazed to speak, but my companions took everything as a matter of course. They had expected to see strange things in the outer world, and they were not surprised when they saw them. My mind was not capable of understanding the existence of an establishment like this on a little island in mid-ocean. But it was useless for me to attempt to reason on this apparent phenomenon; and, indeed, there was no time for it, for Mrs. Lecks walked boldly up to the front door and plied the knocker, stepping back immediately, so that she might not drip too much water on the porch.

"When they come," she said, "we'll ask 'em to let us in the back way, so that we shan't slop up their floors any more than we can help."

We waited for a couple of minutes, and then I, as the member of the party who dripped the least, went up on the porch and knocked again.

"It's my belief they're not at home," said Mrs. Lecks, after we had waited some time longer, "but perhaps we'll find some of the servants in." And she led the way to the back part of the house.

As we passed the side of the mansion, I noticed that all the window shutters were closed, and my growing belief that the place was deserted became a conviction after we had knocked several times at a door at the back of the building without receiving any answer.

"Well, they're all gone out, that's certain!" said Mrs. Lecks.

"Yes, and they barred up the entrance to the island when they left," I added.

"I wonder if there's another house in the neighborhood?" asked Mrs. Aleshine.

"I don't believe," said I, "that the neighborhood is very thickly settled; but if you will wait here a few minutes, I will run around this wall and see what there is beyond. I may find the huts of some natives or workpeople."

I followed a path by the side of the garden wall, but when I reached the end of the enclosure, I could see nothing before me but jungle and forest, with paths running in several directions. I followed one of these and very soon came out upon an open beach, with the reef lying beyond it. From the form of the beach and the reef and from the appearance of things generally, I began to think that this was probably a very small island and that the house we had seen was the only one on it. I returned and reported this belief to my companions.

Now that Mrs. Aleshine had no fear of appearing in an untidy condition before "genteel folks," her manner changed very much. "If the family has gone into the country," said she, "or whatever else they've done, I want to get into this house as soon as I can. I expect we can find something to eat. At any rate, we can get ourselves dry and lay down somewhere to rest, for not a wink has one of us slept since night before last."

"I should think," said Mrs. Lecks, addressing me, "that if you could manage to climb up to them second-story windows, you might find one of them that you could get in and then come down and open the door for us. Everybody is likely to forget to fasten some of the windows on the upper floors. I know it isn't right to force our way into other people's houses, but there's nothin' else to be done, and there's no need of our talkin' about it."

I agreed with her perfectly, and taking off my coat and shoes, I climbed up one of the columns of the veranda and got upon its roof. This extended nearly the whole length of two sides of the house. I walked along it and tried all the shutters, and I soon came to one in which some of the movable slats had been broken. Thrusting my hand and arm through the aperture thus formed, I unhooked the shutters and opened them. The sash was fastened down by one of the ordinary contrivances used for such purposes, but with the blade of my jackknife I easily pushed the bolt aside, raised the sash, and entered. I found myself in a small hall at the head of a flight of stairs. Down these I hurried, and groping my way through the semidarkness of the lower story, I reached a side door. This was fastened by two bolts and a bar, and I quickly had it open.

Stepping outside, I called Mrs. Lecks and Mrs. Aleshine.

"Well," said the latter, "I'm sure I'll be glad to get in, and as we've squeezed most of the water out of our clothes, we won't make so much of a mess, after all."

We now entered, and I opened one of the shutters.

"Let's go right into the kitchen," said Mrs. Lecks, "and make a fire. That's the first thing to do."

But Mrs. Lecks soon discovered that this mansion was very different from a country dwelling in one of our Middle States. Externally, and as far as I had been able to observe its internal arrangements, it resembled the houses built by English residents which I had seen in the West Indies. It was a dwelling in which modern ideas in regard to construction and furnishing adapted themselves to the requirements of a tropical climate. Apparently there was no kitchen. There were no stairs leading to a lower floor, and the darkened rooms into which my companions peered were certainly not used for culinary purposes.

In the meantime I had gone out of the door by which we had entered, and soon discovered, on the other side of the house, a small building with a chimney to it, which I felt sure must be the kitchen. The door and shutters were fastened, but before making any attempt to open them I returned to announce my discovery.

"Door locked, is it?" said Mrs. Aleshine. "Just wait a minute."

She then disappeared but in a very short time came out, carrying a bunch of large keys.

"It's always the way," said she, as the two followed me around the back of the house, "when people shut up a house and leave it, to put all the door keys in the back corner of some drawer in the hall and to take only the front-door key with them. So, you see, I knew just where to go for these."

"It's a poor hen," said Mrs. Lecks, "that begins to cackle when she's goin' to her nest; the wise ones wait till they're comin' away. Now we'll see if one of them keys fit."

Greatly to the triumph of Mrs. Aleshine, the second or third key I tried unlocked the door. Entering, we found ourselves in a good-sized kitchen, with a great fireplace at one end of it. A door opened from the room into a shed where there was a pile of dry twigs and firewood.

"Let's have a fire as quick as we can," said Mrs. Lecks, "for since I went into that shet-up house I've been chilled to the bones."

"That's so," said Mrs. Aleshine; "and now I know how a fish keeps comfortable in the water, and how dreadfully wet and flabby it must feel when it's taken out."

I brought in a quantity of wood and kindling, and finding matches in a tin box on the wall, I went to work to make a fire and was soon rewarded by a crackling blaze. Turning around, I was amazed at the actions of Mrs. Lecks and Mrs. Aleshine. I had expected to see them standing shivering behind me, waiting for the fire to be made; but instead of that, they were moving rapidly here and there, saying not a word but going as straight to cupboard, closet, and pantry as the hound follows the track of the hare. From a wild chaos of uncongenial surroundings, these two women had dropped into a sphere in which they were perfectly at home. The kitchen was not altogether like those to which they had been accustomed, but it was a well-appointed one, and their instincts and practice made them quickly understand where they would find what they wanted. I gazed on them with delight while one filled a kettle from a little pump in the corner which brought water from a cistern and the other appeared from the pantry, carrying a tea caddy and a tin biscuit box.

"Now, then," said Mrs. Lecks, hanging the kettle on a crane over the fire and drawing up a chair, "by the time we've got a little dried off, the kettle will bile, and we'll have some hot tea, and then the best thing to do is to go to bed."

"We'll take time to have a bite first," said Mrs. Aleshine, "for I was never so near famished in my life. I brought out a box nearly full of biscuits, and there's sardines in this, Mr. Craig, which you can easy open with your knife."

I piled on more wood, and we gathered close around the genial heat. The sunshine was hot outside, but that did not prevent the fire from being most comforting and refreshing to us.

As soon as the kettle began to simmer, up jumped Mrs. Aleshine. A sugar bowl and some cups were placed upon a table, and in a short time we were cheered and invigorated by hot tea, biscuits, and sardines.

"This isn't much of a meal," said Mrs. Aleshine, apologetically, "but there's no time to cook nothin', and the sooner we get off our wet things and find some beds, the better."

"If I can once get into bed," said Mrs. Lecks, "all I ask is that the family will not come back till I have had a good long nap. After that, they can do what they please."

We now went back to the house and ascended the main stairway, which led up to a large central hall.

"We won't go into the front rooms," said Mrs. Lecks, "for we don't want to make no more disturbance than we can help; but if we can find the smallest kind of rooms in the back, with beds in 'em, it is all we can ask."

The first chamber we entered was a good-sized one, neatly furnished, containing a bedstead with uncovered mattress and pillows. Opening a closet door, Mrs. Lecks exclaimed, "This is a man's room, Mr. Craig, and you'd better take it. Look at the trousers and coats! There's no bedclothes in here, but I'll see if I can't find some."

In a few minutes she returned, bearing blankets, sheets, and a pillowcase. With Mrs. Aleshine on one side of the bedstead and Mrs. Lecks on the other, the sheets and blankets were laid with surprising deftness and rapidity, and in a few moments I saw before me a most inviting bed.

While Mrs. Aleshine held a pillow in her teeth as she pulled on the pillowcase with both hands, Mrs. Lecks looked around the room with the air of an attentive hostess. "I guess you'll be comfortable, Mr. Craig," she said, "and I advise you to sleep just as long as you can. We'll take the room on the other side of the hall; but I'm first goin' down to see if the kitchen fire is safe and to fasten the doors."

I offered to relieve her of this trouble, but she promptly declined my services. "When it's rowin' or swimmin', you can do it, Mr. Craig, but when it's lockin' up and lookin' to fires, I'll attend to that myself."

My watch had stopped, but I suppose it was the middle of the afternoon when I went to bed, and I slept steadily until some hours after sunrise the next morning, when I was awakened by a loud knock at the door.

"It's time to get up," said the voice of Mrs. Lecks, "and if your clothes are not entirely dry, you'd better see if there isn't somethin' in that closet you can put on. After a while, I'll make a big fire in the kitchen and dry all our things."

I found my clothes were still very damp, and after investigating the contents of the closet and bureau, I was able to supply myself with linen and a light summer suit, which fitted me fairly well. I even found socks and a pair of slippers.

When I entered the kitchen, I first opened wide my eyes with delight, and then I burst out laughing. Before me was a table covered with a white cloth, with plates, cups, and everything necessary upon it; at one end was a steaming teapot, and at the other a dish of some kind of hot meat, and Mrs. Aleshine was just taking a pan of newly baked biscuits from a small iron oven.

"I don't wonder you laugh," said Mrs. Lecks, "but our clothes was still wet, and we had to take just what we could find. I'm not in the habit of goin' about in a white muslin wrapper with blue ribbon trimmin's, and as for Mrs. Aleshine, I did think we'd never find anything that she could get into; but there must be one stout woman in the family, for that yeller frock with black buttons fits her well enough, though I must say it's a good deal short."

"I never thought," said Mrs. Aleshine, as she sat down at the teapot, "that the heathens had so many conveniences, specially bakin' powders and Dutch ovens. For my part, I always supposed that they used their altars for bakin', when they wasn't offerin' up victims on 'em."

"Have you got it into your head, Barb'ry Aleshine," said Mrs. Lecks, looking up from the dish of potted beef she was serving, "that this house belongs to common heathen? I expect that most of the savages who live on these desert islands has been converted by the missionaries, but they'd have to take 'em from Genesis to Revelations a good many times before they'd get 'em to the p'int of havin' force pumps in their kitchens and spring mattresses on their beds. As far as I've seen this house, it looks as if the family had always been Christians and probably either Catholics or Episcopalians."

"On account of the cross on the mantelpiece in our room, I suppose," said Mrs. Aleshine. "But whether they're given to idols or prayer books, I know they've got a mighty nice house; and considerin' the distance from stores, there's a good deal more in that pantry than you'd expect to find in any house I know of when the family is away."

"It is my opinion," said I, "that this house belongs to some rich man, probably an American or European merchant, who lives on one of the large islands not far away and who uses this as a sort of summer residence."

"I thought it was always summer in this part of the world," said Mrs. Lecks.

"So it is in effect," I replied, "but there are some seasons when it is very unpleasant to remain in one of those towns which are found on the larger islands, and so the owner of this house may come up here sometimes for fresh sea air."

"Or it's just as like," said Mrs. Aleshine, "that he lives somewhere up in the iceberg regions and comes here to spend his winters. It would do just as well. But, whichever way it is, I can't help thinkin' it's careless not to leave somebody in the house to take care of it. Why, for all the family would know about it, tramps might break in and stay as long as they like."

"That's just what's happenin' now," said Mrs. Lecks, "and for my part I ain't goin' to find no fault. I don't suppose the people would have been so hardhearted as to turn us away from their doors, but I've seen enough of folks in this world not to be too sure about that."

"How do you suppose," said Mrs. Aleshine, addressing me, "that the family gets here and goes back? Do they keep a private steamboat?"

"Of course they have a private vessel of some kind," I answered, "probably a yacht. It is quite certain that ordinary steamers never touch here."

"If that's the case," said Mrs. Lecks, "all we can do is to wait here till they come, and get them to send us away in their ship. But whether they've just gone or are just a-comin' back depends, I suppose, on whether they live in a freezin' or a burnin' country; and if they don't like our bein' here when they come back, there's one thing they can make up their minds to, and that is that I'm never goin' to leave this place on a life preserver."

"Nor me nuther," said Mrs. Aleshine, finishing, with much complacency, her third cup of tea.

When breakfast was over, Mrs. Lecks pushed back her chair but did not immediately rise. With an expression of severe thought upon her face, she gazed steadfastly before her for a minute, and then she addressed Mrs. Aleshine, who had begun to gather together the cups and the plates. "Now, Barb'ry Aleshine," said she, "don't you begin to clear off the table nor touch a single thing to wash it up till we've been over this house. I want to do it now, before Mr. Craig goes out to prospect around and see what else is on the island, which, I suppose, he'll be wantin' to do."

I replied that I had that intention, but I was quite willing to go over the house first.

"It's come to me," said Mrs. Lecks, speaking very gravely, "that it's no use for us to talk of the family bein' here or bein' there till we've gone over this house. If we find that they have, as far as we know, gone away in good health and spirits, that's all well enough; but if anything's happened in this house, I don't want to be here with what's happened—at least, without knowin' it; and when we do go over the house, I want a man to go with us."

"If you'd talked that way last night, Mrs. Lecks," exclaimed Mrs. Aleshine, "I'd never slept till after sunup and then got up and gone huntin' round among them frocks and petticoats to find somethin' that would fit me, with the quiet pulse I did have, Mrs. Lecks!"

To this remark Mrs. Lecks made no reply, but rising, she led the way out of the kitchen and into the house.

The rooms on the first floor were very well furnished. There was a large parlor and back of it a study or library, while on the other side of the hall was a dining room and an apartment probably used as a family room. We found nothing in these which would indicate that anything untoward had happened in them. Then we went upstairs, I leading the way, Mrs. Lecks following, and Mrs. Aleshine in the rear. We first entered one of the front chambers, which was quite dark, but Mrs. Lecks unfastened and threw open a shutter. Then, with a rigid countenance and determined mien, she examined every part of the room, looking into every closet and even under the bed. It was quite plain that it was in one of the chambers that she expected to find what had happened, if anything had happened.

The room on the other side of the hall was very like the one we first examined, except that it had two beds in it. We next visited the chamber recently occupied by my two companions, which was now undergoing the process of "airing."

"We needn't stop here," remarked Mrs. Aleshine.

But Mrs. Lecks instantly replied, "Indeed, we will stop; I'm going to look under the bed."

"Merciful me!" exclaimed Mrs. Aleshine, putting her hand on her friend's shoulder. "Supposin' you should find somethin', and we sleepin' here last night! It curdles me to think of it!"

"It's my duty," said Mrs. Lecks severely, "and I shall do it."

And do it she did, rising from the task with a sigh of relief.

My room was subjected to the same scrutiny as the others, and then we visited some smaller rooms at the extreme back of the house, which we had not before noticed. A garret, or loft, was reached by a steep stairway in one of these rooms, and into its dusky gloom I ventured by myself.

"Now, don't come down, Mr. Craig," said Mrs. Lecks, "till you're sure there's nothin' there. Of all places in the house, that cockloft, after all, is the most likely."

I had none of the fears which seemed to actuate the two women, but I had a very unpleasant time of it groping about in the darkness and heat, and, as the place was only partly floored, running the continual risk of crashing down through the lath and plaster. I made myself quite sure, however, that nothing had happened in that loft, unless someone had suffocated there and had dried up and become the dust which I raised at every step.

"Now, then," said Mrs. Lecks, when I descended, "as there is no cellar, we'll go wash up the breakfast things; and if you want to take a walk, to see if there's any genuwine heathens or anybody else a-livin' in this island, we're not afraid to be left alone."

For the whole of the rest of the morning I wandered about the island. I investigated the paths that I had before noticed and found that each of them led, after a moderate walk, to some wide and pleasant part of the beach. At one of these points I found a rustic bench; and stuffed in between two of the slats which formed the seat, I found a book. It had been sadly wet and discolored by rain and dried and curled up by the wind and sun. I pulled it out, and found it to be a novel in French. On one of the flyleaves was written "Emily." Reasoning from the dilapidated appearance of this book, I began to believe that the family must have left this place some time ago and that, therefore, their return might be expected at a proportionately early period. On second thoughts, however, I considered that the state of this book was of little value as testimony. A few hours of storm, wind, and sun might have inflicted all the damage it had sustained. The two women would be better able to judge by the state of the house and the condition of the provisions how long the family had been away.

I then started out on a walk along the beach, and in little more than an hour I had gone entirely around the island. Nowhere did I see any sign of habitation or occupation except at the house which had given us shelter, nor any opening through the surrounding reef except the barred passageway through which we had come.

When I returned to the house, I found that Mrs. Lecks and Mrs. Aleshine had been hard at work all the morning. They had, so to speak, gone regularly and systematically to housekeeping and had already divided the labors of the establishment between them. Mrs. Aleshine, who prided herself on her skill in culinary matters, was to take charge of the cooking, while Mrs. Lecks assumed the care of the various rooms and the general management of the household.

This arrangement was explained to me at length, and when I remarked that all this seemed to indicate that they expected to remain here for a long time, Mrs. Lecks replied, "In my part of the country I could tell pretty close, by the dust on the tables and on the top of the pianner, how long a family had been out of a house; but dust in Pennsylvany and dust on a sea island, where there's no wagons nor carriages, is quite different. This house has been left in very good order, and though the windows wants washin' and the floors and stairs brushin'—which will be easy considerin' that none of 'em has carpets—and everything in the house a reg'lar cleanin' up and airin', it may be that the family hasn't been gone away very long, and so it may be a good while before they come back again. Mrs. Aleshine and me has talked it over, and we've made up our minds that the right thing to do is just to go along and attend to things as if we was a-goin' to stay here for a month or two; and it may be even longer than that before the people come back. And I don't think they'll have anything to complain of when they find their house in apple-pie order, their windows washed, their floors clean, and not a speck of dust anywhere."

"For my part," said Mrs. Aleshine, "I don't see what they've got to find fault with, anyway. I look on this as part of the passage. To be sure, we ain't movin' a bit on our way to Japan, but that's not my fault, nor yet yours, Mrs. Lecks, nor yours, Mr. Craig. We paid our passage to go to Japan, and if the ship was steered wrong and got sunk, we hadn't anything to do with it. We didn't want to come here, but here we are, and I'd like to know who's got any right to find fault with us."

"And bein' here," said Mrs. Lecks, "we'll take care of the things."

"As far as I'm concerned," added Mrs. Aleshine, "if this island was movin' on to Japan, I'd a great deal rather be on it than on that ship, where, to my way of thinkin', they didn't know much more about housekeepin' than they did about steerin'.'"

"I think your plans and arrangements are very good," I said. "But how about the provisions? Are there enough to hold out for any time?"

"There's pretty nigh a barrel of flour," said Mrs. Aleshine, "a good deal of tea and coffee and sugar, and lots of things in tins and jars. There's a kind of cellar outside where they keep things cool, and there's more than half a keg of butter down there. It's too strong to use, but I can take that butter and wash it out and work it over and salt it and make it just as good butter as any we got on board the ship."

"But," said I, "you have given me nothing to do. I shall not be content to stand about idle and see you do all the work."

"There's nothin' in the house," said Mrs. Lecks, "which you need put your hand to; but if you choose to go out into that garden and see if there's anything can be done in it or got out of it —that is, if you know anything about garden work—I'm sure we'd be very glad of any fresh vegetables we could get."

I replied that I had been accustomed to garden work in an amateur way and would be glad to do anything that was possible in that direction.

"I never seed into that garden," said Mrs. Aleshine, "but of all the foolish things that ever came under my eye, the buildin' a wall around a garden, when a picket fence would do just as well, is the foolishest."

I explained that in these countries it was the fashion to use walls instead of fences.

"If it's the fashion," said Mrs. Aleshine, "I suppose there's no use sayin' anything ag'in' it; but if the fashion should happen to change, they'd find it a good deal easier to take down a barbed-wire fence than a stone wall."

This conversation took place in the large lower hall, which Mrs. Lecks had been "putting to rights" and where Mrs. Aleshine had just entered from the kitchen. Mrs. Lecks now sat down upon a chair, and, dusting cloth in hand, she thus addressed me: "There's another thing, Mr. Craig, that me and Mrs. Aleshine has been talkin' about. We haven't made up our minds about it, because we didn't think it was fair and right to do that before speakin' to you and hearin' what you had to say on one side or another of it. Mrs. Aleshine and me has had to bow our heads to afflictions and to walk sometimes in roads we didn't want to; but we've remembered the ways in which we was brought up and have kept in them as far as we've been able. When our husbands died, leavin' Mrs. Aleshine with a son and me without any, which, perhaps, is just as well, for there's no knowin' how he might have turned out—"

"That's so," interrupted Mrs. Aleshine, "for he might have gone as a clerk to Roosher, and then you and me would 'a' had to travel different ways."

"And when our husbands died," continued Mrs. Lecks, "they left us enough and plenty to live on, and we wasn't the women to forget them and their ways of thinkin', any more than we'd forget the ways of our fathers and mothers before us."

"That's so!" said Mrs. Aleshine fervently.

"And now, Mr. Craig," continued Mrs. Lecks, "we don't know how you've been brought up nor anything about you, in fact, except that you've been as kind to us as if you was some sort of kin and that we never would have thought of comin' here without you, and so me and Mrs. Aleshine has agreed to leave this whole matter to you and to do just as you say. When us two started out on this long journey, we didn't expect to find it what you call the path of roses, and, dear only knows, we haven't found it so."

"That's true!" ejaculated Mrs. Aleshine.

"And what we've had to put up with," continued Mrs. Lecks, "we have put up with. So, Mr. Craig, whether you say dinner in the middle of the day at twelve, as we've always been used to, or at six o'clock in the afternoon, as they had it on board that ship— and how people ever come to turn their meals hind part foremost in that way, I can't say—we are goin' to do it; if you've been brought up to six o'clock, you won't hear no complainin' from us, think what we may."

I was on the point of laughing aloud at the conclusion of this speech, but a glance at the serious faces of the two women, who, with so much earnest solicitude, awaited my reply, stopped me, and I hastened to assure them that dinner in the middle of the day would be entirely in accordance with my every wish.

"Good!" exclaimed Mrs. Aleshine, her eyes sparkling amid the plumpness of her face, while an expression of calm relief passed over the features of Mrs. Lecks.

"And now I'll be off and get us somethin' to eat in less than no time," said Mrs. Aleshine. "We didn't know whether to make it lunch or dinner till we had seen you, so you can't expect much to-day, but tomorrow we'll begin, and have everything straight and comfortable. I'm goin' to get up early in the mornin' and bake a batch of bread, and you needn't be afraid, Mr. Craig, but what I'll have you a bit of hot meat every night for your supper."

In the afternoon we all visited the garden, which, although a good deal overgrown with luxuriant weeds, showed marks of fair cultivation. Some of the beds had been cleared out and left to the weeds, and we found some "garden truck," as my companions called it, with which we were not familiar. But there were tomato vines loaded with fruit, plenty of beans of various kinds, and a large patch of potatoes, many of which had been dug.

From the lower end of the garden, Mrs. Aleshine gave a shout of delight. We went to her and found her standing before a long asparagus bed.

"Well!" she exclaimed. "If there's anything that settles it firm in my mind that these people is Christians, it's this bed of grass. I don't believe there ever was heathens that growed grass."

"I thought that was all settled when we found the bakin' powders," said Mrs. Lecks.

"But this clinches it," answered her companion. "I can't tell from a sparrowgrass bed what church they belong to, but they're no idolators."

The next morning I delivered to the genial Mrs. Aleshine a large basket full of fresh vegetables, and we had a most excellent dinner. Somewhat to my surprise, the table was not set in the kitchen, but in the dining room.

"Me and Mrs. Aleshine have made up our minds," said Mrs. Lecks, in explanation, "that it's not the proper thing for you to be eatin' in the kitchen nor for us neither. Here's tablecloths and good glass and china and spoons and forks, which, although they're not solid silver, are plated good enough for anybody. Neither you nor us is servants, and a kitchen is no place for us."

"That's so!" said Mrs. Aleshine. "We paid our money for first-class passages, and it was understood that we'd have everything as good as anybody."

"Which I don't see as that has anything to do with it, Barb'ry Aleshine," said Mrs. Lecks, "for the steamship people don't generally throw in desert islands as part of the accommodation."

"We didn't ask for the island," retorted Mrs. Aleshine, "and if they'd steered the ship right, we shouldn't have wanted it."

When we had finished our dinner, Mrs. Lecks pushed back her chair and sat for a few moments in thought, as was her wont before saying anything of importance.

"There's another thing," said she, "that I've been thinkin' about, though I haven't spoke of it yet, even to Mrs. Aleshine. We haven't no right to come here and eat up the victuals and use the things of the people that own this house, without payin' for 'em. Of course, we're not goin' to sleep on the bare ground and starve to death while there's beds and food close to our hands. But if we use 'em and take it, we ought to pay the people that the place belongs to—that is, if we've got the money to do it with—and Mrs. Aleshine and me has got the money. When we went down into our cabin to get ready to leave the ship, the first thing we did was to put our purses in our pockets, and we've both got drafts wrapped up in oil silk and sewed inside our frock-bodies; and if you didn't think to bring your money along with you, Mr. Craig, we can lend you all you need."

I thanked her for her offer but stated that I had brought with me all my money.

"Now," continued Mrs. Lecks, "it's my opinion that we ought to pay our board regular each week. I don't know what is commonly charged in a place like this, but I know you can get very good board where I come from for six dollars a week."

"That is for two in a room," said Mrs. Aleshine; "but havin' a room to himself would make it more for Mr. Craig."

"It ain't his fault," said Mrs. Lecks, somewhat severely, "that he ain't got a brother or some friend to take part of the room and pay part of the expense. But, anyway, the room isn't a large one, and I don't think he ought to pay much more for having a room to himself. Seven dollars is quite enough."

"But then you've got to consider," said Mrs. Aleshine, "that we do the cookin' and housework, and that ought to be counted."

"I was comin' to that," said Mrs. Lecks. "Now, if me and Mrs. Aleshine was to go out to service, which you may be sure we wouldn't do unless circumstances was very different from what they are now—"

"That's true!" earnestly ejaculated Mrs. Aleshine.

"But if we was to do it," continued Mrs. Lecks, "we wouldn't go into anybody's family for less than two dollars a week. Now, I've always heard that wages is low in this part of the world, and the work isn't heavy for two of us; so, considering the family isn't here to make their own bargain, I think we'd better put our wages at that, so that'll make four dollars a week for each of us two to pay."

"But how about Mr. Craig?" said Mrs. Aleshine. "He oughtn't to work in that garden for nothin'."

"Fifty cents a day," said Mrs. Lecks, "is as little as any man would work for, and then it oughtn't to take all his time. That will make three dollars to take out of Mr. Craig's board and leave it four dollars a week, the same as ours."

I declared myself perfectly satisfied with these arrangements, but Mrs. Aleshine did not seem to be altogether convinced that they were just.

"When a woman goes out to service," said she, "she gets her board and is paid wages besides, and it's the same for gardeners."

"Then I suppose, Barb'ry Aleshine," said Mrs. Lecks, "that we ought to charge these people with our wages and make 'em pay it when they come back!"

This remark apparently disposed of Mrs. Aleshine's objections, and her friend continued: "There's a jar on the mantelpiece there, of the kind the East Indy ginger comes in. It's got nothin' in it now but some brown paper in which fishhooks is wrapped. We came here on a Wednesday, and so every Tuesday night we'll each put four dollars in that jar, under the fishhook paper; then if, by night or by day, the family comes back and makes a fuss about our bein' here, all we have to say is, 'The board money's in the ginger jar,' and our consciences is free."

Mrs. Lecks's plan was adopted as a very just and proper one, and at the expiration of the week we each deposited four dollars in the ginger jar.

While occupying this house I do not think that any of us endeavored to pry into the private concerns of the family who owned it, although we each had a very natural curiosity to know something about said family. Opportunities of acquiring such knowledge, however, were exceedingly scarce. Even if we had been willing to look into such receptacles, the several desks and secretaries that the house contained were all locked, and nowhere could Mrs. Lecks or Mrs. Aleshine find an old letter or piece of wrapping paper with an address on it. I explained to my companions that letters and packages were not likely to come to a place like this, but they kept a sharp lookout for anything of the kind, asserting that there could be no possible harm in reading the names of the people whose house they were in.

In some of the books in the library, which were English and French in about equal proportions, with a few volumes in German, I found written on the blank pages the names "Emily" and "Lucille," and across the title pages of some French histories was inscribed, in a man's hand, "A. Dusante." We discussed these names but could not make up our minds whether the family were French or English. For instance, there was no reason why an

Englishwoman might not be called Lucille, and even such a sur-
name as Dusante was not uncommon either among English or
Americans. The labels on the boxes and tins of provisions showed
that most of them came from San Francisco, but this was likely to
be the case, no matter what the nationality of the family.

The question of the relationship of the three persons, of whose
existence we had discovered traces, was a very interesting one to
Mrs. Lecks and Mrs. Aleshine.

"I can't make up my mind," said the latter, "whether Emily is
the mother of Lucille or her daughter, or whether they are both
children of Mr. Dusante, or whether he's married to Lucille and
Emily is his sister-in-law, or whether she's his sister and not hers,
or whether he's the uncle and they're his nieces, or whether Emily
is an old lady and Mr. Dusante and Lucille are both her children,
or whether they are two maiden ladies and Mr. Dusante is their
brother, or whether Mr. Dusante is only a friend of the family
and boards here because no two women ought to live in such a
lonely place without a man in the house."

"Well," said Mrs. Lecks, "whether Mr. Dusante comes back
with two nieces, or a wife and daughter, or Mrs. Dusante and a
mother-in-law, or a pair of sisters, all we've got to say is, 'The
board money's in the ginger jar,' and let 'em do their worst."

In my capacity as gardener I do not think I earned the wages
which my companions had allotted to me, for I merely gathered
and brought in such fruits and vegetables as I found in proper
condition for use. In other ways, however, I made my services
valuable to our little family. In a closet in my chamber I found
guns and ammunition, and frequently I was able to bring in a few
birds. Some of these were pronounced by Mrs. Aleshine unsuitable
for the table, but others she cooked with much skill, and they were
found to be very good eating.

Not far from the little wharf which has been mentioned, there
stood, concealed by a mass of low-growing palms, a boathouse in
which was a little skiff hung up near the roof. This I let down and

launched, and found great pleasure in rowing it about the lagoon. There was fishing tackle in the boathouse, which I used with success, the lagoon abounding in fish. Offerings of this kind were much more acceptable to Mrs. Aleshine than birds.

"There's some kinds of fishes that's better than others," said she, "but, as a gen'ral rule, a fish is a fish, and if you catch 'em, you can eat 'em; but it's a very different thing with birds. When you've never seen 'em before, how are you goin' to tell but what they're some kin to an owl, a pigeon hawk, or a crow? And if I once get it into my head that there's any of that kind of family blood in 'em, they disagree with me just the same as if there really was."

One afternoon, as I was returning in the boat from the point on the other side of the island where I had found the rustic seat and Emily's book, I was surprised to see Mrs. Lecks and Mrs. Aleshine standing on the end of the little wharf. This was an unusual thing for them to do, as they were very industrious women and seldom had an idle moment, and it seemed to be one of their greatest pleasures to discuss the work they were going to do when they had finished that on which they were then engaged. I was curious, therefore, to know why they should be standing thus idly on the wharf and pulled toward them as rapidly as possible.

When I had rowed near enough to hear them, Mrs. Aleshine remarked with cheerful placidity, "The Dusantes are comin'."

The tide was quite low, and I could not see over the reef; but in a few moments I had grounded the skiff and had sprung upon the wharf. Out on the ocean, about a mile away, I saw a boat, apparently a large one, approaching the island.

"Now, then, Barb'ry Aleshine," said Mrs. Lecks, "you'll soon see whether it's his two nieces or his daughters, wife, and sister-in-law, or whatever of them other relationships which you've got so pat."

"Yes," said Mrs. Aleshine; "but, what's more, we'll find out if he's goin' to be satisfied with the board money we've put in the ginger jar."

3. Mrs. *Lecks* and Mrs. *Aleshine* *Win* a Fight and *Make* a Match

WHEN THE BOAT which we saw approaching the island had come near enough for us to distinguish its occupants, we found that it contained five persons. Three sat in the stern, and two were rowing. Of those in the stern, we soon made out one to be a woman, and after putting our eyesight to its very best efforts, we were obliged to admit that there was only one female on board.

"Now, that's disapp'intin'," said Mrs. Aleshine, "for I've wondered and wondered which I should like best, Emily or Lucille, and now that only one of 'em has come, of course I can't tell."

The boat came on, almost directly toward the passageway in the reef, and it was not long before the two women had been able to decide that Mr. Dusante was an elderly man, and that the lady was moderately young and in all probability his daughter.

"It may be," said Mrs. Aleshine, "that the mother, whether she was Emily or whether she was Lucille, has died, and for that reason they are comin' back sooner than they expected."

"Well, I hope you're wrong there, Barb'ry Aleshine," said Mrs. Lecks, "for they'll see lots of things here that will freshen up their affliction, and that won't make 'em any too lively people to be with."

"On the other hand," said Mrs. Aleshine, "it may be that Emily, or else Lucille, has got married and has gone away with her husband to travel, and by the time she's got a little baby she'll come here to live on account of the sea air for the child, and that'll make the house pleasant, Mrs. Lecks."

"I'd like to know how long you expect to live here," said Mrs. Lecks, regarding her friend with some severity.

"That's not for me to say," replied Mrs. Aleshine, "knowin' nothin' about it. But this I will say, that I hope they have brought along with them some indigo blue, for I nearly used up all there was the last time I washed."

During this dialogue I had been thinking that it was a very strange thing for the owners of this place to visit their island in such a fashion. Why should they be in an open boat? And where did they come from? Wherever they might live, it was not at all probable that they would choose to be rowed from that point to this. From the general character and appointments of the house in which we had found a refuge, it was quite plain that its owners were people in good circumstances, who were in the habit of attending to their domestic affairs in a very orderly and proper way. It was to be presumed that it was their custom to come here in a suitable vessel and to bring with them the stores needed during their intended stay. Now, there could be little or nothing in that boat, and, on the whole, I did not believe it contained the owners of this island.

It would not do, however, to assume anything of the kind. There might have been a disaster; in fact, I knew nothing about it, but it was my immediate duty to go and meet these people at the passage, for, if they were unable to unlock the bars, their boat could not enter, and I must ferry them across the lagoon. Without communicating my doubts to my companions, I hurried into the skiff and pulled as far as possible into the passage through the reef. The bars, of which there were more than I at first supposed, were so arranged that it was impossible for a boat to go in or out at any stage of the tide.

I had been there but a few minutes when the boat from without came slowly in between the rocks; and almost as soon as I saw it, its progress was suddenly stopped by a sunken bar.

"Hello!" cried several men at once.

"Hello!" cried I, in return. "Have you the key to these bars?"

A stout man with a red beard stood up in the stern. "Key?" said he. "What key?"

"Then you do not belong here?" said I. "Who are you?"

At this, the gentleman who was sitting by the lady arose to his feet. He was a man past middle age, rather tall and slim, and when he stood up, the slight rolling of the boat made him stagger, and he came near falling.

"You'd better sit down, sir," said the man with the red beard, who I saw was a sailor. "You can talk better that way."

The gentleman now seated himself and thus addressed me: "I am, sir, the Reverend Mr. Enderton, lately missionary to Nanfouchong, China, and this is my daughter, Miss Enderton. We are returning to the United States by way of the Sandwich Islands, and took passage in a sailing vessel for Honolulu. About two weeks ago this vessel, in some way which I do not understand, became disabled—"

"Rotten forem'st," interrupted the man with the red beard, "which gave way in a gale; strained and leaky, besides."

"I did not know the mast was rotten," said the gentleman, "but since the occasion of our first really serviceable wind, she has been making very unsatisfactory progress. And, more than that, the whole force of seamen was employed night and day in endeavoring to keep the water out of the tea, thereby causing such a thumping and pounding that sleep was out of the question. Add to this the fact that our meals became very irregular and were sometimes entirely overlooked—"

"Prog was gettin' mighty short," interpolated the red-bearded man.

"You can easily discern, sir," continued the gentleman, "that it was impossible for myself and my daughter to remain longer on that vessel, on which we were the only passengers. I therefore requested the captain to put us ashore at the nearest land, and after more than a week of delay and demur, he consented to do so."

"Couldn't do it," said the man, "till there was land nigh enough."

"The captain informed me," continued the gentleman, "that this island was inhabited, and that I could here find shelter and repose until a vessel could be sent from Honolulu to take me off. He furnished me with this boat and three seamen, one of whom," pointing to the red-bearded man, "is a coxswain. We have been rowing ever since early this morning, with but a very moderate quantity of food and much discomfort. Now, sir, you have heard my story; and I ask you, as one man to another, if you still intend to bar your water gates against us?"

"I did not bar the gates," I said, "and I would gladly unlock them if I could. I belong to a shipwrecked party who took refuge here some two weeks ago."

"And how did you get in?" hastily inquired the red-bearded coxswain.

"Our boat sunk when we were within sight of the island, and we came here on life preservers and so got under the bars."

The two men who had been rowing now turned suddenly and looked at me. They both had black beards, and they both exclaimed at the same moment, "By George!"

"I won't stop here to tell any more of our story," said I. "The great point now is to get you all ashore and have you cared for."

"That's so!" said the coxswain. And the two sailors murmured, "Aye, aye, sir."

The bar which stopped the progress of the larger boat was just under the surface of the water, while another a foot above the water kept my skiff about six feet distant from the other boat. There was some loose flooring in the bottom of the coxswain's boat, and he ordered two of the boards taken out, and with them a bridge was made, one end resting on the bow of the larger boat and the other on the iron bar by my skiff.

"Now," said the coxswain, "let the lady go first."

The elderly gentleman arose, as if he would prefer to take the lead, but his daughter, who had not yet spoken a word, was passed forward by the coxswain, steadied over the bridge by one of the sailors, and assisted by me into the skiff. Then her father came aboard, and I rowed with them to the wharf.

Mrs. Lecks and Mrs. Aleshine came forward most cordially to meet them.

"Mr. Dusante, I suppose?" said Mrs. Lecks, while Mrs. Aleshine hurriedly whispered in my ear, "Is it Lucille or Emily?"

As quickly as possible I explained the situation. For a few moments Mrs. Lecks and Mrs. Aleshine stood speechless. Nothing which had happened to them—the wreck of the steamer, the sinking of the boat, or our experience with life preservers—affected them so much as this disappointment in regard to the problem of the Dusante family. Travel by sea was all novel and strange to them, and they had expected all sorts of things to which they were not accustomed, but they had never imagined that Fate would be so hard upon them as to snatch away the solution of this mystery just as they were about to put their hands upon it. But, in spite of this sudden blow, the two good women quickly recovered themselves and with hearty and kindly words hurried the missionary and his daughter to the house, while I went to bring over the men.

I found the three sailors busy in securing their boat so that it would not be injured by the rocks during the rising and falling of the tide. When they had finished this job, they had to do a good deal of scrambling before they reached my skiff.

"We thought at first, sir," said the coxswain, as I rowed them across the lagoon, "that it was all gammon about your not livin' here and havin' no keys to them bars; but we've come to the 'pinion that if you'd been able to unlock 'em you'd have done it sooner than take all this trouble."

I now related my story more fully, and the men were greatly astonished when they heard that my companions in this adventure were two women. Upon my asking the coxswain why he had come to this island, he replied that his captain had heard that people lived on it, although he knew nothing about them; and that, as it would be almost impossible to get his brig here with the wind that was then prevailing and as he did not wish to go out of his course anyway, he made up his mind that he would rather lose the services of three men than keep that missionary on board a day longer.

"You see, sir," said the coxswain, as we went ashore, "the parson wouldn't never take it into account that we were short of prog and leakin' like Sam Hill; and because things were uncomfortable he growled up and he growled down, till he was wuss for the spirits of the men than the salt water comin' in or the hardtack givin' out, and there was danger, if he wasn't got rid of, that he'd be pitched overboard and left to take his chances for a whale. And then, by sendin' us along, that give the crew three half-rations a day extry, and that'll count for a good deal in the fix they're in."

When I reached the house, I took the men into the kitchen, where Mrs. Aleshine already had the table spread. There were bread and cold meat, while the teakettle steamed by the fire. In a very short time three happy mariners sat around that table, while Mrs. Aleshine, with beaming face, attended to their wants and plied them with innumerable questions. They had not finished eating when Mrs. Lecks entered the kitchen.

"I put that minister and his daughter in the two front bedrooms," said she to me, after hospitably greeting the three men, "which me and Mrs. Aleshine had run and got ready for the Dusantes as soon as you went in your boat to meet 'em. The young lady was mighty nigh worn out and glad enough of the tea and things and to get into bed. But the gentleman he wanted a soft-boiled egg, and when I told him I hadn't come across no hen house yet on this island, he looked at me as if he didn't half believe me and thought I was keepin' the eggs to sell."

"Which it would be ridiculous to do," said Mrs. Aleshine, "in the middle of an ocean like this."

"If he lets you off with soft-b'iled eggs, ma'am," said the coxswain, very respectfully, "I think you may bless your stars."

"Aye, aye, sir," said the two sailors with black beards.

Miss Ruth Enderton and her father did not make their appearance until the next morning at breakfast time. I found the young lady a very pleasant person. She was rather slight in figure, inclined to be pretty, and was what might be called a warm-colored blonde. Her disposition was quite sociable, and she almost immediately stepped into the favor of Mrs. Lecks and Mrs. Aleshine.

Mr. Enderton, however, was a person of another sort. He was a prim and somewhat formal man and appeared to be entirely self-engrossed, with very vague notions in regard to his surroundings. He was not by any means an ill-tempered man, being rather inclined to be placid than otherwise; but he gave so little attention to circumstances and events that he did not appear to understand why he should be incommoded by the happenings of life. I have no doubt that he made existence on board the disabled brig a hundred times more unsatisfactory than it would otherwise have been. With his present condition he seemed very well satisfied, and it was quite plain that he looked upon Mrs. Lecks, Mrs. Aleshine, and myself as the proprietors of the establishment, having forgotten, or paid no attention to, my statement in regard to our coming here.

As soon as she thought it fit and proper—and this moment arrived in the course of the first forenoon—Mrs. Lecks spoke to Mr. Enderton on the subject of the board which should be paid to the Dusantes. She stated the arrangements we had made in the matter and then told him that as he and his daughter had the best accommodations in the house, each occupying a large, handsome room, she thought that he should pay fifteen dollars a week for the two.

"Now, if your daughter," she continued, "can do anything about the house which will be of real help, though for the life of me I don't see what she can find to do, with me and Mrs. Aleshine here, somethin' might be took off on account of her services; but of course you, sir, can't do nothin', unless you was to preach on Sundays, and not knowin' what denomination the Dusantes belong to, it wouldn't be fair to take their money to pay for preachin' of doctrines which, perhaps, they don't believe in."

This financial proposal aroused Mr. Enderton's opposition. "When I came here, madam," he said, "I did not expect to pay any board whatever, and I think, moreover, that your rates are exorbitant. In Nanfouchong, if I remember rightly, the best of board did not cost more than two or three dollars a week."

"I don't want to say anything, sir," said Mrs. Lecks, "which might look disrespectful, but as long as I've got a conscience inside of me I'm not goin' to stay here and see the Dusantes lose money by Chinese cheapness."

"I don't know anything about the Dusantes," said Mr. Enderton, "but I am not going to pay fifteen dollars a week for board for myself and daughter."

The discussion lasted for some time, with considerable warmth on each side, and was at last ended by Mr. Enderton agreeing to pay board at the same rate as the two women and myself and each week to deposit in the ginger jar eight dollars for himself and daughter.

"You may not care to remember, sir," said Mrs. Lecks, with cold severity, "that Mr. Craig and me and Mrs. Aleshine puts in services besides, although, to be sure, they don't go into the jar."

"I only remember," said Mr. Enderton, "that I am paying an unjustifiable price as it is."

Mrs. Lecks and Mrs. Aleshine, however, were not at all of this opinion, and they agreed that, if it should be in their power, they would see to it that the Dusantes lost nothing by this closefisted missionary.

After dinner—and I may remark that the newcomers were not consulted in regard to the hours for meals—Mrs. Lecks had an interview with the coxswain on the subject of board for himself and his two companions. This affair, however, was very quickly settled, for the three mariners had among them only one dollar and forty-three cents, and this, the coxswain explained, they would like to keep for tobacco. It was therefore settled that, as the three sailors could pay no money, as much work as possible should be got out of them, and to this plan they agreed heartily and cheerfully.

"There's only one thing we'll ask, ma'am," said the coxswain to Mrs. Lecks, "and that is that we be put in a different mess from the parson. We've now eat two meals with the passengers, and me and my mates is agreed that that's about as much as we can go."

After this, therefore, the three men had their meals in the kitchen, where they were generally joined by Mrs. Aleshine, who much delighted in their company. But she made it a point sometimes to sit down with us in the dining room, merely to show that she had as much right there as anybody.

"As to the work for them sailormen," said Mrs. Aleshine, "I don't see what they're goin' to do. Of course they don't know nothin' about gardenin', and it seems to me that the best thing to be done is to put 'em to fishin'."

Mrs. Lecks considered this a good suggestion, and accordingly the coxswain and his companions were told that thereafter they would be expected to fish for eight hours a day, Sundays excepted. This plan, however, did not work very well. During the first two days the sailors caught so many fish that, although the fishermen themselves had excellent appetites for such food, it was found utterly impossible to consume what they brought in. Consequently, it was ordered that thereafter they should catch only as many fish as should be needed and then make themselves useful by assisting Mrs. Aleshine and Mrs. Lecks in any manner they might direct.

I found it quite easy to become acquainted with Miss Ruth Enderton, as she was very much inclined to conversation. "It's ever so long," she said, "since I've had anybody to talk to."

She had left the United States when she was quite a little girl and had since seen nothing of her native land. She was, consequently, full of questions about America, although quite willing to talk of her life in China. Society, at least such kind as she had ever cared for, had been extremely scarce in the little missionary station at which she had lived so long, and now, coming from a wearisome sojourn on a disabled sailing vessel, with no company but the crew and a preoccupied father, she naturally was delighted to get among people she could talk to. With Mrs.

Lecks, Mrs. Aleshine, and myself she soon became very friendly and showed herself to be a most lively and interesting young person.

I did all that I could to make Miss Ruth's time pass agreeably. I rowed with her on the lagoon, taught her to fish, and showed her all the pleasant points on the island which could be easily reached by walking. Mr. Enderton gave us very little of his company, for having discovered that there was a library in the house, he passed most of his time in that room.

"You have made a very fair selection of books, sir," he remarked to me, "but it may readily be conceived, from the character of the works, that your tastes are neither ecclesiastic nor scientific."

Several times I explained to him the ownership of the library and the house, but he immediately forgot what I had said or paid no attention to it. When he paid his board, at the end of the week, he handed the money to Mrs. Lecks; and although before his eyes she put it into the ginger jar, beneath the paper of fishhooks, I know very well that he considered he was paying it to her for her own use and behoof. He was comfortably lodged, he had all that he needed—and very nearly all that he wanted—to eat, and I do not know that I ever saw a man more contented with his lot.

As for the coxswain and the two sailors, they had a very pleasant time of it, but Mrs. Lecks and Mrs. Aleshine would not think of such a thing as allowing them to eat in idleness the bread of the Dusantes. After they had been with us a few days, Mrs. Lecks told me that she thought she could show the coxswain and his mates how to dig and gather the garden stuff, which was daily needed.

"To be sure," said she, "that work goes ag'in' part of your board, but fishin' and bringin' in firewood don't take up a quarter of the time of them sailors, and so that the garden work is done, I don't suppose it matters to the Dusantes who does it. And that'll give you more time to make things pleasant for Miss Ruth, for, as far as I can see, there isn't a thing for her to do, even if she knows how to do it."

The three mariners were more than willing to do anything desired by Mrs. Lecks or Mrs. Aleshine, to whom they looked up with great admiration and respect. The latter was their favorite, not only because she was with them a great deal during their meals and at other times, but because of her genial nature and easy sociability. The men were always trying to lighten her labors and to do something that would please her.

One of them climbed to the top of what she called a "palm-leaf-fan tree," and brought therefrom some broad leaves, which he cut and trimmed and sewed, in true nautical fashion, until he made some fans, which were heavy and clumsy; but, as he said, they would stand half a gale of wind if she chose to raise it. The coxswain caught or trapped two seabirds, and having clipped their wings, he spent days in endeavoring to tame them, hoping to induce them, as far as the power in them lay, to take the place of the barnyard fowls whose absence Mrs. Aleshine continually deplored. Every evening the two black-bearded sailors would dance hornpipes for her, much to her diversion and delight.

"I've often heard," she remarked, "that in these hot cocoanut countries the tricks of the monkeys was enough to keep everybody on a steady laugh, but I'm sure sailormen is a great deal better. When you get tired of their pranks and their tomfooleries, you can tell 'em to stop, which with monkeys you can't."

It was about ten days after the arrival of the missionary's party that, as I was going to get ready the boat in which Miss Ruth and myself generally rowed in the cool of the evening, I saw Mrs. Lecks and Mrs. Aleshine sitting on the bench in the shade of some low-growing trees. They were evidently waiting for me, and as soon as I appeared, Mrs. Lecks beckoned to me; whereupon I joined them.

"Sit down," said Mrs. Lecks; "there's somethin' I want to talk to you about. Mrs. Aleshine and me have made up our minds that you ought to be hurried up a little about poppin' the question to Miss Ruth."

This remark astounded me. "Popping the question!" I exclaimed.

"Yes," continued Mrs. Lecks, "and me and Mrs. Aleshine know very well that you haven't done it yet, for both of us havin' been through that sort of thing ourselves, we know the signs of it after it has happened."

"And we wouldn't say nothin' to hurry you," added Mrs. Aleshine, "if it wasn't that the groceries, especially the flour, is a-gettin' low. We've been talkin' to them sailormen, and they're pretty well agreed that there's no use now in expectin' their captain to send for 'em; for if he was a-goin' to do it at all, he'd 'a' done it before this. And perhaps he never got nowhere himself, in which case he couldn't. And they say the best thing we can all do when the victuals has nearly give out, provided the Dusantes don't come back in time, is to take what's left and all get into their big boat and row away to that island, which I don't know just how far it is, that the captain of our ship was goin' to. There we can stay pretty comfortable till a ship comes along and takes us off."

"But what has all that to do," I asked, "with Miss Ruth and me?"

"Do?" cried Mrs. Lecks. "It has everythin' to do. When it's all settled and fixed between you and Miss Ruth, there'll be nothin' to hinder us from gettin' ready to start when we please."

"But, my dear friends," I said with much earnestness, "I have not the slightest idea of proposing to Miss Enderton."

"That's just what I said to Mrs. Aleshine," said Mrs. Lecks, "and that's the reason we let our irons cool and come out here to talk to you. It's just like a young man to keep puttin' off that sort of thing, but this can't be put off."

"That's so!" cried Mrs. Aleshine. "And I'll just let you see how the matter stands. There is housekeepers who allows a pint of flour a day to each person, but this is for farm hands and people who works hard and eats hearty, and I've found that three-quarters of a pint will do very well, if the dough is kneaded conscientious and made up light, so that it'll rise well when it's put into the oven. Now I've measured all the flour that's left, and me and Mrs. Lecks we've calculated that, allowin' three-quarters of a pint of flour a day to each one of us, there's just eight days more that we can stay here—that is, if the Dusantes don't come back before that time, which, of course, can't be counted on. So you can see for yourself, Mr. Craig, there's no time to be lost, even considerin' that she hasn't to make up anything to be married in."

"No," said Mrs. Lecks; "just for us and three sailors, that wouldn't be needed."

I looked from one to the other in dumb astonishment. Mrs. Lecks gave me no time to say anything.

"In common cases," said she, "this might all be put off till we got somewhere; but it won't do now. Here you are, with everythin' in your hands, but just get away from here, and there's an end of that. She's as pretty a girl as you'll see in a month of Sundays, and if she leaves here without your gettin' her, there's no knowing who'll snap her up. When we've got to that island, you may see her once a week, but maybe you won't. She may go away in one ship and you in another, and there may be somebody right there—a missionary, for all I know—who'll have her before you have a chance to put in a word."

"And that's not the worst of it," said Mrs. Aleshine. "Supposin' them Dusantes come back before we go. There's no knowin' what that Mr. Dusante is. He may be a brother of Emily and Lucille. And what sort of a chance would you have then, I'd like to know, with Miss Ruth right here in his own house, and he ownin' the rowboat and everythin'? Or it may be he's a widower, and that'll be a mighty sight worse, I can tell you."

"No matter whether they're widowers or never been married," said Mrs. Lecks, "there'll be plenty that'll want her as soon as they see her ; and if it isn't for the girl's own pretty face, it'll be for her father's money."

"Her father's money !" I exclaimed. "What are you talking of ?"

"There's no good tellin' me anything about that," said Mrs. Lecks, very decidedly. "There never was a man as closefisted as Mr. Enderton who hadn't money."

"And you know as well as we do," said Mrs. Aleshine, "that in them countries where he's been the heathens worship idols of silver and idols of gold, and when them heathens is converted, don't you suppose the missionaries get any of that? I expect that Mr. Enderton has converted thousands of heathens."

At this suggestion I laughed outright. But Mrs. Lecks reproved me.

"Now, Mr. Craig," said she, "this is no laughin' matter. What me and Mrs. Aleshine is sayin' is for your good and for the good of Miss Ruth along with you. I haven't much opinion of her father, but his money is as good as anybody else's, and though they had to leave their trunks on board their ship, what little they brought with them shows that they've been used to havin' the best there is. Mrs. Aleshine and me has set up till late into the night talkin' over this thing, and we are both of one mind that you two need never expect to have the same chance again that you've got now. The very fact that the old gentleman is a preacher and can marry you on the spot ought to make you tremble when you think of the risks you are runnin' by puttin' it off."

"I've got to go into the house now to see about supper," said Mrs. Aleshine, rising, "and I hope you'll remember, Mr. Craig, when your bread is on your plate and Miss Ruth is sittin' opposite to you, that three-quarters of a pint of flour a day is about as little as anybody can live on and that time is flyin'."

Mrs. Lecks now also rose. But I detained the two for a moment.

"I hope you have not said anything to Miss Enderton on this subject," I said.

"No," replied Mrs. Aleshine, "we haven't. We are both agreed that as you're the one that's to do what's to be done, you are the one that's to be spoke to. And havin' been through it ourselves, we understand well enough that the more a woman don't know nothin' about it, the more likely she is to be ketched if she wants to be."

The two women left me in an amused but also somewhat annoyed state of mind. I had no intention whatever of proposing to Miss Ruth Enderton. She was a charming girl, very bright and lively, and withal, I had reason to believe, very sensible. But it was not yet a fortnight since I first saw her, and no thought of marrying her had entered into my head. Had Mrs. Lecks and Mrs. Aleshine or, more important than all, had Miss Enderton any reason to believe that I was acting the part of a lover?

The latter portion of this question was almost immediately answered to my satisfaction by the appearance of Miss Ruth, who came skipping down to me and calling out to me in that free and hearty manner with which a woman addresses a friend or near acquaintance but never a suspected lover. She betrayed no more notion of the Lecks and Aleshine scheme than on the day I first met her.

But as I was rowing her over the lagoon, I felt a certain constraint, which I had not known before. There was no ground whatever for the wild imaginings of the two women, but the fact that they had imagined interfered very much with the careless freedom with which I had previously talked to Miss Ruth. I do not think, however, that she noticed any change in me, for she chatted and laughed and showed, as she had done from the first, the rare delight which she took in this novel island life.

When we returned to the house, we were met by Mrs. Aleshine. "I am goin' to give you two your supper," she said, "on that table there under the tree. We all had ours a little earlier than common, as the sailormen seemed hungry; and I took your father's to him in the libr'ry, where I expect he's a-sittin' yet, holdin' a book in one hand and stirrin' his tea with the other, till he's stirred out nearly every drop on the floor; which, however, won't matter at all, for in the mornin' I'll rub up that floor till it's as bright as new."

This plan delighted Miss Ruth, but I saw in it the beginning of the workings of a deep-laid scheme. I was just about to sit down when Mrs. Aleshine said to me in a low voice, as she left us, "Remember that the first three-quarters of a pint apiece begins now!"

"Don't you think that Mrs. Lecks and Mrs. Alshine are perfectly charming?" said Miss Ruth, as she poured out the tea. "They always seem to be trying to think of some kind thing to do for other people."

I agreed entirely with Miss Enderton's remark, but I could not help thinking of the surprise she would feel if she knew of the kind thing that these two women were trying to do for her.

"Have you taken any steps yet?" asked Mrs. Lecks of me, the next day. On my replying that I had taken no steps of the kind to which I supposed she alluded, she walked away with a very grave and serious face.

A few hours later Mrs. Aleshine came to me. "There's another reason for hurryin' up," said she. "Them sailormen seems able to do without 'most anything in this world except tobacco, and Mrs. Lecks has been sellin' it to 'em out of a big box she found in a closet upstairs, at five cents a teacupful—which I think is awful cheap, but she says prices in islands is always low—and wrapping the money up in a paper, with 'cash paid by sailormen for tobacco' written on it and puttin' it into the ginger jar with the board money. But their dollar and forty-three cents is nearly gone, and Mrs. Lecks she says that not a whiff of Mr. Dusante's tobacco shall they have if they can't pay for it. And when they have nothin' to smoke, they'll be wantin' to leave this island just as quick as they can, without waitin' for the flour to give out."

Here was another pressure brought to bear upon me. Not only the waning flour, but the rapidly disappearing tobacco money was used as a weapon to urge me forward to the lovemaking which Mrs. Lecks and Mrs. Aleshine had set their hearts upon.

I was in no hurry to leave the island and hoped very much that when we did go we should depart in some craft more comfortable than a ship's boat. In order, therefore, to prevent any undue desire to leave on the part of the sailors, I gave them money enough to buy a good many teacups full of tobacco. By this act I think I wounded the feelings of Mrs. Lecks and Mrs. Aleshine, although I had no idea that such would be the effect of my little gift. They said nothing to me on the subject, but their looks and manners indicated that they thought I had not been acting honorably. For two days they had very little to say to me, and then Mrs. Aleshine came to me to make what, I suppose, was their supreme effort.

"Mrs. Lecks and me is a-goin' to try," she said—and as she spoke she looked at me with a very sad expression and a watery appearance about the eyes—"to stretch out the time for you a little longer. We are goin' to make them sailormen eat more fish; and as for me and her, we'll go pretty much without bread and make it up, as well as we can, on other things. You and Miss Ruth and the parson can each have your three-quarters of a pint of flour a day, just the same as ever, and what we save ought to give you three or four days longer."

This speech moved me deeply. I could not allow these two kind-hearted women to half starve themselves in order that I might have more time to woo, and I spoke very earnestly on the subject to Mrs. Aleshine, urging her to give up the fanciful plans which she and Mrs. Lecks had concocted.

"Let us drop this idea of lovemaking," I said, "which is the wildest kind of vagary, and all live happily together, as we did before. If the provisions give out before the Dusantes come back, I suppose we shall have to leave in the boat; but until that time comes, let us enjoy life here as much as we can and be the good friends that we used to be."

I might as well have talked to one of the palm trees which waved over us.

"As I said before," remarked Mrs. Aleshine, "what is saved from Mrs. Lecks's and mine and the three sailormen's three-quarters of a pint apiece ought to give you four days more." And she went into the house.

All this time the Reverend Mr. Enderton had sat and read in the library or meditatively had walked the beach with a book in his hand; while the three mariners had caught fish, performed their other work, and lain in the shade, smoking their pipes in peace. Miss Ruth and I had taken our daily rows and walks and had enjoyed our usual hours of pleasant converse, and all the members of the little colony seemed happy and contented except Mrs. Lecks and Mrs. Aleshine. These two went gravely and sadly about their work, and the latter asked no more for the hornpipes and the sea songs of her sailormen.

But for some unaccountable reason Mr. Enderton's condition of tranquil abstraction did not continue. He began to be fretful and discontented. He found fault with his food and his accommodations, and instead of spending the greater part of the day in the library, as had been his wont, he took to wandering about the island, generally with two or three books under his arm, sometimes sitting down in one place and sometimes in another, and then rising suddenly to go grumbling into the house.

One afternoon, as Miss Ruth and I were in the skiff in the lagoon, we saw Mr. Enderton approaching us, walking on the beach. As soon as he was near enough for us to hear him, he shouted to his daughter: "Ruth, come out of that boat! If you want to take the air, I should think you might as well with me as to go rowing around with—with anybody."

This rude and heartless speech made my blood boil, while my companion turned pale with mortification. The man had never made the slightest objection to our friendly intercourse, and this unexpected attack was entirely indefensible.

"Please put me ashore," said Miss Ruth; and without a word, for I could not trust myself to speak, I landed her; and petulantly complaining that she never gave him one moment of her society, her father led her away.

An hour later, my soul still in a state of turmoil, but with the violence of its tossings somewhat abated, I entered one of the paths which led through the woods. After a few turns, I reached a point where I could see for quite a long distance to the other end of the path, which opened out upon the beach. There I perceived Mr. Enderton sitting upon the little bench on which I had found Emily's book. His back was toward me, and he seemed to be busily reading. About midway between him and myself I saw Miss Ruth slowly walking toward me. Her eyes were fixed upon the ground, and she had not seen me.

Stepping to one side, I awaited her approach. When she came near, I accosted her.

"Miss Ruth," said I, "has your father been talking to you of me?"

She looked up quickly, evidently surprised at my being there. "Yes," she said, "he has told me that it is not—suitable that I should be with you as much as I have been since we came here."

There was something in this remark that roused again the turmoil which had begun to subside within me. There was so much that was unjust and tyrannical, and—what perhaps touched me still deeper—there was such a want of consideration and respect in this behavior of Mr. Enderton's, that it brought to the front some very incongruous emotions. I had been superciliously pushed aside, and I found I was angry. Something was about to be torn from me, and I found I loved it.

"Ruth," said I, stepping up close to her, "do you like to be with me as you have been?"

If Miss Ruth had not spent such a large portion of her life in the out-of-the-world village of Nanfouchong, if she had not lived among those simplehearted missionaries, where it was never necessary to conceal her emotions or her sentiments, if it had not been that she never had had emotions or sentiments that it was necessary to conceal, I do not believe that when she answered me she would have raised her eyes to me with a look in them of a deep-blue sky seen through a sort of Indian-summer mist and that, gazing thus, she would have said, "Of course I like it."

"Then let us make it suitable," I said, taking both her hands in mine.

There was another look, in which the skies shone clear and bright, and then, in a moment, it was all done.

About five minutes after this, I said to her, "Ruth, shall we go to your father?"

"Certainly," she answered. And together we walked along the thickly shaded path.

The missionary still sat with his back toward us, and he being so intent upon his book, I found that by keeping my eyes upon him it was perfectly safe to walk with my arm around Ruth until we had nearly reached him. Then I took her hand in mine, and we stepped in front of him.

"Father," said Ruth, "Mr. Craig and I are going to be married."

There was something very plump about this remark, and Mr. Enderton immediately raised his eyes from his book and fixed them first upon his daughter and then upon me; then he let them drop, and through the narrow space between us he gazed out over the sea.

"Well, Father," said Ruth, a little impatiently, "what do you think of it?"

Mr. Enderton leaned forward and picked up a leaf from the ground. This he placed between the open pages of his book, and closed it.

"It seems to me," he said, "that on many accounts the arrangement you propose may be an excellent one. Yes," he added more decidedly; "I think it will do very well indeed. I shall not be at all surprised if we are obliged to remain on this island for a considerable time, and for my part I have no desire to leave it at present. And when you shall place yourself, Ruth, in a position in which you will direct the domestic economies of the establishment, I hope that you will see to it that things generally are made more compatible with comfort and gentility, and as regards the table, I may add, with palatability."

Ruth and I looked at each other, and then together we promised that as far as in us lay we would try to make the life of Mr. Enderton a happy one, not only while we were on the island, but ever afterward.

We were promising a great deal, but at that moment we felt very grateful.

Then he stood up, shook us both by the hands, and we left him to his book.

When Ruth and I came walking out of the woods and approached the house, Mrs. Aleshine was standing outside, not far from the kitchen. When she saw us, she gazed steadily at us for a few moments, a strange expression coming over her face. Then she threw up both her hands, and without a word she turned and rushed indoors.

We had not reached the house before Mrs. Lecks and Mrs. Aleshine came hurrying out together. Running up to us with a haste and an excitement I had never seen in either of them, first one and then the other took Ruth into her arms and kissed her with much earnestness. Then they turned upon me and shook my hands with hearty vigor, expressing, more by their looks and actions than their words, a triumphant approbation of what I had done.

"The minute I laid eyes on you," said Mrs. Aleshine, "I knowed it was all right. There wasn't no need of askin' questions."

I now became fearful lest, in the exuberance of their satisfaction, these good women might reveal to Ruth the plans they had laid for our matrimonial future, and the reluctance I had shown in entering into them. My countenance must have expressed my apprehensions, for Mrs. Aleshine, her ruddy face glowing with warmth, both mental and physical, gave me a little wink, and drew me to one side.

"You needn't suppose that we've ever said anything to Miss Ruth, or that we're goin' to. It's a great deal better to let her think you did it all yourself."

I felt like resenting this imputation upon the independence of my lovemaking, but at this happy moment I did not want to enter into a discussion and therefore merely smiled.

"I'm so glad, I don't know how to tell it," continued Mrs. Aleshine, as Mrs. Lecks and Ruth walked toward the house.

I was about to follow, but my companions detained me.

"Have you spoke to the parson?" she asked.

"Oh, yes," said I, "and he seemed perfectly satisfied. I am rather surprised at this, because of late he has been in such a remarkably bad humor."

"That's so," said Mrs. Aleshine; "there's no gettin' round the fact that he's been a good deal crosser than two sticks. You see, Mr. Craig, that Mrs. Lecks and me we made up our minds that it wasn't fair to the Dusantes to let that rich missionary go on payin' nothin' but four dollars a week apiece for him and his daughter, and if we couldn't get no more out of him one way, we'd do it another. It was fair enough that if he didn't pay more he ought to get less; and so we gave him more fish and not so much bread, the same as we did the sailormen; and we weakened his tea and sent him just so much sugar and no more; and as for openin' boxes of sardines for him, which there was no reason why they shouldn't be left here for the Dusantes, I just wouldn't do it, though he said he'd got all the fresh fish he wanted when he was in

China. And then we agreed that it was high time that the libr'ry
should be cleaned up, and we went to work at it, not mindin' what
he said; for it's no use tellin' me that four dollars a week will pay
for a front room and good board and the use of a libr'ry all day.
And as there wasn't no need of both of us cleanin' one room, Mrs.
Lecks she went into the parlor, where he'd took his books, and begun there. And then, again, we shut down on Mr. Dusante's dress-
ing gown. There was no sense includin' the use of that in his four
dollars a week, so we brushed it up and camphored it and put it
away. We just wanted to let him know if he undertook to be
skinflinty, he'd better try it on somebody else besides us. We could
see that he was a good deal upset, for if ever a man liked to have
things quiet and comfortable around him, and everything his own
way, that man is that missionary. But we didn't care if we did
prod him up a little. Mrs. Lecks and me we both agreed that it
would do him good. Why, he'd got into such a way of shettin'
himself up in himself that he didn't even see that his daughter was
goin' about with a young man and fixin' her affections on him
more and more every day, when he never had no idea, as could be
proved by witnesses, of marryin' her."

"Mrs. Aleshine," said I, looking at her very steadfastly, "I believe, after all, that you and Mrs. Lecks had your own way in regard to hurrying up this matter."

"Yes," said she, with happy complacency; "I shouldn't wonder
if we had. Stirrin' up the parson was our last chance, and it
wasn't much trouble to do it."

Mrs. Lecks, whose manner toward me for the last few days had
been characterized by cold severity, now resumed her former
friendly demeanor, although she was not willing to let the affair
pass over without some words of reproach.

"I must say, Mr. Craig," she remarked the next morning,
"that I was gettin' pretty well outdone with you. I was beginnin'
to think that a young man that couldn't see and wouldn't see what
was good for him didn't deserve to have it; and if Miss Ruth's fa-

ther had just come down with a heavy foot and put an end to the whole business, I'm not sure I'd been sorry for you. But it's all right at last, and bygones is bygones. And now, what we've got to do is to get ready for the weddin'."

"The wedding!" I exclaimed.

Mrs. Lecks regarded me with an expression in which there was something of virtuous indignation and something of pity. "Mr. Craig," said she, "if there ever was anybody that wanted a guardeen, it's you. Now, just let me tell you this. That Mr. Enderton ain't to be trusted no further than you can see him and not so fur, neither, if it can be helped. He's willin' for you to have Miss Ruth now, because he's pretty much made up his mind that we're goin' to stay here, and as he considers you the master of this island, of course he thinks it'll be for his good for his daughter to be mistress of it. For one thing, he wouldn't expect to pay no board then. But just let him get away from this island, and just let him set his eyes on some smooth-faced young fellow that'll agree to take him into the concern and keep him for nothin' on books and tea, he'll just throw you over without winkin'. And Miss Ruth is not the girl to marry you against his will, if he opens the Bible and piles texts on her, which he is capable of doin'. If in any way you two should get separated when you leave here, there's no knowin' when you'd ever see each other again, for where he'll take her nobody can tell. He's more willin' to set down and stay where he finds himself comfortable than anybody I've met yet."

"Of course," I said, "I'm ready to be married at any moment; but I don't believe Miss Ruth and her father would consent to anything so speedy."

"Don't you get into the way," said Mrs. Lecks, "of beforehand believin' this or that. It don't pay. Just you go to her father and talk to him about it, and if you and him agree, it'll be easy enough to make her see the sense of it. You attend to them, and I'll see that everythin' is got ready. And you'd better fix the day for tomorrow, for we can't stay here much longer, and there's a lot of housecleanin' and bakin' and cookin' to be done before we go."

I took this advice and broached the subject to Mr. Enderton.

"Well, sir," said he, laying down his book, "your proposition is decidedly odd; I may say, very odd, indeed. But it is, perhaps, after all, no odder than many things I have seen. Among the various denominational sects I have noticed occurrences quite as odd, sir. For my part, I have no desire to object to an early celebration of the matrimonial rites. I may say, indeed, that I am of the opinion that a certain amount of celerity in this matter will conduce to the comfort of all concerned. It has been a very unsatisfactory thing to me to see my daughter occupying a subordinate position in our little family, where she has not even the power to turn household affairs into the channels of my comfort. Tomorrow, I think, will do very well indeed. Even if it should rain, I see no reason why the ceremony should be postponed."

The proposition of a wedding on the morrow was not received by Ruth with favor. She was unprepared for such precipitancy. But she finally yielded to arguments; not so much to mine, I fear, as to those offered by Mrs. Lecks and Mrs. Aleshine.

For the rest of that day the three mariners were kept very busy, bringing in green things to deck the parlor and doing every imaginable kind of work necessary to a wedding which Mrs. Aleshine was willing to give into their hands. As for herself and her good friend, they put themselves upon their mettle as providers of festivals. They made cakes, pies, and I never knew half so well as the three sailors how many other kinds of good things. Besides all this, they assisted Ruth to array herself in some degree in a manner becoming a bride. Some light and pretty adornments of dress were borrowed from Emily or Lucille, they knew not which, and after having been "done up" and fluted and crimped by Mrs. Lecks, were incorporated by Ruth into her costume with so much taste that on the wedding morning she appeared to me to be dressed more charmingly than any bride I had ever seen.

The three sailors had done their own washing and ironing and appeared in cleanly garb and with hair and beards well wet and brushed. Mrs. Lecks and Mrs. Aleshine put on their best bibs and tuckers, and Mr. Enderton assumed his most clerical air as he stood behind a table in the parlor and married Ruth and me.

"This," said Mr. Enderton, as we were seated at the wedding feast, "is a most creditable display of attractive viands, but I may say, my dear Ruth, that I think I perceived the influence of the happy event of today even before it took place. I have lately had a better appetite for my food and have experienced a greater enjoyment of my surroundings."

"I should think so," murmured Mrs. Aleshine in my ear, "for we'd no sooner knowed that you two were to make a match of it than we put an extry spoonful of tea into his pot and stopped scrubbin' the libr'ry."

For the next two days all was bustle and work on the island. Mrs. Lecks and Mrs. Aleshine would not consent to depart without leaving everything in the best possible order, so that the Dusantes might not be dissatisfied with the condition of their house when they returned. It was in fact, the evident desire of the two women to gratify their pride in their housewifely abilities by leaving everything better than they found it.

Mr. Enderton was much surprised at these preparations for immediate departure. He was very well satisfied with his life on the island and had prepared his mind for an indefinite continuance of it, with the position of that annoying and obdurate Mrs. Lecks filled by a compliant and affectionate daughter. He had no reasonable cause for complaint, for the whole subject of the exhaustion of our supply of provisions and the necessity of an openboat trip to an inhabited island had been fully discussed before him; but he was so entirely engrossed in the consideration of his own well-being that this discussion of our plans had made no impression upon him. He now became convinced that a conspiracy had been entered into against him and fell into an unpleasant humor. This, however, produced very little effect upon any of us, for we were all too busy to notice his whims. But his sudden change of disposition made me understand how correct were the opinions of Mrs. Lecks and Mrs. Aleshine concerning him. If I had left that island with my marriage with Ruth depending upon Mr. Enderton's cooperation, my prospects of future happiness would have been at the mercy of his caprices.

Very early on a beautiful morning Ruth and I started out on our wedding journey in the longboat. Mr. Enderton was made as comfortable as possible in the stern, with Ruth near him. Mrs. Lecks and Mrs. Aleshine sat facing each other, each with a brown paper package by her side, containing the life preserver on which she had arrived. These were to be ever cherished as memorials of a wonderful experience. The three sailors and I took turns at the oars. The sea was smooth, and there was every reason to believe that we should arrive at our destination before the end of the day. Mrs. Aleshine had supplied us with an abundance of provisions, and with the exception of Mr. Enderton, who had not been permitted to take away any of the Dusante books, we were a contented party.

"As long as the flour held out," remarked Mrs. Aleshine, "I'd never been willin' to leave that island till the Dusantes came back, and we could have took Emily or Lucille, whichever it was that kept house, and showed her everythin' and told her just what we had done. But when they do come back," she added, "and read that letter which Mr. Craig wrote and left for them, and find out all that happened in their country place while they was away; and how two of us was made happy for life; and how two more of us, meanin' Mrs. Lecks and me, have give up goin' to Japan, intendin', instid of that, writin' to my son to come home to America and settle down in the country he ought to live in—why, then, if them Dusantes ain't satisfied, it's no use for anybody to ever try to satisfy 'em."

"I should think not," said Mrs. Lecks, "with the weddin' cards on the parlor table, not a speck of dust in any corner, and the board money in the ginger jar."

"The Storyteller has nothing more to tell about the contents of his pack; it is now the turn of the buyer to have his say."

FRANK STOCKTON
"A Storyteller's Pack"

SELECTED BIBLIOGRAPHY

Works by Frank Stockton

Rudder Grange. New York: Scribners, 1879

The Floating Prince and Other Tales. New York: Scribners, 1881

Ting-a-ling Tales. New York: Scribners, 1882

The Lady or the Tiger? and Other Stories. New York: Scribners, 1884, 1907

A Christmas Wreck and Other Stories. New York: Scribners, 1886

The Casting Away of Mrs. Lecks and Mrs. Aleshine. New York: Century, 1886

The Bee-Man of Orn and Other Fanciful Tales. New York: Scribners, 1887

The Queen's Museum. New York: Scribners, 1887, 1906

The Dusantes. New York: Century, 1888

The Great War Syndicate. New York: Collier, 1889; Dodd, Mead, 1890

The Merry Chanter. New York: Century, 1890

The Rudder Grangers Abroad. New York: Scribners, 1891

The Squirrel Inn. New York: Century, 1891

The Clocks of Rondaine and Other Stories. New York: Scribners, 1892

The Watchmaker's Wife and Other Stories. New York: Scribners, 1893

The Adventures of Captain Horn. New York: Scribners, 1895, 1908

A Chosen Few. New York: Scribners, 1895

A Storyteller's Pack. New York: Scribners, 1897

The Great Stone of Sardis. New York: Harper, 1898

Buccaneers and Pirates of Our Coasts. New York: Macmillan, 1898

The Associate Hermits. New York: Harper, 1899

Afield and Afloat. New York: Scribners, 1900

John Gayther's Garden. New York: Scribners, 1902

Mark Twain and His Recent Works. *Forum,* Vol. XV, August 1893

How I Served My Apprenticeship as a Man of Letters. *The Youth's Companion,* Vol. LXX, March 5, 1896

My Favorite Novelist and His Best Book. *Munsey's Magazine,* Vol. XVII, June, 1897.

Modern Editions

Ting-a-ling Tales. New York: Scribners, 1955
The Casting Away of Mrs. Lecks and Mrs. Aleshine, and The Dusantes.
New York: Dover
The Bee-Man of Orn. New York: Holt, 1964
The Griffin and the Minor Canon. New York: Holt, 1963
The Best Short Stories of Frank R. Stockton (originally A Chosen Few).
New York: Scribners, 1958
Buccaneers and Pirates of Our Coasts. New York: Macmillan, 1967

Biography and Criticism

Chislett, William, Jr. *Moderns and Near Moderns*. New York, 1928
Griffin, Martin I. J. *Frank R. Stockton: A Critical Biography*. Pennsylvania, 1939; New York, 1965
Howells, William Dean. "Stockton's Stories." *Atlantic Monthly*, Vol. LIX, January 1887
   "Stockton and His Works." *Harper's Weekly*, Vol. XLI, May 29, 1897
   "The Novels and Stories of Frank R. Stockton." *Book Buyer*, Vol. XX, February, 1900
Johnson, Robert Underwood. *Remembered Yesterdays*. Boston, 1923
Stockton, Marian E. "Memoir of Frank R. Stockton, with a Bibliographical List of His Writings." *The Captain's Toll Gate*. New York: Appleton, 1903
Van Doren, Carl. "Frank R. Stockton." *Dictionary of American Biography*. Vol. XVIII. New York, 1936